SIMHA'S ROAR

Praise for *Simha's Roar*

'Those who know history—though what happened in Vathapi is not certain—will anticipate the denouement in the third volume of this trilogy. However, this is fiction, and Arun Krishnan's masterly portrayal of Bharatavarsha (a geographical part of it) from that era leads the reader up to the final clash between the young lion, Narasimhavarman Pallava, and the old Chalukya king Pulikeshi. Right at the end (the Epilogue), the reader wonders, what all this was in aid of? In the end, there was only darkness wrapped in darkness. But there is an inevitability in the way the author depicts the protagonists and their actions, like a Greek tragedy. A great example of how historical fiction should be written.'

—**Bibek Debroy**, author and chairman, PM's Economic Council

'In the climactic third instalment of The Battle of Vathapi series, prepare to be thrust into the heart of war, where the clash of swords and the roar of battle drums echo with vivid intensity. As the lines between righteousness and ambition blur, the characters grapple with the weight of their decisions, torn between conflicting dharmas. Yet, amidst the chaos of conflict, it is the common soldier who emerges as the unsung hero, navigating the harrowing terrain of love and death, their sacrifices echoing through the generations. A poignant reminder that in war, it is often those left behind who bear the deepest scars.'

—**Anand Ranganathan**, author and scientist

'Prepare to be swept away by the grandeur and intrigue of *Simha's Roar*—the final book of The Battle of Vathapi trilogy. In the third instalment, the saga reaches new heights, weaving together history and imagination with breathtaking skill. The author's meticulous research and vivid storytelling bring ancient India to life in all its glory and complexity. The denouement is poignant and worthy of the finale. A must-read for anyone who loves epic historical fiction!'

—**Amish Tripathi**, bestselling author

'*Simha's Roar* sees the political, emotional and personal trajectories of the Pallava and the Chalukya emperors, along with those near and dear to them. The high-stakes battle plays out till one of the lions must be laid to rest. Pages turn at breakneck speed, yet the rasa lingers in the readers' minds long after the book has been finished. Intertwining high-octane action and soul-stirring nuance has been Arun Krishnan's strength and the craft comes to a crescendo along with the pace of expert storytelling. Do read the three unputdownable books in sequence to experience an epic in the making.'

—**Saiswaroopa Iyer**, author

'It comes down to one last battle, an inexorable force drawing the reader and events to the culmination of years of struggle, to one operatic showdown between two emperors, the Pallava king Pulikeshi and the Chalukya king Narasimhavarman, in the city of Vathapi. *Simha's Roar* does not disappoint. A grand, page-turning end to The Battle of Vathapi trilogy, *Simha's Roar* is a befitting finale to this magnificent saga.'

—**Abhinav Agarwal**, author

'The Battle of Vathapi reaches its climax in *Simha's Roar*. As the final chapter of Arun Krishnan's mesmerizing trilogy unfolds, ancient realms collide with contemporary, and past comes alive in all its splendour and strife. Against the backdrop of a land steeped in rich history and intricate politics, the fate of heroes and warriors hangs in balance as they navigate treacherous waters to secure their legacy. The third and last instalment of this glorious trilogy is a triumphant finale that will leave readers spellbound, longing for more, yet satisfied by the epic conclusion of this extraordinary saga. With meticulous attention to detail and an unparalleled flair for storytelling, Arun Krishnan leaves an indelible mark in the genre of historical fiction.'

—**Sunanda Vashisht**, writer and columnist

'With The Battle of Vathapi trilogy, Arun Krishnan joins the august ranks of writers who successfully tell the real story of Bharat using fiction form. The itihasa of the southern part of Bharat needs to reach a wider audience, especially outside the south. His narration of wars with a glimpse of dharma that we followed on the battlefield is quite vivid.'

—**Ratan Sharda**, author and columnist

THE BATTLE OF VATHAPI BOOK 3

SIMHA'S ROAR

ARUN KRISHNAN

HarperCollins *Publishers* India

First published in India by HarperCollins *Publishers* 2024
4th Floor, Tower A, Building No. 10, DLF Cyber City,
DLF Phase II, Gurugram, Haryana – 122002
www.harpercollins.co.in

2 4 6 8 10 9 7 5 3 1

P-ISBN: 978-93-5699-946-6
E-ISBN: 978-93-5699-757-8

Typeset in 11/13.7 Adobe Garamond Pro at
Manipal Technologies Limited, Manipal

Printed and bound at
Manipal Technologies Limited, Manipal

FSC www.fsc.org MIX Paper | Supporting responsible forestry FSC™ C043100

This book is produced from independently certified FSC® paper to ensure responsible forest management.

सरस्वति महाभागे विद्या कमललोचने ।
विद्यारूपे विषालाक्षि विद्यां देहि नमोस्तुते ।।

I pray to Goddess Saraswati, the most glorious one with lotus eyes, the divine manifestation of knowledge, to bless me with wisdom and intelligence.

The Battle of Vathapi Trilogy

Nandi's Charge (Book 1)
Varaha's Vengeance (Book 2)

Contents

List of Characters

The Pallavas

Mahendravarman Pallava: Father of the current king of the Pallavas.

Narasimhavarman Pallava: The current Pallava king. Also known as Mamalla after whom Mamallapuram or Mahabalipuram is named.

Paranjyothi: Commander of the armed forces of the Pallava kingdom. Later on in life, he became one of the sixty-three Nayanmars (Shaivite saints), under the name Siruththondar.

Ilanthiraiyanar: General in the Pallava kingdom reporting to Commander Paranjyothi.

Nalankilli: The prime minister of the Pallava kingdom.

Elango: Captain in the Pallava army.

Muthuvel: Captain in the Pallava army.

Kannan: Captain in the Pallava army.

Sanghamitra: Daughter of a professor at Nalanda University.

Raman: Sergeant in the Pallava army reporting to Kannan.

Suriyan: Sergeant in the Pallava army reporting to Kannan.

Senthan: Captain in the Pallava army.

Karivalan: Captain in the Pallava army.

Bhatta: Soldier in the Pallava army in Kannan's unit.

Murugan: Soldier in the Pallava army in Kannan's unit.

Devadutta: Pallava spy based in Vathapi.

Kiruba: Pallava spy working for Devadutta.

Duraisingham: Raja of Thagadur.

Annamalai: A young captain in Duraisingham's army.

Vedam: Mamalla's factotum.

The Chalukyas

Pulikeshi: The current Chalukya king.

Naganandi: The Chalukya spy chief.

Vishnudutta: A captain in King Pulikeshi's personal guard.

Siddhadharma: A Chalukya spy.

Vedaraya: Prime minister to King Pulikeshi.

Satyaki: Commander of the Chalukya army.

Mangalesha: The Chalukya finance minister.

Kubja Vishnuvardhana: King of Vengi, brother of King Pulikeshi.

Prathapa: Commander of the Vengi army.

Aditya: Eldest son of King Pulikeshi.

Chandra: Second son of King Pulikeshi.

Ranaragha: Third son of King Pulikeshi.

Vikrama: Fourth son of King Pulikeshi.

Jayasimha: Youngest son of King Pulikeshi.

Captain Madappa: A captain in the Chalukya army.

The Pandyas

Jayanthavarman: The current Pandyan king.

Maravarman: The Pandyan prime minister.

Nedumaran: Younger brother of the Pandyan king.

Perumvellan: A general in the Pandyan army.

The Korkais

Chandrasekaran: Raja of Korkai.

Gopala: A retainer of the Raja of Korkai.

Thaamarai: Daughter of the Raja of Korkai.

Vanavarayan: Commander of the Korkai forces.

The Gangas

Srivikrama: The current Ganga king.

Paravikrama: Son of Srivikrama and the crown prince.

Somanna: Prime minister of the Gangas.

Narasimha: Commander-in-chief of the Gangas.

Shivabasappa: Finance minister of the Gangas.

Krishnappa: Commander of the fort at Asanur.

Jayaprakasha: Second-in-command to Krishnappa at the Asanur fort.

Indumathi: Krishnappa's daughter.

Devanna: A Ganga soldier.

Thimmappa: A Ganga soldier.

Mahesha: A captain in the Ganga army.

Vighnesha: A captain in the Ganga army.

Bidappa: A captain in the Ganga army.

Basavaiyya: A retired sergeant in the Ganga army.

The Banas

Krithavarman: The current Bana king.

Dasappa: Commander of the Bana forces.

Bhadrachala: Prime minister of the Banas.

Venkata: Archer in the Bana army.

The Lankans–Manavamma's men

Manavamma: The dethroned ex-king and half-brother of Tribhuvana.

Thissa: Senior commander in Manavamma's army.

Chaminda: A captain in Manavamma's army.

Nayaka: A captain in Manavamma's army.

Kushala: A soldier in Manavamma's army.

The Lankans–Tribhuvana's men

Tribhuvana: The current Lankan king of Anuradhapura.

Abhayanaga: Tribhuvana's prime minister.

Mahasena: Tribhuvana's commander-in-chief.

Hathurasingha: Captain of a ship in Tribhuvana's navy.

Premanayaka: Admiral of Tribhuvana's navy.

Karunaratna: A general in Tribhuvana's army.

Bandara: A captain in Tribhuvana's army.

Warnakula: A captain in Tribhuvana's army.

Srimana: A captain in Tribhuvana's army.

Other Characters

Sadaiyan: A thief and pickpocket.

Anjaneya: A warrior of the Banakulas.

Jabali: A warrior of the Banakulas.

Jamba: A warrior of the Banakulas.

Harshavardhana: Emperor, based out of Kannauj.

Vishnuvarma: King of Ujjain, a vassal of King Harshavardhana.

Author's Note

The last book of the trilogy brings with it a sense of closure, tinged with conflicting emotions—happiness and sadness. Happiness at having been able to complete the story, while sadness at having to bid adieu to all the characters that have lived with me for so many years.

I started writing this book around 2011 after reading Amish's Meluha series, feeling inspired to try my hand at telling stories that have not been told yet. Historical fiction, as a genre, has always appealed to me. I've long been fascinated by old structures, temples and monuments. I would stand in front of the Periya Kovil (Big Temple) in Thanjavur in Tamil Nadu, the land of my father, and let my imagination wander about how it would have looked a thousand years ago when it was inaugurated by the great Raja Raja Chola. *Did he stand at this very spot where I am standing now*? I would think.

Thus, the fascination with history. The urge to tell these stories owes a lot to how our history textbooks ignored most of the stories of yore that didn't happen in and around Delhi. A couple of years before I started writing this trilogy, my wife and I toured Karnataka—Hampi, Aihole, Pattadakal, Badami. Visiting Aihole and Badami turned my mind towards the great Kalki's *Sivagamiyin Sabatham*, which narrates the tussle between the Pallavas and Cholas. I loved that story, even more so than his famous *Ponniyin Selvan*. We also explored Sri Lanka and saw many historical sites in that lovely country. It was then when I decided to write that story, but in my own way.

However, when I actually started writing, one difficulty that arose was the lack of a villain. There were really no villains in The Battle of Vathapi who could have been made the fulcrum of the readers' displeasure and ire. Moreover, since the trilogy ends with the victory of the Pallavas, it would have been easy to caricature the Chalukyas as the villains. For this particular book, I actually wrote the last chapter first. I don't know why, but I wanted to make sure I ended it the way I wanted to, and then wrote the story from the beginning. I have never done that before, and I don't know if I will ever do it again.

I have learnt a lot along the way, and it has been a great journey. I have read somewhere that authors ought not to fall in love with their own characters, but I can't help it. There are some characters who stay on in one's mind. I shall miss them, and I hope that you, the readers, will too.

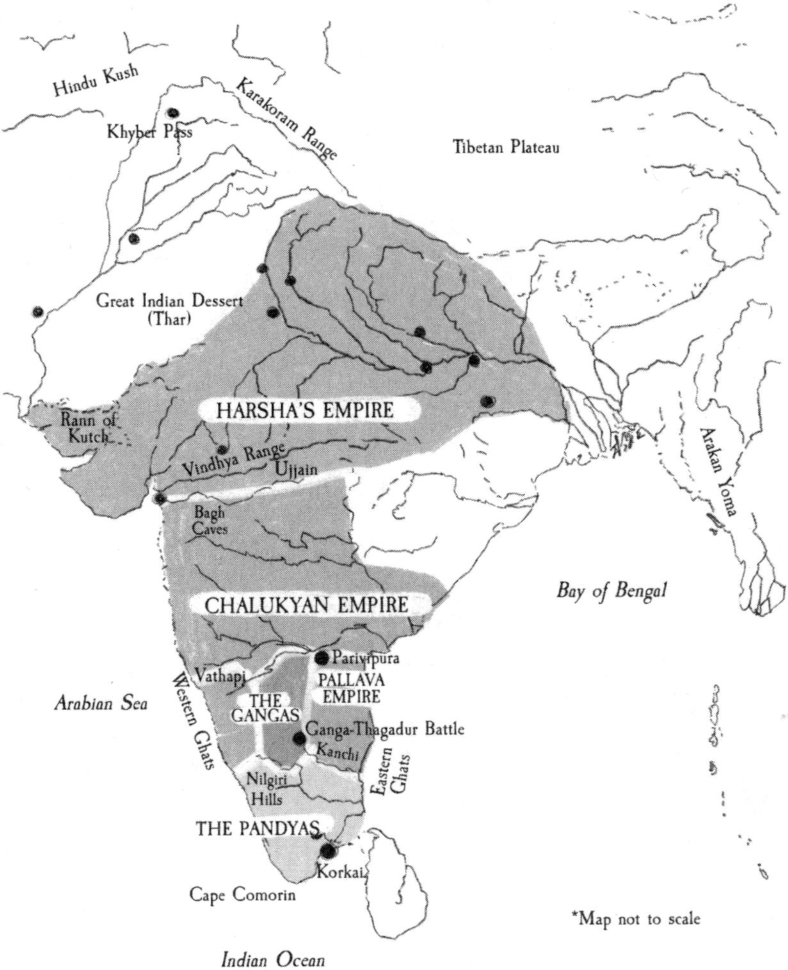
Hindu Kush
Khyber Pass
Karakoram Range
Tibetan Plateau
Great Indian Dessert
(Thar)
HARSHA'S EMPIRE
Rann of
Kutch
Vindhya Range
Ujjain
Bagh
Caves
Arakan Yoma
Bay of Bengal
CHALUKYAN EMPIRE
Parivipura
Vathapi
PALLAVA
EMPIRE
Arabian Sea
Western Ghats
THE
GANGAS
Ganga-Thagadur Battle
Kanchi
Eastern
Ghats
Nilgiri
Hills
THE PANDYAS
Korkai
Cape Comorin
*Map not to scale
Indian Ocean

Battle of Suramara

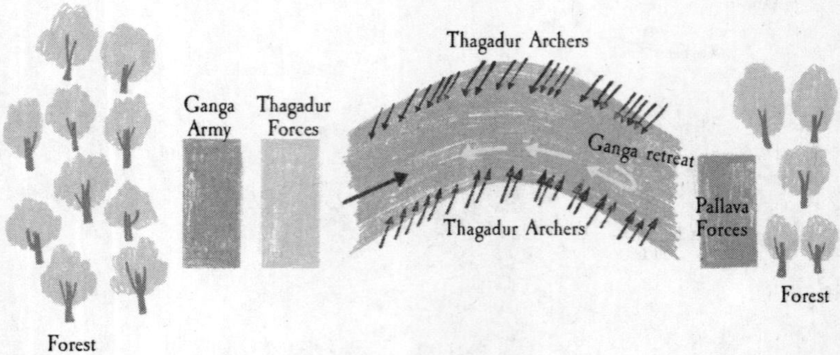

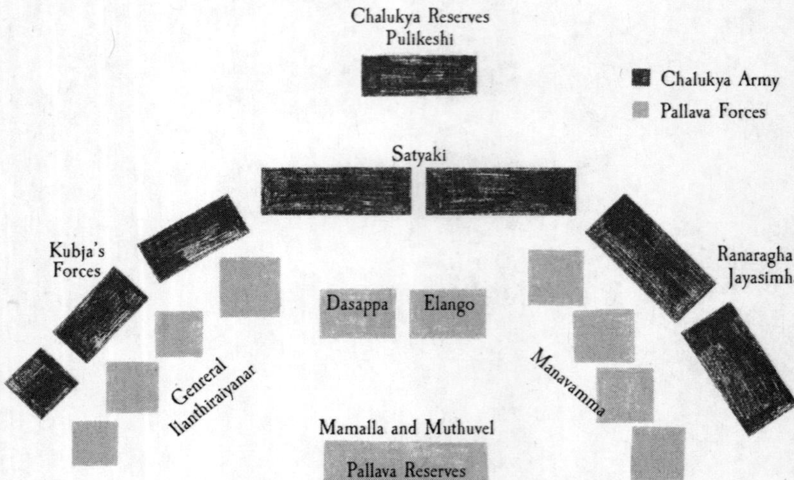

Battle of Manimangala

1

Escapade on the High Seas

Off the coast of Korkai, November 641 CE

The night that Captain Hathurasingha considered the most humiliating of his career started off like any other night of the past month. A cool breeze was doing its bit in dispelling the oppressive heat caused by the sun burning bright at these latitudes. The captain had finished his dinner and was taking a turn about the deck, not just to cool himself or get some exercise but also to ensure that his vessel was in good condition.

Hathurasingha was captain for many reasons, one of which was his fastidiousness when it came to running his ship. He frowned on laxity of any sort among his crew and his attention to detail was legendary. He was spoken of by new recruits in the Lankan navy in terms of utmost reverence.

Hathurasingha was in his late thirties. His long, jet-black hair was tied together at the top by a band encircling his head. He had a broad forehead, wide-set, clear eyes, a slightly bulbous nose, characteristic of his race, set over a small mouth with even, pearly-white teeth. He did sport a moustache but eschewed the beard, more out of vanity than any other reason. His stubble showed signs of white, scattered among the jet black, and he felt that he hadn't yet reached the age to grow a salt-and-pepper beard.

The deck moved gently under his feet, the ship riding the swells easily. The vessel lay closer to the Korkai shores, now. He had earlier been in charge of blockading Korkai, and ensuring that relief supplies did not get to the town when it was under siege by their allies, the Pandyas. Now that the port town had fallen, the blockade was no longer in force. His job now was to ensure that no ships threatened the town. He looked to his right and left, and saw the other two ships that were part of his group, led by two younger captains who reported to him.

Hathurasingha was brought up short by a creaking noise from a plank that he had just stepped on. He repeated the action, trying to locate the source of the sound. He found two misaligned planks and immediately called out to one of his men and pointed it out to him.

'Get it repaired first thing tomorrow,' he said as he resumed his pacing.

He could make out the lights of the town of Korkai as well as of the fort walls. *This is not what I hoped to be doing as captain of a ship*, he thought. *I wish there were some action. Perhaps I need to send a message to the admiral to reassign me to chasing pirates.*

The young lad up in the crow's nest of Hathurasingha's ship shifted this way and that in his perch, trying to get comfortable for the night. He had drawn the night shift this week and was immensely glad for it. Night shift in the crow's nest was much sought after and he and the other boys usually gambled for it.

For one, it was much cooler high above the ship than down below the decks. Moreover, there really wasn't much to do at night, especially when the ship was anchored, and the skies were clear of any rain clouds.

He looked up and saw that the moon was but a sliver and any light from that direction was notional. There were a few scattered clouds that flitted across the sky, obscuring even that little bit of the moon from time to time. He had been trained to not look towards the city when he was on watch, especially at night. He had been told that it would destroy his night vision. So, he studiously put the town at his back and looked into the darkness. Into nothingness.

There really wasn't anything to see. He caught occasional flashes of white if he looked down at the sea as the froth-crested waves lapped around the vessel.

The young lad wedged himself into a comfortable supine position, his back tucked down into the basket, and his legs hanging over it. He started dreaming about his girl back home, the one who gave him naughty little glances and smiles. Gradually, his eyes closed as he was rocked to sleep by the gentle swaying of the ship.

The boats had left the islands a few hours earlier. There were about thirty of them, each holding twenty armed fighting men. The men also doubled as oarsmen. The boats were capable of putting on sails but the men had decided against it. A sail, while it allows for speed, also increases the height of the boat and makes it visible from afar.

Visibility was something that the men on the boats weren't very keen on tonight, hence the use of the oars. Usually, the oarsmen were goaded into pulling in rhythm by the beats of the boatswain but these men were not regular oarsmen. Their trade and lives depended on their ability to remain undetected. They had trained themselves into pulling together without any verbal commands or cues.

The oars dipped silently into the water and pushed the boats forward, moving quietly but urgently, the bows of the boats cutting through the gentle ocean swells, leaving white streaks of froth in their wake. The lack of moonlight helped them stay hidden, as the boats almost disappeared into the sea.

The men at the helm first noticed the masts of the ships and then the hulls as they pulled closer. Chaminda, who was standing towards the front of one of the boats, wondered about that and asked one of the men.

'The earth is curved,' the man had whispered, showing the curved surface of his palm to illustrate. 'So when it comes up, you first see the mast and sails and then the rest of the ship.'

Chaminda had marvelled at how he, who was supposed to have had a good education, had had no clue about this while this man, a pirate, who had probably never seen the inside of a school, knew all about it. Then he realized that the man practically lived on the sea and would have learned about it from his fellow seamen. *And I never paid attention when the monks taught geography or geometry anyway,* he thought, a grin splitting his face. He had always been more interested in learning the more practical arts—like archery, swordsmanship and horse-riding.

He snapped out of his reverie and paid attention as the boats closed in on the ships. The oarsmen had automatically decreased the strength of their pulls and the boats had slowed down perceptibly. The man deputed by the pirate chief to lead the raid was a swarthy individual with an evil-looking scar on the left side of his face. The fact that he was of a normally cheerful disposition enhanced the apparent evilness of his looks because his smile ended up making him look more sinister. His name was Arivu, meaning intelligence.

He turned around and moved his hands vigorously a few times, in a prearranged signal. Ten boats each peeled off from the main body towards the two ships at the ends. The rest of the boats, including the one with him and Chaminda, moved towards the central ship.

The oarsmen had shipped their oars now as the boats glided silently forward of their own accord. The men aboard stood ready with grappling hooks in their hands, their mouths clasped tightly around the blades of their swords. Chaminda let Arivu and his men take the lead, given their expertise.

Once the boats reached the ships, the men in front put their hands out and gently pushed against the hulls, ensuring that the boats did not make a sound by bumping into them. The boats were spread out along the length of the ships. Then, without any overt signal, the grappling hooks were thrown over the ship with the men hauling back on the other end of the ropes till they heard the *click* sound that indicated that the hooks had caught on something and wouldn't dislodge.

They quickly shimmied up the sides of the ship, almost walking up, and landed lightly on its deck.

Hathurasingha was asleep in his cabin. He was a light sleeper and his eyes flew open. He lay there for a few seconds cursing himself and his propensity to wake up every time the ship creaked or waves lapped the hull.

He wondered what had woken him up now. He knew the normal sounds on a ship—the creaking of the boards, the straining of the masts, the flapping of sails, the slapping of the waves against the ship, the calls of the seagulls, the roar of the waves, the whistling of the wind, the clink of bottles as his men drank and their loud voices.

He searched his mind as to the sound that had woken him. It was none of the usual sounds, he decided. It was a *thud* followed by a *click*. That bothered him. In his years of experience, he had never heard those two sounds on any ship that he had served on. He *had,* however, heard those sounds when they had attacked other ships.

He got up with a start. He knew exactly what those sounds were. There was a pull rope next to his bed, attached to a bell, which was to be pulled only in case of an emergency. It was most definitely an emergency. Hathurasingha pulled on the rope, jumped out of bed, picked up his sword and bounded out of his cabin on to the deck.

The scene that greeted him filled him with dismay. He saw several attackers already on board the ship. His men were scrambling on to the deck, looking half asleep, their swords still in their scabbards. As the first few men came up and realized that they were under attack, they grabbed despairingly at their swords. That was the last action that they took because the attackers plunged their swords into them and they crumpled and fell, blood gushing from their wounds.

Hathurasingha screamed at his men to look alive as he jumped over the railing separating his cabin from the rest of the ship and landed on the deck, his sword raised in defiance. He quickly engaged a couple of attackers even as he tried to rally his men.

'To me, men. Look alive. Don't give up. For Maharaja Tribhuvana!'

Hathurasingha fought hard, for his king and country of course, but also for his ship and his pride. Ultimately, all human endeavour boils down to one's ego and Hathurasingha's ego wouldn't allow him to surrender tamely. He set upon the attackers, fighting skillfully, leaving bodies on the deck in his wake. His heart rate and breathing were both controlled, through long years of yoga and practice, while his sword arm beat a staccato against his opponents' swords. He knew that it was a lost cause, since he couldn't find too many of his men still standing. And yet, he fought on. Almost singlehandedly.

His opponents, realising that he was the main impediment to their quick victory, rushed at him in numbers. He engaged two men simultaneously and was pushed back by them until he found himself up against the main mast. As he parried an attack from the man on his right, the man on his left slashed down with his sword on Hathurasingha's sword arm, leaving a deep gash there. Hathurasingha's fist opened involuntarily, and his sword clattered to the floor. Immediately, the man on the left whipped his sword up and held its point under Hathurasingha's chin, hissing, 'Call off your men, Captain. We don't need more bloodshed.'

The other man on the right had raised his sword to bring it down on Hathurasingha's neck when the first man cried out, 'Stop! The man is disarmed. You will not strike him,' pushing the other man away. He immediately turned his attention back towards Hathurasingha.

'As I said, Captain, please ask your men to stop. I would hate to kill my fellow Singhalese,' Chaminda said with purpose, the grim expression on his face giving further weight to his words.

Hathurasingha gazed at him, his eyes stone cold, before he moved his head to one side, without breaking eye contact with his captor, and yelled, 'Throw down your swords, men. We will live to fight another day!'

The same scene was taking place aboard the other two ships. Here too, Manavamma's soldiers ensured that there was no unnecessary bloodshed as they took over the ships.

Hathurasingha stood defiantly as he was tied to the main mast while his men were herded and tied together before being shut in the bilge, below deck. His eyes never left the man who had captured him. He was cursing himself for being all sorts of a fool and for not having anticipated an attack on him from this side. He was being too harsh on himself, of course, but Hathurasingha had not become one of the elite captains in the Lankan navy by going easy on himself. He seethed inside as he wondered what this would do to his reputation.

He looked at Chaminda and asked, 'So you are one of Manavamma's men?'

Chaminda paused midstride and turned back towards him.

'Yes,' he said, a little smile playing on his lips.

'I should have known. Only you guys would get together with pirates and other such riff-raff.'

Chaminda shrugged. 'We find what allies we can in war. You people have no right to talk anyway, the way your king attacked ours surreptitiously and defeated him. Manavamma is, after all, the legitimate ruler of the land.'

Hathurasingha snorted and then asked, 'What is to become of me and my men?'

'You will be taken ashore and, after a few days, released on a lonely beach. You can find your way back to Anuradhapura.'

'Are you sure that you will not kill and burn us on that lonely beach?'

Chaminda's eyes flashed. 'We don't make war that way. Ideally, you would be kept as prisoners, but we don't have the men or the time for that.'

'So all this was to lift the blockade?'

Chaminda smiled. 'What else? Your friends at Korkai are in for a surprise.'

2

Refugee Travails

Kanchipuram and Parivipura, November 641 CE

The large coach rattled along on the *rajapattai* or king's road, going down south towards Kanchi. King Krithavarman of Parivipura and his wives sat in the chariot, their faces identically grim. The princes were in a coach behind them while the lead coach contained Sanghamitra and her two companions.

The journey had not been excessively tough on them. The Pallava general Ilanthiraiyanar had received the message from Sanghamitra and had dispatched a detachment of troops to pick up the king and his entourage and guide them safely to Kanchi.

They had had to walk in the forest for at most a week. The Pallava soldiers had found them soon after. The queens were ecstatic that their walking days were over. So, secretly, was Krithavarman.

No, it wasn't the toughness of the journey that was the reason for their grim visage. They were lamenting the loss of their kingdom and prestige, of becoming refugees in another kingdom. Neither Krithavarman nor his queens had ever faced hardship before. The kingdom had been a protectorate of the Pallavas for a couple of generations, with the result that it had not faced any significant adversity over the past half a century or so. Even during Pulikeshi's campaign to Kanchi twenty years earlier, he had given Parivipura a miss, dismissing any threats from that quarter as negligible.

And now this. Having to run away from their kingdom, leaving behind their comfortable lifestyles. They had hardly taken a tenth of their jewellery with them. That, more than anything else, explained the glumness that had descended upon the two queens. The thought of Chalukya soldiers taking over their clothes, jewellery, vessels and rooms was maddening.

The queens had tried to explain their angst to their husband, but Krithavarman was in a funk of his own, and had responded rather testily to their plaintive cries. The women had subsided into a glum silence from which they would emerge with an occasional sniff and a whisper or two, lamenting their fate to one another.

The coach rattled on, the charioteer hastening the horses forward with occasional cries of *hyah hyah* as they sped towards Kanchi.

Sanghamitra sat alongside Anjaneya, Jabali and Venkata, her eyes closed, but far from asleep. She was pensive and the reason was her deep worry about Elango. She wished she could rush back to Parivipura and get together with Jamba to figure out a way to free him. But Elango had entrusted her with the task of getting the Parivipura royals to safety and she was not going to fail him.

She was glad that she was in a separate coach along with the two Banakulas and the young archer. The wailing and whining that the queens had done in the initial days of their escape had set her teeth on edge. Not one to suffer fools gladly, it took all her self-control to not snap back at royalty. She had tried to keep herself away from the women and from King Krithavarman himself. *He is an inveterate grumbler. A fit husband for those two whiner wives of his*, she thought, perhaps a trifle ungraciously.

The only saving grace for her was the presence of the three young men. They had tried to bring some levity into the bleak and dreary atmosphere by clowning around even more than usual. It had helped Mitra maintain her sanity. They made her predicament bearable.

When the Pallava soldiers had shown up, she had suggested that the young men ride with her. This way she could ensure her distance from the royal whining.

Two days later, they sighted the gates of Kanchi. Krithavarman had been here a couple of times and hence knew what to expect. His queens, however, had never been to the fabled city and they were agog with curiosity. As the chariots rumbled through the city lanes, moving towards the palaces, the queens forgot their misfortunes and took in the sights that the city had to offer, the wares being sold in the various shops and the profusion of foreign-looking folks—Chinese, Malays, Arabs, Romans, Greeks and those from lands further west.

The chariots finally came to a halt in front of the gates of a large house surrounded by high walls. Mitra got down from the chariot and whispered something to the guard, who nodded, saluted and then raced inside the house. A short wait later, General Ilanthiraiyanar came out in a hurry.

'Welcome, Sire. Welcome to Kanchi. I am sorry that your arrival here is under these unfortunate circumstances, but rest assured that we are working on it.'

Krithavarman got down from the chariot sporting a peevish look on his face, something that the general did not fail to notice.

'Sire, if you will follow me, we have this next palace all set up for your visit.'

Kritavarman's lips curled up derisively. 'Visit?'

'Why yes, Sire,' said the general with a smile, 'we consider this trip of yours, unfortunate though it is, merely a visit. You will soon be able to go back to your kingdom.'

Kritavarman's face lost its petulance and visibly brightened. His queens broke excitedly into the conversation.

'Do you really mean that …'

'Are you sure …'

'Yes yes, Your Majesties. Let's go in. You must all be very tired. Kindly take the rest of the day to recuperate. I shall inform the maharaja of your arrival. He is looking forward to meeting you and personally conveying his intent to see that your kingdom is restored to you.'

Ilanthiraiyanar gestured to his men to take the visitors inside. As they passed by, he noticed that Sanghamitra was standing to one side. The general jerked his head at her to follow him. He hurriedly left the palace, turned into the gates of his own residence and led her to his chamber.

The general turned around as they entered the chamber and took Sanghamitra's hands in his own, a gentle smile on his face.

'How are you doing, my dear? You look all in.'

'I am alright, Sir.'

'You sure?'

Sanghamitra gave him a long, steady look and then sighed. Ilanthiraiyanar led her to a divan on the floor and bade her to sit down. He took his own seat and then asked her, 'Elango?'

Sanghamitra's eyes widened in surprise. 'How … how did you know, Sir?'

The general smiled.

'Call it age or wisdom. It is pretty obvious from what you both said in your different messages to me. Or rather, what you both left unsaid.'

Sanghamitra smiled. She ought to have known that there was no way of hiding anything from the general. She told him the whole story of the fall of Parivipura, their escape through the hidden chamber and tunnel, Elango's insistence on her going with the royal family and his instruction to her to ensure that they were seen safely through to Kanchi.

'Now that I have done that, I would like to request your permission to go back there, Sir.'

The general stroked his moustache gently, deep in thought.

'It might not be a bad idea for you to go back there. However, we will be having a council meeting tomorrow. I want you to be present when Commander Paranjyoti and I, along with Prime Minister Nalankilli, meet with the maharaja. King Krithavarman will also be present, although honestly, between you and me, I do not know how useful he is going to be.'

Sanghamitra was too well-trained to respond to every comment made by her superiors, but the look on her face was enough to let the general know what she thought of the king of Parivipura.

Deep underground, in the dungeons beneath the city of Parivipura, an unkempt, dirty and bearded man sat on the floor of his cell, exercising. He went through the series of yogasanas that he had been doing from the day of his incarceration. He knew that he would be in here for a while, and that it was up to him to ensure that his body and mind did not wither away.

Every morning—and the only way he knew it was morning was by the type of meal provided to him, since the dungeon was in almost perpetual darkness—he would sit and do his asanas. He would then meditate for an hour or so, observing his breath, letting it get slower and slower till he went into a deeply meditative state, from which he would emerge to then eat his breakfast, a very watery gruel.

He had lost a lot of weight. He was much thinner now, and those once splendid muscles of his had started to whittle down. Only the asanas that he religiously practised, every day without fail, kept his muscles from dissipating.

Elango spent the rest of the day in contemplation. He was dirty and grimy from not having had a bath in weeks. He knew that cleanliness kept diseases at bay and had tried to ask his gaoler, the man who got him his meals three times a day, to get him a bucket of water, but to no avail. There was a hole dug in the ground that he used to relieve himself, and a small pail of water that was replenished daily, for his ablutions as well as for drinking.

He would wet his dirty *veshti*[1] and wipe his face and torso with it, so as to at least feel like he had cleaned himself. The dungeon was damp and Elango had developed a cold over the last week or so. He had a nasty, hacking, wet cough that just didn't seem to go away. Yet he continued with his routine. He

---

1 Lower garment worn by men, fastened at the waist.

was a warrior and knew the value of routine and discipline. And so, he soldiered on.

Jamba lounged around in front of the entrance to the dungeon. The guards there were used to his presence now.

After leaving Sanghamitra, he had made his way across the river and into the city under the pretext of searching for a job. He knew that a newly conquered city that had been subjected to bombardment would be in need of labourers, and he had volunteered to help in clearing the stones and debris from the streets. He had gradually worked his way towards the dungeons.

Once he had made some money from the work, he had quit and had taken to going out into the forests outside the city every other morning, to hunt. He would invariably come back with a deer or pig and that gave him enough money to spend the rest of the day just loitering around the place.

The guards outside the dungeons had got to know him fairly well. They were curious about him once they learnt that he was from the Dandakaranya, that forbidding forest of which they had merely heard tales.

He, a normally taciturn man, would nevertheless regale them with stories of the forests, the hunts that he had been on, and tales of the various fearsome beasts, some true, many imaginary, that he had made up on the spot. The guards hung on to his every word. He would occasionally buy liquor for the guards, who would surreptitiously tuck it into the folds of their veshtis and go inside the dungeon to hide it.

He had asked to be shown the insides of the dungeon and a guard with whom he had become very friendly had done so one night. The path descended about fifty feet or so before it levelled and entered a long tunnel. On either side, were small chambers, most of which were occupied. As they neared the end of the dungeon, Jamba recognised Elango. He seemed to be sleeping, and Jamba could make out that he had lost a lot of weight since he had last seen him.

He was at least reassured that Elango was still alive. He knew that it was up to him to rescue his friend. A plan began to form in his mind.

3
Chalukyan Moves

Parivipura, November 641 CE

The period after dinner and before sleep is often the best time to sit back and relax. The people gathered in the king's tent were doing just that. Pulikeshi was surrounded by his sons Aditya, Ranaragha and Jayasimha and his brother Kubja Vishnuvardhana. Commander Satyaki was also there in the tent. All of them were sprawled on their respective divans, cups of wine in their hands. The only other member of the tent and the only one without a cup of wine in his hands was the redoubtable Chalukya spy chief Naganandi who was a teetotaller. He didn't lounge on the divan either but sat in a *padmasana* pose, legs crossed and his back ramrod straight.

There were four torches stuck in torch holders that illuminated the interior of the tent. The shadows they threw bobbed and wobbled along with the motion of the flames.

Naganandi watched their chatter impatiently. His was a businesslike nature and idle chitchat bored him. Still, this was his king, and he maintained his silence. His face conveyed absolutely nothing. The spy chief's face always conveyed exactly what he wanted it to show. Naganandi had joined them a week or so earlier. He had had news of the victory at Parivipura and of Pulikeshi camping there. His spies had told him that King Harsha, for all his posturing with his armies north of the Narmada, had not shown any intention of crossing the river. It was probably because of the presence of the Chalukya army that Pulikeshi had sent up north.

Naganandi had then decided that he couldn't contribute anything more by sitting in Vathapi. Taking a couple of soldiers as bodyguards, he had started for Parivipura. They had made good time and reached Parivipura in a week or so. He had found Pulikeshi, his brother and sons sitting there celebrating their victory.

It had incensed Naganandi to see this. *The old king has probably lost his desire for battle*, he had thought rather uncharitably. *Why is he not pressing home his advantage?*

Naganandi himself had not wasted any time. He had reached around dusk and had immediately met his king.

'My King,' he had said with a perfunctory bow as he barged into his tent. Pulikeshi was resting and had been angered by the temerity of the person who had barged in. However, seeing that it was Naganandi, his anger had turned into surprise.

'Naga! What are you doing here?'

'I thought I could be of more use to you here than listen to the lunatic ravings of your womenfolk,' said the spy chief in his own charming manner.

Pulikeshi had smiled.

'Can we get together your brother, sons and the commander?' he had asked, without any of the pleasantries that normal people are wont to exchange when meeting someone after a hiatus.

Pulikeshi had raised his eyebrows.

'Now?'

'Why? Are they doing something so important that they can't be disturbed?' Then, noting the look of annoyance on his king's face, he had said, 'We need to discuss our future course of action, Ereya.'

Pulikeshi had nodded. The name Naganandi used was a name by which he had been known in his childhood. None but Naganandi even remembered it now. All those who had called him by that name were long gone.

He had sent for his brother, sons and Satyaki to assemble in his tent. They were to see the spy chief there and, after acknowledging his presence with bows, looked towards Pulikeshi for an explanation. Pulikeshi however, was enjoying their momentary discomfiture and refused to supply any.

'Thank you for coming here on such short notice, leaving aside the many important activities you all were engaged in,' started Naganandi, more than a hint of sarcasm in his opening statement. 'The maharaja called you here at my request.'

The others had waited for him to continue.

'First, let me congratulate you all on a splendid victory and for the capture of the fort.' Then, lest the assembled company start feeling too full of itself, he continued, '… the capture of an admittedly minor fort of a small feudatory of the Pallavas. I was expecting it to take less time, but you are the experts in warfare, and I am sure you knew what you were doing,' he finished ungraciously, his eyes raking the men.

Pulikeshi suppressed a smile. He was used to the idiosyncrasies of his spy chief, as was Commander Satyaki to a certain extent, but the others looked rather shocked.

'The point, however,' continued Naganandi, 'is about what you are planning to do now.'

The princes looked at one another and at a look from the crown prince Aditya, his brothers Ranaragha and Jayasimha kept mum. It was Kubja Vishnuvardhana who answered, 'We sit here waiting for the Pallavas to attack us. We know they are duty-bound to support Krithavarman. Once they attack us here, we will crush them.'

'How?' asked the spy chief.

'How what?'

'How will you crush them? How do you know they will not crush you? Why do you assume that a fort that has been taken by you once cannot be taken from you by someone else?'

Kubja subsided into a sullen silence. It was then that Naganandi turned to Pulikeshi and said, 'My King, this is not the moment to feel satisfied with what you have achieved. We need to strike while the momentum is on our side. The Pallavas are reacting to us now. If we wait here, we hand over the momentum to them. They can then choose the time and method of attack. We will be like those clay birds that kids knock off in fairs with their little bows and arrows. All arranged in a row and ready to be picked off!'

Pulikeshi's brows puckered at this. He looked towards Satyaki and asked, 'What do you think, Commander?'

Satyaki, who was feeling slightly abashed that he hadn't thought of this on his own, said, 'I agree with the spy chief, Sire. We need to attack them while we are in command.'

'What would you suggest then?' Pulikeshi asked, looking back at Naganandi.

'Where is our Ganga army?'

'Waiting at the border is what I hear.'

'Let us push on south and link up with them. We can then jointly move towards Kanchi and attack the Pallavas.'

'Wouldn't that be the obvious choice?' asked the king.

'Yes. But it is the prudent one. My spies tell me that Jayanthavarman is ensconced in Korkai and I don't expect any help from his end in the near future. Tribhuvana is having his own issues with Manavamma. That means that we need to have overwhelming force to win. And we can only do that if we combine our forces.'

'What about Parivipura then?' asked young Jayasimha.

He nearly quailed under the glare that the spy chief directed at him. That was his usual stare, but Jayasimha wasn't used to it.

'We will leave a token force at Parivipura, to hold the place and keep the populace under subjugation. The bulk of the forces must start south, to link up with our allies.'

Naganandi kept quiet after this, allowing the king some time to ruminate on what he had said. He knew his king. He knew he was a careful and deliberate man when it came to taking a decision. Pulikeshi would think through the pros and cons of any suggestion. He wasn't going to jump on a scheme just because it had come from his spy chief. But Naganandi also knew that his king did give a lot of importance to his views. Years of struggling together had built that trust between them. So he had waited.

Eventually, Pulikeshi spoke. 'We march tomorrow. Let's get moving.' Then, looking around at the others, he had asked, 'Do you have someone whom we can trust to protect Parivipura with a token force?'

'Commander Prathapa,' Kubja had replied. 'A stable man. He can hold the fort.'

Pulikeshi nodded his assent. Then, looking at Satyaki, he said, 'Commander, prepare for us to depart early tomorrow morning.'

Pulikeshi looked at Naganandi and asked, 'Satisfied?'

Naganandi gave a barely perceptible nod. His face was impassive, but the king, who had worked a long time with his spy chief, was probably the only person who could even discern what was going on in his mind behind that wooden facade.

'Looks like you have something on your mind, Naganandi avare,' he said, smiling.

Naganandi nodded. There was no hiding anything from his king.

Pulikeshi threw back his head and laughed. The others looked at him, startled into silence. 'Naganandi avaru has something to say to us,' said Pulikeshi.

'Thank you, Your Majesty,' said Naganandi. 'We need to have a discussion.'

'Go on. We are all here.'

Naganandi hesitated momentarily and then said, 'No, Sire. Just you and I.'

Pulikeshi looked puzzled but he nevertheless indicated to the others to vacate the tent. Once they were alone, he asked, 'What is it, Naga?'

'It is about our plan.'

'What about it?'

'I wasn't completely honest with you all.'

'Why not?'

'I didn't want it to be known early enough. There are always spies in any army and I didn't want what we wanted to do to reach the ears of the Pallavas this early in the game.'

Pulikeshi sat up, interested. His eyes sparkled. He felt alive and young. This was what it used to be like in the old days—the wily spy chief and him discussing how to go about defeating their enemies.

'What do you have in mind?'

Naganandi told him.

4

Discussions in Kanchi

Kanchi, November 641 CE

Prince Mahendravarman rushed into the chambers of his father, Maharaja Narasimhavarman Pallava, also known as Mamalla. The king, he could see, was dressing. His mother stood dutifully by her husband's side, waiting to apply the *tilak*[2] on his forehead and place the crown on his head before he headed out for the day.

Narasimhavarman looked up as his son entered and his face split into a smile.

'What are you doing here now? Don't you have your training?'

The prince, a young lad of about eighteen, grinned. 'We had special training in the morning. Swimming across the river. We finished early and amma told me that you were having a council of war today. I was hoping to be able to join it,' he said eagerly.

---

2 Vermillion paste. A religious mark.

Mamalla pursed his lips, one eyebrow raised, and looked sideways at his son as his wife applied the tilak to his forehead.

'Are you sure your captain will not mind you absconding like this? In my days, I couldn't even go to pee without his permission.'

'Maharaja!' said his wife, slapping his arm playfully as her son burst out into laughter.

'It is still the same, appa. It is just that I am a bit lucky today. The captain dismissed us for the day.'

Mamalla grinned and bent his head so that his wife could place the crown on it. He waited patiently as she fussed about trying to position it correctly.

'Are we done yet?' he asked his wife.

'No, we aren't,' she snapped, adjusting the crown this way and that. Then, with a final tug and a smile, she said, 'Now we are done.'

'Yes, My Queen,' said Mamalla, bowing to her and then putting his arm around her waist and pulling her to him. He planted a resounding kiss on her cheek. The queen reddened in embarrassment even as her son rolled his eyes.

'Appa, can you not do that in front of me?'

'What? Kiss my wife? Where do you think you came from?' asked Mamalla, a wicked grin on his face. The remark caused a further reddening of the queen's cheeks as she hit him on his arm in mock anger.

'Get going. You are incorrigible, you know. And in front of our son at that!'

Mamalla chuckled and then, turning to his son, asked, 'Coming, my boy?'

The prince laughed delightedly. 'So, I can attend the council meeting then?'

'If you are going to ask questions like that, perhaps I had better not take you to the council, after all.'

'Alright. Alright. I shall keep my trap shut and listen.'

Mamalla grinned and put his arm around his son's neck, pulling him close playfully, before planting a kiss on his head.

'Perhaps it would do you good to attend after all. You might well learn something,' he said as they left the chambers for the council room.

The others were already in place when Mamalla entered, followed by his son. As the king took his place on his throne, Prince Mahendravarman went around the room, bowing to King Krithavarman and then to Commander Paranjyothi and General Ilanthiraiyanar. As he stood straight after bowing to the general, he said, 'We have been left free for the rest of the day, Sir, and I requested permission from the king to attend the council meeting. I hope it is alright with you.'

Ilanthiraiyanar looked up at Mamalla, who winked at him. The general turned back to the young prince, a cadet in his army, and said, 'I wouldn't want any young cadet to attend the meeting …'

The prince's face fell.

'… but,' he continued, 'the prince of this kingdom can certainly attend. There would be much to learn here.'

Mahendra's face lit up on hearing these words. He looked around for a place to sit and noticed a beautiful and intelligent-looking woman sitting to one side of the general. He could barely take his eyes off her. He had no idea who she was but, in his mind, anyone invited to a council meeting must be important. He gave her a quick little bow and then sat on the other side, opposite her. This way, he could keep looking at her. And she was spectacular to look at.

Mitra saw the look of adoration on the young prince's face and dismissed it from her mind. She was used to men, young and old, giving her more than a passing glance. It used to bother her at one time, but not anymore.

Mamalla called the meeting to order.

'Friends, let me begin by first welcoming our guest, the king of Parivipura, Raja Krithavarman. He has come here under rather trying circumstances and is an honoured guest of our land. However, I would like to assure the raja that we will not rest until he is restored to his throne and takes back what rightfully belongs to him.'

Cries of 'hear hear' broke out in the chambers. Krithavarman bowed to Mamalla and sat back, looking relieved.

'Let us now focus on what we need to do next. For the past several months, we have been on the receiving end of the Chalukyan offensive. We have lost Korkai to Jayanthavarman. Parivipura has fallen to Pulikeshi. Tribhuvana and his men have blockaded the coast. The fort at Asanur has been retaken by the Gangas, and what's more, they have recaptured the fort at Guddahalli.'

'What has happened to the Raja of Thagadur?' asked Mahendra.

'He escaped,' said the general. 'We hear that a gallant soldier in his army, by the name of Annamalai, held off a numerically superior Ganga force for over three days, allowing the raja to find his way back to our side of the border.'

'And what about Annamalai?' asked the prince.

'Neither he nor any of his men made it. They fell to a man, going down fighting.'

Silence reigned in the chambers for some time. Looks of profound sorrow crossed the faces of Paranjyothi and Mamalla. Presently, Mamalla spoke. 'Make sure to raise a hero stone for Annamalai.'

The general nodded and then said, 'To continue what His Majesty was saying, the Ganga soldiers did not stop with annihilating Annamalai's forces. We hear that they have been joined by a contingent of Chalukya soldiers and are even now camped just outside our borders.'

'Why?' asked the prince.

'Why don't you try answering the question, young man?' asked Paranjyothi.

Mahendra was thrown into some confusion at suddenly being made the centre of attention. He frowned as he thought long and hard. Presently, he said, 'I suppose they are waiting for something?'

'Alright, but what?'

'An attack from us?'

The commander shook his head.

'If that were the case, why would they stop on their side of the border? They would march into our lands and take the fight to us. They have a decent-sized army.'

'Pulikeshi,' said Mitra softly.

All the assembled heads jerked towards her.

'Explain,' said Ilanthiraiyanar.

'I need answers to a couple of questions first, Sir. Is Jayanthavarman still at Korkai?'

The general nodded.

'Has Tribhuvana landed his forces on the mainland?'

'Not that we know of. I have spies along the coast and would have heard about it, if he had.'

Mitra smiled.

'They are waiting for reinforcements, Sir. Since we know that neither Jayanthavarman nor Tribhuvana is coming to their aid, there is only one other place from which they can hope for reinforcements.'

'Aah,' said the general. 'Pulikeshi.'

'Yes, Sir.'

'But isn't Pulikeshi ensconced at Parivipura after his victory there?' interjected Mahendra, looking at Mitra. He felt the urge to prove his intelligence to her.

Mitra gave him a cool glance and then turned towards the generals and Mamalla to reply, bringing a dark flush of anger to Mahendra's face. No young man likes to see a pretty woman treat him like a child and it was obvious that that was how Mitra saw him.

'Do we have any intelligence that says that he is ensconced there? I haven't heard anything, and I doubt if their spies could have crossed us without me noticing.'

As she said this, there was a commotion outside. Ilanthiraiyanar turned around and, with a gesture of his hand, asked the guard to find out what it was about. The guard came back shortly thereafter and bowed to the assembled members and said, 'There is a man who claims to have some information for you, General. Says his name is Kirupa.'

The general's face brightened as he heard the name. 'Ask him to come in.'

A bald man with a flowing beard entered the room and stood gazing at the others, a bit awed. His eyes widened as they caught sight of the maharaja. Kirupa bowed deep to his king and then to the others as well. In his mind, anyone who was part of this group around the king was worthy to be bowed to. Who was he to figure out whom to bow to and whom not to?

'Sit down, Kirupa,' said the general, in a kindly tone.

'Aah, that's okay, Sir. I have some news that I thought was urgent and critical enough for me to pass it on to you immediately.'

'Have you just come to the city?'

'Yes, Sir. I was riding all night.'

His face reflects the journey, thought Ilanthiraiyanar.

'Go on. What is this news that is both urgent and critical?'

'The Chalukyas are coming to attack us.'

If he thought that this would elicit stunned and surprised responses and reactions from the others, he was disappointed. The others in the room looked pensive and even thoughtful, but not surprised.

It was Mitra who responded to this revelation, 'When you say attack us, do you mean Kanchi directly?'

'Yes. They are on their way to Kanchi.'

'How do you know this?'

'After my last visit here to apprise the general of the fact that Pulikeshi was marching for war, I went back and came across them, on their way to Parivipura. I joined the group, posing as a cook, and got an opportunity to be part of their campaign. I was there during the siege of Parivipura.'

'And the army has now moved out?'

'Yes, Sir. Two weeks ago, the king ordered a large portion of the army, barring a few brigades who were left to maintain control of Parivipura, to decamp. We were told that we were on our way to link up with the Gangas.'

'So, they *are* going to link up with them,' said Ilanthiraiyanar.

'That's what it looked like, Sir. But a week ago, the army suddenly wheeled south-east. There was no way that we were going to link up with the Gangas in that direction. I asked around and the general word in the camp was that we were on our way to Kanchi. I felt that I needed to get this to you as quickly as possible. I waited for the night, stole a horse and started riding back. The last three days I flogged the poor horse almost to its death.'

'Thank you, Kirupa,' said Mamalla. 'Well,' he said, looking at Mitra, 'it seems that you are right, young lady.'

'It seems so, Sire. We now know why the Gangas are waiting.'

'Them and their Chalukyan contingent,' said Kirupa.

'What was that?' asked young Mahendra.

'The Chalukyas divided their army into two, with the larger portion with Pulikeshi and a smaller, but by no means insignificant one, joining Srivikrama and the Gangas.'

'That is a fair-sized army then, Your Majesty,' said Paranjyothi.

Mamalla nodded, his face clouded in worry.

General Ilanthiraiyanar vocalized his thoughts. 'What we need to think about is where we want to fight them. For fight them we must.'

'We now know that we have to fight them on two fronts, Sir,' said Mitra. 'We are, or maybe I should say *I* was, working under the assumption that the Gangas are waiting to link up with the Chalukyas. That is obviously not the case. With Pulikeshi coming straight down south to attack us, the Gangas will surely try and hit us from the flank, with Jayanthavarman bringing up the rear, like the previous time.'

'That is more serious then,' said Mamalla. He looked over at Paranjyothi and Ilanthiraiyanar and asked, 'Can we expect any help from Manavamma? At least to bottle up Jayanthavarman so he can't come to Pulikeshi's aid?'

'I will try and find that out as soon as I can, Sire.'

'Also, what is happening with Harsha?'

Kirupa, who had tried to merge into the background as these deliberations were ongoing, cleared his throat gently and said, 'Ahem. Sire, I heard that King Harsha has amassed his forces along the north bank of the Narmada and that has led to Naganandi dispatching some of their army to the north.'

'Can we expect anything more from King Harsha?' asked Mamalla.

Ilanthiraiyanar shook his head slowly as he answered, 'I don't think so, Sire. I don't think his heart is in another fight. He is more interested in the spiritual now. I hear that he is preparing for a big Buddhist convention at Kanyakubja in a year or so. His mind is more involved in that than in picking another fight with his strong neighbour to the south. Also, King Harsha is getting on in years, and the desire to fight decreases with age.'

Mamalla smiled. 'Is that what's happening to you both as well?'

Paranjyothi and Ilanthiraiyanar looked at each other and then at Mamalla.

'Ah, my King, we don't think we are that old yet,' said the general with a smile of his own. Then, spying Kirupa still standing around, he asked, 'Kirupa, do you have anything more to tell us?'

'No, Sir.'

'You may leave then.'

Kirupa bowed and left the chambers.

'I suppose you don't want him to know what your plan is?' asked Mamalla.

'I don't have a plan yet, Your Majesty. But I do believe that King Pulikeshi might not be as strongly placed as he seems to think he is. If we can stop Jayanthavarman from helping him, given that his forces are split, we can, in my opinion, inflict a crushing blow on his campaign. Give me a couple of days, Sire, and I shall get all the information we need to formulate a plan.'

5
Hope Awakens

Korkai, November 641 CE

Muthuvel, Thaamarai and Sadaiyan sat on the sand, on a lonely stretch of beach along the sea, looking out into the distance. The dark, nearly moonless night accentuated the luminescence of the froth on the waves as they crashed repeatedly on to the beach.

Thaamarai sat close to Muthuvel, to his right, her arms wrapped possessively around his upper arm. Sadaiyan lay a couple of feet to Muthuvel's left, his feet stretched out in front of him, head nestling on his palms as he gazed up at the sky.

'You think he will come, anna?' he asked.

'That's what the message said.'

'But we have been doing this for three days now without any sign of him.'

'He said this week. He wasn't clear about which day, though,' said Muthuvel. It had been over ten days now since a messenger had delivered the message from Chaminda where he had promised that he and his army would be coming to their assistance.

Muthuvel looked at Thaamarai as she nestled her head against his arm and said, 'You are oddly quiet today, love.'

Sadaiyan sniggered.

'Oh, will you stop it?' asked Muthuvel. 'You ought to be used to that by now.'

'I don't know, anna. Still brings a chuckle to hear you say that.'

'Sadaiyan, if you don't shut up, I shall whack you on the head,' said Thaamarai, momentarily lifting her head off Muthuvel's arm.

'Yes, akka[3],' said Sadaiyan with a grin that the others couldn't observe. He closed his eyes and let the waves lull him to sleep.

'You didn't answer my question,' said Muthuvel, gently squeezing her arm with his left hand.

'Mmm? What was the question again?' she asked, dreamily.

'I said that you were oddly quiet.'

'That wasn't a question,' she said, infuriatingly logical.

'Alright. Why are you oddly quiet?'

She gave a happy little sigh as she adjusted her head into a more comfortable position on his arm.

'I don't know. This feels nice.'

'What does?'

'This. You. Me. Sitting on the beach. The sound of the waves around us. It almost feels carefree, decadent. I could get used to this.'

Muthuvel gently freed his right arm from hers and then put it around her, his hand snaking around her waist as she settled her head against his chest.

---

3 Elder sister—often used as a term of respect.

'Mmmmm. This is nicer.'

She glanced over at Sadaiyan to check his reaction, but the evenness of his breathing told her that he was fast asleep.

'I could get very used to this, you know,' she said.

'What? Living like this? On the run? Sneaking around? Don't you want your old life back, princess of Korkai?'

'I really don't know. Yes, we have been on the run, but then again, I have had you to myself. Who knows what will happen if we go back to our old life?'

'If? You mean when, right?'

'When,' she said. Then, after a brief pause, she added, 'And if!'

She closed her eyes as her mind went over the events of the past few weeks.

They had been on the run ever since Sadaiyan had sneaked them out in the cart, under the load of dirty laundry. The young thief had driven the cart westwards as fast as he could, without arousing suspicion, trying to put some distance between them and the city. That first night, they had taken rest in a palm grove. The lacerations on Muthuvel's back were still raw and the hurried departure hidden in a cart meant more for goods than for transporting humans had not helped.

He had slept fitfully through the night, moaning in pain. Thaamarai had not slept much that night either, waking up whenever he moaned, which was often.

Sadaiyan had scouted the road before they had resumed their escape and had returned with disquieting news. The road was swarming with enemy soldiers who seemed to be searching specifically for them. He held a hurried, whispered conference with Thaamarai and they had decided that the safer way to travel was by boat. Sadaiyan had driven the cart slowly towards the seashore and stopped when they reached the next village. They had left the cart under some trees and walked into the village.

Thaamarai didn't exactly know what Sadaiyan had said to the villagers, but whatever it was, it seemed to have had the desired effect. Soon a few men came along, following Sadaiyan and bearing a makeshift stretcher. They had loaded Muthuvel on to it and then taken him inside one of their huts. They had spent the day in the hut, with the women rubbing some herbal poultices on Muthuvel's back, which seemed to lessen his pain and had enabled him to drift off to sleep. Sadaiyan, however, had sneaked away to keep an eye on the road and was missing for the rest of the day.

He came back as the day turned to dusk, and told them that the road was still full of soldiers but that they were ranging further west. The village headman had spoken to Thaamarai.

'Princess,' he began, as Thaamarai looked worriedly at him. Noticing her look, he raised his hand in reassurance as he continued, 'Please do not have any fear in your mind, Princess. We are loyal subjects of your father. It is our duty to ensure that you are taken care of.'

'Thank you, *aiyya*[4],' she said, her face reflecting the relief she felt.

'I don't think it is safe for you all here. This place is too close to the city and the soldiers are sure to come here searching for you.'

She nodded in response. 'What do we do?'

---

4 A term of respect for an elderly person.

'I have a plan. My sister lives about twenty miles or so west. She is married to a fisherman in that village. We can take you there in our boat. It shouldn't take more than three hours to get there, and we don't think the soldiers will range that far away looking for you.'

Thaamarai had given her assent to the plan and the three of them had been duly taken by boat to the other village. They had spent much of the intervening days here. Muthuvel had slowly regained his strength as his wounds had healed. They had heard news of the happenings in Korkai from the fishermen. Thaamarai's family, along with Nedumaran and several soldiers, had been imprisoned in the dungeons.

Jayanthavarman had been particularly incensed by the inability of his men to find Muthuvel. Thankfully, he had not taken it out on Thaamarai's family. Jayanthavarman was still camped in Korkai and was showing no signs of returning to Madurai.

Muthuvel mused on how his life had changed over the past several months, ever since the general had handed him his assignment. It had taken him to Lanka and back, given him experiences to remember, near-unbearable pain but also unimaginable happiness in the form of Thaamarai. He glanced down towards her and noticed that she had fallen asleep on his shoulder.

As he gazed out towards the sea again, his keen eyes noticed something that had not been there earlier—a dark blotch that seemed to move up and down along with the undulations of the sea. Slowly, the contours of the boat became sharper. He could also make out the silhouettes of three people in the boat, two of whom were plying oars while the third man stood at the prow of the boat.

Eventually, the boat neared the shore and the man who was standing jumped off the boat, into waist-deep water, and then waded his way towards them.

Muthuvel nudged Thaamarai awake and she sat up, rubbing her eyes. Muthuvel jumped to his feet and ran towards the man walking towards the shore. Chaminda and he hugged and laughed and Muthuvel winced as Chaminda slapped him on his back. The commotion woke Sadaiyan up, and he raced towards them and jumped into Chaminda's arms. Thaamarai hung back, unwilling to intrude upon a meeting of friends.

The trio walked back and Chaminda nodded quizzically towards her.

'Are you going to introduce us?' he asked Muthuvel.

'This is Princess Thaamarai,' Muthuvel said formally.

Sadaiyan sniggered again and said, 'She and anna are also, ummm, how can I put it, in love ...'

'Is that so? Congratulations, my friend,' said Chaminda, grinning. 'I can only say all the very best to you, though,' he said, looking at Thaamarai.

Thaamarai gave a wicked and unselfconscious laugh.

'I am going to like him,' she told Muthuvel, who looked relieved.

After the customary catching up had been dispensed with, Muthuvel asked Chaminda, 'What's the news from your king? Have you figured out a way to help us?'

Chaminda gave a delighted laugh before proceeding to tell the story of the lifting of the blockade.

'So, you can land your army at the port now?'

'Without a doubt. But the ships have gone back to pick up the army. We will land in two days' time.'

6

A Parting

Forests west of Thagadur, November 641 CE

Indumathi couldn't sleep. She turned this way and that, trying to get herself into a comfortable position, but it didn't matter. It wasn't the bare ground that made sleep difficult to come by. It was the distance that had emerged between her and Kannan that was keeping her awake through the night.

She could see his silhouette from her position. He wasn't sleeping either. He had his back against a tree and seemed to be gazing into the distance. Indu sighed and closed her eyes. He hadn't spoken a word to her since the day she had told him about her role in the attack on him and his men.

She had nursed him back to health after the attack. Him and Bhatta, specifically. Basavaiyya's knowledge of medicine had been of immense help. Without him, the wounded wouldn't have stood a chance. He had worked feverishly night and day to save soldiers whom he knew belonged to an enemy state. He would have fought them himself if he were younger, but in these circumstances he was a *vaidya*, a doctor. And so he did what he could to save their lives.

Even so, many soldiers passed away. Basavaiyya treated the death of every man under his care as a personal affront to his abilities and would increase his workload. He often went off into the forest in search of obscure herbs that only he could identify. He ground some into pastes to be applied as poultices, while others, he made into foul-smelling and bitter-tasting concoctions to be ingested by the patients. Even in the middle of the night, he would roam along the lines of the wounded, tending to them. Here a gentle hand on their forehead, there a rub on their arms. He would adjust what passed for their pillows under their heads, attempting to fluff the bundle of clothes that acted as headrests.

Bhatta had opened his eyes about a week after the battle and Kannan, a day longer. Time and again, she had thought that he wouldn't ever wake up and would drift away. Her own breath would grow ragged when she heard him struggling for air. She had taken to being near him, night and day. She had even taken to sleeping right next to him so that she could respond quickly if she ever heard him in distress. Murugan, that indefatigable giant, had offered to take over so she could get some sleep, but she had refused.

Kannan had eventually opened his eyes one afternoon, and the first thing that he had seen had been her face, looking anxiously down at him. He had told her later that his first thought had been that he must have died and gone to heaven. He had then instantly been terrified because if she were in heaven along with him, it meant that she had died too.

Once he realized that it was indeed Indu, he had shown remarkable progress in his recovery. He was still very weak. Food was not aplenty here and was carefully rationed by Murugan and so he had become much thinner.

One evening, as they sat together, Indu resting her back against a tree and Kannan leaning his head on her shoulders, he had broached the topic.

'Indu, it is wonderful having you here, but I have been meaning to ask ... How are you here? How did you know where we were and how to find us?'

Indu had dreaded this moment. She knew that she ought to tell him the truth and had never figured out how to bring up the topic. But now that he had asked her outright, she couldn't lie to him.

So she told him everything—her going to her prime minister with news of Kannan and his army's movements. Of her then deciding to follow him because she knew that she could well have written his death sentence. Of Basavaiyya, her old guardian and a friend of her father, who had agreed to escort her to him. Of her coming upon them in the aftermath of the battle. Of staying with them to help tend to the wounded.

Kannan had sat up from her shoulder when he heard that she had gone to the prime minister with details of his movements and whereabouts. He had moved slightly away from her as she had continued her tale, a hard look in his eyes as he gazed into the distance. She had tried to take his hand, but he had pulled it away from her. As she finished her story, she had reached out tentatively and put her hand on his shoulder, but he had shrugged it away angrily. He had turned towards her, the light of love missing entirely from his eyes. There was anger and hurt in them. Anger, since her actions had resulted in the deaths of hundreds of his men. Hurt, because he felt betrayed by her.

He had stood up slowly and then, glancing down, uttered just one line as he moved away, 'You are dead to me.'

Kannan sat looking into the distance. His thoughts kept returning to Indu. *How could she do it? How could she betray me like that? And then to come here and pretend like it was all going to be fine just because she helped to heal some of my men? The men whose wounds were a result of her actions?*

He shook his head to clear his mind of these thoughts. He had been thinking about this almost every minute of every waking hour. He had tried to put her presence out of his mind. But she was right here, going around tending to the wounded along with Basavaiyya. He had remonstrated with Murugan to ask her to go away but the latter had pointed out bluntly that if Kannan wanted to kill more of his men, then sure, *he* could send them away, but he was damned if he, Murugan, was going to do that.

Kannan had muttered curses under his breath but knew that Murugan was right. He put up with her presence. He made a resolution to not look at her but then, his eyes followed her movements of their own violation, as she went around tending to his men.

Presently, he heard footsteps approaching and looked up to see the familiar pair of Murugan and Bhatta. Bhatta seemed to have become even thinner if that was possible. He looked gaunt but his steps were firm, and he appeared mentally strong. *Which can't be said for me*, thought Kannan.

The two men sat down in front of him, their legs stretched out, leaning on their arms behind them. It was Bhatta who started the conversation in his usual forthright manner.

'Boss, we need to talk about this situation between you and the lady.' He always referred to Indumathi as 'the lady', never by her name.

Kannan glanced sharply at him.

'That isn't going to stop me from talking about it, Boss,' said Bhatta. 'You can glare at me all you want, but we need to talk about this.'

'It's none of your business,' said Kannan abruptly.

'Aah, actually it is, Boss,' said Murugan. 'You know how this excuse for a soldier and I rarely agree on anything. But on this matter, we are of one mind.'

'Why thank you, my goofy friend. What a pleasant surprise that your mind is capable of appreciating the thought processes of your betters, for once,' riposted Bhatta.

Murugan ignored this with lofty disdain as he turned back towards Kannan and said, 'Boss, we think you are doing wrong by Indumathi.'

'Really? After what she has done to our comrades?'

'She hasn't done anything.'

'Do you absolve her of blame for all this? Who was it who gave away our whereabouts to the Gangas? Don't you think that what we have here, with hundreds of our friends killed and scores more wounded and dying, is a direct result of her actions?' asked Kannan heatedly.

'No, Boss, we don't,' said Bhatta. 'The lady did what anyone with an iota of love for her land would have done.'

'And what of her love for me?'

'She followed you here, didn't she?' asked Murugan.

'Maybe it was just to assuage her guilt at handing us on a platter to our enemies.'

'Boss, that statement is not worthy of you, and you know it,' said Murugan.

'She had a conflict between her dharma as a citizen and that of a lover. It mustn't have been an easy decision for her. She did what she had to do as a citizen but then, as someone who loved you, she came down to find you. She is a rare lady, Captain,' said Bhatta, a note of profound respect in his voice.

'You should be very proud of her, Boss,' spoke Murugan, quietly. 'Such women are rare. She has shown courage and dignity under the gravest of circumstances. I remember when she saw you and Bhatta here lying wounded. She did shed a few tears initially, but after that, she was all businesslike. You both are alive today because of her determination to not let you die. She would sit next to both of you and talk to you as if you could hear her every word. She would tell you stories of her childhood. She would talk to you about her journey to find you. But I hadn't ever heard her apologize to you for telling her prime minister about us.'

'What would you have done in her place, Boss?' asked Bhatta, quietly. 'Wouldn't you have put your land and king above all else? Wouldn't you consider it your patriotic duty? Why do you then grudge her that? You should be proud that such a lady chose you as her man.'

Kannan was silent, trying to digest what he had heard from the two men closest to him.

Indu woke up with a start as she felt someone's hand tapping her shoulder. She looked disbelievingly at Kannan, hunched over her.

The dawning of hope quickened her heartbeat. *Has he come to forgive me for what I have done?* she thought. Kannan sat down slowly. Indu reached her hand out to help him instinctively and was pleasantly surprised when he didn't pull away but gripped her hand tightly as he sat next to her.

Her breath caught in her throat as he gazed at her with a look in his eyes that she had feared she would never see again.

'Indu,' he whispered gently. 'Will you ever forgive me?'

Indumathi couldn't believe the words that she was hearing.

'Forgive you, Kannan? It should be you forgiving me for the harm that I have caused.'

'No, Indu. You did what any good citizen of a land would have done. Two irascible friends of mine just spent some time getting that through my thick skull.' He smiled affectionately as he looked back towards where Murugan and Bhatta were sitting, watching them.

'You guys can go get some sleep now, if you have finished eavesdropping on our conversation,' said Kannan.

Indu smiled and made a vow to thank them personally for their efforts on her behalf.

'Can I at least have a hug now?' she asked.

Kannan smiled affectionately at her as he pulled her into a bear hug. They sat for some time like that in a warm, comforting embrace. Eventually Kannan broke the silence and said, 'I need you to go back to your kingdom.'

Indu stiffened as she heard these words and drew back from him, gazing up into his eyes.

'You are sending me away,' she said flatly.

'Indu,' he replied gently, 'there is a war coming. I am a warrior. I need to go and join my army and fight on their side. Where will I take you now?'

'You want me to go back and do what?'

'Wait.'

'Wait?'

'Wait. Wait for me to come back. I promise I will come back.'

Indu gave a hollow laugh. 'Can anyone ever promise to come back when going off to war? You are lucky to have survived this last battle. Do you want me to live my life in a never-ending wait for you?'

'No. I want you to go ahead and live your life if I don't come back. Marry someone else. Someone lucky enough to get you as a wife. But if I come out of the war alive, I *will* come for you.'

'Do you think it is easy for me to just forget you and live my life with another man?'

Kannan prudently kept quiet.

'Listen to me, Kannan. You are the only man in my life. That's it. I understand what you are saying, but don't you dare tell me to get on with my life with someone else. I shall wait for you to come to me after the war. If you don't come, I shall live out my life with your memories.'

She hugged him fiercely. Kannan had a lump in his throat as he held her tight.

Indu and Basavaiyya left a week later. Indu hugged Kannan tightly and for a very long time. But there were no tears in her eyes.

'Come back safely to me,' she whispered in his ears as she pulled away from him reluctantly and then, followed Basavaiyya back towards their land. She didn't turn to look at Kannan even once, and then she was lost from view.

Murugan and Bhatta wore forlorn expressions on their faces and were even a little misty-eyed as they watched her walk away. Kannan looked at them and asked, 'Are you both crying?'

'Of course not, Boss,' sniffed Bhatta.

'Not at all,' said Murugan, wiping his nose and eyes with the end of his turban.

'If you both are quite done, can we discuss what we are going to do next?'

'Do you have a plan, Boss?' asked Murugan.

'I do. Here is what we are going to do,' said Kannan and began to outline his plan.

7
A Friend in Need

Parivipura, November 641 CE

The departure of the majority of the Chalukyan army from Parivipura had initially filled the hearts of its citizens with hope. That hope died down fairly quickly when they realized that there was still a sizeable force present, to keep control of the city.

There was, however, one good that came out of the reduced size of the army. The soldiers were more intent on protecting the fort from any attacks than policing the city. The upshot of it was that the citizens suddenly found their lives returning to some semblance of normality.

Jamba spent more time loitering in front of the dungeons than in hunting. He would still go out to hunt every day, but now, instead of trying to sell the haul in the market, he had taken to selling it directly to the soldiers in front of the dungeons at outrageously low prices. This had enabled him to strike up a friendship with them.

They no longer viewed him as an outsider or someone to be guarded against. Their increasing familiarity with him resulted in their including him in their regular and extended sessions of drinking. Jamba, as confirmed a teetotaller as one can be, pretended to take part in the sessions. He would barely sip at his drink and would tip it into some nearby shrubs when no one was watching.

This particular morning, after a night of spectacularly heavy, drunken carousing, the guards sat in the shade of the portico, holding their heads in their hands.

'Aaaaaaaarrrrrrggghhhhh,' groaned one of them.

'Having a headache, are we?' asked Jamba solicitously.

'Shhhhhhhhh, don't shout. Please!' said the other one.

'I think I remember telling you both to ease back a bit.'

'Yes, yes, you did,' groaned the first guard.

'Well, I don't want to tell you I told you so, but, I told you so.'

The guards just buried their heads in their hands and continued to groan. Presently, one of them raised his head and looked at Jamba with bleary eyes.

'Can you do us a favour?'

'What is it?'

'Can you go and give the prisoners their breakfast?'

Jamba exulted secretly.

'Sure,' he shrugged his shoulders nonchalantly.

'You see that bucket there? That has the gruel. Dump one ladleful of gruel into the pan that is kept in each cell. Just one ladleful though.'

Jamba nodded, picked up the bucket with the ladle and walked into the dungeon.

Elango had not slept well. There were a couple of rats in his cell that kept scuttling across the floor, and he had spent a considerable portion of the night trying to kill them with his pan, but to no avail. The lack of light made it an almost impossible task.

He searched for and found the bucket of water that was his daily quota. It was less than a quarter full. He reached in, took some water in his palm, rinsed out his mouth with it and spat it in the general direction of the hole that was his toilet. He wished he had the neem sticks[5] with which he used to clean his teeth every morning. His mouth felt unwashed, and it stank. *Oh well. If I ever get out of here … When I get out of here, the first thing that I will do is take a bath and clean my teeth*, he thought with a wry grin.

He heard footsteps. *The morning meal. That watery gruel that passes for it at least.* The footsteps sounded different, somehow. They were not the typical heavy thud that he had become used to. These were almost silent, and it was only his training as a soldier that had made him pick up on them.

He heard the sounds of the ladle hitting the insides of the bucket and then being scooped into the little bowls that each prisoner had. He took his bowl, kept it near the gate, and sat beside it. He was hungry and watery gruel was better than no gruel.

The guard continued his job but strangely, passed his cell without pausing.

'Hey,' shouted Elango. 'What about me?'

---

5 Sticks from the margosa or neem tree. Used since time immemorial in India for cleaning teeth.

The guard ignored him and kept moving to the other cells. Elango sat back, feeling a moment of despair. *Are they going to starve me now?*

He heard the whispered sounds of the guard's footsteps as he walked back. This time, the guard stopped in front of his cell. Elango felt his hopes rising as he turned towards him. The guard knelt and brought the torch near his face. Elango smiled widely as he recognized Jamba. It was only due to his immense self-control that he did not give a whoop of delight. Jamba ladled the gruel into his bowl until it was full and whispered, 'Tonight.'

And then he was gone. Elango picked up his bowl and attacked it with relish. *Tonight, I shall be free.*

'This giving food to the prisoners is not easy work. For one, that place stinks. I don't know how those people stay there,' said Jamba. It was around noon, and he was seated outside the prison with the two guards who now appeared to be in somewhat better shape than earlier. The passage of time, a quick bath followed by drinking a foul-smelling concoction that Jamba had brewed for them had rendered them functional.

'Like they have a choice,' chortled the skinny man, too skinny to have been considered for any army. *Probably the cousin of a captain or something*, thought Jamba.

His companion, a stouter man, laughed coarsely. 'The stink is basically of their own making.'

These two could make a pair of comedians. Not that they would be very good at it, but at least they have the physical characteristics for it. Aloud, Jamba said, 'I feel the need for drinks tonight.'

'You?' asked the skinny one, his face registering disbelief. 'Weren't you the one educating us this morning about the perils of drinking?'

'That was before I went down there. I think I understand now why you men drink so much.'

The two guards burst into loud guffaws.

'We told you,' said the bulky one. 'Alright, we will get some more wine.'

'Lots of it,' said Jamba.

'Lots of it.'

'And I will go out to hunt. I'll see if I can come back with a nice, big fat deer. We could get the cook to make us some delicious curried meat.'

'Ooh,' said the thin one, licking his lips in anticipation.

'See you in the evening,' said Jamba, springing to his feet and walking away. He had not just baited the trap, but his prey were in their cages now. *I will shut the trap doors on them tonight.*

The man taking care of the stables was wolfing down his afternoon meal when he saw Jamba walk towards him.

'Ho, Jamba, what brings you here? I see you had a good hunt,' he said, looking at the carcass of the deer that hung across his shoulders.

'It was alright. I wanted to talk to you about something.'

'Tell me.'

'I want to buy a couple of horses. Good ones.'

'Whatever for?'

'I seem to be running through the stock of deer and wild boar near the fort. Each succeeding day, I find that I have to go deeper into the forest to get the meat.' Then, glancing furtively to his left and right and lowering his voice dramatically, he said, 'These Chalukya soldiers have an insatiable appetite.'

'And not just for food, I bet,' muttered the stable owner darkly.

Jamba winked and then sighed.

'We have to make a living though, however much we may dislike them.'

'You said a mouthful there, brother. We have families to feed.'

'Yes. Why do you think I bring them meat if not to make some money? You know that I am from the forest and we forest-dwellers don't have it easy.'

'You don't say! How *do* you live in the forest without any of the amenities?'

Jamba shrugged. 'We manage. But it is tough. That's why the need for some money. So, can you sell me a couple of horses?'

'How much money have you got?' asked the stable owner in a businesslike fashion, friendship cast aside for the moment, his eyes glittering and shrewd.

'How much are the horses?' countered Jamba.

'Thirty *pana*s each.'

'Thirty! And I thought you were my friend.'

'Business is business. I have a family to feed too, you know.'

They haggled for a while and the man settled for forty-five panas for the two horses.

'Hold them for me, will you? I shall take them early tomorrow morning.'

Soldiers seem to know a lot of bawdy songs, thought Jamba. *The drunker they get, the bawdier the songs.* He had been listening to the two guards getting drunker by the minute. He had handed over the deer that he had hunted to the cook, telling him that he could take a portion of it for himself, which had made the cook a very happy man.

The guards had started drinking as soon as night had set in, and even before the cook had finished cooking the deer. They had picked up a few flagons of wine and were busy trying to ensure that they went through their entire stock before the new day dawned.

Jamba acted as if he were matching them drink for drink, but, in his usual fashion, was surreptitiously watering the plants and shrubs behind him. The guards got more and more sloshed. The levels in the flagons got lower. The songs got bawdier.

The cook brought out the rice and spiced deer meat and the men ate it with relish, the gravy dripping all over them as their liquor-addled brains could not quite control their hands. It was around midnight that the guards finally fell asleep. Surprisingly, it was the fat one who dropped unconscious first. The skinny one, belying expectations, stayed awake a few minutes longer, before he, too, fell back insensate.

Jamba waited a while to make sure that they were well and truly asleep before he moved. He knelt next to the fat one and removed the large ring containing all the keys from the man's waistband. He got up and, hurrying over to the dungeon door, opened it. He had decided not to take a torch with him, lest the light wake any of the other prisoners. He closed the door once he stepped in and stood at the top of the stairs leading down into the dungeon, to give his eyes time to adjust to the darkness.

He headed down the stairs, his feet making nary a sound. He moved like a wild animal, with caution, making sure not to step on anything that would make a sound, before putting his foot down. He had already scoped out the path that he would take to Elango's cell when he had come down earlier in the morning. He had used that trip to clear the path of any sticks or stones.

He moved steadily forward. He needn't have worried about being discovered. The prisoners were all fast asleep. Sleep was their only relief from the constant hunger, and they slept the sleep of the exhausted. An uninterruptible deep sleep.

He reached Elango's cell and bent down. He had clutched the keys tight against his right hand so that they wouldn't jingle. He took out the ring and then slowly, very slowly, passed his fingers over the keys. He had no way of knowing which key fit which lock and so started to insert one key after another into the one on Elango's cell to find the correct key. It took him a while but eventually he found the key that fit. There was a loud *click* as the lock opened. Both Jamba and Elango froze. The sound had seemed unnaturally loud to their ears but the snores from the different cells told them that it hadn't woken anyone up.

Elango stepped out of his cell. Jamba closed the gate and locked it. He then turned to lead the way back up, but Elango stopped him with a hissed 'wait'.

Jamba turned around, surprised.

'We need to get Commander Dasappa. He is in the cell next to mine,' whispered Elango.

Jamba whispered his agreement and moved to the next cell under Elango's guidance, then fumbled with the keys and eventually found one that fit. Elango opened the gate noiselessly and then whispered, 'Commander. Commander Dasappa.'

Dasappa stirred and then sat up groggily. He could barely make out the two men in the darkness.

'Who is it?' he asked, louder than either Jamba or Elango wished for.

'Hush! It is me, Elango.'

'Elango! My boy! What? How?'

'No time for explanations, Commander. Follow us.'

Saying so, Elango turned and let Jamba lead the way up the stairs and through the door, out into the world.

He baulked as he saw the guards sprawled in front of them but then noticed that they were comatose. Jamba bent down and replaced the key bunch in the fat one's waistband and then led the way towards the western gate. There was a small *mandapam*[6] very near the stables where he had bought the horses. A couple of men were asleep there and Jamba, Elango and Dasappa lay down beside them.

They weren't worried about the guards raising an alarm. The guards wouldn't discover that the prisoners were no longer in their cells till well into the next morning, by which time they hoped to be free of the city.

The next morning, even before the city stirred into wakefulness and activity, Jamba, Elango and Dasappa walked towards the stables. The stable owner was sleeping in one corner. Jamba asked Elango and Dasappa to wait outside and then gently prodded the owner awake.

'Whaaa. Eh, who?' said the man, waking up with a start. 'Oh, it's you.'

'Come to take my horses,' said Jamba.

The owner nodded and then got to his feet and stretched, letting out a long and loud yawn. He then shuffled towards the two horses and untied them. Jamba caught hold of the reins and led them out, handing one of them to Elango.

6 A kind of roofed porch, open on all sides, often used as travellers' rest stops.

'I didn't know about the commander here yesterday and only bought two horses,' said Jamba.

'Maybe we can persuade the stable owner to part with one more?' asked Elango.

The stable owner had emerged from the stable and was looking at Elango curiously. There was something familiar about the man, but he couldn't figure out where he had seen him.

Jamba turned to the stable owner, 'We need one more horse.'

'You only paid for two,' said the owner.

'I know. But I need one more.'

'It will cost you,' said the owner, shrewdly divining that it was a seller's market at this point.

They haggled briefly. Jamba dug into his waistband, pulled out the necessary coins and handed them over to the stable owner, who, in turn, went over and untied another horse, a weak-looking one at that, and handed it over to Jamba.

'You are kidding me, right? This pathetic excuse of a horse is not worth what I paid,' Jamba said furiously.

The stable owner smirked. 'This is the only one I have. Take it or leave it.'

'Let's go, Jamba. It's alright. Let's take it for now,' said Elango.

'You,' said Jamba ominously, looking at the stable owner. 'I shall remember this. And I shall be back!'

The stable owner wet his lips nervously and watched them lead the horses away. There was another man with them who also looked vaguely familiar to him. But it was still fairly dark, and he couldn't make out the face.

Elango and Dasappa mounted their horses and followed Jamba towards the gates. They walked their horses through the gates just as the gates had opened for the day. As they passed through, Elango turned and took a long look at the city that he had failed to defend. *I will be back*, he told himself. He glanced across at Dasappa and could see the same look of determination on his face. They made their way to the river and found a boat that would take them across, on their way south. They were free!

8

A Surprise for Jayanthavarman

Korkai, November 641 CE

The sun was just about peeking over the horizon. Its rays fell on the water, turning it into a shimmering sheet of fire. Tiny boats bobbed up and down on the waves as the fishermen made their way out to sea.

There were a few boats, however, that were not there for the purpose of fishing. One of these boats was occupied by four people, a boatman, a soldierly-looking man, a young boy, and a pretty girl who had wrapped the end of her saree over her head and face.

The boatman had taken his net and made a show of throwing it overboard. He repeated the process from time to time while the three others in the boat sat watching him. Occasionally, the young boy would get up to help him pull in the net so that they could cast it again in a different location. They did catch some fish, which the boatman put into a basket at his feet, but his whole approach to the process was perfunctory.

Eventually, the sun rose and the other boats' occupants started to wrap up their work for the day and make their way back to shore. The boatman pulled in his net and followed in their wake, as did the other boats that were part of the group.

When the boats reached closer to shore, the soldier and the young lad took the ends of their turbans and wrapped them around their faces to obscure them. The same was done by some of the men in the other boats. When the vessels neared the shore, the man and the boy jumped down first, into ankle-deep water. The man helped the young woman off the boat by grabbing her by the waist and lifting her off the boat. She landed in the water with a splash and gave a happy little laugh.

The three of them thanked the boatman and then walked towards the fort gates. All around them, men from their group were making a beeline for the city.

They joined the line of fishermen and women going towards the market. The market was a daily affair and the soldiers at the gate paid them scant attention. The group had taken the baskets containing the fish that had been caught and set up their own impromptu shops, in the same row as the others.

While the rest of the members of their group made a show of trying to sell their catch, the young lad seemed to treat this extremely seriously and worked assiduously to make some money.

'Not so fast, Sadaiya,' hissed Muthuvel. 'We do want to make the fish last till noon at least?'

'How can I let the others make more money than me, anna?' he whispered back.

'The money is not important,' snapped Muthuvel.

'It is always important,' grinned Sadaiyan, going on to shout out his wares.

Muthuvel glowered at him but then felt Thaamarai's hand clutching his arm and suddenly, all was right with the world again. They sat down to wait.

The mid-afternoon sun beat mercilessly down on the port of Korkai. It didn't seem to bother the fishermen. Their day started early and finished early as well, at least the fishing aspect of it. They were sitting in their huts or under the shade of their boats, disentangling their nets. One of the men was working on his boat, cleaning the keel. As he paused briefly to wipe some sweat off his brow, he noticed something that brought a surprised 'Oy' from him. His fellow fishermen heard that and looked out to sea. They could make out the masts of three ships rising over the horizon.

As they continued watching, the rest of the ships came slowly into view. The fishermen were dumbstruck. The last time that they had seen ships this big coming in to the port had been before the beginning of the siege. They knew of the naval blockade imposed by King Tribhuvana of Lanka, of course. So, what were these ships doing here?

The guards on the fort walls would have seen it earlier than the fishermen if they had paid attention, given the added advantage of the height of the fort walls. They had, however, been taking shelter from the midday sun and it was only after they heard a series of startled shouts that they had stepped out on to the fort walls to investigate the reasons for the commotion.

The sergeant in charge of the southern gate took a panicked look at the ships and called for one of his younger soldiers to run to the palace and inform King Jayanthavarman about them.

'What is it?' asked Jayanthavarman in an irritated voice, when the young guard had been led into his presence.

'Your Majesty, this young lad says that the sergeant at the southern gate sent him with an urgent message.'

'Well?' asked the king, targeting the young man with a look of annoyance.

'Your Majesty, there are ships coming in. Three big ships. And a number of smaller boats.'

'Ships?'

'Yes, Sire.'

'Did the sergeant say anything about what type of ships?'

'No, Sire. But we did see a number of armed men disembarking from them. That is when the sergeant sent me to inform you.'

The youngster noted that this information seemed to have had the desired impact on the king, whose eyes bulged in shock.

'You may go,' said Jayanthavarman with a curt nod before yelling at the guard, 'tell my bodyguards to get my horse ready.'

Jayanthavarman stood atop the southern gate and looked down at the men amassed on the beach. *There must be at least four or five thousand of them*, he thought, giving an involuntary shudder. The newly arrived men were all armed with swords and shields and several of them had bows and quivers full of arrows. He noticed that the men were still not pitching tents. That left him puzzled.

As he was taking in the scene, he saw a small group walking towards him. The two men walking in front seemed to be grizzled veterans while there were a couple of younger folks alongside them.

The men stopped about twenty yards away from the closed southern gates. They looked up and, seeing Jayanthavarman, bowed to him.

'Greetings, Your Majesty,' said the bearded man, pleasantly. 'We come bearing news from Lanka.'

Jayanthavarman's eyes narrowed as he looked keenly at them.

'How did you know I am the king?' he asked.

The bearded one smiled. 'I fought with you all those years ago when King Pulikeshi had invaded the Pallava lands. I was a young lad then and very junior, so I doubt that you would even know me. Moreover, King Tribhuvana had given us your description. A very accurate description, actually.'

Jayanthavarman stayed quiet, still looking at them suspiciously. His eyes lingered on the man standing beside the bearded one. Something about him was familiar but he couldn't quite place him.

'And why have you decamped here with all these soldiers?' he asked. 'One would think that this is an invasion.'

The bearded man laughed.

'King Tribhuvana has sent us here to aid King Pulikeshi, Sire. He promised him help against those Pallava rats. We are the help,' he said, gesturing at the men around him.

'What do you want?'

'We just want entry into the city, Sire. And then we will be on our way to join the Chalukyas.' Saying this, the bearded man waited. Jayanthavarman took his time thinking about it. His fingers tapped a nervous beat on the fort wall. He stood there, chewing his lip. He looked towards the men assembled on the beach, bearing Tribhuvana's standard. He realized that he couldn't deny entry to an ally and ordered his men to open the gates.

The gates swung open slowly and the group that the bearded man belonged to moved forward. Jayanthavarman, his brows puckered, glanced down again at the men now nearing the gates. He noticed the familiar-looking man he had spotted earlier. His walk. Something about his walk. That peculiar way of rolling his shoulder. Where had he seen that before? And then it hit him.

'Manavamma!' he yelled.

It seemed like the universe exploded into action at that point. Manavamma, who had been walking behind Thissa, glanced up as he heard his name being called and realized that the ruse was over.

'Through the gates! Come on, men!' he shouted.

At the same time, Jayanthavarman yelled out, 'That's the enemy! Shut the gates. Shut the gates, now!'

The men who had pushed the heavy gates open tried to get them shut again, but it is always much easier to push than to pull. Before they could get the gates moving again in the opposite direction, the air above Jayanthavarman's head was thick with arrows as Manavamma's archers let loose. Jayanthavarman ducked and his bodyguards immediately surrounded him and ushered him down. As Jayanthavarman reached the bottom of the fort walls, he noticed his soldiers trying vainly to close the gates. But already, they were being pushed back by the Lankans. There were just too many of them. At this point, Jayanthavarman knew that the city was lost to him.

'Sire! We need to go,' shouted the leader of his troop of bodyguards. Jayanthavarman leaped on to his horse and raced towards the northern gate, his bodyguards escorting him on their horses.

The Madurai monarch suddenly brought his horse to a stop near the northern gates and turned towards his bodyguards.

'Nedumaran. I need Nedumaran. Let's get him from the dungeons.'

He started to turn his horse that way but found his path blocked by the captain.

'Sorry, Your Majesty. But we just don't have the time. There is a real danger that you will get caught in the melee. The Lankan soldiers are possibly already at the palace. We cannot risk having you caught here. We can always take back this fort, but we need to get you to safety.'

Jayanthavarman suppressed his momentary annoyance as he realized that the captain was correct. There was no glory in being captured in this fort. He could always raise an army and come back. And so he turned his horse towards the northern gate and passed through it at a gallop. They raised a trail of dust as they sped away from Korkai, back towards Madurai.

Earlier, Muthuvel, Sadaiyan and Thaamarai had made their way slowly towards the palace. They were still covering their faces. There were just too many people here who knew Princess Thaamarai and they didn't want to be discovered even accidentally. Muthuvel had tried to convince the princess to stay back along with the other soldiers who had accompanied them, but to no avail.

'Your life is going to be interesting, anna,' Sadaiyan had smirked. 'Akka here is not likely to listen to much of what you say.' He evaded the intended cuff from Muthuvel but heard a delighted little tinkle of laughter from Thaamarai.

They were now loitering in the vicinity of the palace which seemed to be only sparsely guarded. With a majority of the Korkai soldiers having been killed, or having fled the fort after the fall of the city, and with the royal family incarcerated in the dungeons, Jayanthavarman did not expect any attacks from inside the fort. The soldiers weren't particularly alert. There were very few of them in front of the palace.

These guys ought to be fired, thought Muthuvel. *Allowing strangers to loiter in front of the palace is just unpardonable. Can't complain though. Good for us, I suppose.*

It was around noon that he saw Jayanthavarman rush out of the palace, mount his horse and gallop away towards the southern end of the city. A scant half an hour or so later, he heard a huge commotion from that direction. He had a good vantage point from which he could see the road leading to the northern gates. He heard hoofbeats and saw a few horses dashing across, northwards. He thought he had glimpsed Jayanthavarman's horse flash past.

Shortly thereafter, the tumult to the south increased in volume. He wasn't to know that Manavamma's army had overcome the token resistance at the gates and was pouring in. He had, however, surmised that this might well be the case. He noticed the soldiers in front of the palace were looking south, towards the direction of the noise. It had increased to a roar now as the Lankan soldiers came gushing through, on their way to the palace.

The Pandya soldiers took one look and abandoned their positions. There was bravery. There was foolhardiness. And then there was plain foolishness. Standing up to fight with the odds stacked so heavily against them was simply untenable, and the soldiers threw down their weapons and surrendered.

'Come on,' said Muthuvel as he rushed towards the soldiers, stooping to pick up a sword. Sadaiyan was close behind him with Thaamarai following them both. With no one to stop them, they hurried through the gates. Muthuvel asked Thaamarai to lead the way to the dungeons. Thaamarai set off around the palace to the back. A narrow path led from the back of the palace between thick woods. They ran up the path until they came to a building made of stone. There were a couple of soldiers guarding the place. Muthuvel moved forward, thrusting Thaamarai behind him. Sadaiyan stood to one side of him.

'Throw down your weapons, men. Your king has run away from the city. Manavamma's men are here.'

The soldiers looked disbelievingly at him.

'Look, we can do it the easy way. Or the hard way. I am giving you the option of escaping while you have the chance.' He cocked his head to one side. The hullabaloo was audible now.

'You hear that? That, my friends, is the city being retaken. I say again, step aside and try and make good your escape or you *will* have to fight me.'

The two guards gulped and looked at each other and then back at Muthuvel.

'Well? What will it be?'

The swords clattered down to the ground and the guards sidled out of there, giving Muthuvel a wide berth and then breaking out into a run. He noticed that they did not run down the path that they had taken but had escaped into the woods.

Thaamarai rushed past Muthuvel and into the dungeons. The place was dark, and it was Sadaiyan who had the presence of mind to pick up one of the torches at the entrance. Muthuvel had grabbed a huge bunch of keys that he had found hanging on a nail. They moved down a flight of stairs and came to a line of cells.

'Appa! Appa!' cried Thaamarai as she searched for her father.

'Thaamarai? Is that you?'

'Yes, appa, where are you?'

'Here! Here, my child.'

They looked around until Thaamarai spied her father and mothers in a cell. Muthuvel went over and fumbled with the keys, trying to find the right key for the cell as Thaamarai watched impatiently. They finally heard a *click* as the key turned the tumblers in the lock. Thaamarai opened the gate and rushed into her father's arms.

9
Ilanthiraiyanar Prepares

Kanchi, November 641 CE

General Ilanthiraiyanar had been closeted with Commander Paranjyothi all day. They had been interrupted a couple of times by the general's man, who had brought them the occasional snack or food. The food had mostly consisted of fruits and water. The general was a drinking man but that was only when he was off duty. Today he needed his faculties about him. Heavy meals were a precursor to a slowing of the mind, and he didn't want that. Not today.

There were maps painted on silken cloth spread out in front of them. Maps of Kanchi and its surrounding regions, of Suramara where the Ganga and Chalukya soldiers were waiting for them, and of all the southern kingdoms.

They both wore serious expressions as they looked down at the maps. All around them were *olai*s, collections of rectangular-cut palm leaves that they would use to write down their thoughts and orders. There were styluses placed near them.

Ilanthiraiyanar leaned back in exhaustion.

'I can't make up my mind,' he admitted.

'There are just a few options, no?' asked Paranjyothi.

'Yes, but the repercussions of getting the decision wrong are so grave that my mind keeps wavering between them.'

Paranjyothi smiled that gentle smile of his. His kindly eyes looked across at his old friend.

'Why don't you go over it again for me? Perhaps recapping the whole thing might trigger a solution.'

Ilanthiraiyanar nodded. However, before he could begin, a knock sounded on the door.

'Yes?' he asked with irritation.

'Sir, the maharaja wishes to see you both.'

'Oh great. That's what was missing. Pressure from our lord and master.'

'Oh, come on,' smiled Paranjyothi. 'You know that His Majesty has a keen brain. Recapping our deliberations in front of him might well lead to a solution.'

'Alright,' said the general in a resigned voice. 'Let's go then.'

Mamalla was waiting for them in the council chambers along with Prime Minister Nalankilli and Prince Mahendra. Mahendra was looking around the room.

'You searching for someone, my boy?' asked Ilanthiraiyanar, a knowing twinkle in his eyes.

Mahendra blushed. 'I thought Lady Sanghamitra was part of the group deliberating on our plans,' he said.

Ilanthiraiyanar suppressed a smile. *Aah to be young again*, he thought.

'Not really, lad. We plan. She executes her part well. That's how it is. Don't you have some drills to attend to?' he asked with raised eyebrows.

'Aah, I thought that I could get to understand what our plans are, Sir.'

'Soldier, you might be the prince, but you are still part of the army. When the plans have been made, they will be communicated to your captain, who will let you and your comrades know in due course. You are dismissed,' he said curtly, not caring in the least that he was talking to the future king of this land.

Mamalla looked away as he tried to hide his smile from his son. The boy looked suitably chastened and crestfallen and left after bowing to all four of the men in the room.

'I am glad to see that you aren't going easy on him just because he is the prince,' said Mamalla with a smile.

'You asked me not to, Sire,' said Ilanthiraiyanar.

'That, I surely did.'

'Anyway, you sent for us, Your Majesty?'

'I want to hear about your plans for our campaign.'

Ilanthiraiyanar and Paranjyothi exchanged glances.

'What's the matter?' asked Mamalla.

'We are stuck,' said Paranjyothi, after a brief pause. 'We haven't been able to figure out what to do.'

'Tell me,' said Mamalla.

Paranjyothi looked towards Ilanthirayanar. The general started speaking.

'Well, there are multiple options that we are thinking of. The easiest one is to do nothing but stay here and build up our forces. We can then choose where to meet Pulikeshi. But that runs the risk of getting caught between the Ganga and Chalukya forces.'

Mamalla nodded.

'The second option is to take our forces and move forward, meeting Pulikeshi where he won't expect us to. That does have the element of surprise, but again, we haven't accounted for the Gangas at our flank.'

Ilanthiraiyanar paused to see if Mamalla would say something, but the king merely waited for him to continue.

'The third option is to split our forces. Have one part of our army attack the Gangas, while the other one engages Pulikeshi.'

'Where?'

'Could be here. Or could be somewhere else, like in option two.'

'What about Jayanthavarman?' asked the king.

'Oh, I forgot to tell you,' said Paranjyothi, slapping his palm on his forehead. 'We got news from the south a short while ago. It seems that Manavamma has not only lifted the blockade but has also taken the fort at Korkai and freed the king and his family.'

'Jayanthavarman?'

'He escaped to Madurai along with most of his army.'

'How did his army escape?' asked Mamalla with a frown.

'Most of the army was still outside the fort. When the king escaped, the army packed up and left after him. Manavamma decided not to engage them or pursue them since he wanted to make sure that he had control of the fort. He has sent word that he now intends to mount a siege on Madurai.'

'Good. That will keep Jayanthavarman off our backs,' said the king.

'I wonder though …' started Paranjyothi.

'What, Paran?'

'I wonder if there is a way for Manavamma to keep Jayanthavarman bottled up in the fort in Madurai while also sending troops here.'

'Split up his forces? Does he have enough men?' asked Nalankilli.

'My spies tell me that he has roughly around four to five thousand men.'

'He can easily leave a thousand men to besiege Madurai and keep Jayanthavarman occupied, while sending the rest of his men to support us, I would think,' said Nalankilli.

Paranjyothi nodded and said, 'That still leaves us with the question of what we would want to do.'

'I do not like the thought of the Gangas and the Chalukyas catching us in a pincer yet again,' said Mamalla with a wry smile. 'We went through that twenty years ago and I am not going to allow them to do that again.'

'So, splitting our forces seems to be the way to go then?' asked General Ilanthiraiyanar.

'Yes, but that still leaves us with the question of where we want to meet Pulikeshi,' said Paranjyothi.

'I think we should let him come closer to us,' mused Mamalla.

Ilanthiraiyanar looked keenly at him.

'Stretch their supply lines?'

'Once they come close to us, we cannot just stretch, but cut off their supply lines altogether. With the tail gone, we can then deal with the head. But that requires that the Gangas be neutralized, first.'

Ilanthiraiyanar took out a silk roll from his waistband and spread it on the ground in front of him. The others got up from their seats and crowded around the map.

'Here we are,' he said, pointing to Kanchi on the map, 'and this is the likely route that Pulikeshi will follow to come down south to Kanchi.'

The others looked keenly at the route that he had traced with his finger. It was Paranjyothi who said, 'We can't allow him to come right down to Kanchi. We don't want him pitching his tents and getting comfortable with a siege. That will lock up our army inside the fort walls, and the force that would have gone to fight the Gangas will also not be able to help much.'

'What do you suggest?' asked Mamalla.

'We have to harass them along the way. Make life difficult for them. Have small groups of soldiers that keep attacking their rear and flanks as they march down. That will keep them on tenterhooks. They will be on edge. We keep doing it so that they don't get a direct route to Kanchi.'

'Keep pushing them eastward?'

'Yes, why not? Keep pushing them off the path that they would like to take.'

Mamalla pulled at his lower lip as he frowned in thought. 'We would need to break our forces into three pieces then. One to Suramara. One to wherever we want to finally meet them, which, I might remind you, hasn't been decided yet. And the third one, to harass Pulikeshi's troops.'

'I could lead the troops to Suramara against the Gangas, you could hold the bulk of the troops in reserve for the main battle, and Ilan here could lead a smaller force to make Pulikeshi's life miserable as he moves down south,' said Paranjyothi.

'Also, don't forget that we are expecting Manavamma's forces here, once I get a message across to him,' said Ilanthiraiyanar.

'How long do you suppose it will take Pulikeshi to come down south from where he was last when he made a move towards Kanchi?'

'Given the size of their army, it should take them between two and three weeks.'

'If not harassed,' said Mamalla.

'If not harassed,' agreed Ilanthiraiyanar with a grin.

'Your Majesty,' interjected Nalankilli. 'Don't you think we also need an army here at the fort, just in case ...?' he trailed away.

'Just in case we get beaten?' asked Mamalla, the smile robbing the question of the edge that it contained.

'We do need to plan for worst case scenarios as well, Sire.'

'You are right, Prime Minister,' said Mamalla gravely, giving due weightage to the words of a man that he respected.

'Do we expect any other armies to take a hand?' asked the general.

'What about Tribhuvana?' asked Nalankilli.

'You think he will attempt something?'

'He would be seething, wouldn't he? His blockade has been lifted. You also told us that Manavamma had beaten his army at Puttalam. Don't you think he would want to get some of his own back at Manavamma?'

'The important point, though, is whether he has the army whose size is commensurate with his anger,' said Mamalla.

'Perhaps we should ask Manavamma to split his forces into three as well. One piece that is left at Korkai to act as a deterrent to Tribhuvana. Another, that besieges Madurai and bottles up Jayanthavarman and a third that bypasses Madurai and comes here,' said Commander Paranjyothi.

'That sounds like a plan,' agreed Mamalla. 'Let's get the pieces moving.'

10

A Surprise for the Gangas

Forests west of Thagadur, November 641 CE

The men merged into the tall *darbha* grass, their bodies completely hidden as they peered through the stalks. They had been waiting for the sun to go down. In front of them was a large army camp, set out in typical style. *Army camps all over the world are probably laid out in the same manner*, thought their leader. The generals and kings were at the hub, in large tents. The further one was down the hierarchy, the farther they were from the centre. The elephants were placed at the back of the camp and some distance away from it. It was better to be careful where elephants were concerned, especially war elephants. They were temperamental creatures and given to stampeding at the slightest chance.

The cooks and other support staff were placed to one side, to the far left of where the men lay waiting. They had no quarrel with the cooks and wouldn't attack unarmed men. They did, however, want to inflict significant pain, suffering and loss on the soldiers of this army.

They had trekked for a week to get here. It had been slow going at first, as the men were giving their bodies some time to heal and recover from their travails. They had had to be careful as well, keeping an eye out for enemy scouts who might discover their presence. They needn't have worried, though. The scouts, if any, were not paying attention to their rear.

They weren't a large group. They were barely thirty or so in number and they knew that it would be futile, not to mention foolish, to go up against this army. Their immediate need was horses and they had decided to get some from their enemies.

The place where they waited was directly in line with the stables where the horses were tethered. While the horses of the kings and generals were kept near their tents, most of the infantry's horses were kept here.

The sun had touched the tops of the trees. Still the men waited. They knew that dusk would come fast. Torches would be lit, and those would destroy the night vision of the enemy.

The sun went down below the trees and the camp subsided into darkness, punctuated by the hundreds of torches that had been lit. The torches threw light within the camp, but they also threw shadows—shadows that allowed for concealment.

The men lying in the grass started crawling forward. The darkness made it easy for them; the lack of alertness of those in the camp made it doubly so. They were crawling from a direction that was downwind of the horses, who couldn't smell the men and hence continued munching peacefully on their meal of oats and hay.

The leader stood up quickly as they reached the edge of the camp and stooped between the wooden railings that made up the stable fence. His men followed suit—swiftly, noiselessly. A couple of men cut the ropes that held the wooden railings together and gently lowered the blocks to the ground.

The men then walked on soft feet towards the horses. The animals looked up inquisitively, but the men stroked their flanks with their hands, whispering softly. A couple of the horses shied away and snorted and snickered when they felt unfamiliar hands on their bodies and scented the unfamiliar smells of the men.

The men untied the ropes that yoked the horses to the railings and, speaking softly all the while, started leading them out. As the last man exited the stables with his new horse, a stable hand, who had come to look in on the horses, saw the empty stalls and the backs of the men leading the horses out, and raised the alarm.

'Thieves! Thieves! Help!' he cried.

It was too late though. The men jumped on the horses and galloped away into the night and the surrounding forest.

The soldiers who had rushed towards the stables on hearing the shouts of the stable boy gave up the idea of following the men in the dark. They would go looking for them in the morning, they decided. Their sergeant asked the stable boy only one question.

'How many horses were taken?'

'About thirty,' said the boy, doing a quick count. The sergeant walked away to report to his captain.

A couple of miles from camp, the men pushed their horses ever deeper into the woods, until they reached the clearing along the little pond that was their camp.

The leader got off his horse, groaning a little from the pain he still felt in his back as his muscles moved.

Kannan's face split into the familiar wide smile as he remarked, 'Well boys, I must say that went quite well, don't you think?'

The sergeant who had spoken to the stable boy led some of his men into the forest early the next morning. They had tried to follow the trail left by the horses, but the forest floor was dry and they soon lost sight of any tracks. The jungle was also thick, and they spent a considerable amount of time going back and forth, trying to find a path forward. Eventually, the sergeant called it a day, and his dispirited men followed him back into camp.

He reported to his captain his failure to find the horses or the men who had taken them. The captain ticked him off properly before getting to his feet and walking slowly towards the tent of General Narasimha, the army chief of the Gangas. He didn't particularly look forward to the task of telling his general that thieves had stolen thirty of their horses.

As expected, the general blew his top and bawled him out for a few minutes. Eventually, regaining his composure somewhat, he asked, 'Who do you think these thieves were?'

The captain took his time answering.

'I think they might not be petty thieves, Sir. At least not in the middle of the jungle, here,' he said, pointing around.

'That's what I thought as well,' said the general. 'You may go.'

The captain saluted and left.

Narasimha walked out of his tent and towards the king's.

The king was reclining on his bed when Narasimha entered unannounced. The guard at the gate was not brave enough to stop his general from going into the king's tent.

'You look angry, Narasimha avare,' said King Srivikrama.

'You will be too, Your Majesty, once you hear what I have to say.' He narrated the events of the previous night and the loss of the horses.

'Thirty horses isn't such a big number, is it?'

'No, Sir. But it's not about the number of horses that we lost. It is more about the fact that men could come into our camp and coolly leave with so many horses, without being detected or challenged.'

'Do we know anything about who they were?'

'No, but we don't think they were your run-of-the-mill thieves. They had to be soldiers of some sort.'

'Who?'

'If you want me to hazard a guess, I will say, possibly survivors of the Pallavan army that we annihilated.'

'Aah. I too have some news for you, Narasimha avare,' said the king.

'What about, Sire?'

'I received a message from Maharaja Pulikeshi last night.'

Narasimha waited for his king to elaborate.

'The maharaja asked us to start moving towards Kanchi but to plan it so that we reach there in about two weeks' time. The maharaja and his men are even now moving towards Kanchi. He wants us to attack from the flank while the maharaja takes them head-on.'

Narasimha smiled.

'Looks like a rehash of a familiar old plan.'

It had taken the men a day's hard riding to get to Thagadur. Their horses had been well rested, and they got to the city in time before the gates closed for the day. The soldiers of Thagadur had baulked at the sight of thirty mounted men, clearly soldiers, going by their bearing, entering the city gates. They had been stopped by a sergeant and it was only after Kannan had shown him the amulet that identified him as a captain in the Pallava army that they were allowed to enter.

He had led his men to an eatery at the edge of the city and they all bedded down for the night under the stars.

The next morning, Kannan, Murugan and Bhatta rode their horses towards the palace. They dismounted near the gates and Kannan requested an audience with the raja.

'He is asleep,' said one of the guards, insolently.

'When does he wake up?' asked Kannan at his polite best.

'I don't know. Come back at noon,' the guard replied in his most offhand manner.

Kannan could sense Murugan getting fidgety behind him.

'Friend,' he said. 'You see this?' he asked, showing him his amulet. 'I am a captain in the Pallava army, personally sent by Maharaja Narasimhavarman Pallava. The maharaja is none too happy about the way your king and your soldiers let the Gangas take back the fort at Guddahalli and has asked me to come here and find out the reasons for it. Do you really want to stop me from entering the palace and talking to your king?' He looked long and hard at the soldier.

The soldier blanched. A slow trickle of sweat rolled down from his forehead, along the side of his face and to his neck.

'Ah, wait here please, Captain. I shall go in and find out.'

'You do that. But don't be too long. I am not a man of infinite patience,' he added menacingly.

The soldier was back in short order.

'The raja will see you now.'

'Oh, so he *was* awake after all,' said Bhatta with a grin.

The soldier grinned back sheepishly as he led them inside the palace.

Raja Duraisingham of Thagadur sported a peevish look on his face. He wasn't happy with the news that the guard had given him. Ever since their hasty retreat, facilitated by Annamalai and his men, Duraisingham had been fearful of the reaction from Kanchi. And it looked like it had come in the form of this captain. A captain! And him a raja! His face radiated his disgust at the circumstances as he welcomed the men. He had sent for his generals when he heard who was at the gate, and they were all seated around him.

'To what do I owe this pleasure? A visit from members of the Pallava army is not very common here.'

Kannan debated on what to tell the raja and then decided to tell him the truth.

'Sire, we haven't come from Kanchi.'

'What?' asked Duraisingham, relief momentarily chasing the peevishness from his face.

'Why did you make that claim to my guard?' he asked angrily.

'We didn't think there was any other way to see Your Majesty.'

'So where are you from?'

'We are what's remaining of the army that started off from Asanur to come to your aid, Sire,' said Kannan quietly.

'Our aid? Where?'

'We were following the Ganga forces as they were following you, Your Majesty. We were hoping to come to your aid, but …' he trailed off.

'What?'

'We were ambushed. Most of our troops were annihilated. We started off with nearly five hundred men. Only thirty of us survived,' said Kannan, his face and voice reflecting the pain in his heart.

Duraisingham perked up considerably on hearing this. Someone had had it rougher than him.

'What do you want from me?'

'The Ganga forces are barely two days' march away from here, Your Majesty.'

'Yes, yes I know,' said Duraisingham, testily. 'I have scouts too.'

'What are you proposing to do about it, Sire?'

'Me? What can I do? Have you seen the size of that force? I was hoping that Kanchi would come to my assistance but if you are it, I fear that even Commander Paranjyothi and General Ilanthiraiyanar have given up.'

Kannan hid the irritation he felt at this upstart king sullying the names of men he revered in such a cavalier manner.

'I am sure there is a plan, Your Majesty. But we need to do our part as well.'

'I have no intention of going up against that army. They would grind me to dust. I was hoping that *your* army would help us.'

Kannan noticed the stress on 'your' but decided to ignore it.

'Your Majesty, there is much that we can do. After all, your soldiers fought heroically to facilitate your own escape from the Ganga forces.'

'How did you hear about that?' snapped Duraisingham.

'We came across the place where they had fought the battle. There was a huge pile of ash and impromptu hero stones that had been erected. The Ganga soldiers may have decimated your men, but they do know how to give respect to their enemies. It was clear that there had been a protracted struggle there, before the final denouement.'

Kannan looked at the generals sitting around the king as he said those words, trying to get through to them. He noticed one or two of them shifting in their seats.

'So that young Annamalai did die in battle. We can at least go and tell his family that,' said a moustachioed general.

'You mean you haven't told them yet?' asked Kannan.

'We weren't sure,' said the man, defensively. 'They could have been captured as well. We still don't know if some of them were captured.'

Kannan took his time responding.

'If the Ganga soldiers move towards Kanchi, they will not allow Thagadur to stand at their rear,' he said.

'Yes, yes we know that,' said Duraisingham.

'What are you going to do about it then?'

'Sue for peace.'

'Sue for peace?' bristled Kannan.

'Sue for peace!' said Duraisingham.

'But you are allied to Kanchi!'

'Look, young man. Right now, the Ganga forces are closer to us than the Pallava army is. I must look out for my city. I don't think we can last out a siege here. The only option I can think of is to sue for peace.'

Kannan looked at the generals seated on either side of the king.

'Is that your opinion as well?'

The generals looked everywhere but at him.

'Your Majesty, Generals. Your men died gloriously in battle. Died so that they could buy you time. They might have died but they succeeded in what they set out to do. Don't you want to avenge their deaths? They left behind wives, mothers, sisters, parents, kids, relatives and friends, whose lives will never be the same again. Surely their deaths ought not to go in vain. Wouldn't future generations talk about us derisively if we were to do nothing? How would you face your own men, knowing that you did nothing to avenge the deaths of their comrades?'

The generals looked around uneasily at one another.

'What can we do?' said one of them, finally breaking the uncomfortable silence that had followed Kannan's words. 'They are a huge army, as the raja said.'

'We can hold out for a siege and tie them up here. I shall send a message to the generals at Kanchi. They are sure to send an army to assist us. The Gangas cannot proceed further until they have conquered us, and we shall not make it easy for them. We owe it to your men, Sire.'

'I agree with the young man, Your Majesty,' said a general, finally breaking his silence. 'My troops will never forgive me if we give in so easily, especially given the sacrifices of Annamalai and his men.'

Duraisingham looked at his generals. The others, he noticed, had nodded their heads in agreement at what the general had said.

'Alright,' Duraisingham said petulantly. 'Let us prepare for a siege.'

11
Muthuvel Leaves for Kanchi

Korkai and Madurai, November 641 CE

'I don't know why you have to go to Kanchi now,' stormed Thaamarai, her eyes flashing dangerously. She was standing with Muthuvel atop the fort walls, looking out over the port. It was a moonlit night and they had strolled all along the fort wall to end up to the south. They could see the ships tied near the jetties. A refreshing breeze had sprung up, which made Thaamarai's locks fly around her face.

'Very pretty,' said Muthuvel.

'What?' flared Thaamarai.

'Your hair. Flying about like that. Very pretty,' he said, raising his fingers to move them off her face.

Thaamarai's eyes softened momentarily and then she brushed his hand away.

'None of that now. I am still angry with you.'

'Sure,' he said reasonably. 'You go on being angry with me. Doesn't mean I can't touch your hair or slip my hand around your waist, like this,' he said as his arm snaked around her.

She freed herself from his hold and took a step away, breathing hard.

'I can't think when you do that.'

'Well, don't then.' He attempted to put his arm around her again, but she escaped once more and stood a couple of feet away from him, her arms folded across her chest, looking out at the sea, her upthrust chin indicative of her determination to not be sidetracked.

Muthuvel sighed.

'Look, it is not like I have a choice. I am a soldier and I need to follow orders.'

'Did the message from Kanchi order you to get back to Kanchi? Did it?'

'No.'

'That's right. There was nothing in the orders about you going back to Kanchi. I was in the room too, remember? All it said was to ask Manavamma to divide his army in three and to rush with the largest segment to Kanchi.'

'Well, what do you suppose I should do when there is peril facing my king? Stay on here and avoid the fight?'

'There is peril here too!'

'Who from?'

'Tribhuvana.'

Muthuvel scoffed. 'What's he going to do? We have ships now to counter him. Maybe not on the high seas but closer to shore. And he will have nowhere to land. Even if he is able to land and seeks to lay siege to the place, you all ought to be able to hold him off fairly easily.'

Thaamarai knew all this. On a logical plane, she knew that Muthuvel needed to be with his army and men when Pulikeshi was attacking Mamalla, but when has logic ever been able to triumph over human feelings?

Muthuvel was smart enough to realize this. He came close to her and turned her to face him, holding her upper arms.

'Thaamarai,' he said softly. 'I *have* to go. You know that. I know you know that. I promise that I will come back.'

She leaned into him, her head buried in his chest. His arms went around her waist. She clung to him fiercely. She mumbled something, but the wind blew her words away so he couldn't quite catch them. What she had said was, 'Alive. Come back to me alive.'

They left the next morning. Muthuvel, Manavamma, Thissa, Chaminda, Nedumaran and Sadaiyan were riding in front of the army as they made their way out of the gates, towards Madurai. Sadaiyan had insisted on going along with Muthuvel. Muthuvel had tried to dissuade him but Sadaiyan was having none of it.

'What am I going to do here, anna? The siege has been lifted. I don't have any coconuts to sell now,' he grinned. 'I can't even make money that way. If I come along with you, it will be a great experience for me. I notice that wars are a good time for some people to make a lot of money, and I don't want to miss that opportunity,' he said, his eyes shining brightly.

Muthuvel had given in. Secretly, he was delighted that the young thief would be with him. He had grown very fond of the boy. Moreover, the young rapscallion could be very useful. His knowledge of the seamier side of society and his ability to not let certain ethical or moral values cloud his decision-making could be very useful in times of war.

Manavamma had decided to leave about five hundred men at Korkai and take the rest with him. His plan was to leave another fifteen hundred men to besiege Madurai and take the remaining men with him to Kanchi.

It would take them three days to get to Madurai. Muthuvel, Chaminda and Sadaiyan rode together just behind Manavamma, Thissa and Nedumaran, who was wearing his typical, and some would say habitual, scowl. Anyone going at the head of an army to lay siege to a city that he believed was his for the taking ought to have been in a more cheerful mood. The reason for Nedumaran's petulance and irritability was Thaamarai.

Ever since he had seen his wife's younger sister blossom into a beautiful woman, he had set his heart on marrying her. After all, it was not unheard of for a prince to marry sisters. His wife wouldn't be too unhappy since he was only bringing her sister home as the step-wife.

However, the increasing closeness between Thaamarai and Muthuvel and her rebuffing his advances had left him in an almost permanent ill temper. That she had dared to pick someone whom he classified as a common soldier, over him, piqued him no end. He had observed them coming back to the palace late the previous night, their arms around each other.

He glowered into the distance as he thought of that. He had already developed possessiveness towards the girl and resented the fact that Muthuvel had had his arms around her.

He was pulled back into the present by Manavamma's voice.

'Huh? What did you say?'

'I asked what the plan was. We don't have siege engines. So, what's the plan for breaching the fort? Do you know a way in? Some secret gate perhaps?'

'There is a secret gateway, but my brother is sure to have blocked it. He knows I am with you.'

'Well then? Is there any other way? Someone inside maybe who can help you?'

Nedumaran was silent. The only person in Madurai who had sided with him was Gopala and that too because of his loyalty to Nedumaran's wife. And he was dead, killed during the siege of Korkai. Nedumaran rued the fact that he didn't have more friends within Madurai. He hadn't felt the need when he was the prince. He wondered now if that had been a mistake.

Roughly a hundred miles north of where they were, Jayanthavarman sat in his council chambers along with his ministers and generals. The mood in the room was sombre. They had received a message from Pulikeshi, asking for their assistance in the upcoming war against the Pallavas.

The army chief, General Nedunchezhiyan, looked pensive while Prime Minister Maravarman read out the olai the messenger had brought.

'This had to come at this time,' muttered Nedunchezhiyan. 'Just when we have also heard that Manavamma is advancing on Madurai with his forces.'

The king looked startled.

'When were you going to inform me of that?'

'I just heard it this morning, Your Majesty.'

'How large an army?'

'Fairly large, Sire.'

'And I suppose that my brother is with them?'

Nedunchezhiyan nodded in response.

'Can we afford to send a force to Pulikeshi's aid in these circumstances?'

'If we must, we need to send them out right now, before we are besieged,' said the army chief.

'How long before Manavamma gets here?'

'Another couple of days.'

'Can we withstand a siege?'

'I think we can, Sire. For one, I don't think Manavamma is going to spend his time here. He is probably going to take the bulk of his forces north, to link up with the Pallavas.'

'Aah. So, Nedumaran will be besieging here with a smaller force?'

'Yes. With some of Manavamma's troops and some of the Korkai forces.'

'Does that mean that we can send some of our troops north and still defend the fort?'

Nedunchezhiyan shrugged. 'We can defend alright, Your Majesty, but we won't be able to defeat them if we send our forces off to the north. And if, somehow, the Pallavas are successful, Manavamma will be back along with the Pallava forces. We might be in trouble then.'

'What do you suggest?' asked his king.

'I think that our first duty is to protect ourselves. We need to sit this one out.'

The preparations for the siege had gone off without a hitch. They had reached Madurai on the third day and had surrounded the city walls, splitting into four groups, each group making their way to the four city gates. About five hundred soldiers were positioned outside each of the gates. The contingent that went around to the north was much larger. A small force started setting up camp outside the north gate while the rest of the force peeled off and headed north-east towards Kanchi.

Nedumaran had placed himself in front of the southern gate along with some of Gopala's men. The soldiers had set up camp in a leisurely manner. The Pandyas standing on top of the fort walls had watched them, aware that they were out of arrow range. There was a lot of banter and chitchat between the two sets of soldiers.

Inside the city, Jayanthavarman had spent a considerable amount of time atop the northern, eastern and western gates before making his way to the south. He reached there mid-morning, and noticed a large tent that he was sure was his brother's. He smiled derisively as he noticed Nedumaran coming out of his tent. Obviously, word had been sent to his brother that he was atop the southern gates.

The brothers looked at each other over the intervening distance, the distance in their hearts much wider. Jayanthavarman spit over the fort walls, signifying his contempt for his brother. He knew that that would infuriate Nedumaran. He understood his brother's insecurities and fully intended to play upon them.

Muthuvel, Chaminda and Sadaiyan rode their horses hard. They had separated from Manavamma and the rest of the army and were on their way to Kanchi.

They slowed down to a walk every hour or so to give their horses a break from the tough pace. Muthuvel was in a hurry to get to Kanchi and to give them the message. He knew that it would take the army at least another three weeks of hard riding to reach Kanchi. He wanted to get there earlier. Much earlier. If there were to be a war against the Chalukyas, he wanted to be a part of it right from the beginning.

They were covering over thirty miles every day. They hoped to be in Kanchi in another week or so. Muthuvel couldn't wait to be back in his city. It had been a long time since he had left the place on the direction of General Ilanthiraiyanar. He wondered how the others were doing—Kannan and Elango. He had heard that Kannan had taken Asanur and then had set out towards Guddahalli but hadn't heard anything else after that.

His knowledge of Elango's whereabouts was even sketchier. He hoped to see them again. *Yes, even Elango*, he thought with a smile. Perhaps he had grown over the last few months. He didn't get the same feeling of dislike when he thought about Elango. He was certain that Thaamarai had something to do with it. She had changed him—of that, he was sure. What surprised him was that he didn't mind at all. He gave himself up to thinking about Thaamarai to pass the time as they rode on.

12
War of Attrition

En route to Kanchi, November 641 CE

Maharaja Pulikeshi was reclining in his chariot along with his brother Kubja. The air was still and drowsy in the stifling heat of the afternoon. The army had just started moving again, post their halt for lunch. They advanced slowly, as lethargy—born of a heavy lunch—gripped them. The chariot trundled ahead, and the cavalry followed at a slow walk, with even the horses hanging their heads as they ambled forward. The infantry shuffled along half asleep, while the elephants swayed their way ponderously behind them all.

The path they were on meandered its way through the terrain, the sluggishness of its turns mimicking the somnolence and listlessness of the men. A herd of buffaloes, half submerged in the muddy waters of a pond, munched on grass and masticated the food, keeping time with the movement of the Chalukya army. Bees buzzed lazily and flitted about, lingering from flower to flower. Even the birds seemed to have taken a pause from their usual industriousness in the oppressive heat.

The stillness was shattered in the most brutal fashion. A volley of arrows arced over the ground and thudded into the king's bodyguards and their horses, who were positioned as a protective barrier around Pulikeshi's chariot. Some of the bodyguards toppled over with a cry and a grunt. Others were dead before they hit the ground. Many horses went down on their knees, neighing, with arrows stuck into their sides like pins in a cushion.

It took a few seconds for everyone to fathom what had happened. The contingent marching in front of the king's chariot consisted of his sons and a few high-ranking members of the army. They had been dozing upon their horses but were startled into wakefulness by the death cries of the soldiers. By the time they realised what had happened, a fresh set of arrows was already in the air and coming towards them.

Prince Aditya was the first to react.

'Take cover!' he yelled as he jumped off his horse and used it to shield himself from the arrows. The others followed suit. One of the captains who was a little late got an arrow in his thigh as a reward for his tardiness.

'Archers!' cried Aditya. 'Get our archers here! Shoot back!'

He noticed that the archers shooting at them were just outside the tree-line. There were maybe a hundred of them keeping up a relentless barrage at the Chalukyan army. More men and animals went down. The cavalrymen were having trouble controlling their horses, who, nostrils flaring and eyes dancing wildly, wished to pound out of there but were being held firmly in check by their masters. Several horses succumbed while providing protection to their riders. It took a couple of minutes for the archers from the Chalukya side to start shooting back.

The enemy archers kept their salvo going for a bit longer but eventually, they decided to let valour wait on prudence. They stepped back into the trees and were soon lost from sight. The archers on the Chalukya side kept shooting arrows, somewhat aimlessly, into the trees, before Aditya called a halt to that.

King Pulikeshi emerged from his chariot, enraged, his face glowering, his eyes red, and ready to vent at whoever had wrought this. He saw his wounded and dying men and let out a growl.

'You!' he shouted at his sons. 'Take a few men and see if you can chase down those people.'

The princes jumped with speed at his command. They got on to some uninjured horses and selected a few men they trusted to go along with them. A few archers jumped up behind the riders. The group then rode towards the forest, their very beings alert and cautious. There was every possibility that the other archers were waiting to ambush them.

Closer to the tree-line, the Chalukyan archers dismounted and moved forward on foot, their heads turning from side to side, their eyes constantly searching for a glimpse, a glimmer, a flash of something that was out of place, that ought not to have been there.

The horses followed behind them. They found the spot where the enemy archers had knelt to shoot. Close by, they found the spot where several horses had been tied to trees. It appeared to be a sort of impromptu corral. Ranaragha, who was the best tracker among the brothers, got down and surveyed the ground.

'How many?' asked Aditya.

Ranaragha pursed his lips. 'Slightly difficult to say but looks to have been well over a hundred. Maybe even as many as two hundred.' He looked up at his brother.

'What do you say? Should we go on?'

Aditya mulled it over in his mind. After a few seconds of silence, he said, 'No. I don't think we are going to catch them, and given that this is a forest and they have been here, they hold all the advantages. They can set up an ambush for us anytime they want. I am not foolish. Let's go back and report to Father. I think this needs some serious discussion.'

General Ilanthiraiyanar, second only to Commander Paranjyothi in the Pallava military hierarchy, sat on a tree stump. The rest of the tree lay near it, on its side, perhaps having been felled by a storm. The trunk itself was rotting, but the stump seemed sturdy enough. He eyed his troops as they lolled on the ground.

It had been a satisfying day. They were a small force of around three hundred men, and had ridden hard and fast to catch up with Pulikeshi's army. They had tracked the enemy for a couple of days, always keeping within the forest and out of sight. The Chalukya scouts seemed to be more interested in what lay ahead of them than to their flanks, and hence, they had remained undetected.

Their attack had gone as planned. The idea, as discussed earlier in Kanchi, was to harass the Chalukya troops as they came down south, and to slowly push them eastwards, extending their supply lines. Ilanthiraiyanar wanted to do this with a minimal loss of men. These sorts of hit-and-run tactics, while not particularly valorous, were still a necessity of war. He wanted to ensure that by the time the Chalukya army arrived in the vicinity of Kanchi, they would be a bedraggled lot.

He had posted scouts all around. He didn't want to be caught by the Chalukya soldiers, who were bound to try and follow them. He could have prepared for an ambush but had decided against it today. Today was just a sample of what they were going to put the Chalukyans through. He knew that a sufficiently enraged Pulikeshi *would* eventually send his men into the forest in numbers to try and take them out. He would wait for that, he decided.

He heard the rustling of leaves behind him, and turned around to see one of the scouts standing stiffly between two trees.

'What is it?' he asked, noting the look of terror on the man's face.

'Oh, nothing much,' said a bearded man, stepping into the clearing from behind the scout, holding a knife to the scout's back. A tall, dark individual with a warrior-like bearing stood next to him.

The soldiers who had been lounging in the clearing got to their feet immediately, swords and knives drawn. They were confused by the ease with which the general sat and even more so when his face widened into a grin.

'Aah, Elango, my boy, welcome back!'

'I nearly didn't recognise you there. You have changed a lot. That beard, I am sorry to tell you, doesn't suit you at all. Also, you ought to eat up a bit. You look positively skinny.'

Elango smiled back at him. It was very difficult to throw the general off his usual sangfroid. He removed the knife from the scout's back and said, 'Sorry about that. Didn't mean to frighten or hurt you.' The scout gave him a tentative, hesitant smile, and took leave of the gathering to return to his post.

'I didn't have much of a choice, Sir. It's not like I went on a self-enforced diet,' Elango said to the general.

He narrated the story of his captivity and eventual escape and introduced Jamba and Commander Dasappa to him.

The general got up from his seat and bowed first to the Banakula. 'I have heard a lot about you from someone else.'

'Sister Mitra?'

'That is correct. It looks like you have been of great service to her and Elango.'

'They saved my life,' said Jamba succinctly, as if that one statement were an answer to everything that he had done or would ever do for them.

Ilanthiraiyanar nodded. He understood the code under which men such as Jamba functioned.

He then clasped Commander Dasappa's hands and said, 'Sorry about the loss of your fort, Commander. I hear your men held out for a long time and fought bravely till the end.'

'Thanks in large measure to your man Elango here,' said Dasappa.

Ilanthiraiyanar smiled a quiet smile of pride.

'How did you find us?' he asked Elango.

'Happenstance. We were proceeding towards Kanchi at a fair clip and ran into the back of the Chalukya army. We were trying to figure out a way to go around them and then saw the mayhem today. We surmised that if someone attacked the Chalukya army, it had to be ours. So, we slipped around their rear and then came looking for you. Jamba here could follow a fish through water or a bird in the sky. So following three hundred or so soldiers through the forest posed no difficulties for him.'

Ilanthiraiyanar nodded. 'Are you still intent on proceeding towards Kanchi?'

'What? And miss all this? I have a score to settle with the Chalukyas,' said Elango.

As the group disbanded, Elango heard a slight commotion. The noise he heard was coming from a fight between one of the sentries guarding their little area of the camp, and someone else. He heard raised voices and presently snippets of the conversation drifted over to him.

'I need to see him ...'

'And I have told you that you can't. Not at this time of the night.'

'But I know him.'

'Yeah, sure. Everyone knows him. The more important question is, does he know you?'

'Of course he knows me,' said the first voice heatedly. 'Why don't you call him over and ask him?'

'Privates like myself don't call out to captains and ask them to come over!'

Elango had had enough of this. 'Who is it?' he called out.

There was a sudden hush as both the voice of the person trying to enter and the sentry went quiet. Then, the voice called out, 'Elango, Sir. It's me. Venkata.'

'Venkata!' exclaimed Elango. 'Let him in,' he told the sentry. Venkata walked past the sentry, giving him a mocking grin, and then made straight for Elango.

'Sir! It is good to see you. I just heard from someone that you were in this camp. I *had* to come and meet you,' said Venkata.

Elango pulled the young lad into a warm hug. Venkata disengaged himself and then bowed to his commander, Dasappa.

'Glad to see that you made it out too, Sir,' said Venkata.

Dasappa nodded in return.

Elango asked the question uppermost on his mind. 'You were with Mitra. Where is she? Is she alright?'

Venkata grinned and nodded his head vigorously.

'Yes, Sir. We escorted King Krithavarman and his family to Kanchi, along with Anjaneya and Jabali.'

'Yes, Jamba did tell me that he had sent them along with Mitra. So, where is she?'

'I don't know, Sir.'

'Don't know?'

'She was called to General Ilanthiraiyanar's office …' he said, pausing momentarily as he looked at the general, and then continued, '… and then left, saying she was going to help the general. She also told me that I needed to go with the general on a campaign, and here I am.'

Elango looked across at General Ilanthiraiyanar who nodded his head slightly as if to say, 'Let's continue this conversation later.'

'But gosh! I am so glad to see you safe and sound, Sir. It would be good to fight together once again!' exclaimed Venkata.

Elango smiled at the enthusiastic young man.

'That we surely will, Venkata. Go and get some rest. We could all use some,' he said.

No sooner had the young man left than Elango walked across to the general.

'I wanted to ask you about Mitra, Sir,' he said. 'I mean Sanghamitra,' he corrected himself.

The general let a small smile appear on his lips.

'What about her?'

'You heard what Venkata said. Can you tell me what she is doing?'

The general told him.

'Are we absolute imbeciles? Am I surrounded by nincompoops? How could we let this happen? We were moving into enemy territory, and we had scouts looking only to the front? What kind of an army is this? What is the need for generals and princes when an enemy can attack our forces with impunity? Do I need to personally take over the reins of the army?' Pulikeshi thundered, looking at Commander Satyaki.

The others in the room, Aditya, Ranaragha, Jayasimha and even Naganandi to an extent, cowered under the verbal onslaught unleashed by Pulikeshi. The king presented a striking picture, standing in the middle of the tent, in the flickering circle of light thrown by the four torches. He stood with his hands balled into fists on his hips. His eyes flashed fire. His breathing was heavy as emotion took him in its grip. His head swivelled on that thick neck, set atop massive shoulders, as he looked from one to the other.

Everyone looked anywhere but at him, afraid to meet his eyes. Almost everyone, actually. Naganandi looked back at him steadily, unwaveringly. He and the maharaja had been through much together and he was no stranger to the king's outbursts. He knew that the outbursts stemmed from a desire for action and decisiveness. Indecision and incompetence bothered him. In this instance, it was incompetent decision-making and complacency on their part that had stirred Pulikeshi's emotions to a fever pitch.

'Well?' asked Pulikeshi, latching on to the eyes of the only person meeting his own eyes.

Naganandi shrugged. 'It was a mistake, Your Majesty. It was complacency on our part. We thought that the Pallavas would sit back and wait for us to come down south before they met us and …'

'Shouldn't we have anticipated this?' interrupted Pulikeshi.

'Yes. Perhaps.'

'What are you all doing then?'

'Maharaja, if I may suggest …'

'What?'

'What has happened has happened. We are all angry and upset. It would be much better to channel that anger into what we need to do now.'

Pulikeshi glared at his spy chief. Naganandi looked back in return, his face impassive. The tension in Pulikeshi's body seemed to gradually decrease. His hands came off his hips. His fists unclenched. His shoulders rolled forward. The king walked towards his chair and sat down, his face much calmer now. He had always been action-oriented and what Naganandi said appealed to him.

He gave a long sigh and then nodded at Naganandi.

'You are right. Let's focus on what we need to do. This is going to slow us down, you know?'

Naganandi nodded and shrugged his shoulders at the same time. It couldn't be helped. And what wasn't in his control, Naganandi never worried about.

13

Thagadur Prepares

Thagadur, November 641 CE

Kannan paced slowly atop the fort walls, pausing ever so often to check on the work being carried out. Thagadur had never actually prepared for a siege in many years, and it showed. The walls had cracks or were so weak that even a small battering ram could quite easily break through.

As he looked into the distance, he could see rows of carts going up to and returning from the surrounding hills, filled with stones and rocks. The hills were basaltic in nature and there was a surfeit of rocks there which would serve the purpose of shoring up the fort walls.

When Kannan had appealed to Raja Duraisingham's council to put up a fight, he had expected some of the generals to take the lead. They had all, however, deferred to him, knowing that he had more actual fighting experience than any of them, and in modern tactics at that. They had prevailed on the king to put Kannan in charge of strategy while they themselves would oversee the defences. Duraisingham had agreed, happy that they hadn't asked his advice on strategy and tactics.

Kannan had spent some time detailing his plans to the generals. Only one of them was somewhat competent, perhaps past fighting age, but competent enough to understand military necessities and act on them. This general, named Rayappa Devar, was the one to whom Kannan depended on to get things done. The other generals he either ignored or gave trivial tasks to, so that they wouldn't pout and mope around all day, feeling left out.

It was Rayappa's responsibility to repair the fort walls. Kannan and he had gone around the walls identifying the weak spots, and had decided upon reinforcing those areas with stones stacked on the inside of the fort, against the cracks. That was the best that they could hope to do, given the lack of time.

Kannan estimated that the Ganga army would be upon them in a week to ten days' time. Meanwhile, they not only had to repair the walls, but also stock up on food for an extended siege. He had tasked a couple of semi-competent generals with going out into the countryside and commandeering food from the hapless villagers. He felt bad doing that, but it was a necessity, and he was a practical man. Tough situations called for tough choices to be made and it was the commander who had to make them. It so happened to be Kannan, in this case.

He had made sure that one or the other of his men was also part of any group to which he had given a task. Murugan, for example, was the one who was in charge of collecting food grains from the villages. The generals whom he shepherded were present more to give legitimacy to their cause. Any villager would resent having his foodgrains taken away. The resentment is increased if perfect strangers come and demand it. By taking the generals along with him, Murugan and the others were able to lower the degree of anger among the populace.

Bhatta and a few of the others were tasked with filling the land outside the fort with caltrops and other such pointed devices, that would make life miserable for horse and soldier alike, were they to approach the walls. He was also in charge of ensuring an increase in the production of arrowheads and spears.

Kannan paid attention to all these facets as he continued his pacing. One didn't become a captain in the Pallava army merely for one's fighting abilities. Kannan was good at his job because he not only was able to delegate work to his trusted lieutenants but he also had a keen eye for detail and kept track of all the work that needed to be done.

There was something, however, that was bugging him. Something intangible—a faint ghostly touch at the back of his mind that disconcerted him. He went over his plans again and again. Was there something that he had missed? He decided to talk it over with Murugan and Bhatta at the end of the day.

The next morning saw the three of them, mounted on their horses, leaving the fort gates, picking their way carefully through the obstacles that Bhatta had laid out. He was in the lead since he knew the way through that veritable maze.

It was Murugan's idea to take a journey outside the city, to survey the lay of the land, when Kannan had mentioned that nagging feeling to him.

They rode on, along the path leading west, past rice fields and tilling farmers. The day was pleasant since the sun had barely cleared the horizon. The farmers were already hard at work. The land was dotted with rocky hillocks, containing giant granite boulders, and was sparsely vegetated. The air was thick with birds going about their early morning activities, tittering and chirping noisily. Goatherds and cowherds led their charges towards grass-covered patches.

Murugan approached one of the cowherds.

'Anna, is there a way up this hillock?'

'You see that big rock there? Go around it. There is a path that winds its way to the top.'

Murugan nodded his thanks and jerked his head towards the others to follow him.

The path, if it could be called that, allowed for only one person to walk along it. Kannan and Bhatta trailed Murugan single file, and they followed the twists and turns of the path on its way up the hill. The hillock was sparsely covered by bushes. The path itself was rocky and the men kept their feet gingerly in between the sharp-edged stones dotting the ground.

It took them roughly a half hour of twisting, turning and wending their way up the path to get to the top. The sun was well clear of the horizon by then. Its golden rays blazed across the verdant fields and groves. Here and there lay liquid pools of silvery water as the rays reflected off the surface. The faint sound of bells being rung in nearby temples reached their ears.

The men stood silent as they drank it all in.

'Beautiful, isn't it?' said Bhatta.

'Do you have to state the obvious?' asked Murugan.

'It's a habit born of association with an uncultured ignoramus like you,' said Bhatta with obvious satisfaction at having bested his friend in their recurring game of repartee.

Murugan scowled, but his attention had already turned towards Kannan, who stood looking towards the fort, a frown on his face. He nudged Bhatta and then slanted his eyes towards Kannan.

'Something troubling you, Boss?' asked Bhatta.

'The fort.'

'What of it?'

'It isn't defensible,' said Kannan.

'It isn't the strongest fort that we have ever seen, for sure,' added Murugan. 'But we knew that.'

'That is an understatement,' said Kannan. 'I have had this nagging feeling over the last few days, despite all our efforts to strengthen the defences of the fort. It is as if we were dressing up a pig to play the role of a princess in a play.'

'Raja Duraisingham wouldn't be very happy to hear you describe his dear city in that fashion, Boss,' said Bhatta.

Kannan snapped his fingers. 'That's to the dear old raja. Look at the city. No moat. Walls made of mud and brick and while we are trying to shore it up with stones, look at the approaches to the fort.'

Bhatta looked. So did Murugan.

'Easy approaches,' said Murugan, laconically.

'Precisely.'

'I see what you mean, Boss. We can't hold that place against a small force, let alone the Gangas and Chalukyas together,' said Bhatta. 'What do you suggest we do?'

Kannan swivelled his head as he surveyed the land. The path from the west caught his attention. They had travelled that way just a few days ago. He recognised several of the hills and hillocks that dotted the route.

'There,' he pointed to a place where the path was lost from view as it dived between two hills. 'Remember that?'

'Yeah,' said Murugan. 'Two hillocks split by the path.'

'The perfect place then,' said Bhatta.

'For?'

'For? Why, you dunce. For an attack of course,' replied Bhatta.

Murugan looked afresh at the hillocks and then all along the path.

'I agree, Boss. Seems like the only place. But aren't they going to expect that? I am sure they would have sent their scouts ahead.'

'Let us assume that they have. We can bottle them up there, can't we? If they don't attack us, they can't proceed further. And if they do, then we have the upper hand,' said Kannan.

'They could climb the hills too …' said Bhatta.

'… and it will be very costly for them,' finished Kannan. 'They might overwhelm us eventually, but it will finish them as a threat to Kanchi. And that is what we want, don't we?'

Murugan and Bhatta looked at each other and then at Kannan. And then back at each other again.

'Well,' said Murugan, 'we had better inform Raja Duraisingham, then. He isn't going to be very happy about it though.'

'I can live with that,' said Kannan shortly, starting to descend the hillock.

Paranjyothi rode at the head of his army. He could have taken a chariot for himself if he liked, but he was a soldier's soldier. He had come up through the ranks. His prowess on the battlefield was legendary. Young soldiers were often told tales of the many campaigns in which he had taken part. His chest and arms bore the marks of numerous battles, the healed scars a telling testament to his abilities.

He was at the head of an army of about two thousand men. Kiruba had mentioned that the combined Ganga and Chalukya forces numbered around three thousand. He was confident that with his men and those of the Raja of Thagadur, he would be able to more than hold his own against the enemy forces.

But holding his own was not what he had set out to achieve. His goal was to decimate the enemy forces. He remembered the previous campaign when the Chalukyas had attacked them during King Mahendravarman's reign. The Ganga and Pandya forces had caught them in a vice-like grip and, despite some brave fighting by the Pallava soldiers, they had been routed. He was determined to prevent that from happening again.

That evening, as he rested in his tent, two messengers reached him. The first one had come from Kanchi and had been sent by the king. It informed him that their man Muthuvel had reached Kanchi with news that Manavamma's men were on their way. He had also mentioned that Madurai was under siege and that Jayanthavarman would not be able to move out and come to Pulikeshi's assistance.

The second messenger reached him later in the night. This one had come from the west, from Thagadur, but the message was not from Raja Duraisingham. It was from Kannan. The messenger told him that the captain had decided that Thagadur was not defendable and that they needed to take the fight to the enemy. He had identified a place ideal for them to ambush the Ganga forces.

Paranjyothi smiled to himself. His old pal Ilanthiraiyanar chose his men well. He had noticed that Kannan had not really asked for permission from the commander but was informing him of the decision that he had taken in the field. *A capable young man and one who knows his mind*, thought Paranjyothi, as he retired for the night.

14
Siege of Madurai

Madurai, December 641 CE

Prince Nedumaran stood outside his tent, looking at the southern gates of the fort enveloping his beloved city of Madurai. They had been camping outside the fort walls for over a week now and it bothered him that there was an impasse. They didn't have any siege machines with which to break down the fort walls. Moreover, even if they had had those, he would have been loath to use them against his beloved city. He wanted to take over the kingdom, not destroy the city that he had grown up in. He knew that his position would become untenable among his few supporters were he to harm the city or its citizens.

And so they were camped here, day after day, doing nothing, while they waited for his brother to do something. Do what? Capitulate? Why would he? There was likely enough grain stored within the city to last at least a month or so.

Nedumaran wasn't a patient man. He wanted the throne *now*. It didn't occur to him that patience was oft a virtue that was rewarded in due course. His other major grouse was the fact that, while nominally, he was the head of this army, it was Thissa, the Lankan general, who called the shots. He himself didn't have any troops of his own. The troops loaned by his father-in-law—mostly Gopala's men—treated him with distant respect. They seemed to listen more to that blasted Lankan general than to him.

Nedumaran's eyes narrowed as the many slights, real and imagined, from Gopala's men flickered through his mind. A man quick to take umbrage, his mind quickly conjured up a list of the many grievances that he felt were legitimate. His lips tightened and his nostrils flared in fury as he worked himself up into a perfect storm of anger and hatred.

His mind directed this ire at Thissa. *He* was the one who was supposed to help Nedumaran take the fort and he had done nothing but sit on his bottom since coming here. Nedumaran seethed in helpless rage at this injustice done to his cause by a general of his ally. He decided to go and confront the man himself.

He called for his horse and, mounting it, rode around the eastern side of the fort towards the northern gates where Thissa was camped. The soldiers saw him coming and alerted the general, so that when he rode up to his tent, Thissa was standing outside, waiting for him. He bowed courteously to Nedumaran, and said, 'Alight and come inside, Your Highness.'

Nedumaran dismounted and followed his host into the tent. Thissa bade him sit in the well-bolstered divan that he himself used. Nedumaran sat down, a sneer on his face, and said, looking around the tent, 'Looks like you have made yourself very comfortable here.'

If Thissa noticed the slight intended behind these words, he pretended not to understand them and said, 'One does what one can in the midst of a campaign, Your Highness.' He then added with a smile, 'Age and rank do have some small advantages in any army.'

'Does that include sitting on one's ass and doing nothing?' asked Nedumaran, a little crudely.

Thissa, a man of a generally placid disposition, could feel the irritation mount within him toward someone he considered a popinjay. He fought a rising tide of revulsion and said mildly, 'Sieges are often like that, Sire.'

'Really? I thought the purpose of a siege was to try and attack the fort and take it …'

'Or to wait and tire out the men within the fort,' interrupted Thissa.

'Oh! Is that what this is supposed to be?'

'That's the general idea,' said Thissa, his patience starting to wear thin.

'How long do you think that will take?'

'I would suppose a couple of months, depending on how much food they have inside the fort, which I don't think will be much. We didn't really give them enough time to go about stockpiling food.'

'Well, I suggest that we find out ways to attack them.'

'With what, Your Highness?' asked Thissa with exaggerated patience.

'Battering rams or catapults.'

'We don't have catapults or the expertise in this army to build them. As for battering rams, you know the size of those gates. We would need humungous trees. And even if we did attack those gates with a battering ram, do you think the people on top of the fort walls wouldn't be dropping things on us? Nasty things like hot oil or boiling water? How many men should I sacrifice for this?'

'As many as required,' said Nedumaran arrogantly.

'I am sorry, Your Highness. These are *my* men. And *my* orders, from *my* king, are to ensure that your brother Jayanthavarman cannot go to Pulikeshi's aid. Taking the fort is of secondary importance to me.'

'But not to me.'

Thissa gave Nedumaran a long and steady look and then said, 'In that case, Your Highness, you might need to raise an army of your own. While I am perfectly willing to lay siege to the fort, I am not going to actively disobey the orders of my king.'

Nedumaran snorted his disgust and got up from the divan, making uncharitable remarks about Thissa, his king and Lankans in general.

Thissa bristled at this but held his peace.

'Under other circumstances, Your Highness, I would not have taken this slight to my king and country. I shall let it pass this time. I do wish, though, that we meet someday under different circumstances, when I will be able to repay you for what you have just said.' The menace in his voice was evident.

Nedumaran walked out without replying. He yanked the reins of his horse from the hand of the soldier holding them, jumped on to the horse and then, lashing its flanks savagely with the ends of the reins, raced away.

Any man who whips his horse that way needs whipping himself, thought Thissa in disgust.

Nedumaran seethed the rest of the day. *How dare a minion, a servant of a Lankan king without a kingdom, speak to me like that? How dare he?* His thoughts were in a ferment as he paced up and down his tent, growling. Despite his servants stepping fearfully around him all day, they were at the receiving end of several tongue-lashings from him.

He wanted a go at his brother. His mercurial nature now directed all his ire at his brother, Jayanthavarman, a man who, he felt, had denied him a shot at the throne. That he, Jayanthavarman, was the rightful heir to the throne seemed to escape him. Nedumaran was like a horse with blinders attached. He had lost all perspective on why he had set out to rebel against Jayanthavarman in the first place. His being was consumed with acquiring the Madurai throne.

The next morning, he sent a messenger to the gates, under a peace flag, asking for a meeting with Jayanthavarman. Jayanthavarman appeared at the gates an hour or so later. An hour that Nedumaran spent in restlessness.

He was alerted to Jayanthavarman's arrival by one of his men. He rushed outside to see his brother silhouetted against the sky, hands placed jauntily at his hips. Nedumaran walked forward alone, deliberately, as if showing his disdain to his brother. As he neared the gates, he noticed the archers placed along the walls, with their bows pulled taut and the arrows pointing at him.

'Is this your bravery, aṇṇa?' asked Nedumaran with a sneer.

Jayanthavarman put his hands out and asked his men to lower their weapons. He then waited for Nedumaran to come closer.

'You wanted to talk to me?'

'I wanted to tell you not to be such a coward and to come and fight me like a man.'

Jayanthavarman bristled.

'A coward? I could squash you like the worthless bug that you are if I wanted to.'

'Is that why you are hiding behind the fort walls and your soldiers?'

Jayanthavarman laughed.

'All this bravado of yours was in marked absence when you were rotting in the dungeons of Korkai, dear *thambi.*'

Nedumaran's face darkened as he remembered his days of incarceration.

'Yes, well, now the tables have turned, haven't they?'

'Turned?' asked Jayanthavarman. 'So you have some allies helping you. You were a beggar then. You are a beggar now. You had to beg a foreigner from Lanka to help you. And worse, you had to beg your own father-in-law for some soldiers. Moreover, what can you do to me? You can stay out there in discomfort in those little tents. Me? I am well ensconced here. We have enough food grains. I will be warm in my bed while you will have to face the night chill and the cold winter mornings in that tent of yours.' He laughed out loud.

'I challenge you to a fight,' replied Nedumaran, realising that he was getting the worst of the verbal exchange.

'A fight? With you? Fights are between equals. By what stretch of the imagination are you my equal? Just because we were both born of the same womb doesn't make you equal to me. Point me to a single deed of yours that is worthy of me duelling with you.'

'All your words are just to hide your cowardice.'

Jayanthavarman threw back his head and laughed.

'I was not born yesterday, little brother. When I decide to fight, it will be at my convenience, not yours,' he said, turning away abruptly, leaving a fuming Nedumaran standing in front of the gates.

Jayanthavarman had gone back and called for a council meeting. General Nedunchezhiyan and Prime Minister Maravarman were present. The king told them about his encounter with his brother and asked them for suggestions.

'It is obvious that he is getting frustrated, Your Majesty. Let him,' said the prime minister.

'Not so fast, Prime Minister,' said the army chief. 'We are not out of the woods yet. We have barely a couple of weeks of food left. We didn't have time to prepare for this siege. What do you suppose happens when we start running out of food?'

'Hmmm …' mused Maravarman.

'Can we attack him?' asked the king. 'I really want to crush that bug.'

'Ah, Sire. He still is your brother,' said Nedunchezhiyan.

'He lost any privileges that he had as my brother by raising the banner of revolt against me,' said Jayanthavarman harshly.

'An attack on only him won't be feasible, Sire. You forget that we are surrounded on all four sides by their army,' said Maravarman. 'They are sure to come to the support of our comrades.'

'Hmmm. I am not trying to beat the entire army. Just Nedumaran. Can we launch a limited attack?'

The others were sunk in thought for a while before Maravarman said, 'Perhaps there is a way, Sire.'

15

Sadaiyan and Muthuvel

Kanchi, December 641 CE

Kanchi, at midmorning, presented its usual busy appearance with traders, businessmen, officials, armed forces and ordinary citizens jostling for space in the streets. Two horses were making their way slowly through the traffic. Their riders had contrasting expressions on their faces. Muthuvel, who hated crowds in general, wore a weary look, while Sadaiyan's eyes were bright and shining. He was in his element in a crowd, and he hadn't seen these many people congregated together in a long time.

Korkai, for all its attractions, lacked the one thing that a thief and pickpocket yearns for—jostling, bustling crowds that allow honest members of that profession to ply their trade. Sadaiyan's fingers twitched involuntarily as he eyed several potential marks—men and women with fine jewellery and heavy purses whose contents he was desirous of possessing. He glanced out of the corners of his eyes at the man riding next to him and decided that now was not the time to act on increasing his own wealth. Muthuvel was rather straitlaced and his views on property rights were somewhat traditional.

Muthuvel for his part was finally glad to be back in his own city, even with the crowds. He looked around to see if any changes had taken place in his absence. The *gopurams*[7] of the old temples still towered over the city. The people seemed to be blissfully unaware of what was happening in the outside world. The fact that events had been set in motion that would result in a war between two powerful neighbouring states seemed to be absent from the collective consciousness of the citizens of Kanchi.

Sadaiyan and Muthuvel weaved their way through the crowds to the city centre, making a beeline for the offices of General Ilanthiraiyanar. There were crowds of people here too, as horses, chariots and soldiers fought for space. Muthuvel got down from his horse and Sadaiyan followed suit. As he got down, he squared his shoulders and dashed against a prosperous-looking citizen who nearly went down. Sadaiyan clutched the man's arms and pulled him up with an apology. The man gave him a disdainful look and rushed away, leaving his heavy purse in a grinning Sadaiyan's hand.

Muthuvel noticed it and frowned his disapproval. He extended his hands towards Sadaiyan, who placed the purse in them with a grin.

'Just trying to keep in practice, anna,' he said. 'I'm making sure that the old skill hasn't deserted me. After all, when all this is over, I will need to go back to my old profession.'

'We shall see about that,' said Muthuvel, as he called out to the man whose possessions had been divested from him.

'Sir, you dropped this just now,' said Muthuvel.

---

7 Temple towers

The haughty-eyed man stopped as if gobsmacked and then came towards them.

'Thank you,' he mumbled, taking the purse from Muthuvel and starting to count the coins. Once he was satisfied that nothing had been pilfered, he moved away, again throwing a thankful look towards Muthuvel, who watched him with disgust.

'You know, I actually wish I hadn't given the purse back to that ass,' he said.

Sadaiyan laughed. 'I think, anna, that maybe you are also starting to think like a thief now.'

'Never, thambi, but perhaps I do have a slightly better understanding of why you do what you do.'

They returned to the task at hand with Muthuvel asking for an audience with the general from the guard outside the offices. As they waited, a man came from inside General Ilanthiraiyanar's building and, recognising Muthuvel, said, 'Hi Muthu. I haven't seen you in a while. Where have you been?'

'Oh, here and there,' said Muthuvel evasively.

'I see. Anyway, I hear you are waiting to speak to the general. Unfortunately, he is away.'

'Do you know if Commander Paranjyothi is in?'

'Why do you ask?'

'I have news from the south that I need to give to either the general or the commander.'

'I see. Well, neither of them is here.'

'Can you tell me where they have gone?'

'Come on, Muthu, you know I can't tell you that.'

'Well, what I have to say IS important.'

'Would the maharaja do?' the man asked, a twinkle in his eyes.

'What do you think?' asked Muthuvel.

The man chuckled and slapped Muthuvel on the back. 'Come on, let me take you to him. Horses?' he asked.

'No. Let's walk. We have been on horses for a while now,' said Muthuvel.

'Oh yes!' Sadaiyan said, with feeling.

'Who is he?' asked the soldier.

'My brother,' said Muthuvel. 'He was with me through all my travels and probably knows even more about certain events than I do.'

'Oh, alright. Come along then.'

Sadaiyan smiled inwardly and his eyes filled with tears. He had noted how Muthuvel had introduced him and for someone who had grown up as an orphan to be called a brother, and that too by a man he idolised, was gratifying.

They walked over to the palace and were shown into the large hall on the ground floor. The man who had led them there took his leave. Muthuvel and Sadaiyan waited, the former patiently, the latter with wide-eyed curiosity.

'These kings do live well, don't they, anna?' he asked.

'Hmmm?' asked Muthuvel absent-mindedly, his thoughts on other things.

'These kings. Look at the size of this place. And all these golden items,' he said, pointing at several vases and cups that glinted in the sunlight falling on them from the skylights above the hall. 'This is the life,' he said, a happy smile playing on his face. 'Nothing to worry about and all the money in the world, servants to do your every bidding. I think I could get used to it.'

'You think so, do you?' asked a voice from the stairs leading down from the first floor.

Muthuvel and Sadaiyan looked up and Muthuvel stood to attention and bowed when he recognised his king. Sadaiyan stood gaping at Mamalla until, prodded by a stiff finger from Muthuvel, he too bowed hastily.

'Well, young man? You haven't answered my question,' asked Mamalla with mock seriousness.

Sadaiyan hesitated, unsure of how to answer, but then, his natural impishness took over.

'Well yes, Your Majesty. Sounds like a great life,' he said with a grin.

Mamalla guffawed aloud even as Muthuvel glowered at Sadaiyan. Mamalla noticed the look and said, 'It's alright, young man. I rarely get an opportunity to listen to such uninhibited comments. So, what is it that you would like to talk about?'

'Sire, we have just come from Madurai.'

Mamalla's eyebrows rose. 'Manavamma's army is there, right?'

'Well, part of it, Your Majesty. The rest are on their way to Kanchi. We,' he gestured towards Sadaiyan and himself, 'rode on ahead to see if we could be of some use here.'

Mamalla was silent as he heard Muthuvel's request. A gentle breeze wafted across the hall, ruffling his hair. He leaned forward thoughtfully, his eyes measuring the man and the boy in front of him. Evidently, he liked what he saw, for, after what seemed like hours but was probably only a minute or so, he said softly, 'I would like you to meet up with General Ilanthiraiyanar and inform him of the location that we have selected for our battle with Pulikeshi's forces.'

'Sire,' said Muthuvel, bowing to him.

'They might be a little difficult to find though, since the general and his men are harassing Pulikeshi's flanks and rear.'

'We will find them, Your Majesty,' said Muthuvel.

'Make sure you take a couple of fast horses. I want you to reach them as quickly as possible so that the general can start steering Pulikeshi's army towards the place. 'Will he be staying here?' Mamalla asked, pointing at Sadaiyan.

'No, Sire. The young lad will come with me.'

'Is it wise?' asked Mamalla, his eyes flicking to Sadaiyan and back again to Muthuvel.

'He rescued me when I was caught by the Pandya soldiers at Kodimunai. He was the one who came with me to Lanka and showed me how to get in touch with Manavamma. He wormed his way into Jayanthavarman's army disguised as a coconut-seller and helped me burn their catapults. He also helped in rescuing me, again,' and this time he looked at Sadaiyan affectionately, 'from the Pandya camp.'

A smile played upon Mamalla's lips. 'The young man certainly seems to have bailed you out enough times, hasn't he? No wonder you like to travel with him.'

Muthuvel smiled in response. 'That I do, Sire.' Sadaiyan preened with pride and bowed to the king.

'Alright then,' said Mamalla. 'Get some rest today. You can leave in the morning.'

Pulikeshi relaxed in his tent. There was a beehive of activity outside as the soldiers set up camp for the night. His tent was always the first one to be pitched. *Prerogatives of a king*, he thought.

The previous few days had been tough for the army. The incessant attacks by the Pallava soldiers on their flanks and rear had tested them, and caused their nerves to stretch near breaking point. There was no set pattern to these attacks. Sometimes the enemy attacked at the end of a day, like now, when they were involved in setting up camp. On some occasions, they would attack at sunrise, when sleep had not yet dissipated from the eyes of the soldiers. There were still other days when they attacked during lunchtime or during that somnolent period post-lunch, when the army moved sluggishly on its way.

Pulikeshi had tasked the crown prince, Aditya, with defending them against these attacks. To be fair to him, conceded Pulikeshi, he had been somewhat successful. He and his brothers had taken turns with small detachments that rode away from the main bulk of the army to suss out any potential danger and to deter direct attacks on them.

As they had moved out of the forested areas, into the more flat and open lands further east, the frequency of attacks had come down. There wasn't any place for the enemy to hide and to ambush them. They would have to come across open land and that would have been suicidal. *And the Pallavas are definitely not suicidal*, thought Pulikeshi.

What the attacks had done though was slow them down. They ought to have been in Kanchi by now, if not for these attacks. They still had nearly a hundred miles to go and at the rate at which they were going, it would take them at least another week, if not ten days. Pulikeshi frowned. *This is giving them far too much time to prepare for us.*

As he sat contemplating the present and trying to peer into the fog of the future, he heard footsteps outside his tent, followed by the tall, thin and angular presence of his spy chief, Naganandi. The emperor motioned to him to sit down on one of the other divans in the tent.

'This is taking too long,' said Naganandi, coming to the point in his abrupt manner. 'We should have been in Kanchi by now.'

Pulikeshi smiled. 'Yes, I know. I was thinking the same. I don't think we can do anything about it though.'

'Why not? We are now on open land. Let's increase the pace. I doubt that the small contingent that Narasimhavarma has following and harassing us will dare to attack us across open land.'

'Can we not force them into a conflict and annihilate them?'

'I doubt it. For one, we don't know where they are exactly. They could be behind us, or in front of us, for all we know. They know this land better than us. No point in foolishly spending our time trying to find them.'

Pulikeshi noted the use of the adjective but did not react. Naganandi, by virtue of his long association with the king and his steadfastness to his cause, had a latitude in the way he spoke to the emperor that was not allowed to others.

'Alright. I agree. Let us step up the pace then.'

16

Friends Reunite

Lands north of Kanchi, December 641 CE

They had come across the Chalukya army when they were still about seventy miles or so from Kanchi. They had seen them from afar as the army wended its way south-eastward, stretching miles into the distance. Muthuvel noticed smaller groups of soldiers who were ranging away from the main column, obviously as lookouts.

'Looks like General Ilanthiraiyanar and his men have made them very nervous, anna,' noted Sadaiyan.

Muthuvel slapped his hand on Sadaiyan's back in response.

'How do we find our men?'

Muthuvel pursed his lips and shrugged. 'They could be anywhere. On this side of the Chalukya army or the other side. We will just need to ask around.'

They had spent quite some time going into small villages and hamlets asking villagers or farmers tending to their fields whether they had seen some of the Pallava soldiers around. Muthuvel had taken to identifying himself first as a

Pallava soldier before asking for information, knowing that the farmers, especially this close to Kanchi, would not want to divulge any information to the enemy. Sometimes the identification took a while depending on how suspicious the villager or farmer was.

It was Sadaiyan who eventually got information on the whereabouts of the general and his men. Early on, frustrated by how long it was taking them to win the trust of the villagers, Sadaiyan had suggested that they split up.

'I might be able to get them to open up faster than you can, anna. You look too forbidding for them to trust you. Me? I am lovable,' he said, the usual wicked grin splitting his face.

They had decided to meet up at the end of the day at one of the villages. When Muthuvel reached their meeting point after sunset, he found Sadaiyan waiting impatiently for him.

'It took you long enough,' he said accusingly.

Muthuvel gave him a weary look and got down from his horse. He put his hands above his head and stretched, then bent down to touch his toes and work the kinks out of his body. An involuntary groan escaped his throat as he stood up again.

'You are getting old, anna,' was Sadaiyan's rather trenchant comment, an observation that caused Muthuvel to pick up a pebble and chuck it at the young lad.

'Don't worry, you will get there in due course,' said Muthuvel, still twisting his body this way and that.

'Aren't you going to ask me whether I found anything?'

'You will tell me if you found something, I am sure.' Muthuvel could not quite see Sadaiyan's face clearly in the dark but could make out the youngster's suppressed excitement from the way he was hopping from foot to foot.

'Alright. Spill it.'

'I know where they are,' said Sadaiyan, trying to sound nonchalant, but the glee in his voice failing to conceal his feelings.

Muthuvel deliberately kept quiet.

'Aren't you curious?'

'Oh, well. I don't really believe you, but sure, tell me what you have found out,' said Muthuvel disingenuously.

'They are on the other side of the marching columns, barely a couple of miles from where we are.'

'Are they now? And how did you find that out? Met a helpful farmer or villager, did you?'

'Nothing of that sort. A cagey bunch, these villagers. I saw some horse tracks and followed them. Sure enough, they led me to another village on the other side. Looks like our men are camping there for the night.'

Muthuvel grinned, his white teeth showing clearly on his dark face. 'What are we waiting for then? Lead on. Let's go meet the general.'

The duo rode cautiously, not wanting to blunder their way into the Chalukya camp, or their scouts. As they neared the village where Sadaiyan had spied the Pallava forces, they became even more wary and watchful. It wasn't long before they found their way blocked by a couple of sturdy-looking men.

'Hold on. Hold on there. Where do you think you both are going?'

Muthuvel's temper was on a rather short leash after a long day of mostly fruitless riding, but he controlled his anger as he replied, 'We are on our way to meet with General Ilanthiraiyanar, Corporal.'

'Yeah? Does the general want to meet you ...?'

'Captain,' supplied Muthuvel. 'The word you are looking for is "captain" and if you do not take me to the general quickly, I will make sure that you are busted down to a private, understand?'

The men baulked at this note of authority in the stranger's voice. They looked at each other uncertainly.

'Well? What's it going to be?'

'We can't let you in,' said the second man, stubbornly.

Sadaiyan, seeing the ferment in Muthuvel, stepped in smoothly.

'Aah, look. Why don't one of you keep an eye on us here and the other one can go and inform the general that Captain Muthuvel wants to meet him?'

The suggestion appealed to the soldiers. The one who had stopped them left to convey the message to the general while the other one kept a wary eye on them, his sword unsheathed from its scabbard.

It wasn't too long before the first soldier came back at a run and said to his partner, 'The general asked me to bring them to him.' Then, bowing to Muthuvel, he said, 'My apologies, Sir. But we have been dodging Chalukya patrols for a while now and I had to be sure.'

'That's alright, Corporal. I must admit that I did overreact. It has been a long day.'

They got off their horses and followed the man into the village. At the centre of the village was a large banyan tree, as there is in every village. A square platform surrounded the tree and on it, were a few men, resting. Lit torches were mounted on poles that were fixed to the ground. One of the men got off the platform and walked up to him. Muthuvel stiffened and smacked his fist against his chest as he recognised General Ilanthiraiyanar.

'Welcome back, my boy,' said the general, giving him a bear hug.

As the general released Muthuvel from his grasp, Muthuvel noticed the man who had silently walked up behind the general. It was a much thinner and gaunter Elango than he remembered from several months ago. Muthuvel and Elango looked at each other and it was as if all those years of petty animosities fell away in a flash. The experiences of the past several months had changed both men. They enveloped each other in a long hug and as they disengaged, Elango said, 'It is good to see you again, Muthu.'

'Likewise, my friend,' said Muthuvel with genuine warmth and feeling in his voice and eyes. He introduced Sadaiyan to the others, recounting the stories of Lanka and Korkai, while not revealing details of Sadaiyan's more disreputable past, something for which Sadaiyan was glad.

He then looked around and asked, 'Is there any food left? We have been trying to trace you all day and are very hungry.' The remark brought much laughter from his friends. The general asked for food to be brought for the two and as they wolfed down their meal, the general and Muthuvel updated each other on what had been happening.

'Did you actually meet King Harshavardhana? How is he?'

'Inspiring, but old,' said Elango with a smile.

'Looks like we have both been through our own trials and tribulations, haven't we? You at Parivipura and me at Korkai,' said Muthuvel, looking at Elango.

'You at least got to see Korkai come back into our hands. Parivipura though …' Elango trailed off.

'Will be back in our hands in due course,' said General Ilanthiraiyanar. 'I have no doubts about that.'

'I hope so, Sir,' said Elango.

'You doubt me, my boy?'

'Ah no, Sir. Not you. But the world is a funny place especially when it comes to war and conflict.'

'You are letting the fall of Parivipura weigh too heavily on you, son.'

Elango kept quiet. Muthuvel, noticing Elango's evident distress, changed the topic.

'The emperor sent me here with a message for you, Sir.'

'Oh?'

'He said that they have decided on the place to face Pulikeshi.'

'Which is?'

'Manimangala.'

Ilanthiraiyanar furrowed his brows. 'That village about twenty-five miles or so north-east of Kanchi?'

'Yes, Sir.'

'Why that place?'

'Three reasons, Sir. First, we push them further away from Kanchi and to the east. Stretches their supply lines. Second, there are no major water bodies there. We don't want them near the river, is how the maharaja put it.'

Ilanthiraiyanar was sunk in thought for a bit before he responded.

'I agree. Both valid points. We had discussed this before I left and it looks like the maharaja has chosen wisely. What was the third reason?'

'Manimangala is also known as Ratnagrahara.'

'I am aware of that,' said the general.

'I don't get it,' said Elango.

'It is known for exporting jewels. One of our best kept secrets. Well actually, no. I am sure Pulikeshi would have heard about it.'

'Aah. So, you think he wouldn't mind coming by that route?'

'That's the hope,' said Muthuvel.

'I wish there was a way to somehow influence them into following that route,' mused General Ilanthiraiyanar.

'You mean send someone into their camp?' asked Elango.

'But who?' queried Muthuvel.

'I could go, anna,' said Sadaiyan.

'Out of the question,' replied Muthuvel immediately.

'I could go too,' said a hitherto silent voice. They looked around for the speaker.

'I could go with the young lad,' said Jamba. 'They are sure to need meat for their soldiers. I could hunt a few deer and supply them.'

'And I could go along as his assistant,' said Sadaiyan with enthusiasm. 'As his nephew or something. I could ferret out information as well as feed them some misinformation. I am very good at ferreting things out. Ask anna if you don't believe me,' he said, looking at Muthuvel.

Muthuvel's face was undecided. 'It is too dangerous,' he said.

'I will have this man to protect me,' said Sadaiyan, looking at Jamba. 'And he looks like he could protect lots more people than just me,' he continued, eyeing Jamba's impressive physique.

There was a bit of discussion but eventually Muthuvel perceived that his opinion was in a minority. The general gave permission to Jamba and Sadaiyan to infiltrate the Chalukya camp.

The night sky was bright. A near-full moon shone brightly over the earth, casting stark and dark shadows on the ground. In a small, secluded mandapam, Sanghamitra lay down, looking up into the night sky. Lazy, wispy clouds drifted across the face of the moon.

She sighed a sigh of loneliness and discontent. She had been lonely before, of course, but ever since that fateful trip up north with Elango, she had gotten used to having someone around who cared for her. Solitude was overrated, she decided. She liked being in love. She liked the thought of caring for and having someone care for her. Having grown up without a family, it felt nice to finally be a part of someone else's life.

She sat up, letting her feet hang over the edge of the mandapam, her hands by her side. The moon seemed to be in motion while maintaining a fixed position in the sky, an illusion, she knew, caused by the relative movement of the tendrils of cloud across its face.

It had been hard for her to leave Elango in Parivipura, knowing that he might be captured or worse, killed, but she could not ignore his entreaties to her to save the Parivipura royal family. He had known exactly what to say to get her to leave. She gave a little smile that made the dimples in her cheeks dance. Not that there was anyone to see it, of course.

She wondered how Elango was doing. She had got word from General Ilanthiraiyanar that he had been able to escape from Parivipura with Jamba's help and she had heaved a sigh of relief when she heard that. Of course, she had no idea of what he had gone through in captivity. Had he been treated well? Had he suffered any physical injuries? She wished that the general would not be so businesslike when passing information, but then again, she thought, he didn't get to be a general by gossiping like attendees in a village fair.

I wish I could have Elango hold me just once. She blushed prettily at the thought, the only witness being the benignly shining moon. She missed having his arms around her, missed placing her head on his chest and listening to his heartbeat. She missed the smell that was unique to him. Most of all, she missed that feeling of comfort that only he could give her.

She sighed again and then admonished herself angrily. *Look at me. Mooning about like a lovesick village maiden. For God's sake, Mitra, get a grip on yourself.*

The moon, however, continued to shine on her angst and dreams.

17

One Foot through the Door

Vathapi, December 641 CE

The southern gates of the city of Vathapi saw a steady stream of people throughout the day. Travellers, visitors, merchants, mendicants, pilgrims, traders and students from lands to the south used the gates to make their way into the city.

Among the many who entered the city this morning was a trio of *bhikshus*[8], shaven-headed and dressed in ochre robes. The lead bhikshu moved in a stately manner with the other two following, clearly subservient to the leader.

They had been walking for over three weeks now and had finally reached their destination. As they entered the city, the other two peeled off together to go their separate ways. The leader moved towards a different part of town. People bowed reverently as the bhikshu passed through the streets. In a city where Buddhists, Jains, Shaivite and Vaishnavite leaders lived

8 Monks

amicably together, the reverence shown towards the Buddhist guru wasn't out of place.

The bhikshu walked on past them, through a maze of narrow lanes, acknowledging their bows with a gentle nod of the head, before finally turning into an even smaller lane that led to a nondescript single-storey apartment that had seen better times, and knocked on the door.

The door was opened by a thin, bearded man with a hooked nose and a scar running from his forehead to his nose. The bhikshu gave him an olai, which the thin man took with him to an inner room, leaving two large, well-muscled men to watch over the bhikshu.

Hook-nose was back in a short while and nodded to the bhikshu to follow him inside. As they entered, Devadutta rose from his seat and welcomed the bhikshu with a deep bow.

'Welcome back. I did not expect to see you here, with things the way they are and certainly not in this state.'

'We all do what we have to do.'

'True, true. Do you have any specific instructions for me?'

'I will need to know everything there is to know about the fort and the city. Entry and exit points. What are the strengths and weaknesses? Are there any architectural diagrams of the fort?'

'Mmmmm, I am not very sure of that. The fort is old, and any diagrams would not be accessible to the general public, in any case,' said Devadutta.

The bhikshu mused on this for a while.

'Is there a way to get inside the northern ridge?'

The northern ridge was where the king and his family lived. It also held all the administrative offices.

'You are thinking of the administrative offices, I presume?'

The bhikshu nodded.

'Entry into the north wing is severely restricted. In all my time here, I have been there only once.'

'I will find a way in,' the bhikshu said with some confidence.

Queens Mangalamma and Visalakshi sat in their respective palanquins, waiting to be carried down the steep stairs leading out of the gates for the northern bastion.

It was the younger queen's idea to go into the city. Ever since the men had left on their campaign, they had been bored. One could only spend so much time wandering around the palace and the gardens on top of the rocky cliff that was their home.

They had proceeded to the temple of Bhagwan Ganesha to pray for the well-being of their husband and sons. Till Naganandi had been there, they had at least had periodic information about how the campaign was going. News of the victory at Parivipura and the recapture of the forts at Asanur and Guddahalli had reached them. They had thanked the Gods profusely.

However, Naganandi's departure had cut down on the information they received. The prime minister, Vedaraya, only gave them vague and general updates, leaving both the queens unsatisfied.

'Of all the close-mouthed men, Vedaraya probably tops the list,' Visalakshi had fumed to Mangalamma. 'It is so hard to get any information out of him.'

'I will go mad if I have to stay put in the palace for one more day,' said Mangalamma.

Visalakshi's eyes had suddenly brightened as she said, 'Akka, why don't we go into town and visit the temples on the southern ridge? It has been a while since we have been there, and it will do us good. One of the maids has been telling me about a new bhikshu who has arrived and is supposed to have miraculous powers.'

Mangalamma merely rolled her eyes at Visalakshi's ability to view every mendicant who came to the city as a revered guru, but she had brightened at her suggestion to go out, and plans had been made to go to the temples the next day. Prime Minister Vedaraya had to be informed, of course, and he had agreed with alacrity to the suggestion. It was quite possible that he had been harried by the repeated requests from the queens for information about the campaigns and was glad to get them out of his hair for a day.

The palanquin bearers picked up their loads and started down the steps, their gaits causing the palanquins to sway. As they neared the bottom of the cliff, the queens could see the steps leading up the southern cliff. They could make out the ant-like figures of the devotees as they made their way to the top. There was no path between the two cliffs, riven as the top was by deep ridges and the only way to go from one cliff to the other was through the city.

The palanquins made their way to the Bhoothanatha temple on the eastern bank of the Agastya Lake. The queens had a dip in the lake, whose waters were supposed to wash away the sins of the devotees who bathed in it. They then proceeded to the ancient Bhoothanatha temple, which had existed from time immemorial, although the current structure was supposed to date from only a couple of hundred years earlier.

They came out of the temple and glanced up towards the southern cliff. Mangalamma noticed a large congregation of devotees at the far end of the lake, near one of the several caves dotting the area.

'Is that where your bhikshu is?' she asked Visalakshi.

'That's what the maid told me,' replied Visalakshi.

'Should we go up to the cave temples on the hill before visiting the bhikshu?'

'That would be too tiring, akka.'

Mangalamma nodded and then got into her palanquin. She had thought about walking up the cliffs initially, but the day was turning out to be unusually hot for this time of the year, and she didn't fancy a walk in the searing heat. The palanquin bearers exulted silently at not having to climb up the steep sandstone steps.

They neared the cave around which the people had gathered. The guards parted the crowd, announcing the arrival of the queens. The queens walked towards the cave entrance, acknowledging the greetings of the people with stately nods of their heads. The cave itself was dark and the brightness of the midday sun made it appear even darker from outside.

The queens squinted on entering the cave, trying to adjust their eyes to the sudden darkness inside. At the far end of the cave, they saw a seated figure.

'The bhikshu,' whispered Visalakshi to the elder queen, stating the obvious. There were two other similarly clad figures hovering near the bhikshu, but all the attention of the queens was on the monk.

They got down on their knees and bowed to the bhikshu, who blessed them with a raised hand.

'Akka, ask the monk about the success or failure of the campaign,' whispered Visalakshi, nudging Mangalamma.

Mangalamma shrugged her hand off and then, looking at the bhikshu, asked, '*Swami.*[9] Can you tell us if the campaigns

---

9 A term of reverence

that our husband and sons have gone to will be successful? Will they return victorious?'

The bhikshu motioned to one of the men. He came over, sat down beside the queens, and said, 'The guru has taken a vow of silence and will not speak for the next month. You can come back in a month and ask the question again.'

Mangalamma's face fell in disappointment, but Visalakshi leaned over to her and whispered something in her ear. Mangalamma nodded and then, looking at the bhikshu, said, 'We understand. But can you do us the honour of staying within the palace grounds? There is a small mandapam there that you can use.' She looked expectantly at the bhikshu, who had listened to her with eyes closed, but now opened them and gestured something to the disciple.

'The guru would like to take you up on the offer but that would not be fair to all the other people who would like to visit us.'

'The mandapam is on the lower level of the palace grounds. We can make sure that it is open for devotees from sunrise to sunset,' said Mangalamma, making a mental note to talk to Prime Minister Vedaraya about it.

The bhikshu heard her proposition and bowed to her in acceptance.

As the queens got up and turned to make their way out of the cave, a small smile played on the bhikshu's lips. *One foot through the door.*

18
Jayanthavarman's Gamble

Madurai, December 641 CE

Jayanthavarman brooded. It had been a boring week. Safe and secure, yes, but boring. The siege, for what it was, consisted mostly of his brother's forces sitting around in their tents outside the Madurai fort walls, while his men loitered desultorily atop them, shouting down occasional insults at Nedumaran and his men. Nedumaran's men had neither the expertise nor the knowledge to build siege engines and catapults. Hence, they were reduced to shooting arrows over the fort walls. The men on the walls responded in kind and after an hour or so of such pleasantries, both sides would stop shooting at each other and retire for the day.

He would occasionally join them in shouting insults and needling his brother. He could see, even at a distance, that it incensed Nedumaran, and that was what he hoped to do. His brother wasn't a great strategist, and an incensed Nedumaran had even poorer judgment than usual. He also understood that Nedumaran did not have the trust of his army. The army was not his. Most of them belonged to the Raja of Korkai and their efforts were half-hearted at best. The rest belonged to Manavamma, and while they were probably a much better fighting unit, their goal was completely different from Nedumaran's. All they wanted was to ensure that Jayanthavarman was cooped up inside the city. They were not particularly interested in attacking the city.

This had gone on for several days. While life went on as usual inside the ancient city, the citizens of Madurai were starting to feel the pinch of food being rationed. Jayanthavarman's ministers were warning him that stocks were running dangerously low and that if the siege went on for a week or more, then they would have to take some steps.

Jayanthavarman's eyes narrowed in anger as his thoughts turned towards his younger brother. *The traitor. After all I did for him! Maybe I should have killed him in Korkai when I had the chance. Then I wouldn't have to deal with this siege. I could have easily come to an arrangement with Manavamma and Narasimhavarma.*

He seethed at his inability to teach a lesson to that upstart brother of his. He needed to ensure that Nedumaran wouldn't be a threat to his son when he took over, if not for anything else. A plan slowly started to form in his mind. He stroked his moustache absentmindedly as he thought through the contours of the plan. *Yes. It might just work. It might just work at that.*

Nedumaran rinsed his mouth with water and spat it out to one side. He had just finished his morning ablutions by the side of a well that had been dug by his men. The water table here was quite high and they had hit water barely twenty feet or so down.

The well was placed at the back of the camp and Nedumaran had primacy when it came to using it.

He trudged back to his tent, and servants scurried behind him with a covered plate that contained his breakfast. He went in and sat down while a banana leaf was placed in front of him and he was served his meal. Nedumaran ate moodily, his mind preoccupied. He was a man who prized his creature comforts. He had lived the good life and so, hanging around in tents outside his own city was not his idea of fun.

Dark thoughts ran through his mind, primarily about the men leading his army. They didn't seem to be doing anything to take the city. The daily exchange of arrows did nothing to advance their cause. He had tried to reason, cajole, and even shame them into action, but they had advanced all manner of excuses from 'We don't have the siege engines' to 'How can we try and climb that fortress with all those men waiting for us with boiling water and hot oil?'

He himself had had very little experience of war. Truth be told, he had had *no* experience of war. But his whole mien and demeanour were based on a carefully constructed image he had of himself—an image that was at odds with what he was in reality, a reality that he refused to acknowledge.

Nedumaran completed his breakfast and got up to wash his hands in a bowl that a servant brought for him. He wiped his mouth with his angavastram when he heard horseshoes striking against pebble, followed by footsteps.

Thissa entered his tent. It was a daily occurrence. It gave Nedumaran the illusion of being in charge of the army. Thissa had been asked by Manavamma to keep up appearances. And so, he showed up every day at the same time ostensibly to report to Nedumaran.

There wasn't much to report. After all, what *can* one say about a day spent doing nothing but waiting outside the fort walls. Thissa listened quietly, as usual, to Nedumaran's fulminations against his brother and his tirade against his generals, including himself, and their inability to force the issue.

Once Nedumaran fell quiet, Thissa stood up, bowed to him, got on his horse and went back to the northern gates and to his men. He didn't relish spending any more time with Nedumaran than he had to.

Shortly thereafter, there was a long sharp blast of trumpets. Nedumaran heard it and rushed outside his tent to see the gates swing open.

The cavalry rushed out of the gates before they had swung fully open. Jayanthavarman himself was in the lead, making his way towards the besieging forces.

The men in Nedumaran's camp had certainly not expected this. They had expected a day like any other, filled with occasional bouts of activity, but mostly a sort of paid holiday, where they could play dice and chess and wager money that they had been guaranteed. The sudden opening of the city gates and the rush of cavalry came as a rude shock to them. Many of them had an initial look of annoyance on their faces, almost as if to admonish the Madurai forces for spoiling the even tenor of their day.

The next instant, they were scrambling inside their tents, grabbing their swords, shields and other weapons. It was too late though.

The Madurai cavalry thundered across the open ground and was quickly among them. Jayanthavarman and his men smashed through the camp, cutting a long furrow right through the centre. Men were cut down before they could even realize what was happening. Jayanthavarman had Nedumaran's tent in his sights as he hacked his way towards it. Men fell outside their tents half-clothed, some of them clutching weapons in their hands. Many of the tents collapsed on their inhabitants as the ropes holding them up were cut by the horsemen, causing them to flounder inside the tent and leaving them unable to take part in the hostilities. It would save their lives though.

There were a few men, true professionals, who did react quickly to the threat, and engaged the enemy by pulling them off their horses, and knifing them to death. The horses thundered on through the camp, riderless, but these were few and far between. Nedumaran's men, dealing with the suddenness and savagery of the attack, were suddenly faced with a new threat that utterly demoralised them.

Elephants appeared behind the cavalry, trumpeting furiously. They moved at a run, following in the wake of the horses. The mahouts had been given one instruction, and that was to cause as much disarray as they could in the camp. There were soldiers sitting on top of the elephants with bows and arrows, who were there to protect the mahouts and to shoot at any enemy soldiers who posed a threat. The bulk of the damage was done by the elephants, who trundled into the camp, running over and through the tents, crushing men and material under their feet.

Nedumaran stood aghast as he watched the destruction of his army. He looked around uncertainly, wondering what he could do but already, he could see his soldiers with their hands up in the air, surrendering. He didn't have much time to look around though, because the horses were already upon him. He saw his brother galloping towards him, sword held aloft.

Nedumaran knew that he ought to protect himself. His sword was in his tent. He knew that he ought to go in and get it and try and fend off his brother. Or he could just raise his hands and surrender. He knew what needed to be done, but strangely, his body seemed to be frozen in place. His brain was sending him frantic signals to move. It gave him both options, but he stood immobile, looking at his brother bearing down upon him.

He could see Jayanthavarman's face contorted in anger. His eyes were drawn hypnotically to the rhythmic pattern of the horse's feet, thudding into the ground.

Fifty feet. Forty. Thirty. Twenty. Ten feet.

Nedumaran looked directly into his brother's eyes, and he saw in them anger and the desire for revenge. As the horse neared him, Jayanthavarman stood up in his stirrups. His hand flashed upward. The sword glinted gold as it caught the sunlight and then flashed down hard in a savage downstroke. Nedumaran's last thought was that it looked so pretty. The sword bit into the side of his neck and cut his artery. Blood gushed out in a fountain, but the sword edge carried on, unmindful of the damage it had already done. It severed the tendons of his neck and then emerged from the other side, decapitating his head.

Nedumaran's head flew off to one side and fell near one of the pins to which his tent was tethered, even as his body crumpled. Nedumaran's eyes were still open and wide, and his mouth twitched as his head lay there by the side of the tent, forlorn. Eventually, the twitching stopped.

Janyanthavarman had reined in his horse sharply after decapitating his brother. He stepped off the horse and grabbed Nedumaran's head by his hair and held it aloft, letting out a primeval roar. His men cheered. Then Jayanthavarman, cognizant of the danger posed by the other army units belonging to Manavamma, gave a sharp order for his forces to retreat. The cavalry obeyed his orders with speed. One of the horsemen picked up Nedumaran's headless torso and slung it across his horse as he raced back towards the gates.

The elephants took a while longer to be turned around, but eventually, they all made their way back in. Shortly thereafter, Nedumaran's head, mounted on a spear, made its appearance over the southern gates. It stayed there, a grim reminder of Jayanthavarman's anger.

That was how Thissa found Nedumaran later on. He had made his way back to his own camp and the first knowledge he had that something had happened at the southern gates was the sudden appearance of a bloodied soldier in their camp, carrying news of the surprise attack.

Thissa had thought that he had heard some commotion and trumpets, but Madurai was a big city and he had not attributed it to anything dangerous or calamitous.

Upon hearing the news, he had taken a small retinue and rushed to the southern gates, only to see a devastated camp. Men tended to their wounded mates, while rows of dead bodies spoke of the carnage that had been inflicted. He directed his gaze towards the southern gates where he saw the grim view of Nedumaran's head mounted on a spear.

Thissa cursed himself. He knew it wasn't his fault, but the consummate professional that he was, he still chided himself for allowing it to happen. He had seen the laxity with which Nedumaran's forces had arrayed themselves in front of the gates. The daily shooting matches apart, there was a lack of security consciousness among the troops. They had been lulled into such a state of complacency that it was no surprise that they had been caught napping by Jayanthavarman.

Thissa's face darkened, the more he gazed at Nedumaran's head. He had never liked the man, but he had been an ally, and his death incensed him. He would make life hell for the citizens of Madurai, he decided.

19

The Gangas Prepare for War

Madurai, December 641 CE

'Are you sure about this?' asked King Srivikrama.

'Yes, Your Majesty,' responded the scout.

They were all seated in Srivikrama's large tent, barely a day's march from Thagadur. As was the practice, their scouts had ranged ahead to check the lay of the land, and for any hidden surprises or ambushes. This scout had just returned with news that the Thagadur forces were waiting at the other end of a large open area.

'You could see their tents?'

'Hundreds of them, Sire.'

'How large is their army?' asked Srivikrama.

'Not as large as ours, Your Majesty. Maybe slightly less than half of ours.'

'Could you get close enough to see how the army was arrayed?' asked General Narasimha.

'No, Sir. We were too far away. We would have to get on open ground to get closer to them and there is no way to do that without being observed.'

'Alright. Dismissed,' said the general curtly. Then, turning to the king, he said, 'I am intrigued by this, Your Majesty.'

'Intrigued?' asked Captain Madappa.

'Yes. Intrigued. What are they doing this far from Thagadur?'

Captain Madappa rubbed his chin with his hand, his eyes squinting in concentration.

'Preparing for an attack, obviously.'

'That sounds reasonable,' said Srivikrama. 'After all, no one wants an enemy army to be camped outside their city walls.'

'Yes, but does that mean that they are more confident of meeting us on open ground? That too, with an army only half our size, if our scouts' reports are to be believed?' asked the general.

'Their fort must be very easy to take, I suppose, if they think that meeting us on open ground with an army half our size is better than letting us lay siege to their city,' said Madappa.

'Well, what do we do?' asked the king.

'We can attack them ...' said General Narasimha.

'But?'

'But we need to think this through a little bit. I don't want to attack them until we know how they are arrayed.'

'How do we find that out?' asked Srivikrama.

'By arraying ourselves of course,' said Narasimha with a smile. 'If they see us preparing for an attack, they are bound to take up positions as well. That should give us an indication of what they are planning.'

'That is smart thinking,' said Captain Madappa, his face displaying his respect for the older soldier.

'Let us not show them all our soldiers though. We can do a mock array. Place our horses in the centre.'

'No elephants?' asked Madappa.

'No elephants. Let's keep them as a nice little surprise, shall we?'

Kannan walked through the rows of tents and made his way to the front. The private who had called on him to come to the front was much shorter than he was, and struggled to keep up with his long steps as he marched forward.

'When did they first start congregating there, Corporal?' he asked.

'About a minute before I was told to come and fetch you, Sir,' said the young lad in a squeaky voice. *I wonder if he is even old enough to be in the army*, thought Kannan, as he strode rapidly ahead towards the frontline.

He reached the front and looked across the field. He could see a large body of men gathered on the other side. The cavalry was placed at the centre. Behind them, and at the flanks, he could see infantry. *Where are the elephants? Looks like they are deliberately hiding them.*

A couple of Raja Duraisingham's generals had walked up beside him. He turned to them and said, 'Generals. Can you please get our men ready for battle? It looks like they,' he pointed in the direction of the Ganga forces, 'sure are getting ready for it.'

'Cavalry in front and infantry behind?'

'Yes, sure.'

The generals left to deploy their troops. In short order, the army was ready. The men waited for the enemy to advance so that they could meet them in the middle of the field, but the Ganga forces did nothing of that sort. They stood around all ready for battle, but there was no forward movement.

'What are they doing?' asked one of the generals.

Kannan shrugged. 'Maybe they are waiting for us to move.'

'Well, let's move then.'

'Alright. Let's move fifty feet and see if they reciprocate.'

The generals gave the command, and the army began to move forward. Kannan glanced keenly at the far end.

'They aren't moving,' said the general walking beside him.

'Yes. It looks like they don't want to fight today.'

'What on earth were they parading themselves for then?'

'Maybe to test our army,' said Kannan, a thoughtful expression on his face. 'Let's go back. I don't think we are going to be fighting today.'

'They seem to be dependent on their cavalry and infantry alone,' said General Narasimha.

'Couldn't they be keeping their elephants hidden, just like we have done?' enquired Captain Madappa.

'Possible. But I don't think so. They are the ones who have chosen the battlefield. I would expect them to have arrayed in full formation when we started deploying. The fact that even then they didn't have elephants tells me that the Thagadur forces don't have our strength in terms of heavy cavalry.'

'What about the Pallava forces?' asked King Srivikrama, worry writ large on his face.

'We haven't received any word about them from our spies, Your Majesty,' interjected Madappa.

'But that doesn't mean that they aren't there …'

'No, Sire. But we also don't have any indication that they are. If they were, I would expect them to draw us in towards Thagadur, and then attack us. The fact that they have come out here is possibly a sign that they haven't got the expected help from the Pallavas,' said Narasimha.

The king pondered on this for a while. Ultimately, it was his call whether to attack the forces of Thagadur or to wait it out. He knew that Pulikeshi was advancing on Kanchi and if they had to strike at the Pallava flank, they needed to get past Thagadur. After what seemed to General Narasimha and Captain Madappa an eternity, the king spoke.

'Let's do it then. Tomorrow?' he asked, looking at his general.

'Tomorrow,' his general agreed.

Dark, inky blue skies took on orange and yellow hues as the burning disc that was the sun rose into the sky on its daily path through the heavens. The commotion of birds tittering and leaving their nests was accompanied by the sounds of armies preparing for war.

The Ganga army started getting ready at first light, with the infantry and cavalry putting on their armour and taking up their weapons. The soldiers had used the previous night to sharpen their swords, spears and arrowheads. The captains started to lead their regiments towards designated areas. The cavalry was placed at the centre in two columns with a gap in between. Directly behind the cavalry were placed the bowmen. They had selected longbows because they knew that any initial thrust had to be accompanied by a shower of arrows. The shorter bows were slung across their shoulders, and would be used later for close-quarter combat. The infantry stretched out on both sides slightly behind them.

Kannan's scouts had alerted him to the Ganga army's moves, with the result that there was a corresponding hum of activity on their side. Their deployment mirrored that of the Gangas, with the cavalry placed in the middle and the infantry stretching out to the sides. There were, however, two significant differences between the Thagadur and Ganga deployments. For one, their numbers, both in terms of infantry and cavalry, were much smaller than the Gangas. The second major difference was that the Thagadur cavalry was bunched up at the centre in one solid column.

Kannan stood with three other Thagadur generals and studied the Ganga forces. The generals, while outranking him, deferred to him in military matters, not just because the raja himself had put Kannan in charge, but also because they appreciated Kannan's superior knowledge of military tactics.

'To them we must look like a small army that can be crushed easily,' said one of the generals.

Kannan smiled. 'That's exactly what we want them to think.'

'Why is there a gap in their cavalry deployment?' asked another general.

'Elephants, of course.'

The general sucked in his breath.

'Elephants? You knew this? They would tear through our ranks!'

'Relax,' said Kannan. 'We aren't going to directly engage with them. They will bring their elephants out through that gap only after we have committed our forces to battle. When they do that, here's what I want you to do,' he said, and he bent his head and gave out his instructions to the generals, who listened intently and nodded occasionally.

'You think it will work?' asked the general who had been worried about the elephants.

'Trust me, Sir.'

'I am always worried when someone says that to me,' he muttered.

Kannan grinned, showing his even white teeth. He even whistled somewhat tunelessly. He had a score to settle with the Gangas, for all his men. It was time.

20
Mamalla's Plans

Kanchi, December 641 CE

Narasimhavarman Pallava, emperor of Kanchi, stood looking out over the city from his terrace, leaning on the parapet. The sun was setting fast and the sky, near the horizon, changed its colours from saffron to ochre to dark red to deep blue and finally to black.

Temple bells sounded across the city as the evening prayers commenced. Thousands of torches lit up the palaces and houses in Kanchi. It reminded the king of another night like this, more than a decade ago—the night when his father had passed away. He could almost hear Chittan's tread, as he came up the stairs, asking him to hurry over to the king's room.

Today, however, it was his son Vedam who had sent someone with a lit torch to the terrace to ensure that the king was not enveloped in darkness. Mamalla let him fuss with the torch in the torch-holder and then turned his gaze back to his beloved city. It was his invariable practice every evening to watch the sun go down from his terrace. He prized the few moments of solitude that he could steal from days that were usually filled with activity.

He heard someone walking across the terrace towards him. The sound of anklets told him that it was his wife who had joined him in his solitude.

The queen put her arm around him. Instinctively, Mamalla lifted up his left arm and the queen ducked under it. His arm snaked around her waist.

'You still have a delectable waist,' he noted playfully.

'And you still lie well enough,' she said. 'I am sure you have noticed that my waist has thickened over the years.'

'Aah. But it fits so well in my hand,' he said giving the exposed flesh on her waist a gentle pinch.

She laughed and put her head against his shoulder. They stood like that for some time, watching the city dress itself up for the night. Presently, she sighed, and Mamalla looked down at her.

'What is it, my dear?' he asked.

'The war.'

'Worried?'

'Mmmm.'

'You have so little faith in your husband?'

'I have every faith in my husband,' she flared up and then said, more quietly, 'War is uncertain. Capricious. Who knows what can and will happen? A chance stroke. An unlucky arrow. All women worry when their menfolk are about to go to war.'

'Yes, but you are the queen.'

'I am also a woman,' she snapped.

Mamalla turned his back to the parapet and leaned against it, pulling her into his arms. He tilted her head up with a finger under her chin.

'We have it planned this time around.'

The queen gave a very un-queenly snort.

'You doubt us?'

'I know who you mean when you say "we". Do remember though that both your commander and your general are confirmed bachelors and don't have any women to worry about them. You do.'

Mamalla laughed, his arm tightening around her.

'When are you off?' she asked, after a while.

'Soon,' he said. 'Within the next three or four days.'

Before she could respond to that, they heard footsteps coming quickly up the stairs. The queen tried to detach herself from Mamalla, provoking a protest from him.

'It is only Vedam, and I am sure he knows that you and I love each other dearly,' he said.

It was indeed Vedam. He stood at the head of the steps and said, 'General Ilanthiraiyanar is here to see you, Sire.'

'Ilan, here?' His brow furrowed as he mused on the news.

'Wasn't he supposed to be on some campaign?' asked the queen.

'That's right. I wonder what he is doing back,' replied Mamalla. Then, looking at Vedam, he said, 'Seat him in my office, will you? I shall meet him there.'

'Whatever are you doing back here, Ilan?' asked Mamalla, as he entered the room.

General Ilanthiraiyanar, who had been standing near a window and looking out into the garden, turned around and gave him a weary smile, before they hugged.

'Not much for me to do there anymore,' he said.

'What do you mean?'

'Pulikeshi and his army are now out in the open and I am not going to ask my small force to make suicidal attacks on them. I have asked them to merely follow the main army and see if they can prove to be irritants to them from time to time, so that they slow down their progress. Besides, Elango and Muthuvel are there, and you don't really need a full general to be in command with those two around.'

'Is that all?'

'Well, I also felt the need to come back here and talk to you about our plans for Manimangala.'

'What about them?'

'Have you given any thought as to how we are going to deploy our forces?'

'I have been doing nothing but that,' said Mamalla. 'From your reports, I gather that our forces are roughly going to be equal?'

'Yes. With Manavamma's forces to support us, it should be about equal.'

Mamalla slapped his forehead. 'Let's get Manavamma in here as well. Whatever plans we make will surely involve him.'

The king sent for Vedam and asked him to send someone to request Manavamma to come over to the palace. Manavamma had reached Kanchi only the previous day, and he and his men were camping outside town. Mamalla had requested Manavamma to stay in one of the palaces near his own, but the Lankan king had declined the offer, preferring instead to stay with his men.

As they waited for Manavamma to arrive, the king asked the general, 'Have you eaten yet?'

Ilanthiraiyanar shook his head. The king sent for some food for both of them, and they sat eating and drinking some wine.

It was about half an hour or so later that Manavamma was shown into the room by Vedam.

'Sit down, sit down, my friend,' said Mamalla. 'Vedam, please get the Lankan king some food as well.'

'Hello, Your Majesty,' said Ilanthiraiyanar with a formal bow. 'So nice to see you after all these years.'

'Likewise, Ilan. I think we can drop the formal modes of address here?' said Manavamma, smiling. 'I hear that you are now a general.'

'All kings make mistakes,' said Ilanthiraiyanar, smiling affectionately at his king.

'I don't think this one was that egregious a mistake, though,' said Mamalla.

They all laughed and spoke of trivialities until the business of food was over. Mamalla brought the discussion back to preparations for war.

'Manava. I requested your presence here since the general has just returned from his skirmishes with Pulikeshi's forces, and has, I suspect, gleaned more information about the make-up of his army. Why don't you go ahead, Ilan?'

'As I was telling you earlier, the armies are almost equally matched in size, especially with the Lankan forces swelling our numbers,' said Ilanthiraiyanar, looking gratefully at Manavamma, who gave a small bow in return.

'But?' asked Mamalla.

'Why do you think there is a "but"?' countered the general.

'Just the way you left that statement. There is always a "but" after such statements.'

Ilanthiraiyanar smiled. 'That there is. While we are evenly matched in terms of numbers, there are areas where the Chalukyas are stronger.'

'And areas where we are too?' asked Mamalla.

'That is that, of course.'

'Good. So what areas are the Chalukyas stronger in?'

'Elephants.'

'Their elephant brigade outnumbers ours?'

'By a lot. They are heavily dependent on their elephants.'

'What about their cavalry?' asked Manavamma.

'With yours and ours, we have a significantly higher count in terms of cavalry.'

'I faced a not too dissimilar scenario in Lanka against Tribhuvana's forces. They had an overwhelming superiority in elephants. We didn't have too many horses either.'

'How did you beat them?'

'We used the terrain to our advantage. A small clearing in a densely wooded area. We had two groups hidden in the forests and they attacked from the flanks once Tribhuvana's forces had committed. We annihilated them that day,' said Manavamma with relish.

'That won't work here,' said Mamalla. 'Manimangala is a flat land. As flat as it gets. There isn't any place to hide entire divisions.'

Silence descended upon the room as the three men bent their minds to the problem. It was Ilanthiraiyanar who broke the silence and said softly, 'When I was a young lad, I had come across a *yavana*[10] soldier-turned-trader. We got talking one evening in a tavern.'

'What were you doing in a tavern?' asked Mamalla with a raised eyebrow and a twinkle in his eyes. 'And why wasn't I there with you?'

Ilanthiraiyanar laughed. 'You were probably doing princely things and Paran was probably doing saintly things.'

---

10 Foreigner

'Well, what about the yavana?' asked Manavamma.

'We were swapping stories of battles and wars. I was telling him about the different formations that are described in our texts, especially the Mahabharata. He was quite fascinated by the *chakravyooha*[11] as I recall. Anyway, he told me about several famous battles in his country. One particular battle stood out for me. It was fought nearly a thousand years ago,[12] by his reckoning. The general faced a very similar conundrum, although in his case, the numerical superiority of the enemy was much higher. However, he too had a very strong cavalry that he used to devastating effect.'

'What was the terrain like?' asked Mamalla.

'Flat.'

'Interesting. So, you think that would work in our case as well?'

'I believe it will.'

'What did the general do?' asked Manavamma, curiously.

Ilanthiraiyanar cleared the table in front of him and then, using several small objects and flags, started telling them about that battle. The three men conversed late into the night, at the end of which they had a plan of action.

---

11 A famous circular formation that was used in the Mahabharata during the Great War.

12 Alexander's defeat of Darius at Gaugamela.

21
Battle of Suramara

Suramara, December 641 CE

Kannan sat tall on his horse, surveying his opponents It was a cool day. Winter seemed to have set in and the usual sweltering heat was in abeyance. His horse was bobbing its head and snorting, while swishing flies away with its tail. Kannan's horse had taken a liking to him ever since he had stolen it from the Gangas. He was a kindly master who gave him a rub every morning and evening, fed him well and never used the lash on him. What more could a horse ask for?

Each of the horses among the Thagadur forces was carrying two men—a horseman and an archer sitting behind him. Kannan knew that they needed to get close to the enemy cavalry so that their longbows could prove ineffective. No side wants to risk injuring its own soldiers. He knew that if they got close enough, the longbows would have to stop shooting. He was also counting on his archers to provide cover while they raced across the turf towards the enemy lines.

He looked around at his men. The cavalrymen mimicked his posture on their mounts. The infantrymen looked alert enough and anyway, if things went according to plan, they wouldn't come into play much, if at all.

A long bugle call sounded from the opposite side. One of his men raised a similar blast in response. Immediately, the two armies started moving towards each other, at a slow canter. Kannan concentrated on the Ganga centre. He knew that the arrows would come from there as soon as they got within range. The smell of the dust rising from the feet of the horses reached his nostrils and he wrinkled his nose.

'Arrows in the sky!' he shouted as the first volley went up from the enemy. Immediately, his entire cavalry broke into a gallop. As the Ganga arrows reached the tops of their arcs, the Pallava cavalry was already racing ahead and were well inside the range of the falling missiles. The longbow archers among the Gangas had already discharged a second volley without accounting for the increased speed of the Pallava cavalry. The arrows sailed over their heads and landed behind their lines, falling harmlessly to the ground.

Kannan gave the signal to slow the horses as the enemy came within range of their arrows. The bowmen slipped off the backs of the horses and let fly their own volley towards the Ganga soldiers, almost as soon as their feet touched the ground. The arrows arched away towards the Ganga front line. Kannan expected them to cower down under their shields, but instead, they veered off to either side, a large opening appearing at the centre of the Ganga line, followed by the trumpeting of elephants.

'The elephants are coming,' he yelled, even as he directed his archers to keep shooting towards the centre. They had barely had time to shoot another couple of rounds when the elephants came careering through the gap and charged at them. Kannan sounded two short blasts on his conch. Immediately, the archers jumped on to the backs of their respective mounts and the Pallava cavalry split in two, making a sweep to either side in a tight turn. The horses raced back towards their own lines, pursued by the elephants, the archers sitting behind the mahouts loosing periodic volleys of arrows at the retreating Pallava cavalry.

Some of the arrows did find their marks. Some of the cavalrymen and their bowmen went down under the barrage but most of them kept out of range. As they got back to their lines, the bowmen on the horses again slid down their horses and turned around, facing the onrushing army. Their arms moved in a coordinated fashion, whipping back, plucking arrows from the quiver, mounting them on the bowstrings, and letting them fly into the air.

The mahouts tried hard to keep the arrows away from their heads by holding aloft wooden shields. Some of the arrows struck the elephants, who, already mad with the fury of the charge, became completely enraged. They rushed forward shrieking, their trunks swinging pendulously from side to side, their heads lowered in a charge.

Captain Madappa smiled in triumph, his teeth tightly clasped. He was sitting atop the lead elephant as it charged towards the enemy forces, having earlier eschewed riding behind the elephants as part of the horse cavalry. He wanted this. He wanted the destruction of this Pallava army. He turned to look back and saw the princes Chandra and Vikrama seated on horses in the first line of the cavalry immediately following the elephant troops.

His gaze travelled further back, towards the rear of their forces, and he saw the chariots carrying King Srivikrama and General Narasimha at the back, their pennants fluttering in the breeze.

He turned to the front just as his mahout shouted out, 'Incoming arrows!'

Madappa hurriedly ducked under a shield. He had a spear in his hands and was waiting to get in range of the troops before hurling it at them. But then he saw a strange sight as the Pallava cavalry wheeled away and back the way they had come. *Are they retreating? Or have we taken them by surprise with our tactics? Maybe hiding our elephants from them till now has worked*, he exulted.

'Onward, men!' he cried. 'Let us crush those retreating cowards.' He took out his conch and gave a series of short blasts and the elephants raced on ahead.

Then he noticed the Pallava men getting off their horses and turning around with their bows raised.

This time it was he who shouted, 'Incoming arrows!' The mahouts all held aloft their larger wooden shields as he and the archers seated behind him took shelter under their smaller shields. He heard the *thwacks* of the arrows on the wooden shields. He also heard the metallic clangs of the arrows against the smaller shields that they all held up.

Why are they doing this? They are going to get run over by us. He then saw why. The Thagadur infantry was scrambling behind them, retreating pell-mell. The archers were providing them with some time to get away, hoping against hope to stop the onrushing elephants.

As the gap between them narrowed, the archers got up from their kneeling stance and jumped on to the backs of the waiting horses. The cavalrymen sped off. Madappa saw that they were getting away and realized that his elephant troops were stopping his cavalry from pursuing the fleeing enemy.

He asked his mahout to slow down and then turned around and motioned to Chandra and Vikrama.

'They are getting away. Chase them!' he pointed towards the enemy troops. Then, turning towards the elephant cavalry, he shouted, 'Mahouts! Let the cavalry pass.'

The mahouts were heard giving crisp orders to their elephants, without much success. The war haze was on the elephants, and they continued their mad dash towards the Pallava army. Somehow, the mahouts managed to slow them down enough for the cavalry to pass in between their ranks and chase the fleeing enemy.

Madappa noticed that the wide field had narrowed considerably and that their army was starting to bunch together. The enemy was lost to view because of a bend up ahead. He could see his cavalry start to outpace his elephants. They reached the bend a few hundred yards ahead of Madappa and his mount, and were soon out of sight. Madappa sat impatiently as his elephant trundled on.

He saw that the path was narrowing alarmingly up ahead. The terrain had also changed. The clearing in which they had started the battle lay between two hilly ridges, which, while almost flat near the scene of the battle, had grown in height within a mile or so. As his elephant neared the bend, he saw that the path had narrowed tremendously and was now passing in between two cliffs formed by those ridges. It was then that he started having some misgivings.

Kannan and his cavalry raced ahead through the gap in between the cliffs. The way forward was clear because the infantry had, instead of retreating along the path, climbed the ridges on both sides. He looked ahead, up and to his left, and saw tiny, ant-like figures climbing the cliff. He turned his gaze to the opposite side and saw the same.

The path led between the cliffs for a quarter of a mile and then started to broaden slowly. He chanced a quick look back and could see the dust cloud being raised by his pursuers.

'Come along now, suckers,' he muttered under his breath as he bent low over his horse, trying to streamline his body along his horse's back to cut down any drag. His horse pumped its powerful muscles as it galloped forward.

A further quarter of a mile or so ahead was a wooded area to which Kannan and his men were headed. He turned back again and could see that their enemy had gained on them. He looked to his left and grinned at the man riding next to him, one of the younger captains in Raja Duraisingham's army. The captain grinned back. As they reached the woods, the men pulled their reins in a flourish and the horses came to a halt, their forelegs rising and pawing the ground. Kannan and his men turned their horses quickly and sat waiting for the enemy to catch up with them.

Bhatta lay on his stomach, peering warily over the edge of the southern cliff. He saw his mates gallop through the narrow gap between the cliffs. He recognised the man in the lead. His boss was hard to miss. He saw the enemy cavalry following, perhaps a couple of hundred yards behind Kannan's men.

He gazed off into the distance and could see the charging line of elephants and then the infantry behind them. It would take them another few minutes to come through the gap. Bhatta looked across the gap towards the northern cliff. He could make out the hulking figure of his friend Murugan, lying similarly prone on the edge of the cliff, observing the proceedings.

Bhatta gave a low whistle which made Murugan look towards him. He held up the fingers of his right hand and then pointed towards the rest of the Ganga forces. Murugan nodded. Bhatta looked back over his shoulder and saw his archers lying down on the cliff, not wanting to get silhouetted against the sky and give away their positions. He gestured with his hands to them to lay still.

The noise from the pursuing troops became louder as the pounding of the horses' hooves echoed in the space between the cliffs. The trumpeting of the elephants and the sounds of their heavy treads were also getting ever closer. The Ganga cavalry charged on, now clearly in sight of the Pallava horses up ahead. Bhatta ignored their passage and waited for the infantry and elephants to show up in between the cliffs. Their work would start then.

Princes Chandra and Vikrama pulled the reins of their horses to slow them down as they saw the scene in front of them. The Pallava cavalry—after giving them a run through the cliffs—had now turned around and was facing them. Chandra, the elder of the brothers, gestured to his sibling to stop. They sat there taking in the scene, their swords hanging limply in their hands.

He could see the Pallava soldiers sitting erect on their horses. He saw them slowly take out their swords from their scabbards and hold them aloft. Their swords glinted and glittered as the burnished metal caught the sunlight. He heard the soldiers cry out 'Hara Hara Mahadeva' as they started to charge at them.

'Jai Varaha,' cried Chandra as his heels dug into the sides of his horse. His mount took off as if shot from a catapult, streaking across the ground towards his enemies. His brother Vikrama was close on his heels, followed by the rest of the cavalry.

The two cavalries smashed into each other, swords clashing against swords, spears emptying saddles, as they sliced through their opponents' armours. Chandra felt the heady rush of battle as he engaged first one enemy, and then another. He had been taught well and was a good swordsman, as was his brother. In between shifting his attention from one enemy to another, he chanced a quick glance to see how his brother was faring and was gratified to see him holding his own against his foe.

Their cavalry was greater in number, and it seemed like their opponents were moving back under the sheer ferocity of their onslaught. Chandra wielded his sword expertly, cutting and slicing his way through. Not for him the heavy overhanded strokes. He used his sword like a goldsmith used his engraving chisel, not like a blacksmith used his hammer. His master had taught him never to overextend himself and to keep his thrusts minimal. As he disposed of yet another opponent, he noticed a burly man who was creating havoc in their ranks.

His style was remarkably different from Chandra's own. He was more heavy-handed, but his movements were swift, precise and debilitating. The power that radiated from his shoulders transferred itself smoothly through his sword arm to his sword as he slashed and cut his opponents apart.

The opponents noticed each other almost at the same time, guiding their horses towards one another. Chandra held his sword in front and thrust up and to the left, trying to wound his opponent's forearm and slice through the tendons, but the man simply rotated his wrists at the last instant and parried his sword away. Chandra hadn't expected that subtlety from someone as large as his opponent and glanced at him in surprise. His opponent wore a little smile of satisfaction.

Chandra moved his horse around more warily now. This wasn't just some big, hulking oaf who used his size to his advantage. He recognised now what he had missed earlier—the quiet confidence of a supreme warrior. As he circled, a deep long blast on a conch sounded, and it was as if a storm broke over them.

22

Battle of Suramara—The Finale

Suramara, December 641 CE

Commander Paranjyothi had led his men from Kanchi towards Thagadur. A messenger from Kannan had arrived when he was halfway to his destination, giving details of what Kannan was planning, and he was in agreement with the plans. As far as Paranjyothi was concerned, the man on the ground took the tactical and operational decisions.

Moreover, he knew that Ilanthiraiyanar trusted Kannan, and he, in turn, trusted his general completely. So he merely sent back a response agreeing to whatever it was that Kannan had planned. The only change he made was in the speed with which he and his men were marching towards Thagadur.

They had reached Thagadur the previous afternoon, even as an anxious Kannan waited for them. His plan depended, to a large extent, on the presence of Paranjyothi's army at the rear. Paranjyothi had ridden out with Kannan the previous evening to survey the terrain. The commander had nodded appreciatively as Kannan explained where he wanted Paranjyothi's forces to be stationed. He approved.

He had moved his forces here under cover of darkness, just in case some of the Ganga scouts were around, although Kannan had assured him that there was only a very slim chance of that. But a slim chance was a chance nevertheless, and Paranjyothi was not known for negligence.

They had been waiting in the woods all through the initial skirmishes and then the retreat by Kannan's men. When Kannan and his men had stopped near the edge of the woods and re-engaged the Ganga cavalry, they had got ready. The plan was for them to attack only once the Ganga cavalry was fully engaged.

At the appropriate time, Paranjyothi had blown his conch and his men had poured out of the forest, surrounding the Ganga forces.

Murugan could see Paranjyothi's men entering the fray and bolstering Kannan's cavalry with their numbers. He looked towards the west where the Ganga elephant brigade was entering the narrow path in between the cliffs. The infantry followed close behind.

Murugan glanced across at the southern ridge and gave a low whistle. It was loud enough to attract Bhatta's attention but soft enough to go unnoticed by the enemy troops rushing beneath them.

In response, Bhatta motioned to his archers, who scrambled over on their haunches, silently, to the edge of the cliff. The archers on Murugan's side of the cliff did likewise.

The two friends looked at each other and then, almost as if they were of one mind, gave the order to their bowmen. The archers stood up at the edges of the cliff, notched their arrows and then let fly. There was none of the lazy arcing of arrows that usually accompanied volleys on a battlefield. The enemy here was directly beneath them, and the archers let fly at the soldiers in almost a straight line.

The strength of their hands, the elasticity of their bowstrings, and the force that pulled all objects down to the earth combined in creating fast-moving missiles. The speedy arrowheads cleaved through wood and steel, bone and sinew, as they embedded themselves in humans, horses and elephants. The arrows sliced through the ranks effortlessly. Men and animals alike staggered and fell in mid-step. Elephants went down as the arrows penetrated their brains, their legs folding under them. As they fell on their sides, they crushed the infantrymen running past them.

It took a while for those bringing up the rear to understand what was going on. They searched for targets to attack and found none. They looked and they died in the hundreds, as arrows bore down on them mercilessly.

The elephants didn't last too long. The men lasted a mite longer, trapped between two towering walls of rock, trying to retreat but coming up against their own companions, who pressed forward unaware of the danger.

Some of them tried to use the carcasses of the elephants and the dead bodies of their own comrades to shield themselves from the deadly onslaught. A few of the more intrepid ones tried to take up their bows and shoot at their tormentors up above, on the cliffs, but that was like the last desperate gulp that a drowning man takes as water rushes down his throat—doing something for the sake of doing something. The arrows never reached the tops of the cliffs and the brief instant for which they were exposed proved to be their undoing. Intrepidness lost out to self-preservation.

For the men who were still alive, injured or trapped, the situation was about to get even worse.

Chandra and Vikrama did a double take when they saw fresh troops coming out of the woods. Hundreds and hundreds of them. Perhaps thousands. All the numerical superiority that they had assumed was theirs when facing the Pallava cavalry fell away under the sheer weight of the numbers that the woods disgorged, in a seemingly unending stream.

Chandra, who had been engaging Kannan, knew that there was not a moment to lose. He understood that they were in trouble, and that every second that they delayed there would mean utter annihilation. He took out his conch, stood up in his stirrups and blew the signal to retreat.

He saw Vikrama's head whip around as he heard the sound.

'Let's go, men. Let's go!' yelled Chandra as he turned his horse around in a jiffy and started galloping towards the opening in between the cliffs. His men followed suit, disengaging from their individual fights.

Their horses thudded across the open ground and bunched together as they neared the cliffs. Chandra looked around and saw that the Pallava cavalry wasn't pursuing them. They were instead, walking their horses slowly towards the opening. His brows furrowed. *Why are they doing that?* His brain, caught up in a storm of emotions and thoughts, was unable to process this new information.

As his horse raced in between the cliffs, he saw the host of dead men, horses and elephants lying on the ground. Before he could comprehend what had happened, arrows rained down on him and his men. Chandra acted instinctively. He jumped off his horse and hit the ground in a roll, even as his horse crashed to the ground, whinnying, pierced by multiple arrows.

Chandra crawled over to one side of it and used its body and his shield to protect himself from the hail that was descending on them. He wanted to check on how Vikrama was doing. He raised his head, using the shield to protect it from the arrows coming from above and saw that Vikrama was crouched along one edge of the cliff under an overhang that protected him from the arrows. Vikrama gestured to him to come over. Chandra, realising that staying in the open increased the probability of a chance arrow finding him, ran over in a crouch and joined his brother under the overhang. He checked to see if he had been hit by any of the arrows but seemed to have miraculously escaped.

'We can't stay here for long,' he told his brother. 'Look over there!'

Vikrama turned around to see the direction indicated by his brother and saw the Pallava cavalry, with whom they had been fighting not too long ago, walking towards them, most probably to finish the job.

'We have to go, now!' yelled Vikrama. Chandra nodded and then as Vikrama dashed out from under the overhang, he followed him. Vikrama had picked up a couple of shields and was holding them up above his head, while he zigzagged his way through the ravine. Chandra followed suit, as did more of their surviving men.

Arrows whistled dangerously past them. Many embedded themselves in the shields held aloft with loud *thwack*s. The princes ran past the dying and the dead. The groans of their men filled them with dismay, but there was nothing that they could do. Staying there meant certain death.

At last, they reached the edge of the ravine where the path opened out. They found the remnants of their army there, milling about, unable to decide what to do. They spotted the chariots belonging to King Srivikrama and Commander Narasimha at the back. They approached them and saw the king jump off his chariot.

'Oh, my boys! I thought that I had lost you,' he said, hugging his grandsons, clasping their blood-stained bodies to him.

Chandra gently disengaged from his grandfather and asked, 'What are you doing here, Grandfather?'

'What?' spluttered the king.

'We need to go,' said Vikrama. 'They will soon be upon us.'

'Who?' asked the bewildered king.

'The Pallava cavalrymen, of course. The men on top will realise soon enough that there is no one else in that ravine worth shooting at. They will stop, and then the cavalry will come through.'

A panicked look spread over Srivikrama's face as he glanced back at Narasimha.

'I have been trying to tell you, my King, that we need to leave now. This battle is lost. Let us save what we can of the army.'

Srivikrama hesitated, but the combined glances of the princes and his commander proved too much for him. He sighed, and then got on to his chariot, a broken man. The remaining members of the Ganga army retreated the way they had come, across the open field and into the woods on the far side.

23

The Bhikshu's Ruse

Suramara, December 641 CE

Life had settled down to a predictable pattern for the three of them. The bhikshu was ensconced in a little mandapam next to the temple to the west of the palace. They had initially been given a place on one of the lower levels, but the bhikshu had manoeuvred to get the queens to move them to a mandapam near the palace.

There, the royal family would gather every day to sit at the feet of the master. They would sing *bhajans*[13] in praise of the Gods, with the bhikshu maintaining a studied silence in a meditative posture. There was an aura about the master, or so the bhikshu had heard the members of the Chalukya royal family whisper to each other, as they gathered at the mandapam every morning and evening.

The two attendants ensured that their master was well-fed and rested. They would stop people from intruding on the

13 Religious songs

bhikshu's rest hour in the afternoons. In a few days, they had the run of the place, and could come and go as they pleased.

The clean-shaven attendants, in their white clothes, would wander up and down the steps leading to the palace from the fort gates. They would frequently foray outside the fort as well, mingling with the crowds and traversing all over the extensive city.

One day, the three of them sat in the mandapam, enjoying some much-needed rest after a heavy lunch. The bhikshu was lying on a thin mat made from woven sticks. The other two were lying down nearby, fanning themselves with hand-held fans that had been donated to them by the devotees.

One of the attendants spoke up, 'I was walking down to the fort earlier this morning and noticed this building off to one side.'

'Mmmm,' murmured the bhikshu.

'I noticed people going in and out of that building.'

'What kind of building?' asked the bhikshu.

'You know. Looked like an office. I peeked in, and there were a bunch of people sitting at low desks writing something on manuscripts. But we did see the prime minister spend a lot of time there. I spoke to a couple of guards stationed there. They said that it was the prime minister's office.'

'I wonder if we will find anything interesting there,' said the bhikshu.

'I wouldn't know, even if I could get inside the office. I can't read.'

'Or write,' chimed the second man.

'Or write,' agreed his companion. 'Not as if you can read or write either.'

'Better than you, I bet,' was the derisive reply.

'Well, at least I spent the time usefully trying to find some information. What did you achieve today?' he asked his companion, with what he felt was justifiable heat.

'I discovered something,' said the second man, a smug grin spreading across his face.

'Yeah? And what would that be?'

'That there is an underground room.'

'What? Where?' asked the bhikshu, sitting up now.

'You know that house in the distance?' he pointed in a westwardly direction.

'Mmhmm.'

'You see what looks like a walkway in front of it, due east of the house?'

'Yes.'

'There is a room under that walkway, it seems.'

His companion snorted in disgust.

'There is!' said the other man, with a touch of exasperation.

'I bet there is nothing of the sort. Must be his usual fanciful stories,' he said, turning towards the bhikshu.

'Let's listen to what he has to say.'

'That's right,' said the raconteur, encouraged by the words of the bhikshu. 'I was walking along it last evening, trying to juggle with a few pebbles, when one of them fell down and gave a hollow sound. That piqued my interest.'

His companion snorted again.

'You can scoff, but I am telling the truth. Anyway, I was intrigued and so I dropped a few more pebbles, and sure enough, there was a hollow *thunk* whenever a stone hit the path.'

'That could just be from the construction. Maybe some missing bricks.'

'All over the path? I took my staff and started tapping my way over that. For about twenty yards or so, I heard a thump but not after that. There *is* something hollow underneath that path and I bet it is a room.'

'Do you know whose house it is?' asked the bhikshu softly.

'I found out. It seems it is the house of someone named Naganandi.'

The bhikshu gave a gasp of surprise. Naganandi's house! The famous or infamous spy chief of the Chalukyas, depending on whose side one was on. *A secret room perhaps? In the basement? How do I get into it? Surely there must be a way.* The bhikshu was deep in thought. The attendants looked at one another in surprise and then shrugged their shoulders. Their task was to bring bits of information to the bhikshu. What the master did with it was not their concern.

They lay down again and let the coolness of the mandapam lull them to sleep. The bhikshu, however, lay awake thinking.

The two men walked towards the seamier part of town, where the bhikshu had visited Devadutta. They weren't particularly concerned about any threat of bodily harm. They knew that they could take care of any such troubles. They, however, hoped for a peaceful trip. It wouldn't do for two monks to be seen fighting in the streets of Vathapi.

Devadutta looked up in surprise as they were let into his inner room by his servant.

'What are you both doing here?' he asked.

'The bhikshu sent us.'

Devadutta waited for them to continue. When they didn't, he responded impatiently. 'Well? Why did the bhikshu send you?'

'We have found a secret room in Naganandi's house.'

'You mean I found out about it,' said the other man.

'Yes, yes, you found out about it,' replied his companion testily.

'I don't care who found it. Will you get on with it?' snapped Devadutta irritably.

'Don't yell at me. He interrupted me,' said the first man. Then, noticing signs of ferment in Devadutta, he hastened to add, 'The bhikshu thinks that there is a way to get inside. But once inside, there is no one else who can go into the hidden chamber and see what information might be hidden there.'

'What about you both?'

'Er ...' said the first man.

'Er ...' said his companion.

'The thing is ...'

'The thing is, we can't read or write,' said the second man, a little shamefacedly.

Devadutta gave a little nod, not wanting to say anything that might make them feel worse than how he surmised they already felt.

'Tell the master that I will be there tomorrow towards the end of the morning prayers. Now tell me what the plan is to get us inside the building.'

Today is the day, thought Devadutta as he walked his horse slowly towards the palace gates at the bottom of the northern spur. He got off his horse and tied it to the hitchrail. The guards at the gates allowed him in after he showed them the palace pass that the bhikshu's attendants had given him.

Devadutta started walking up the steep stone steps. He was puffing in very short order. *I really am getting old*, he thought, as he stopped on a step, gasping for air and squinting his eyes as he looked up. He knew he still had at least another quarter of a mile to climb.

He muttered a curse under his breath and started climbing up. He had been doing this for the last three days, ever since that first day when he had come here to meet the bhikshu. The bhikshu, who had been hitherto silent, had burst out into a song when he went to prostrate himself at the master's feet, much to the amazement of the crowd of royals. They hadn't heard the master utter a single word in all these days. And here was the master, breaking into a song just for this one devotee. They looked at Devadutta with profound respect.

The master had then gone into a long discourse about the world, and how to navigate through it. At the end of the discourse, the assembled crowd had plied the master with questions, which had been patiently answered.

From that point onwards, every morning and evening, the master would give a discourse on various philosophies. The adoring crowd would ask their questions, to which they would get well-thought-out answers. This continued for a couple of days.

This morning, however, the master had turned to the topic of *vaastu*[14] and had spoken at length about the positives of ensuring that any building construction ought to be carried out in accordance with its rules. The master had also spoken of the ill effects of ignoring these rules.

'Master,' one of the queens had interrupted the discourse, even as the others looked at one another in consternation.

14 Ancient Hindu science of architecture that promotes a way to bring harmony and a congenial setting to live and work. Somewhat akin to the Chinese concept of feng shui.

However, a queen is a queen, and the usual rules of etiquette do not necessarily apply to her.

'Yes?' asked the bhikshu, with a gentle smile.

'What about our palace here? Do you feel that the vaastu is good?'

'Why do you ask, my child?' the master asked the much older queen.

'Well, Master, there is a war coming, and I want to make sure that nothing here has any negative influences on the conduct of the war.'

Devadutta smiled inwardly as he heard this. This was precisely what the bhikshu had been leading up to. He waited for the answer even though he knew what it would be.

The bhikshu looked around the courtyard, at the palace and the temple and then towards the singularly unattractive structure that was Naganandi's house in the distance. Then, pointing at the house, the master said, 'That house. There is something wrong with its location. Whose house is it?'

The queens looked at each other, undecipherable looks on their faces.

'That belongs to Naganandi,' said Visalakshi, the younger queen.

'Who is he?' asked the bhikshu.

Visalakshi gasped. 'You don't know him?'

'Am I supposed to?'

Some of the ladies in the royal entourage giggled. 'We thought everyone knew him,' said Mangalamma, the chief queen. 'He is a close confidante of His Majesty,' she said.

'Well, that might be so, but he isn't doing you any favours by living in that house.'

'What is wrong with the house, Master?' asked Mangalamma.

The bhikshu's eyes closed in meditation. An expectant hush settled on the crowd before the bhikshu's eyes opened.

'Is there a hollow space underneath the house?'

Mangalamma and Visalakshi exchanged glances.

'A hollow space, Master? You have seen how this place is. It is one giant rock. How could there be a hollow space underneath the house?' asked Mangalamma.

The bhikshu's eyes narrowed into a penetrating gaze as they looked upon the queens, causing them to shift uncomfortably.

'Is there a room there perhaps? An underground room?'

The women looked at each other in confusion. Mangalamma looked back at some of her entourage and queried, 'Do any of you know if there is an underground room in Naganandi avaru's house?'

The ladies gave each other puzzled looks. One of them finally spoke up.

'We don't know, Your Majesty. He doesn't allow any of us into his house. There is only one person who is entrusted with cleaning it and that is the caretaker.'

'Call him here,' ordered Mangalamma.

The girl who had answered got up and rushed towards Naganandi's house. She was back in short order with a middle-aged man, who approached the queens and bowed with his palms folded in front of him.

Mangalamma acknowledged his greeting with a queenly nod of her head and then asked, 'Is there an underground room in Naganandi avaru's house?'

The man looked startled and then passed his eyes over the crowd.

He bent down and whispered softly to the queen, 'Your Majesty, can we discuss this inside? Out of hearing of this large crowd?'

Mangalamma understood what he was trying to say. She got up from her seat and told the assembled crowd in a voice that brooked no dissent, 'With the permission of the master, I would like you all to leave now. We have some important matters to discuss.'

The master called her over and whispered a few words in her ear. The queen immediately turned towards Devadutta and said, 'The master wishes for you to remain.' Devadutta bowed his head in acquiescence.

The crowd disbanded quickly. A master's words had moral weight, but a queen's orders were an injunction to be obeyed. Finally, only the two queens, the master, the two disciples, Devadutta and the caretaker remained. The queen looked at the caretaker and said, 'Well?'

'There *is* a room in the house, Your Majesty,' he said, somewhat reluctantly.

The queens drew in their breaths sharply and turned to bestow the master with looks of utmost devotion.

'That room destroys the harmony of the house and, by extension, this entire area,' said the master ominously.

'What can be done about this, Master?' asked Visalakshi, her eyes big and round with fear.

'There are ways,' said the bhikshu. 'But I will need to look at the room and carry out certain rituals and rites there.'

The caretaker stiffened at these words.

'Aah, Your Majesties,' he said, looking at the queens in alarm. 'I don't think we can go in there without talking to my master. He is very strict about that. He doesn't allow anyone to go into that room, not even me.'

'Well, your master isn't here now, is he? And we can't wait for him to come back to do the puja that is required to cleanse the room,' said Mangalamma.

'But I don't even have the key to the room, my Queen.'

'Then we will break the lock.'

'Break the lock?'

'Break the lock,' said the queen firmly.

The caretaker licked his lips in panic. On the one hand was his fear of what his master would say and do to him if he came to know that strangers—and that included the two queens—had entered his secret underground lair. On the other hand was the incontrovertible fact that his master was absent, and he was faced with the belligerence of the two queens who outranked everyone else around here.

'Well?' asked Mangalamma, impatiently.

'Very well, my Queen,' he said submissively, turning back and leading the way to Naganandi's residence.

It took the caretaker some time to find a crowbar and break the lock on the door leading to the underground room. The door was approached by means of steps that led down from the ground floor. These steps were hidden under a wooden door on the floor, which was kept hidden from sight by a carpet that was laid on top of it.

In the meantime, under instructions from the bhikshu, the queens had made arrangements for the materials required for the rituals, including incense sticks, banana leaves, betel leaves and various other knickknacks, to be brought to the house.

The lock was broken and the bhikshu stood at the threshold and glanced inside, secretly exultant. As far as the eye could see, there were manuscripts. Some on the ground, some on wooden shelves. The bhikshu noticed some large silk rolls tied with threads which could only be maps. The queens tried to follow the bhikshu into the room but were stopped by the master.

'No, my dear children. This is still unsafe. I cannot risk your presence inside since it might impact the well-being of your loved ones.' The queens stepped back immediately, fear writ large on their faces.

'You three,' said the bhikshu, looking at the disciples and Devadutta. 'You can come in. And bring the materials needed for the rituals.'

24

Sadaiyan Reprises an Old Role

Lands Northwest of Manimangala, December 641 CE

Sadaiyan walked through the camp pushing a cart, whistling a bawdy love song that he had picked up from someone in his disreputable journey through life. The cart was piled high with fresh coconuts that he had procured from some of the villages around the camp. His whistling was interrupted by the jaunty salutations that he threw out ever so often:

'Hey, Private, how's it going?'

'Corporal, how about buying a round of coconut water for your entire platoon?'

'Good morning, Captain. You look fine now but I bet by noon you will be hankering for some good old coconut water to quench your thirst.'

'Hi there, Private. The horses are looking peaked. Make sure you feed them well!'

Sadaiyan's progress through the camp left behind a bunch of chuckling soldiers. His sassiness and irreverence towards one and all made him much liked in the camp, which was a sharp contrast to the taciturn man walking next to him. Jamba's demeanour and mien were forbidding. He usually had the carcasses of a couple of deer or boars slung across his shoulders as they made their way through the camp.

Their usual practice was for Sadaiyan to find a good spot to hawk his coconuts while Jamba deposited his burden with the cooks, and returned to sit by the young lad's side with his habitual bland expression.

The young thief seemed to be enjoying this interlude, where he could make some money, although the honesty of it all chafed him.

Sadaiyan and Jamba had debated on how to approach the camp. They abandoned their initial plan of Sadaiyan acting as Jamba's understudy as a hunter. Sadaiyan had pointed out to the older man that going into the camp as a hunter did not give them enough time to loiter around inside it. They would have to go to the cooking area, hand over the meat for the day to the cooks and then leave quickly.

Sadaiyan's experience in Korkai gave him an idea. Coconuts were available here, the same as they were in Korkai. Soldiers got thirsty all the time. So why not use the same ruse as before?

Jamba agreed with his suggestion, and much to Sadaiyan's evident disgust, haggled with a villager and bought a cart from him. The young thief had pleaded with Jamba that such expenses were unnecessary when he was around, and that he could sneak a cart out of one of the villages at night, but the older man would have none of it. Sadaiyan grumbled and muttered under his breath that Jamba was taking away all the fun from their little expedition, but it left Jamba unmoved.

Jamba then bartered some fresh meat that he had hunted for coconuts. They loaded the cart with them and then started walking towards the Chalukya army line. They noticed that the army was bunched together—probably a result of the repeated raids and attacks carried out by General Ilanthiraiyanar and his men. They noticed too the roving bands of men who formed a loose outer perimeter half a mile or so from the main army contingent.

'They seem very suspicious of everyone,' Sadaiyan said.

'Wouldn't you be? If you were being attacked incessantly?' asked Jamba with a small chuckle. His chuckle made Sadaiyan look up at him. Even in the brief time that he had known Jamba, he had never seen the forest dweller so much as smile.

'You seem to be enjoying this, aiyya,' said Sadaiyan.

'I like a good fight,' said Jamba and marched off towards the outer perimeter of soldiers.

They had been able to make their way through to the main camp without much ado. A cartful of coconuts and freshly hunted meat got them easy access. They had been directed to the back of the camp where the cooking fires burned and smoked incessantly.

The cook, a cantankerous old coot, stood in front of the fires, spewing directions at his assistants. He had looked suspiciously as Jamba and Sadaiyan had walked up to him. In keeping with the ruse, Sadaiyan had introduced Jamba as his uncle who was mute and handed over the meat to him. The cook had accepted the meat somewhat dubiously and he had sniffed at it carefully. He had asked one of his assistants for a knife and had sliced off a piece from the deer's thigh. Satisfied about the quality of the meat, he had given a short nod of approval, at which point, the haggling started on the price.

Sadaiyan was in his element, and used his full sales repertoire, as he started with an outrageous opening bid and refused to budge. He well knew that it was a seller's market. There weren't too many other places where they could get fresh meat, and in the end, while he did let himself be beaten down slightly, he still sold the meat for five times what it was worth in one of the villages.

As the assistant handed him the money, Sadaiyan tried to tuck it into the cloth tied around his waist but found that his hand was arrested in its movement by Jamba, who clasped his own huge hand around Sadaiyan's elbow. With his other hand, he opened Sadaiyan's fist and extracted all the money from it and then wordlessly tucked it into the recesses of his own clothing, giving Sadaiyan a wicked grin.

Sadaiyan pouted momentarily, but then grinned and started shouting out, 'Fresh coconuts. Tender coconuts. Coconut water that will quench your thirst like a beautiful woman satisfies your dreams. Water that will leave you feeling that you have taken a dip in the holy Mansarovar lake. Water that will feel like Mother Ganga herself slaked your thirst. Come and get them.'

That first day, he had sold all his coconuts by noon. He had taken to replenishing his cart at one of the nearby villages during lunch and returning around evening. Two cartloads a day was a lot of money for the young lad, and Sadaiyan was ecstatic. The young thief though did not let his fledgling business get in the way of their larger goal. They had started off by positioning their cart at the outer edges of the camp and, over the course of the next few days, worked their way slowly inwards, so that now, he could park his cart almost at the centre, a stone's throw away from the king's tent.

They had seen King Pulikeshi take a walk outside his tent. He had looked towards them and asked one of his men to get him a tender coconut. Sadaiyan had tried to deliver it himself, but the soldiers had prevented him from doing so. One didn't get close to the most powerful emperor of the land that easily.

The princes, however, had taken to coming to his cart a few times during each day. They enjoyed Sadaiyan's quick wit and repartee and his refreshing lack of obsequiousness. He treated them like he treated everyone else in the camp.

'Hoy, Sadaiya,' said Prince Aditya. 'Give us our usual, will you?'

Sadaiyan noticed the prince and his brothers Ranaragha and Jayasimha sauntering up to his cart.

'I am truly blessed today,' said Sadaiyan. 'To have three great princes of the mighty Chalukya dynasty come to taste the wares of this humble peasant.'

'Humble peasant, my foot,' said Ranaragha. 'You earn more money than us.' Then, turning to his brothers, he asked, 'What do you say? Should we ask the king to levy taxes on this young lad's daily revenues?'

'Hmmm,' mused Jayasimha, with a mock frown on his face.

'Come on now, Princes. You know I give you three deep discounts that I don't give to the other soldiers? Why would you want to tax an honest peasant unnecessarily?'

The princes chuckled in response, while Sadaiyan took out his curved sickle and started to hack away at the coconuts, opening a small hole in three of them.

'So what news, Princes? How far are you going to go?' asked Sadaiyan.

'You know where we are going to go?' asked Prince Aditya.

'Oh yes, to Kanchi, I hear,' said the young lad. 'But aren't you way off? Shouldn't you be striking down south now? You are going too far to the east.'

The princes glanced at each other and back at the young lad.

'You know this area well?' asked Prince Jayasimha.

'Know it? Like the back of my hand. Have been all over this place with my uncle here. I usually don't sell coconuts. This is just because of your presence in these parts, else, who will buy coconuts from me? I would barely be able to sell a cartful a week!'

'So you are making money off us?'

'Most certainly,' grinned Sadaiyan. 'Haven't you heard that war is good for business?'

The princes laughed again and then paused to lift their respective coconuts and slurp the cool liquid through the opening. Some of the liquid dribbled past their mouths on to their bare bodies.

'I wish there was some way to drink this without it dripping all over us,' complained Ranaragha.

'Maybe if you brought along some cups, I could pour the water into them,' replied Sadaiyan.

'Too much trouble,' said Aditya, drinking from his coconut again. He finished his in a few gulps and then handed the coconut over to Sadaiyan who, with a few deft blows, opened it up and cut out a small piece of the outer shell to act as a spoon to scoop out the soft, white flesh inside. He handed the scoop and the coconut back to Aditya and did the same for the other two as well.

'So,' said Aditya, returning to the topic after scooping a bit of juicy coconut into his mouth, 'you think we are drifting too far east?'

'Depends on where you want to go. If you want to go east to the coast, then you are on the right track,' said Sadaiyan, impishly. 'Or if you want to go to Ratnagrahara,' he said slyly.

'Eh what?' asked Aditya.

'Ratnagra … what?' asked Ranaragha.

'Ratnagrahara! Don't tell me that you haven't heard of it. I thought you were proceeding this way because your goal was Ratnagrahara,' said Sadaiyan.

'What is Ratnagrahara and why should we go towards it?'

Sadaiyan let a confused look spread across his face.

'Do you mean to tell me that you don't know about the place? Then why on earth are you coming this far east?'

'Will you get to the point?' asked Aditya exasperatedly.

Sadaiyan looked around furtively and said, 'Don't let anyone around know that I told you, alright? They will string me up for being in cahoots with the enemy.'

'Us?' asked Aditya.

'Yes, you. Who else would the enemy be, this close to Kanchi?'

'Alright. Alright. Go ahead,' said Aditya.

'Ratnagrahara,' continued Sadaiyan, lowering his voice conspiratorially, 'is the place where jewels are made and exported to other kingdoms.'

'Jewels!' whispered Jayasimha reverently.

'Yes, tons of it, from what I hear,' said Sadaiyan. 'Goes from there all over the land. I have tried to go there but they won't let non-natives into that area.'

Adita suddenly snapped his fingers and said, 'You. Come with us. I want you to say what you have just told us to the king.'

Sadaiyan bowed and hid a smile. Then, turning to Jamba, he said, 'Uncle, please take care of the cart while I go with the princes.'

Jamba nodded impassively.

Elango and Muthuvel were sitting together under a tree preparing to settle down for the night. The only light in the camp came from the remnants of their cooking fire, which was now slowly dying into reddish-grey embers.

The camp lay in a banana grove behind one of the villages, not too far from the Chalukya army. The soldiers had hunkered down for the night. There were strict orders to maintain silence. A round-the-clock guard was mounted on all sides and especially so facing the south, where Pulikeshi's men were located.

Elango and Muthuvel were discussing the plans for the next day when they heard the rustling of leaves and soft footsteps. They turned to look in the direction of the sounds and spied Sadaiyan and Jamba walking softly into camp, accompanied by two soldiers.

Sadaiyan turned back towards the soldiers who had escorted them in and said, '*Now* will you guys go back to your duties? Didn't I tell you that I know them?'

The soldiers grinned, bowed to Elango and Muthuvel, and went back the way they had come, leaving behind a scowling Sadaiyan gingerly rubbing the back of his head.

'What happened?' asked Muthuvel.

'One of them smacked the young lad on his head,' said Jamba, grinning wickedly as he came forward to hug Elango.

'I bet they did that deliberately,' said Sadaiyan. 'They know who we are.'

The others chuckled and then, even before the newcomers sat down, Muthuvel asked, 'Well?'

'Ratnagrahara enticed them, sure enough. They are moving towards Manimangala. We can send that messenger to Kanchi now,' said Sadaiyan.

Pulikeshi stirred in his bed, trying to fall asleep. The attendants had lit a strong incense in the evening and let the smoke waft all over the tent to drive the mosquitoes away, but that didn't stop a few intrepid insects from finding their way in and feasting on the resting body of the great Chalukya emperor. Not that they knew or cared about who he was, of course.

Pulikeshi slapped his hands against his exposed chest and arms, trying futilely to massacre the whole platoon of mosquitoes. He muttered curses under his breath and sat up when he thought he heard something outside his tent. A tall, wiry figure entered, impatiently brushing aside the queries of the guards.

'Naganandi!' exclaimed Pulikeshi. 'What on earth are you doing here?'

'I wanted to talk,' said the spy chief in his usual abrupt manner.

'Can someone get a light in here?' asked Pulikeshi in a raised voice. Shortly, a man appeared with a lit torch, placed it in a torch holder and left.

'Alright,' said Pulikeshi, 'what did you want to talk about?'

'A few things. Among them, the plan that was discussed earlier in the day.'

'Eh?'

'Of proceeding to Ratnagrahara. Or Manimangala as they call it.'

'What about it?'

'I have been thinking.'

'Ah. And?'

'Something doesn't add up for me.'

Pulikeshi looked keenly at his spy chief. When Naganandi said something, he always paid attention.

'Well? Are you going to stand around all night, or are you going to tell me what's going on in that bald head of yours?'

'That conversation earlier in the day. The coconut-selling kid who came in here with tales of the rich pickings were we to proceed towards Manimangala.'

'What of it?'

'Don't you think it was a little too pat?'

Pulikeshi pursed his lips in thought. 'Why didn't you say something then?'

'I did not want to say anything in front of that young lad,' Naganandi said.

'You don't think he is trustworthy?'

'Rajan. Where is your sense of discernment? We are in enemy territory. Why should we believe anything a local says here?'

Pulikeshi started pacing his tent, a frown on his face.

'So, you think it is disinformation?'

'Could be. Although the town does exist, and it does make jewels.'

'So, send out some scouts and find out what the Pallavas are up to,' said Pulikeshi.

'I did,' replied Naganandi. 'They came back earlier in the day. The Pallava army is paralleling us a few miles to our south.'

'You think we are being funnelled towards Manimangala?'

'Seems like it.'

'Why?'

'I am not sure why,' admitted Naganandi. 'The terrain is the same all across. Flat as a table. With farmlands intruding. I sent scouts immediately after the meeting. They only just returned.'

'And?'

'Flat land,' said Naganandi. 'There is farmland all the way from here to Manimangala. But, near the town, there is a huge area which is shorn of any agricultural land. I believe that that's where the Pallavas want to meet us.'

'But why? Do they have a larger army than ours?'

'Not remotely.'

'So then what's our problem? We can crush them, especially on flat land. And we are yet to have the Ganga forces join us,' Pulikeshi said.

'Aah. Coming to that ...' said Naganandi, and paused. Pulikeshi waited for him to continue.

'I had a messenger come from the west today.'

'Did they retake Guddahalli?'

'Yes, they did,' replied Naganandi. 'And then chased the Pallava feudatory, that pesky Raja of Thagadur, almost to his city.'

'Excellent,' said Pulikeshi, smacking his right fist into his left palm.

'Not really,' said Naganandi.

'What do you mean?'

Naganandi sighed. 'They got caught in a trap between the Thagadur forces and the forces sent by the Pallavas to their aid. Our Ganga allies got decimated.'

Pulikeshi's face darkened with a mix of anger and fear—anger about what had happened to his ally and fear about the fate of his father-in-law, and more importantly, his sons.

'The boys?' he whispered.

'They are safe,' said Naganandi.

Pulikeshi let out his breath in a rush. 'Thank *Narayana*[15] for that!'

'Are they wounded? Did they give a good account of themselves?' asked Pulikeshi the father.

15 Another name of the God Vishnu.

'No, they aren't wounded, other than the little scratches that they picked up during the course of the battle. And yes. They seemed to have been in the thick of things. And escaped by the proverbial hair's breadth.'

Pulikeshi sat down on the bed heavily, a worried frown on his face.

'What do you suggest?' he asked his most trusted advisor, looking up at him.

Naganandi started speaking in a low voice. He spoke for several minutes without being interrupted by his king. At the end of it, he asked, 'So, shall I give the orders?'

Pulikeshi looked at Naganandi and nodded in agreement.

25

Manimangala

Manimangala, December 641 CE

Early that morning, Mahendra bounded into Mamalla's chambers even before his father had finished his morning ablutions, so eager was he to set off for his first battle.

'Appa. Are you just getting up?'

Mamalla gave him an amused smile. 'Have you been up all night, my boy?'

'Well …' said Mahendra, a grin dawning on his face. 'I was too excited to sleep,' he finished, somewhat embarrassedly.

Mamalla smiled. 'I know how it feels, son.'

The queen had walked in on them with a towel in one hand. She handed it to her husband and pushed him towards the bathhouse.

'We are going to be late for our visit to the Kailasanathar Temple,' she admonished him.

Mamalla made a face at Mahendra, careful to keep his wife from seeing it. Mahendra grinned in return. His mother caught that.

'Yes, yes, I know. He made a face. Father and son can only make fun of me,' she said, mock seriously.

Mahendra put an arm around her. 'Would we do that, Amma?'

'You know you would. And that man,' she indicated the departing back of her husband, 'will surely do that. Especially when he is with you!'

Mahendra laughed out aloud. His mother's mock anger evaporated as she hugged her son tightly. 'Be careful, alright?'

'You worry too much, Amma.'

'I am a mother …'

'… and only when I become a parent will I understand, right?' completed her son.

'Yeah, yeah. Make fun of me. Anyway, let me get ready for the trip to the temple.'

She left and Mahendra caught up with his father and asked, 'What about King Krithavarman, Appa? Is he coming with us?'

Mamalla looked at him out of the corner of his eyes. 'I don't think so.'

'Why not? Wouldn't he be looking to regain his kingdom?'

'You don't know Krithavarman well, do you? He is not exactly the type who will go into battle.'

'Aah,' said young Mahendra, with a knowing nod.

'Aah, indeed. So, we shall leave him be.'

The royal family rode out to the temple together, along with General Ilanthiraiyanar and Manavamma, who met them outside the palace gates. The priests chanted sacred mantras to God Shiva, praying for victory for their king. The queen applied the red vermillion paste on the foreheads of the king, her son, Manavamma and Ilanthiraiyanar.

The group then walked their horses back to the palace, where Mamalla and Mahendra took leave of a teary-eyed queen. She hugged her husband somewhat perfunctorily, perhaps keenly aware of the watching eyes of those gathered there, and then her son more tightly.

Eventually, the men started their horses forward as the assembled crowd shouted the familiar war cry of the Tamils, 'Veera Vel! Vetri Vel!'

The road was lined with men, women and children, who showered flowers on the king and his men as they filed out of the city.

General Ilanthiraiyanar threw a glance back at his army. He was riding up front with his king, Mamalla, and Manavamma, the claimant to the Lankan throne. Ilanthiraiyanar thought that Mamalla's hulking form resembled a bull, perhaps even Nandi. The king had disdained riding in a chariot and had accompanied them on his horse. Behind the trio was young Mahendra, Mamalla's son, wide-eyed and looking a bit nervous, by Ilanthiraiyanar's reckoning. After all, he was setting off on his first military campaign.

There was a jauntiness in the steps of the soldiers as they marched towards Manimangala behind their king and their general. They marched for their king but also for themselves. They marched for their pride—a pride that had been battered over twenty years ago when Pulikeshi had laid waste to Kanchi. Sinhala and Tamil soldiers marched together, singing songs, laughing and joking on their way to cover the twenty miles or so to Manimangala.

General Ilanthiraiyanar had decided that they would cover the distance in two days. Ten miles a day was a very relaxed pace for army men and Ilanthiraiyanar had chosen to preserve his soldiers' energies. The messenger from Muthuvel and Elango had informed him that it would take at least four more days for Pulikeshi's army to reach Manimangala. That would leave enough time for his men to be well entrenched and waiting for the Chalukyas.

And then we will have our revenge, he thought. *Revenge for Pullalur, in part.*

The travel to Manimangala was incident-free. Travelling through one's own kingdom rarely brings any danger. Mamalla and Manavamma had renewed and revived their friendship during the ride. They spent a lot of time talking to each other about the political situations in their respective lands. General Ilanthiraiyanar had given them space by dropping back and riding next to the young prince Mahendra.

The young man had shrunk back nervously at the beginning. This was, after all, his commander. He had always been treated by him as a junior member of the staff, a very junior member at that. Yet, out here, on this campaign, something seemed to have changed. Ilanthiraiyanar had conversed easily with him, as if talking to an equal. Mahendra didn't know the reason, of course, but as far as Ilanthiraiyanar was concerned, the young lad had graduated from being a common soldier back to being the crown prince.

The intervening distance to Manimangala was covered swiftly, requiring only a night's halt midway through their journey. They started off early the next morning and were in Manimangala by the afternoon of the same day.

The town had already been evacuated by an advance party of soldiers. All the jewellers had been asked to close their workshops, take their belongings and move away, under armed escort towards Kanchi.

General Ilanthiraiyanar took charge once they reached there, directing the setting up of the camps. The camps were set up roughly a mile back from the designated battlefield, a large open area that spread out in front of them.

Mamalla, Ilanthiraiyanar and Manavamma, with Mahendra tagging along behind them, rode out to the edge of the open area. The king sat straight on his horse, his eyes hooded, gazing out into the distance. The others spread out around him, giving him some space. Eventually, Mamalla broke the silence and glanced at his general. 'Pullalur was a similar-looking place, wasn't it?' he asked softly.

'Yes, Sire,' said Ilanthiraiyanar. 'There is one difference though …'

'Oh? And that is?'

'We are prepared this time around. Well, better prepared,' said Ilanthiraiyanar with a smile.

'And you have allies with you, my friend,' Manavamma chimed in.

Mamalla gave him a smile in return and turned to look back at the field. Then, after a brief pause, he said, 'I sure do hope that your yavana plan works.'

It was around dinnertime that same evening that a fresh batch of forces joined the army camp. Elango and Muthuvel had led their men back towards Manimangala once they realised that the Chalukyas were moving towards the same destination. Commander Dasappa rode with them, hoping to be of some help to the Pallavas.

The bulk of the group settled down towards the back of the camp, but Elango and Muthuvel, accompanied by Sadaiyan, Jamba, Dasappa and a few others, walked over to where the king and the generals were camped.

The guard outside General Ilanthiraiyanar's tent spotted the newcomers and informed the general, who came out and welcomed his men.

'Good to see you again, boys. Hope things went well?'

'No problems, Sir. We slowed them down as usual, but seeing that they started moving towards this place, we cut out,' Elango said.

Hearing their voices, Mamalla and Manavamma stepped out of the Pallava king's tent. Manavamma's face lit up as his eyes fell on Muthuvel.

'Aah, my friend. So good to see you again. You and Chaminda along with this young lad here,' he said, pointing to Sadaiyan, 'had quite a journey back to Korkai, I gather.'

Muthuvel bowed to the Lankan king and said, 'Couldn't have done it without Chaminda's help, Your Majesty.'

Manavamma turned towards Mamalla and introduced him to Muthuvel and Sadaiyan.

'I have already met them,' said Mamalla. 'This young man,' he said, pointing to Sadaiyan, 'seemed to feel that a life in the palace would be nice.'

Sadaiyan grinned back at the king and eventually bowed at a nudge from Muthuvel.

'Let me introduce you to Commander Dasappa of Parivipura. He and this young man, Elango, managed to escape from the fort. Elango is the one who went all the way to Ujjain to meet King Harsha,' said General Ilanthiraiyanar.

Mamalla stepped forward and enveloped first Muthuvel and then Elango in a bear hug. 'Thank you, men, for all that you have done for our kingdom.' Elango and Muthuvel gave embarrassed nods as they stepped back from the king's embrace. He then bowed to Commander Dasappa and said, 'Thank you for being here, Commander. Rest assured that we will get you your fort back.'

Dasappa bowed to him. 'Thank you, Your Majesty. How is my king?'

Mamalla put a bland expression on his face and said, 'He is well. We decided that it would be better for him to remain at Kanchi than come on this campaign.'

Dasappa, looking a trifle embarrassed, nodded his understanding.

Mamalla's eyes fell upon Jamba. 'And who is this man?' he asked.

'He is Jamba, Your Majesty,' said Elango. 'We couldn't have managed to reach Ujjain without his help, especially through the Dandakaranyaka forest. He belongs to one of the forest tribes.'

Mamalla inclined his head towards Jamba with a nod. Jamba did likewise. He wasn't going to bow to any king, but he did manage a respectful-looking nod.

Mamalla then looked up at Ilanthiraiyanar and said, 'Well? Shall we go through our plans again?'

The general nodded and asked Muthuvel and Elango to step into the king's tent. Sadaiyan was eager to go in but a vehement shake of the head from Muthuvel left him outside, sporting a scowl. Jamba grabbed his arm firmly as he led him back the way they had come.

In the tent, the general opened up a large silk map in front of him and started going through the details of the plan with the others as they crowded around the low table, the lights from the torches casting their glow upon them.

A day and a half after their arrival at Manimangala, their scouts came back with news that the Chalukyas had arrived. They brought with them more accurate information about the size of the army and the numbers of the individual elements—infantry, cavalry and elephant troops.

Mamalla, Manavamma, Ilanthiraiyanar, Mahendra, Dasappa, Elango and Muthuvel huddled in the king's tent going over their strategy.

'They outnumber us by a third,' said Manavamma.

'We knew that,' said Ilanthiraiyanar.

'You really think this strategy that we have gone over can help deal with that sort of a numerical superiority, that too on flat land?' asked Manavamma.

'It worked in precisely the same situation,' said the general.

'But you yourself said that it happened over nine hundred years ago,' said Manavamma.

'Things haven't changed all that much over the last few centuries,' said Ilanthiraiyanar.

Mamalla caught Elango and Muthuvel exchanging concerned glances with one another and smoothly intervened, 'Coming back to the issue at hand, our strategy relies on three core elements, a strong mid-section and flanks that can both withstand and counter-punch, right?'

'Yes, Sire,' said the general.

'How do we deploy them, then?' asked Mamalla.

'Sire, I would place myself on the left flank, with Manavamma and his men on the right,' said Ilanthiraiyanar.

'I will take up the centre then,' said Mamalla.

'No, Your Majesty. I would place you at the rear, with the reserve units.'

'You want me to sit out the most important battle of our lives?' asked Mamalla, with some heat.

'Sire,' answered Ilanthiraiyanar calmly, 'the front faces the brunt of the initial thrust. We are quite certain that that would consist of a mix of elephant troops and cavalry moving under heavy arrow bombardment. We can't have you right at the front. If a chance arrow were to come your way …'

'Yes?'

Ilanthiraiyanar kept quiet, unsure of how to complete that statement. Manavamma came to his aid.

'I think, my friend, what the good general is trying to tell you is that wars have been lost when the king has been incapacitated. Troops seem to lose heart when they see their leader wounded or dead on the battlefield.'

Ilanthiraiyanar threw a grateful glance in Manavamma's direction and continued, 'Sire, the Lankan king is right. You are our most precious asset. We have got to keep you safe, at least from the initial onslaught.'

'What about me, Sir?' Mahendra piped up. 'I wouldn't want to miss my first war by being at the rear, with the reserves.'

Ilanthiraiyanar gave him a long and speculative look before saying, 'I agree. You must make your name on the battlefield. You will need to be at the front. Elango, you will need to man the centre along with the prince here.'

Elango nodded. If the prospect of facing the initial charge gave him pause, he didn't let it show on his face.

'General Dasappa,' said Ilanthiraiyanar, looking at the Parivipura man. 'Will you do us the honour of leading the other half of the cavalry regiment at the centre?'

Dasappa bowed low. 'It will be my privilege, General,' he said.

'What about me, Sir?' asked Muthuvel. 'I should be out there with Elango, facing the first wave of attacks.'

The general shook his head. 'I want you at the back, with the reserves, along with His Majesty.'

'But Sir …' Muthuvel protested.

Ilanthiraiyanar held up his hand. 'I know everything you are going to say, young man, and the answer is still no.'

Muthuvel's face fell. Perhaps to assuage his feelings, Ilanthiraiyanar continued, 'This is not going to be a simple battle by any stretch of the imagination. They have the advantage in numbers. We will need to bring even our reserves to bear, for sure. It is only a matter of time. So, Muthuvel, it is not as if I am asking you to sit the battle out. I am asking you to aid and protect our king. When you folks in the rear are called into action, I know what our king will do.' He paused briefly and smiled affectionately at Mamalla, who raised an eyebrow in return.

'You know it, Sire. The bloodlust will be on you. And you will jump in recklessly, trying to singlehandedly decimate the opposition. Muthuvel has a cool head and can help in the situation.'

Then, his tone suddenly turned more sombre as he said, 'I think the rear is going to be hard-pressed, if His Majesty the Lankan king and I can't hold the flanks.'

'I have a lot of trust in both of you gentlemen,' said Mamalla.

'That may be so, Your Majesty, but sometimes the sheer weight of numbers can be difficult to hold. If we do start getting pressured on the flanks, we will fall back as discussed earlier,' said Ilanthiraiyanar.

The others nodded.

'Do you think the cavalry at the centre will follow the elephant troops? Or will they charge alongside them?' asked Elango.

Mamalla smiled. 'I will save the general the trouble of answering that question. They will charge alongside the elephant troops. Given their advantage in numbers, they would want to open as wide a front as possible, right, Ilan?' asked Mamalla, startling his general by slipping into the more familiar form of address.

'Yes, Sire.'

There was a lull in the conversation as every individual in the tent was sunk in his own thoughts about the battle. Eventually, Mamalla said, 'We know what we are facing. And we know what we need to do. No point worrying about what may or may not happen tomorrow. Veera Vel! Vetri Vel!'

'Veera Vel! Vetri Vel!' shouted the men around him.

That night saw two sets of troops moving silently through the land. One of the groups had travelled a long distance. The signs of their exhausting journey would have been visible on their faces if the moonlight had been brighter. Yet, they were soldiers and there was no slouching of backs or rounding of shoulders as they sat astride their horses. They moved forward at a sedate pace—not a full gallop, but at a trot. Their destination was more than thirty miles away. It meant at least another ten hours of travel not including the rest that their horses required. They knew that they would be reaching their destination only by the middle of the following day. The men in the lead were silent now. They didn't want to advertise their movement through the land. One never knew who would be watching.

The second group travelling that night was oblivious of the first. They, however, had only about ten miles or so to travel and were taking it even easier, leading their horses on a gentle walk. They planned to be at their destination by morning. The men appeared rather jaunty in comparison to the other group. Exhaustion didn't seem to have touched them. There was some banter among the men as well, although the sergeants periodically hushed them into silence.

The two groups rode on along their respective paths. Quietly. Doggedly.

26

Battle of Manimangala—The Hostilities Begin

Manimangala, December 641 CE

It is curious how the days that humankind considers important begin like any other day. Nature does not care one whit about what one of its many species does. The sun continues to rise in the east and go along its merry path across the skies. Birds leave their nests and forage for food. So do insects, reptiles, fish and mammals, completely unaffected by a fellow species getting ready for what it thinks is a momentous occasion.

The morning after the Chalukya army reached Manimangala dawned as usual. The sunrise was pretty, if not spectacular. The days were getting shorter as winter progressed. There was a haze across the field as the early morning fog took its time dissipating under the feeble rays of the sun. Eagles wheeled away high above the earth, rising on gusts of air till they were mere pinpoints in the morning sky.

Down below, on the earth, the species known as humans were becoming animated. They were running to and fro, putting on armour and other equipment, tending to their horses and elephants and giving their swords, spears and arrowheads a last, loving sharpening on wet granite stones. Much would depend on the sharpness of their equipment today.

Captains communicated their messages to their sergeants, who commanded their corporals who, in turn, shouted out their orders to that lowest form in the army hierarchy—the poor private. The bustle was uniform, regardless of whether it was the infantry, the cavalry, or the elephant troops. The cavalrymen fed gram to their horses while making conversation with them. Horsemen always talked to their horses, and not in the way that young parents cooed to their young ones, but as equals, detailing their day, and what could be expected from the enemy. The horses neighed softly as they fed and periodically bobbed their heads up and down. Caretakers brushed the animals simultaneously before saddling them.

The elephant troops were a study in contrast. The men who were to sit atop the elephants didn't really know their mounts well or even care to get to know them—that was the duty of the mahouts who brushed them down, fed them sugarcane and balls of jaggery, and spoke to them in gentle whispers while running their palms down their trunks. Every elephant had bells hanging around its neck which jingled and tolled with each movement of the animal's head. The mahouts spoke encouragingly to the animals as they put their iron armours over their heads and trunks and across their backs, hanging to both sides. It would take a very skilled archer to attack the few unprotected spots on the elephant's body, and given how tough their hides were, the mahouts were confident of their elephants being able to withstand any pinpricks from their opponents. Their eyes and the tips of their trunks were the vulnerable spots but there was nothing to be done about those.

This scene was the same whether one looked at the Chalukya camp or the Pallava one, as the armies got ready for what they realised would be one of the most decisive battles of their lives. However, what they didn't know was that this would be a seminal event in this land's history.

Pulikeshi took the help of a stool placed near his horse to get on its back. He would normally have disdained such help, but his advancing years had given him a healthy respect for the limitations of the human body, and he had stopped feeling guilty about using such privileges. He sat astride his horse, straight and proud. This man had conquered huge swathes of territories across the land, had defeated both his preeminent rivals, Harsha and Mahendravarman, and his empire was the largest in Bharatavarsha.

He made a dashing figure, his back straight, his shoulders thrown back, his armour glinting in the morning sun. The paunch brought on by age seemed to add rather than detract from this image.

Beside him, on their horses, sat Commander Satyaki, the king's younger brother Kubja Vishnuvardhana and Pulikeshi's sons Ranaragha and Jayasimha. The expressions on the faces of these men made for an interesting study. While the king, his younger brother and his commander all wore world-weary expressions, the faces of the young princes showed excitement, enthusiasm, eagerness and anticipation in equal measure. Their eyes sparkled. They could barely sit still on their mounts. They were fidgety and constantly played with the bridles in their hands or the swords hanging at their waists. Their eyes darted this way and that, taking in the scene. This was their first big battle, and they were chomping at the bit.

Pulikeshi glanced towards his sons and said, a smile playing on his lips, 'Well, boys. How are you feeling? Ready to take on the Pallavas?'

'Oh yes!' said Jayasimha, his face elated, his eyes shining brightly.

'Not scared, right?' asked Kubja, teasing his nephews.

'I just want my sword to taste lots of Pallava blood today,' said Ranaragha.

The others threw back their heads and roared in laughter.

'Easy there, my lad. There will be plenty of time for that,' said Commander Satyaki. Then, looking at his king, he continued, 'Shall we start deploying our forces, Sire? Or do we wait for the Pallavas to do so first?'

'We have the greater numbers. Let us deploy. We can always modify later depending on how the Pallavas react,' said Pulikeshi.

Satyaki nodded and then gave a series of commands to a few of his soldiers who acted as runners on the battlefield. They left immediately to pass on the messages.

The Chalukya army started moving towards their positions. The elephant troops were at the centre, with the cavalry placed alongside them on both sides. Infantry troops were placed directly behind the elephant and cavalry troops. Further back along the same line stood the archers with longbows. Some of the horses also carried archers who sat behind the cavalrymen. These archers were equipped with short-range bows. The centre was commanded by Commander Satyaki.

The left and right flanks of the Chalukya army consisted entirely of elite cavalry troops with Kubja Vishnuvardhana and his men on the right, while Ranaragha and Jayasimha commanded the troops on the left flank. Pulikeshi himself was at the rear, with the reserve troops.

As he watched, he saw the Pallava army starting to array itself on the battlefield.

General Ilanthiraiyanar had purposely delayed positioning his forces until the Chalukyas had completed their deployment. The king and he had been watching their manoeuvres intently and the general hissed a satisfied 'Yes' under his breath as he watched them deploy themselves in a traditional manner.

'According to plan, then?' asked Mamalla. They were sitting on their horses and watching the opposing forces. Manavamma, Elango and Muthuvel were the others present in their little group.

'According to plan,' said Ilanthiraiyanar, grinning boyishly.

He called his runners to him and passed on the message to the platoon leaders to deploy. The runners saluted and left. Elango looked at the others and then at his king and said, 'We shall meet again after our victory.'

'Veera Vel! Vetri Vel!' said Mamalla, and Elango turned his horse and rode out towards the centre, directing his troops into the precise location he wanted them. Manavamma and Ilanthiraiyanar turned simultaneously towards Mamalla and said, 'Well, I shall be taking off …'

'Allow me to leave, Your Majesty …'

'Go well, my friends. We shall meet again today, and hopefully, victory will be ours.'

They nodded and left, leaving a serious Mamalla and a still slightly disgruntled Muthuvel sitting there. The giant Jamba stood behind them, looking at the departing soldiers wistfully.

He would have loved to be at the front along with Elango, but he had had strict instructions from him to stay near the king and to protect him under any eventuality. So Jamba had stayed.

'Shall we move towards the rear, young man?' asked Mamalla.

Muthuvel sneaked an embarrassed look at his king, hoping he hadn't observed his petulance, and said, 'Yes, Sire. If what the general said is true, we won't have much time to rest. The battle will be upon us soon.'

Pulikeshi frowned. He thought that he had seen everything that there was to see on the battlefield during his long years of warfare. What he was seeing, though, mystified him. He called a runner to him and asked him to request Commander Satyaki to join him. In a short while, Satyaki trotted back on his horse from his position up front.

'You called, Your Majesty.'

Pulikeshi grunted and then pointed towards the Pallava deployment.

'Are you seeing that?'

'Yes, Sire.'

'Well?'

'It does look somewhat different. They seem to be staggered.'

'Huh,' said Pulikeshi as he and his general turned to look towards the Pallavas. Two things caught their attention. For one, except for the centre, which was standing right opposite their own centre, the rest of the Pallava troops were standing obliquely, pointing away from the centre and towards the flanks on both sides.

That, in itself, was something new. Add to that the fact that brigades were now standing in a staggered fashion with each brigade echeloned in such a way that the troops furthest from the centre were in front and each successive brigade was set back.

'I have never seen that before,' confessed Satyaki.

'Neither have I,' said Naganandi, coming up to them and standing beside their horses.

Pulikeshi looked down at him. 'I thought you had decided to stay back until required?'

'I couldn't stand the waiting,' said Naganandi.

'What do you think of that?' asked Commander Satyaki.

'That is certainly new …'

'But?'

'I don't know. You both are the experts on warfare. I just gather information!' snapped Naganandi, obviously irritated that he couldn't figure out the formation.

'It's alright. We will go around them anyway,' said Satyaki, and then, saluting his king, nudged his horse forward, towards the front lines.

A long trumpet sounded from the Pallava lines and was answered by a similar sound from the other side. Battle cries rose from both sets of troops.

'Veera Vel! Vetri Vel!' cried the Pallava soldiers.

'Jai Varaha!' cried the Chalukyas.

Drums started beating from the rear of both armies. The horses whinnied. Many of them stood on their hind legs as the tumult of the war got to them. The elephants started trumpeting, eager to shuffle forward. The mahouts held them in check, waiting for the order to unleash them. As usual, the start was indicated by a perfect storm of arrows that rose up into the air from both sides, the Pallavas a couple of seconds later than the Chalukyas. The arrows whistled into the heavens, looking like a swarm of locusts as they seemed to blot out the sky. Both the armies were well prepared for this eventuality—the second the arrows went up, so did the shields, as the soldiers protected themselves and their mounts.

The arrows showered down on the troops on both sides while the opponents continued to move towards each other. Elango was off to the right of the elephant troops, leading the cavalry. He chanced a look at Prince Mahendra who rode next to him, his eyes wide, his nostrils flaring, the heady mix of youth and his first battle experience bringing a flush to his face.

Young Venkata was seated behind Elango, already letting loose his arrows, his hands going back and forth between his quiver and the bowstring in a blur. Elango saw that the Chalukya elephant troops were more numerous than their own and spread out further. If he and his cavalry continued forward, they would be riding directly into the paths of the mountainous beasts.

'To the right!' he yelled above the tumult. 'To the right and around the elephants!'

His men followed him. Elango sneaked a peek over to the other side to see if Dasappa had done likewise or if he needed to send him word. He needn't have worried. The veteran soldier knew what he had to do and Elango could see the cavalry to his left wheeling away, trying to get out of the range of the elephants.

The charge of the elephants and the horses raised a dust cloud over the battlefield. It had been a particularly dry season and the ground was dry and cracked. The heavy footsteps of the elephants and the forceful pounding by the legs of the horses raised the dust from the ground, making it swirl amidst the men and animals. It caked the sweat-stained bodies of the soldiers and the horses. It got on their faces and into their eyes, their noses and their mouths, making Elango and the other soldiers squint and spit out the tasteless grit.

The two armies crashed with a tumultuous roar. Elephant crashed against elephant. The mahouts screamed at their mounts, trying to goad them into a frenzy. The elephants butted heads, their trunks curling around each other's. The soldiers sitting on top targeted one another with spears while trying to maintain their precarious balance even as the elephants stood up on their hind legs.

Elango and Mahendra led their men at a fast clip, in a race to get outside the line of the elephants' rush. The Chalukyas had spread out their elephants in a long line and it took an extra burst of speed from the horses to get them past the elephants. Some of the horses went down, shrieking in pain and fright as the elephants merely brushed them in their mad dash forward.

Elango had no time to think about what was going on behind him or in other parts of the battlefield. Their opponents were upon them, and his sword was out, slashing, parrying and thrusting. Venkata had slipped off the back of the horse as soon as they had gone past the elephants and Elango was now free to stand up in his stirrups. He held the reins with his teeth and slashed down on his opponents, his standing position giving him greater reach.

This was something that he had learned from an old veteran who had taught him the art of fighting on horseback. He parried an attack with his shield and then hacked down on the shoulder of the man who had attacked him. His sword bit into the man's shoulder and didn't stop until it came up against his rib cage, slicing cleanly through flesh, muscle and bone. Blood erupted from the gash as the man cried out in pain and toppled from his horse.

Elango chanced a quick look around to see how Prince Mahendra was doing. The prince was giving a good account of himself, but Elango noticed that he was in danger of getting isolated as he was getting pulled out of position.

Elango waited till Mahendra dispatched his man and then yelled, 'Mahendra! To me. To me.'

Mahendra quickly turned his horse and rode towards Elango. They were again in the thick of the action as men continued pouring towards them on horseback. The Chalukya infantrymen, meanwhile, had sneaked past the cavalry and were engaging the Pallava infantry. Steel rang on steel. Oaths clashed with oaths. Cries rose and died, cut short suddenly as steel found flesh. Dust enveloped the men, cocooning them in their own little worlds where none existed but their opponents.

Suddenly, Elango heard a cry from his right. Mahendra's horse had gone down as an errantly thrown spear found its side. The young prince had rolled off his horse smartly, but was now on foot, and engaging an infantryman armed with a spear. He was having a rough time of it, parrying desperately as his opponent lunged with the spear again and again. Elango tried to turn his horse to go to his help, but another man was immediately upon him.

He fought furiously, trying to get rid of his opponent so that he could go to the aid of his prince. He eventually ran his sword through the man and turned his horse towards Mahendra. The sight chilled him. Mahendra was being driven back bit by bit by the man with the spear. Unknown to him, there was a body lying on the ground behind him. Before Elango could shout out a warning, Mahendra tripped on the body and fell, his arms windmilling wildly as his body fought for balance.

Elango saw Mahendra's opponent raise his spear up to begin the fatal downward thrust but then the man stopped. The spear hung motionless above him and his hands started to drop. It was then that Elango noticed the spearhead protruding from the Chalukya soldier's back. He moved his horse around and saw the other end of the spear in Mahendra's left hand. The young prince had picked up the spear lying next to the dead man and had thrust upwards with it, catching his opponent through the middle just before he could bring down his own spear.

Mahendra rolled aside and let go of his hold on the spear. The stricken man fell, his weapon falling from his lifeless hands. His body hit the ground with a thud. Elango pointed to a riderless horse and Mahendra grabbed its reins and quickly got up on its back, and they turned together again to face the relentless attack from the Chalukyas.

27

The Battle Rages

Manimangala, December 641 CE

Kubja Vishnuvardhana, king of Vengi and younger brother of Emperor Pulikeshi, was in a quandary. He was leading the cavalry on the right flank of the Chalukya deployment. His brief had been to go around the Pallava left flank, but that seemed to be a more difficult task than he had initially surmised.

He had been confused by the Pallava deployment. He had expected their forces to line up against his in a straight line, and given his advantage in numbers, he had stretched out his own line, to really extend the opposition forces. The Pallavas, however, refused to take the bait, and had instead just pivoted about their central point—the point where their king and reserve forces were stationed—so that they were pointed at an angle towards his forces.

They had also echeloned their forces with each successive layer set back and to the right from the outermost force, forming a series of steps. Kubja had ignored this formation at first, and when the call for attack had been sounded, he and his forces had rushed at the opponents.

However, the echeloned formation of his opponents had broken their own straight line since his forces were now having to forcibly mirror the structure of their opponents to get at the recessed units. This had led to smaller individual units matching up against the Pallava echelons, negating their numerical advantage.

Kubja was frustrated. Battle raged all around him. Men clashed with each other, sweated, grunted, swore, spilt blood, and turned the earth red. Their horses raised dust clouds that hung grimly over their little piece of earth, clouding the battlefield. His men were being stymied as they tried to fight their way forward. Kubja was worried that if his unit thrust deeper, they could be outflanked by the Pallava unit to their right.

We will just have to do it the hard way, he decided. He gritted his teeth and charged ahead, on to the next man.

General Ilanthiraiyanar was leading the Pallava left flank, and had positioned himself at the outermost edge. It was a well-thought-out decision. The general had surmised, upon examining the Chalukya deployment, that they would try and go around him. He knew that his own forces would have to pivot to counter that, and he didn't trust anyone else to ensure that the pivoting was done successfully.

And successful it had been. The Chalukya units had tried to manoeuvre their way around, but the general had pivoted his forces as planned. He smiled as he saw the Chalukyas engage his men. *Good. Now that they have engaged, maybe I can take out their leader.*

He had noticed a man on the Chalukya side giving orders. While he had never met Kubja, he recognised him from descriptions that he had heard. He surmised that the Vengi king would be towards the centre of his forces. During a lull in the battle, that brief period where both sets of foes take an impromptu breather to get their bearings, he motioned to the young captain beside him.

'Sir?'

'Take a small group of men and go find where the Vengi king is fighting. Keep him occupied,' the general said crisply.

'Sir!' said the young man as he motioned to a few trusted comrades. They turned their horses and hurried towards the centre.

With a satisfied smile, Ilanthiraiyanar looked back at the men in his troop and said, 'Alright men. Let's break through this unit now, shall we?'

Saying this, he spurred his horse ahead. A loud chorus of 'Veera Vel! Vetri Vel!' sounded behind him as he spurred his horse towards his nearest opponent.

Prince Ranaragha's eyes shone as he led his men into battle––a moment that he had always dreamed of. He exulted in the rush as his horse galloped forward towards the Pallava forces. His younger brother Jayasimha rode next to him, just off his right shoulder. Ranaragha felt time slow as his horse galloped forward. He felt the wind ruffling his hair. He felt the sun beating down on his back and neck. He felt the drops of sweat making their way down his spine. He noticed the dust motes as they danced lazily around him in the sunlight. His heightened senses could make out every individual Pallava soldier, in their own charge towards them. His mind registered the motion of a soldier shifting in his saddle, trying to get more comfortable, then another soldier tightening his grip on his sword.

His mind identified and categorised the horses rushing towards them by their colours—white, black, brown, grey and mixed. He saw the sun glinting off the swords. He heard the trumpeting of individual elephants and the thumps of their feet on the ground. He felt the design on the handle of the sword that he gripped in his hand. He perceived his own breath and felt the rush of blood in his ears and his heart thumping away inside him.

As the opponents drew closer, he noticed their faces—contorted, twisted with emotion. Hairless faces. Hairy faces. With full beards. With trimmed beards. With short moustaches that ended at the lips and with those that curled across the cheeks. He noticed their armour, and in a small corner of his mind, it registered that these looked very different from the usual ones that the Pallavas wore.

And then, all of a sudden, they were upon him. Masses of men. Men who looked like Lankans. The two armies clashed against each other at speed. Horses went down, shrieking and neighing in that first engagement, throwing riders headlong into the dust. Many were trampled underfoot by horses of both sides.

The brothers fought together, side by side. They fought deftly, as befitted the sons of Immudi Pulikeshi—precise in their movements, working in tandem as they tried to make headway against the Lankan forces. They fought to break through to the back where the Pallava king was. They fought relentlessly, indefatigably, cajoling and encouraging their men in turns. Their arms started to fatigue, but still they fought.

So did Manavamma and his men. They had marched all the way from Lanka for this—to repay their debt to a king who had stood by them through thick and thin. These were battle-hardened troops who had fought at the Battle of Puttalam and then again at Korkai. Their dash across the land, from Korkai to Kanchi, and now to Manimangala, had left them in peak condition.

They also had the advantage of experience, and they brought it to bear against the Chalukya forces. Manavamma rode at the head of the cavalry, with Chaminda to his left. As the two armies clashed, Manavamma's horse buckled under him, and he was thrown over the horse's head. The Lankan king pulled his head in to his shoulder, tucked his feet up into his body and then rolled. Horses thundered past and over him but luckily, none stepped on him. Manavamma noticed an opening, rolled his body towards it, and then stood up in one swift motion, sword in hand.

Chaminda had seen his king go down and swerved his own horse towards him, evading horsemen trying to hack at him with their swords. He parried a couple and then went under the stroke of a horseman while driving his sword horizontally into the soldier's body. The rider was almost lifted off his horse by the force of the blow and tumbled off the rear end of the animal. The horse stalled, perhaps in confusion at the sudden loss of its rider. Chaminda seized its reins and rode swiftly towards his king.

Manavamma, in the meantime, stood with his sword out in front of him. A man was riding towards him, bent low over his horse, his spear extended in his arm. As the rider neared him, Manavamma stepped outside the line of the spear and, getting hold of it, pulled with all his might. The soldier at the other end of the spear ended in a heap at his feet. Manavamma's sword swished once and nearly decapitated the man. Blood gushed out of the wound and the man's feet jerked sporadically before becoming still.

Chaminda had reached Manavamma by then, and the Lankan king took the reins of the riderless horse from him, and leapt on top of the horse. He immediately noticed that the Chalukyas were trying to get around their flanks and gave Chaminda the order to pivot their regiments as planned. The manoeuvre that Ilanthiraiyanar had carried out on the left flank was now repeated by the Lankans.

Manavamma looked around once more and saw two men who looked like princes. He gestured in their direction to Chaminda and then, with him in tow, started fighting his way towards them.

Commander Satyaki rode atop the lead elephant. He had debated upon riding his own horse but had settled on the elephant. He knew that if they were to burst through the Pallava forces, the elephant forces would be the ones doing it. There was an added benefit in being seated on top of the elephant as well—it gave him a good vantage point to observe the battle all around and to give instructions where required.

He looked towards both his flanks and saw that they were already engaged. At the moment, it seemed like both flanks were stymied by the Pallavas, but it was only a matter of time before they could gain the upper hand. He could see that his forces were putting tremendous pressure on the Pallava flanks.

Satyaki turned back towards the centre and concentrated on what he had to achieve. He had taken up a bow even though he had a stack of spears next to him. He was a skilled archer and he focused on the mahouts of the opposing elephants. *Kill the mahouts! Win the battle!* he recalled one of his instructors telling him. And so, he concentrated on the mahouts.

Satyaki crawled out from behind the howdah that he and the other archers were using for shelter, and lay along the elephant's back, behind the mahout. He gestured for the other archers on his elephant to keep up the barrage of arrows. He waited and then rose in one swift motion, notched an arrow to his bowstring and let fly at the opposing mahout. The arrow embedded itself in his chest. The man's hands went up involuntarily, grasping the arrow, and then he toppled over slowly, fell off the elephant and landed on the ground.

The Pallava elephant took a sideways step and landed its foot on the fallen mahout's head, squashing it open. It reacted immediately by lifting both its forelegs up in the air. The archers on the elephant had nothing to hold on to, and tumbled off the elephant's back. The elephant trumpeted loudly as it felt the sudden lessening of weight.

Satyaki's mahout goaded his own elephant forward, nudging it behind the ears with his feet. The elephant charged at the mahout-less, confused Pallava animal. It tried to meet the charge of Satyaki's elephant but without a mahout, it stood no chance. It trumpeted loudly again and then fled from the scene. Satyaki's elephant moved forward even as he shouted instructions to the archers sitting on the elephants next to him to follow his lead.

There were three more ranks of elephants and Satyaki and his men moved forward methodically, relentlessly, targeting the mahouts and rendering the opposition elephants directionless. Once that happened, it was a simple matter of disposing of the opposition archers atop the riderless beasts. One other factor helped Satyaki and his men as they started to ram their way through the Pallava centre. The pivoting manoeuvres by both the Pallava right and left flanks had left gaps between the flanks and the centre and the Chalukya cavalry darted forward through them, attacking the Pallava centre.

In short order, Satyaki and his contingent barrelled through the Pallava elephant brigade, leaving only the Pallava cavalry between them and King Narasimhavarman Pallava.

'Let's go.' Muthuvel heard these words from Mamalla and looked up at him. The king was sitting astride his horse, a position that he had maintained since the beginning of hostilities. Muthuvel and Jamba were standing beside his horse.

Sadaiyan was also there, of course. Sadaiyan was never far away from Muthuvel. He had been given strict instructions to not enter the battlefield, but the young thief had still clothed himself in some ill-fitting armour, no doubt stolen from someone, and had shown up for the battle. He looked a little comical in his borrowed attire, but there was nothing comical about the sword belted at his waist, the knife held in his hand or the intense expression on his face.

Mamalla looked down at Muthuvel and repeated his comment, 'Let's go. They have broken through.'

He said it flatly, seemingly without emotion, but his clenched fists and straight back told a different story.

Muthuvel nodded and quickly jumped on to his horse. He looked enquiringly at Jamba, who shook his head.

'I prefer fighting on foot,' was his simple reply.

Muthuvel nodded in return and then, looking at Sadaiyan, said, 'You, thambi, will remain here. Do you hear me?'

Sadaiyan scowled at him and then his face creased into a beatific smile as he replied, 'Of course, anna. Whatever you say.'

Muthuvel looked suspiciously at the young lad's ready acquiescence but eventually shrugged his shoulders and turned back to face the front lines. He could see the Chalukya elephant brigade deep into the Pallava ranks. They would break through any moment now. Muthuvel looked at Mamalla, sitting tall and straight, and wondered what would be going through the king's mind. He didn't have a lot of time to ponder though. Mamalla interrupted his thoughts.

'Do not ride right at the elephants. Ride around them. I will take the right flank. You take the left. Lead our cavalry away from the elephants and then try and circle them from the back and attack them.'

Muthuvel raised a gentle protest. 'But, Your Majesty, the general insisted that I stay with you.'

'Young man, the general isn't here, and I am the king.'

Muthuvel looked away contritely in response.

'Don't worry, Muthuvel. I will be with the king,' said Jamba.

Muthuvel nodded and then, he and the king gave rapid instructions to the troops waiting behind them. With a final set of instructions and a 'Follow me!', the king and his captain rode into battle.

This isn't going well. This isn't going well at all, thought Ilanthiraiyanar, as he clashed swords with yet another opponent. He was starting to fatigue. A decade ago, he wouldn't have felt this way. He cursed age and the passage of time as he deflected a blow with his sword. Out of the corner of his eyes, he noticed a depression in the ground, and slowly, deftly, started manoeuvring his opponent towards it, backwards. His strokes became more vigorous and eventually, his opponent's horse backed into the depression, causing the soldier to grab his reins wildly as he fought for balance. General Ilanthiraiyanar, who had been waiting for just this moment, calmly ran him through. The soldier toppled from the horse, dead before he even hit the ground.

But it wasn't his own battle that the general was thinking about. As he looked around the battlefield, through the haze of the all-permeating dust cloud, he saw that the Chalukya elephant brigade had broken through. A quick glance backwards and he thought he saw someone who looked like his king riding into battle, but he couldn't be very certain because of all the dust. He turned back towards his own flank and saw how stretched his forces were. They had been able to successfully stop the Chalukyas from out-flanking them, but this had come at the cost of stretching their own front, leaving massive gaps in their deployment.

They had managed to stymie the Chalukyas till now. Ilanthiraiyanar had tried to make his way towards the Vengi king, Kubja, but had been unable to fight his way through. He was, however, satisfied that their line was still holding.

And then he heard a sudden roar from his left, mingled with the thudding of hoofbeats and accompanied by the war cries of men riding into battle. Ilanthiraiyanar looked around and all he could think was, *Who are these men and where did they come from?*

29

A Surprise Arrival

Manimangala, December 641 CE

Prince Aditya was in the lead. They had ridden through the night and had halted amidst a palm grove. It was Naganandi's idea to have a second attacking reserve that would be kept from view of the Pallavas. They had thus peeled off from the main army, under the cover of the night, and had ridden south and then east, waiting for an opportune moment to enter the battle.

They had played spectator to the early clashes. Aditya had seen his uncle, Kubja, try to get around the Pallava flank without much success. It was then that he had decided this was the opportune moment they had been waiting for.

Their assault on the Pallava left flank was ferocious. They came in at a thunderous run and crashed into the Pallava cavalry from their left and slightly to their rear. The cavalry stood no chance. They were already engaged with the army. This new threat didn't register until Aditya and his men were amidst them.

Vast numbers of Pallava men fell in that first assault. Riderless horses dashed hither and thither. Ilanthiraiyanar found his men getting crushed between the new Chalukya forces and Kubja's men, who now fought with renewed vigour.

The Pallava ranks started to waver, if not break. Ilanthiraiyanar had survived the first assault by the new Chalukya troops, but he realised that the only way to keep his men from getting slaughtered was to concentrate his forces. He blew a series of short, sharp signals on his conch. Immediately, his captains took up the signal. The Pallava cavalry started disengaging and falling back in an orderly fashion. They came together, eliminating the gaps, and formed a protective semi-circle around their centre. The semi-circle did not extend across the width of the battlefield but afforded both defensive capabilities and manoeuvrability to the men.

And then they fought. Ferociously. Man to man. They fought for their captains and their general. They fought for their king. But above all, they fought for themselves, for their own pride as fighting men.

Aditya's and Kubja's cavalries merged and formed one large unit that started crushing the Pallava semi-circle inwards. Ilanthiraiyanar's men were exhausted. Many died because their exhaustion caused their arms holding the shields to come up just that little bit late. Their sword arms were just that little bit wearier as they tried to bring them up to parry a thrust. They died as they battled a relentless stream of opponents. They killed one, then the next and the next but eventually fell against a fresher soldier. The dust clouds hung thick. Blood scoured the earth and made it damp. Every soldier still fighting had blood flowing from a hundred little nicks and cuts.

When one soldier fell, the others came together to close the gap. The semi-circle started shrinking and collapsing towards the already stressed centre. And still the Pallavas fought.

Thwack! Elango felt a whisper of wind as the arrow went past his right shoulder. He had just finished dispatching his opponent, the final flick of his wrist nearly slashing across the man's throat. What he hadn't accounted for was another soldier creeping stealthily towards him from his right. His arm had been raised for the fatal blow when the arrow whizzed past him and buried itself in the creeping soldier's throat. The man's sword fell from his hand as he grabbed feebly for the arrow. His hands didn't quite make it all the way up to reach the arrow and his fingers twitched before he toppled over and died.

Elango looked in the direction that the arrow had come from and saw a grinning Venkata waving to him. Elango smiled back and touched the hilt of his sword to his forehead in salute.

All around Elango was carnage. The bodies of soldiers, dead and dying, were strewn around. All the cavalry men under his command were now on foot. All their horses had been killed. Their elephant brigade had been decimated. It was not that the Chalukya forces had not suffered losses. It was just that they had more numbers and hence could bear the losses better.

Mahendra was still fighting beside Elango. The young prince had acquitted himself well. He had a wild gleam in his eyes which would, if Elango had known the way the king fought, have reminded him of Mamalla. He ducked and weaved among the Chalukya cavalry men, going down on his knees to both evade the Chalukya swordthrusts while shearing through the flesh, bones and tendons of the legs of the Chalukya horses. The horses went down shrieking, spilling their riders on the ground. Mahendra would then move grimly towards the fallen man and engage him in a one-on-one combat. He won every time.

Elango shouted at him, 'Mahendra! Fall back! It is too dangerous here!'

The young prince nodded and quickly retreated to stand next to Elango and his other colleagues. The once-cavalry men, now-infantry men, started retreating in an orderly fashion, making things difficult for their opponents.

Elango noticed that the elephants were going past them towards the rear and yelled at Venkata, 'The mahouts! Get their mahouts.'

The young man responded in typical fashion. Three arrows flew and three mahouts went down, leaving their elephants standing, shaking their heads, and sniffing their fallen masters with their trunks.

'Spears!' yelled out Elango, and several of the infantry men in the rows behind him now attacked the elephants and the archers on top. The elephants shrieked with rage and ran amok. The howdahs on top of the elephants shuddered and wobbled and the men in them tried to hold on, but ultimately tumbled off the elephants, some to be crushed by the elephants following them, others to rise, only to be cut down by Elango's men.

And yet, Elango and his men retreated. One step at a time.

Mamalla was exhilarated. *It is all very well being a king and building temples, but nothing, absolutely nothing can equal the thrill that comes from riding into battle*, he thought.

Even if he were riding into danger and almost imminent death. He could see that things were not going great for them. Their left flank was stressed. He had lost sight of the right flank and what it was up to. The centre had given away and was in retreat. *I hope that Ilan's yavana friend knew what he was talking about when he educated him about that age-old battle*, he thought.

Then, Mamalla pushed these thoughts out of his mind. He was riding into battle. It had been a while since he had done so. Once in the thick of things, there was no time to worry about strategy. Strategy occupied one's mind until one engaged an opponent on the battlefield. After that, one just hoped that all the parts of the army were carrying out the duties assigned to them and focusing on the job at hand.

And the job at hand is daunting enough. The Chalukya cavalry and infantry seem to be pouring through the centre. There is only one way to stem that tide, thought Mamalla, as he gave his horse a sharp kick with his heels and urged it forward.

Muthuvel, who was riding just behind him, was surprised by the sudden turn of speed and goaded his horse after him. He was surprised to see the long-striding Jamba nearly keep pace with them as the Banakula ran, his long legs eating up the ground almost as fast as the horses.

Mamalla swung around wide, evading the onrushing elephants as he crashed his horse through the middle of the Chalukya cavalry to the right, clearing a path for himself through sheer momentum. Jamba followed suit, as did several other cavalry men, following in the wake of their king. Muthuvel mirrored his king, going around the elephants on the left flank and eventually running into the Chalukya cavalry. The twin Pallava charges cleaved through the Chalukya cavalry at the centre like a hot knife through butter. Mamalla was at the forefront, his heavy sword leaving a trail of devastation in its wake. Muthuvel was close behind, keeping the opposition off his king's back.

Elsewhere, Jamba was leaving his own trail of destruction, a short sickle in one hand and his own special long spear in the other. Cut. Slice. Thrust. Impale. Slash. Duck. Weave. Thrust. Slice. Cut. There was something very methodical about it.

'Forward!' yelled Pulikeshi as he rumbled forward at the head of his men. He had hoped to not have to commit his reserves, but it seemed to him like the centre needed bolstering. He had glanced at Naganandi to see what his spymaster thought of it and had got a quick nod from him. It was time to commit the reserves.

Pulikeshi's men, almost all of the infantry, heard their king's command and ran on ahead of him, into the middle of the fight. Their men, who had been flailing under the onslaught by Mamalla and his reserves suddenly revived as they saw their own numbers being boosted.

Pulikeshi rode into the fight, his sword swinging from side to side. His strokes were heavy, backed by powerful shoulders and arms, and men fell underneath it. The wiry Naganandi went ahead of his king. He had followed him for a long time, through all those seemingly interminable battles of their youth. And he wasn't going to let his king go into battle alone now. Naganandi's preferred weapon of choice was the spear and he preferred fighting on the ground. He swirled and twirled the spear around him with a deftness that belied his age. He cleared a path for Pulikeshi through the fighting until they emerged into a little lull amidst the carnage.

Naganandi was the one who noticed him and pointed him out to Pulikeshi. The king looked in the direction pointed to by his spy chief and saw the hulking presence of his opponent. Some indefinable sixth sense must have alerted Mamalla of the attention because he glanced towards Pulikeshi almost at the same time. The two lions glared at one another, and then, as if drawn by an invisible string, turned their horses towards each other.

It was then that Pulikeshi heard a voice yelling, 'My King! My King! *Thanthe*[16]!'

They rounded the trees at a trot and stopped momentarily. Their chief looked at the scene and quickly assessed what was happening. He was good at that. After all, he was the commander of all the Pallava forces.

Kannan, Murugan and Bhatta waited with Raja Duraisingham and his generals as Commander Paranjothi observed the battlefield. They had ridden hard the last five days and covered the distance of about a hundred and seventy miles, the last twenty or so of which they had done early this morning. Paranjyothi had been kept regularly informed about the Chalukya troop movement as well as the final choice of battlefield.

He and the rest of the men had started for Kanchi the very next day after the battle of Suramara and here they were. He knew the men were tired from all the riding. He also knew that that wouldn't stop his men from going into battle.

16 Father

He gazed at the battlefield and noticed the collapsed left flank and the melee at the centre. He couldn't see exactly what was happening at the centre because of the cloud of dust that hovered like a cloudbank across the whole battlefield. The right flank was almost hidden from his view, and he decided that the only option open to him was to beat back the Chalukyas on the Pallavan left flank.

He looked at his men and gave a crisp command. His men perked up, and then, with the familiar war cry of 'Veera Vel! Vetri Vel', charged at the enemy.

29
The Rout

Manimangala, December 641 CE

Kubja's men didn't know what hit them as an immense number of horsemen suddenly appeared to their right. They were fully engaged and committed to the fight with the Pallavan left flank and they disintegrated under the sudden onslaught from behind. Hundreds of Chalukya men fell in that first rush by Paranjyothi and his forces.

Ilanthiraiyanar's men, who had been struggling desperately to hold the line, suddenly realised that help was at hand. Their spirits revived as they saw their opponents falter. They fought with renewed vigour, crushing Kubja's men in the pincer. It was a rout. Kubja understood that it was a rout. He had been so close to finishing off the Pallava flank and linking up with Pulikeshi's forces at the centre and then this new army had suddenly poured in on them. He briefly contemplated fighting to the bitter end but thought better of it. It wasn't going to help anyone, especially not his brother. They might at least live to fight another day. He gave the order to his men to retreat, though by then, there weren't many of them left to hear it.

Over on the Pallava right flank, Manavamma had advanced steadily towards the young princes. It hadn't been easy. He had had to fight every step of the way, killing opponent after opponent as he edged his horse ever closer to the spot where the two princes were fighting.

Ranaragha saw him. He didn't quite know who he was, but going by his features, he surmised that this must be the Lankan king siding with the Pallavas. He saw the Lankan man point his sword at him. For some reason, that inflamed him. He spurred his horse forward towards the Lankan.

Their horses danced around as their swords clashed. Manavamma was the better swordsman, a veteran of many battles. The young man in front of him was eager and enthusiastic. He was also skilled, but the skill did not have the advantage of years to be tempered by caution. The first few minutes were spent testing each other out. Manavamma had a derisive smile on his face and that seemed to goad Ranaragha's fury. His strokes became heavier and harder, but also wilder. When fighting an experienced opponent, control is perhaps even more important than vigour. In the heat of the battle, Ranaragha forgot that. A slight overextension of the arm. A minuscule imbalance and Manavamma's sword unerringly found its mark. Ranaragha had turned to deliver a blow and his torso had turned. Hence, Manavamma's strike went in low and to the right of Ranaragha's abdomen.

He gave a cry and clutched his side. Jayasimha, who had noticed his brother moving away from him to fight his opponent, heard the cry. He quickly disengaged from his opponent and raised a cry, 'To Prince Ranaragha! Protect the prince!'

His men heeded the yell and rushed towards their prince along with Jayasimha. Manavamma sat on his horse, watching Ranaragha's hands desperately clutching his sides, trying to stem the copious flow of blood. The prince had sagged on his horse, clutching the reins weakly. Before he could raise his sword to finish the young Chalukya prince, Jayasimha and the other Chalukya soldiers were upon him. Manavamma prudently stepped back as the soldiers formed a cordon around their wounded prince and then slowly backed away, leading him towards the rear. Manavamma knew that this was the chance that they had been waiting for and raised his sword high into the air and screamed, 'Their prince is dead! Forward, men! Forward!'

He flung a quick look back at his men and found what he had expected to find—a berserk unit behind him. The intensity and ferociousness of their attack pushed back the Chalukya soldiers, who were already broken-spirited on seeing their princes retreat.

The Chalukya flank blinked, then faltered and ultimately retreated in disarray. The loss of their young prince demoralised them, and they broke contact with their opponents, retreating haphazardly. Manavamma's men burst through the flank, pursuing their opponents but soon, at Manavamma's signal, they broke off the pursuit and swung around towards the left, in an envelopment that was almost a millennium old—the envelopment that the yavana soldier had told General Ilanthiraiyanar about. The envelopment that would soon take Manavamma behind the Chalukya centre.

Pulikeshi's head whipped around as he heard the panicked 'thanthe'. He saw Jayasimha coming towards him at a full gallop and then suddenly to a halt, the horse whinnying and raising itself on its hind legs, forelegs pawing the air.

'What is it? Where is Ranaragha?' asked Pulikeshi.

'Thanthe. Ranaragha … Ranaragha …' spluttered Jayasimha.

'Is he dead?' asked Pulikeshi, in his usual blunt fashion.

'I don't know,' said Jayasimha miserably. Then, spying Mamalla trying to manoeuvre his horse towards them, he blurted out in a hurry, 'The Pallavas have broken through. Ranaragha is hurt. He went up against the Lankan king and …'

Pulikeshi nodded. Just then, he saw a horse approach them from the right flank. It was his brother Kubja. He was sweating profusely, his body covered in blood, some of it dried. Dust, sweat and blood mingled to cake his body. He was breathing strenuously as he came up to them, his horse pulling a similar stunt to that done by Jayasimha's horse.

'We are doomed,' said Kubja.

Pulikeshi looked at his younger brother. His brother was a very practical man, not given to exaggeration.

'The right flank?' he asked.

'Gone. Fresh troops showed up, I don't know from where. Almost wiped out our men.'

'Aditya?' asked the king, his voice level.

'He is safe,' said Kubja and Pulikeshi let out an audible sigh of relief. 'I have asked him to take the remaining soldiers and retreat. However little the number of men remaining,' he muttered under his breath.

Pulikeshi thought fast. With both flanks collapsing, they were in real danger of being encircled. He glanced back once again at Mamalla. *So near*, he thought. *So near and yet, and yet, should I retreat now? Won't the minstrels have a field day singing about how the great Immudi Pulikeshi left the battlefield? Turned tail and fled? Showed his back to the enemy? Should I not have it out with Mamalla here and now?*

'Anna!' Kubja's insistent voice intruded on his thoughts. 'We need to go. Now!'

Pulikeshi looked once more at Mamalla and then, took out his conch and sounded the alarm to retreat. He would live to fight another day.

Jamba had kept close to Mamalla, to his left, ensuring that no one could surprise the king from that direction. As the Chalukyan right flank had retreated under the onslaught of the fresh troops that had arrived, they had collapsed towards the centre. Some of the Chalukya troops had spied the Pallava king and had decided to take a chance and get at him.

It was at that moment that Mamalla and Pulikeshi had started to move towards each other. Jamba noticed that Mamalla's attention was now focused on something up ahead. Sensing the looming danger, he had leaped into the group of men who were now starting towards Mamalla.

His sickle scythed through the air as Jamba danced amidst the men, leaving carnage in his wake. Limbs and heads rolled under the severity of his attack. He whirled and darted through the enemy ranks. Sometimes jumping up into the air to evade strikes against him. Sometimes sliding on his knees and slashing at the feet of his enemy. The enemy soldiers had never seen anyone fight like this and they simply did not have a response to his virtuosity.

Jamba chanced a quick look back to check on the Pallava king. He noticed that Pulikeshi was turning back and seemed to be in retreat. He exulted, and turned back to finish the man he was fighting. It was then that he felt a sharp pain in his abdomen. He looked down at the rear end of a spear. Puzzled, he dropped his sickle and held it with both his hands. His legs felt weak under him and buckled. He looked up and saw the man who had flung it at him from a distance. The man still stood there, unwilling to approach the stricken Jamba.

Jamba leant forward to maintain his balance. The end of the spear now rested on the ground against the body of a fallen foe, and as he rocked forward, the spear was pushed deeper into him. Jamba died on his feet, impaled on the spear. All around him were the bodies of the men who had died at his hands.

General Satyaki heard the signal to retreat—three long blows on the conch. He recognised the sound of his king's conch. It meant that they had lost. He processed all this in one corner of his mind. And then pushed it aside.

He was in the thick of battle—a battle that every warrior relishes, one against an opponent of equal stature. He had been thrown from the elephant a short while after they had broken through the central Pallava ranks. An arrow had unerringly found his mahout and others had stuck his elephant, which had reared up and upended all of the men perched on its back. He had been fortunate to not get trampled upon by the beast. He had rolled as soon as his feet had hit the ground and come up fighting.

The cavalry was all gone now. The horses lay dead and the cavalry men were now on foot. He preferred it this way. He liked fighting on foot. It was the way of the warrior, according to him. Mother Earth, firm under his feet, and an opponent in front of him. He had killed many today, and inflicted grievous wounds on many others.

And now he faced an opponent worthy of his mettle. He recognised the man. This was the commander of Parivipura. The man who had surrendered to them. He smiled at that recollection and the smile brought a scowl on the face of his opponent.

'You are a bit far from your fort,' he remarked, driving home the barb.

'It is easy to take a fort when you pay traitors to let you in,' retorted Dasappa. 'I didn't see any success from your troops in scaling our walls. Quite a few of your men died trying that, didn't they?'

'Prathapa should have killed you back there,' said Satyaki.

'Why don't you try now?' asked Dasappa and then jumped at him, his shield up, his sword arm raining blows. Satyaki was pushed back initially by the ferocity of the attack but eventually swivelled out of line and waited for his opponent. They circled each other warily, lunging first one way and then the other, waiting for an opening, however slight. They both struck at the same time, their respective shields blocking the blows. Dasappa took this opportunity to use his body and momentum to push Satyaki, who scrambled backwards. He somehow managed to hold his balance but that slight delay gave Dasappa a minuscule edge. A lesser opponent would not have been able to do much with that minuscule edge, but Dasappa was very far from being a lesser opponent.

He followed up his advantage by swinging fast and hard, a series of rapid blows that barely gave Satyaki enough time to ward them off. And then Satyaki stumbled. His heel hit the body of a dead soldier on the ground and he started to go over. His arms spread out, desperately trying to regain balance and that was all the opening Dasappa needed. He bent his left knee, lengthened his step, and thrust hard and low. His sword made a slurping sound as it went cleanly through Satyaki's abdomen. Satyaki gasped in pain and grasped the sword with both hands. Dasappa let it go, not wanting to yank out the Chalukya commander's insides with it.

Satyaki fell backwards, his head, shoulders and back resting on the ground while his hips and legs lay over the fallen soldier. As he looked up, he saw Dasappa's face come into view. Dust continued to swirl around them. He had some difficulty focusing on his opponent's face, which grew progressively indistinct. Satyaki felt like he was falling, and then he expelled a last breath of air into the universe.

All around him lay the dead and dying from both armies. Horses lay dead with spears sticking out of their sides. Men lay dying, some with their limbs chopped off, their stumps gushing blood, others with arrows embedded in them. The injured screamed. The dying whimpered. The dead lay silent.

Eventually, silence triumphed over the screams and whimpers.

30
The Aftermath

Manimangala, December 641 CE

They had been searching for him for a while. In the immediate aftermath of the battle and the sudden flush of having routed a seemingly implacable foe, there had been much jubilation. Elango had turned towards Muthuvel and asked him where he was. Muthuvel had seemed surprised by the question and had turned around quickly to ask the others around him.

Sadaiyan, who had gone into battle, despite admonishments from Muthuvel not to do so, had told them that he had been behind the missing man and had seen him cut a swathe through the enemy ranks.

'Where did you see him last?' asked Elango.

Sadaiyan pointed to a spot on the battlefield and then started running towards it. Elango and Muthuvel followed, picking their way more carefully through the bodies. They found Sadaiyan on his knees, sobbing. Elango saw Jamba, dead, leaning against the spear that had impaled him, surrounded by nearly fifteen bodies of enemy soldiers.

Elango eased Jamba's body to the ground and broke the spear in half. He pulled out the spearhead from Jamba's back, laid Jamba's head on to his lap and gently stroked his forehead with his fingers, again and again. Muthuvel had also bent down next to Sadaiyan and put his arm around the inconsolable young lad. They sat there for a long time, the three of them, honouring their friend and comrade.

The grim task of cremating the dead was being attended to. The army had brought in a lot of men from the surrounding villages. Trees were being cut and bodies piled on top of them. Mass cremations were the order of the day, except for one. Elango had seen to it that Jamba was given a separate pyre. He was unaware of the traditions of the forest dwellers and hoped that this would enable Jamba to attain the feet of Bhagwan Rama.

Muthuvel, Sadaiyan and he were joined by General Ilanthiraiyanar to pay their last respects to the fallen man. Elango walked around the pyre three times before tipping the pot containing the embers on to it. As the pyre lit up and started consuming Jamba's mortal remains, the men bowed to it, their hands folded in respect.

They walked back towards the camp slowly. Elango turned back and cast a last, lingering look at the pyre. He knew that he would need to tell Sanghamitra about how their friend and her guardian had passed away.

There was a reunion in the camp between Elango, Muthuvel and Kannan. The joy of meeting each other after a long interval of time was tinged with the sorrow of having lost many of their comrades. Murugan and Bhatta came up to Elango and

Muthuvel, first saluting their superior officers and then hugging them.

'Muthu,' yelled out a voice and they all turned to see Chaminda making his way towards them, a tired grin on his face. Muthuvel ran to him and hugged him, as did Sadaiyan. Introductions were made. It was Murugan who made the practical suggestion that since they were both celebrating their victory and grieving for the dead, it would be good to use the one specific thing that was capable of handling both these moods.

'I am disgusted by you,' said Bhatta. 'We have all lost men and all you can think of is drinking.'

Having said so, it was Bhatta who went and procured flagons of wine with which they started to simultaneously celebrate their victory and drown their sorrows.

'You think they will write songs about us?' asked Murugan, his face contorted in mock concentration.

'About you? Whatever for? You didn't do anything in this battle. Except be a burden on that poor beast that carried your fat self all over the place,' said Bhatta.

'You are just envious of my fine physique,' said Murugan contentedly.

Kannan looked from the bickering duo to Elango and Muthuvel and rolled his eyes at them. The others smiled indulgently.

They drank well into the night. They drank for a victory that would leave its mark in history. They drank to their king's well-being. They drank for future victories. But mostly, they drank to drown their sorrows at having lost comrades and friends. They knew that it could have been any one of them in battle that day. They were just lucky. And so, they drank to their luck.

It was after dinner that Mamalla gathered his advisors around him. This was a smaller group and consisted only of Commander Paranjyothi, General Ilanthiraiyanar, King Manavamma, Raja Duraisingham of Thagadur and Commander Dasappa of Parivipura. All of them were swathed in bandages, which covered the various cuts that they had received during the course of the battle. None of their injuries were serious—they would eventually heal and perhaps leave scars that would testify to their valour in battle.

Ilanthiraiyanar had wanted to include the three young men who had been so instrumental in the campaign, but Mamalla had asked him not to. He had heard about Jamba falling in battle and had remarked, 'Let them mourn their friend.'

So the six of them sat in the king's tent, nursing cups of wine. Conversation was at a standstill with each man sunk in his own thoughts. Raja Duraisingham broke through the quiet, 'Do you think we should have pursued them and finished it once and for all?'

The others looked thoughtfully into their cups before Paranjyothi responded, 'I don't think so, Your Highness. Our soldiers were all in and with the rush of victory, it would have been difficult to motivate them to ride out again after Pulikeshi and his men. It was a tough battle.'

'Tough,' agreed Ilanthiraiyanar.

'Very,' said Manavamma. 'Although, I did get one of their princes.'

'Killed?' asked Paranjyothi.

'He was wounded pretty badly. My sword found his belly,' said Manavamma coarsely.

'So what are your plans then, Paran?' asked Mamalla, looking at his commander. The others waited, deferring to the Pallava army chief.

'We must follow them, of course,' said Paranjyothi, after a brief pause.

'All the way?' asked Mamalla.

'Of course, Sire,' said Paranjyothi.

'It is a long way to Vathapi,' said Ilanthiraiyanar.

'That it is. But isn't that what this whole thing has been leading up to? The ultimate revenge? Capture Vathapi and finally fulfil the pledge that the king made to his father?'

'Shouldn't we get started then? And catch the Chalukya army as they retreat? Decimate them before they can get to Vathapi and fort up?' asked Manavamma.

'There are three military reasons not to do that,' said Paranjyothi.

'And one non-military reason,' said Mamalla.

Manavamma turned towards the Pallava king and asked, 'What is the non-military reason?'

'I will not pursue and kill an enemy who has fled the battlefield. That wouldn't be dharmic,' said Mamalla.

'It is non-military and non-practical, perhaps?' asked Manavamma.

'Perhaps,' said Mamalla with a nod of acknowledgement. 'But that is how I feel about it.'

Silence reigned in the tent amidst an underpinning of tension. Dasappa was the one who broke it by asking, 'What are the military reasons for not pursuing them?'

Ilanthiraiyanar looked relieved at the lessening of tension in the tent and took up where Paranjyothi had left off.

'Firstly, we are in no condition to go after them immediately. Today was a tough battle. We won, yes, but we barely won. If it hadn't been for Commander Paranjyothi and his men showing up when they did, we might well have not made it through the day,' said Ilanthiraiyanar.

Dasappa looked across at Paranjyothi. 'How did you know to come here on this very day, Commander? Was it happenstance?'

Paranjyothi gave a wry smile. 'My friend. General Ilanthiraiyanar isn't the sort to leave things to happenstance.'

'You mean …?' Dasappa trailed off, his question unasked.

'Yes. He had sent out a man riding in our direction to update us about the events. He met us a couple of days after you left Kanchi. Luckily both he and our troops had ridden hard and so met up when we were only a couple of days' ride from Kanchi. We hared it here after that. I only wanted to commit our forces once we could tilt the battle decisively in our favour.'

'You ran it close, didn't you?' asked Mamalla with a smile. 'For a brief while there, I was not very sure if we would be able to hold out. The Chalukyas fight well.'

'That they do, Sire,' said Ilanthiraiyanar. 'We knew that even twenty years ago, when they whipped us.'

'Coming back to what we need to do,' continued Mamalla, 'we were in the middle of the first of the three military reasons for not pursuing the beaten Chalukya army.'

'Aah yes. Well, today was a tough battle and we all have the wounds to show for it. So do the soldiers. We have several dead and a large number of wounded. We need to tend to them. I don't want us to rush into anything precipitate and make some silly blunders, now that we have the upper hand,' concluded Paranjyothi.

'What is the second reason?' asked Dasappa.

'Parivipura,' he said, looking at Commander Dasappa.

'You mean …'

'Yes. We can't go on to Vathapi and have an enemy fort to our rear. Even though Kubja would have left only a nominal force at the fort, we can't have them harassing our rear as we march up to Vathapi,' said Paranjyothi.

'So you are suggesting that we stop by Parivipura and retake it, before going on to Vathapi?' asked Mamalla.

'Yes, Sire.'

'Why not use a smaller force to do that while the main force marches on ahead to Vathapi?'

'We might not have enough men to take Vathapi then, Your Majesty,' said Ilanthiraiyanar. 'Although, Paran, the maharaja's suggestion does have some value. What if we could use a smaller force to take Parivipura? After all, with Commander Dasappa's knowledge of the fort, it should be easily manageable.'

'Thank you, Ilan. That brings me to the third reason for not pursuing the fleeing Chalukya army.'

'Which is?' asked Ilanthiraiyanar.

'We need more men.'

'Where are we going to get more men?' asked Manavamma.

Commander Paranjyothi and General Ilanthiraiyanar looked at one another, smiled, and then turned back to Manavamma.

'Let me tell you how,' said Paranjyothi.

King Jayanthavarman of the Pandyas was just finishing his dinner along with his queens when a guard entered and whispered something to the palace caretaker who was overseeing the dinner.

The caretaker walked up to the king and, bending down, whispered softly into his ears.

Jayanthavarman looked up, startled, and said, 'What does he want at this hour?'

'He didn't say, Your Majesty.'

'Call the guard,' said Jayanthavarman.

The guard bowed to the king and waited.

'What did he say?'

'He only said that he wanted to talk to you about something urgent. His exact words were, "Tell the king that the news I have is urgent and that it could be for his benefit."'

Jayanthavarman mused on this as he rinsed out his mouth into a basin and then wiped the water off his face and hands. Then, having come to a decision, he told the guard, 'Go to Prime Minister Maravarman and let him know that I desire his presence in the council chambers, immediately. Then go back and tell our visitor to come in.'

The guard bowed, saluted and left.

Jayanthavarman noticed the look of nervousness on the faces of his queens and said, 'Nothing to worry about, my dears. Go to the antahpuram. I shall conclude my meeting and come over.'

The king walked over to the council chambers, which had already been lit with a couple of torches stuck in the torch-holders on the walls. He heard hurried footsteps outside followed by a panting Maravarman rushing into the room.

'The guard said that you wanted to see me urgently,' he huffed.

'Did you almost run here, *mama*?' asked Jayanthavarman of the prime minister who was also his uncle.

'Almost,' said Maravarman, still trying to catch his breath. 'What is the urgency?'

'There is someone who wants to see us,' said Jayanthavarman.

'Who?'

Before the king could reply, they heard footsteps outside the door and saw General Thissa entering the chamber.

Maravarman's eyebrows shot up when he recognised the visitor.

'Your Majesty, Prime Minister,' said Thissa with a short bow.

Jayanthavarman wore a scowl as he looked at the man who had tormented him for nearly a month now.

'What do you want?' he asked, abruptly.

'May we all sit down?' asked Thissa, heading to the nearest chair.

Jayanthavarman nodded with ill grace and sat on his throne. Maravarman took a chair adjacent to the king.

'Well?' demanded Jayanthavarman once they had taken their seats.

'I have news for you, Sire,' began Thissa.

'From?' asked the king.

'His Majesty Narasimhavarman Pallava,' said Thissa.

Jayanthavarman and Maravarman exchanged glances and then Maravarman asked, 'What is the news?'

'The Pallavas have defeated Pulikeshi and his men in a battle at a place near Kanchi.'

'WHAT?' Jayanthavarman jumped out of his seat.

Thissa repeated his statement.

'Yes, Yes. I heard you the first time,' said Jayanthavarman testily. 'Is it true?'

'I wouldn't be here if it wasn't,' said Thissa.

'They were really defeated?' asked Maravarman, disbelievingly.

'It was a rout at the end. They are still fleeing back to Vathapi.'

The king and his prime minister were silent. Thissa let them think through the ramifications of the news that he had just brought them. It would make his job easier.

It was a while before Jayanthavarman stirred. He looked across at his uncle and then at Thissa. 'What do you want?'

'Why, Your Majesty. I didn't say that I needed anything. Yet,' said Thissa.

'Quit stalling, General. Let us hear what it is that you want. You didn't come here to just deliver the news.'

Thissa looked at the king steadily for a few seconds and then said, 'Your Majesty. You have been opposed to the Pallavas for a long time now. King Narasimhavarman hasn't forgotten how you aided the Chalukyas during the battle of Pullalur.'

He paused for effect and saw Jayanthavarman's face darkening.

'However,' he continued smoothly, 'the king is willing to overlook that and extends a hand of friendship to you. There is going to be a war. In Vathapi. King Narasimhavarman would like you to sit that out.'

'Or else?' asked Maravarman.

'I don't like making threats to such eminent personages as yourselves,' said Thissa. 'Let me just say that in the event that you do not take the proffered hand of friendship, the king will take it as a personal affront and *will* turn his attention towards Madurai once the Vathapi campaign is over.'

'And if we do accept this hand of friendship?' asked Jayanthavarman.

'Why, Your Majesty, I shall raise the siege immediately and leave.'

Maravarman and Jayanthavarman glanced at each other. Something passed between them, for, Jayanthavarman turned towards Thissa and said, 'Alright. You have my word that we will not come to the aid of the Chalukyas.'

'May I take that as your promise?' asked Thissa.

'Pandya kings are not known to go back on their word,' said Jayanthavarman curtly.

Thissa nodded as he got up from his seat, bowed to the king of Madurai and walked out.

31

The Retreat

Vathapi, December 641 CE

Pulikeshi sat slumped on his horse, his face grim. His eyes were etched with worry for his son, who was being carried on a stretcher alongside him. The remnants of the army stretched out behind them. There were the walking wounded, who could manage to get about on their own. And then there were those who had progressively deteriorated over the past few days of travel and who couldn't be left on the road. The more able of the men carried their comrades. The horses, fatigued themselves, seemed to sense the lassitude of their riders and plodded along, heads bent.

Naganandi rode alongside Pulikeshi, with Kubja, Aditya and Jayasimha following behind them. They all wore identical expressions—an intermingling of hurt, anger, sorrow and resignation from a comprehensive defeat. They didn't talk much. They couldn't talk much. They didn't have anything to say. Each person was sunk in his own thoughts.

Pulikeshi brooded on the defeat. He blamed himself. That was his nature. He didn't waste much time on recriminations thrown at others. He still did not understand how exactly they had lost. He knew that the other side had got a fresh infusion of reserves and that had tilted the scales. But then again, his left flank had been breached. *Could it be because of that staggered arrangement? Was that the reason that our flanks were unable to get around the Pallava flanks? Is this how it ends? A long reign with victories over one and all now ending in defeat at the hands of a smaller power, one that I had thrashed two decades ago?*

He looked at Naganandi riding beside him. His face was like a rock. *Naganandi never did show his emotions. Not even when we were struggling to stay alive all those years ago.* He turned back to glance at the others. His boys seemed distraught, their shoulders slumped, their bodies covered in bandages and showing the vestiges of the battle.

Pulikeshi then looked at the stretcher carrying his son Ranaragha. He was unconscious and his face was wan. The vaidyas had shaken their heads at Pulikeshi when they had first taken a look at the young prince, giving him slim chances of recovery. Pulikeshi's eyes flashed in anger at seeing his young offspring lying supine on the stretcher. *I wish it had been me,* he thought. *I wish that blasted sword had found me and spared my son.*

The group shuffled slowly forward. They still had a long way to cover to get home. *I hope the Pallavas are not following us,* thought Pulikeshi, as he slumped once more in his saddle with a resigned rounding of his shoulders.

Prime Minister Vedaraya walked from his office along the path leading up to the top of the ridge that housed the palaces. His knees hurt as he ascended the stairs. *Blast old age,* he thought.

I could run up these stairs a decade ago and now my knees hurt just thinking about going up to the palace. He persisted, however. The news he had received was too important for him to delay conveying it to the queens.

He finally reached the small plateau on top of the ridge and walked towards King Pulikeshi's palace. The guards made way for him as he walked through the outer gates and into the palace. The caretaker welcomed him with a bow and then darted inside to intimate the queens of his arrival.

Queens Mangalamma and Visalakshi joined him soon afterwards.

'What brings you here, Prime Minister? Is all well?' asked Mangalamma, noticing the worried look on Vedaraya's face.

Vedaraya bowed to the queens. As he stood up again, there was a look in his eyes that caused the younger queen, Visalakshi, to exclaim, 'Vedaraya avare. Are you alright? Is there some news from our Lord?'

Vedaraya schooled his features and said, 'I am afraid I have some bad news, my queens.'

The queens gasped.

'Is he …?' said Mangalamma.

'I hope …' said Visalakshi.

'He is fine. He is alright,' said Vedaraya, allaying their fears.

'What is it then? Are the boys alright?'

'All of them are alright, except …'

'Except?' asked Mangalamma.

'Ranaragha was injured in the battle.'

The queens gasped again, and their eyes glistened with tears.

'Is he going to be alright?' whispered Visalakshi.

'We don't know, Your Majesties. I was just sent word that we lost the battle near Kanchi.'

The two women sat down on the couches, wiping their tears with the edges of their sarees and hugging each other for comfort.

'What about our Lord?' asked Mangalamma through her tears.

'They are on their way back. They should be here in another three to four weeks. It is a long way from Kanchi.'

'Will they be safe? Are they being pursued?' asked Visalakshi.

'They are not being actively pursued, but …'

'But?'

'But we know that eventually, the Pallavas will come here.'

'Oh Varaha!' whispered Mangalamma. 'What will become of us?'

'Your Majesty, please don't panic. We have a strong fort, and it is not easy to break into. And our citizens will come together to defend this place. Our maharaja has successfully faced worse trials and tribulations in his life. We will come through this as well,' said Vedaraya.

The queens did not look too convinced, but Vedaraya had one more unpalatable bit of news to deliver. He cleared his throat to attract the attention of the women.

'Is there more?' asked Mangalamma.

'Yes, Your Highness. We have some more bad news. This time from your father's kingdom.'

'My father! Is he well?'

'Yes, he is well and so are the princes Vikrama and Chandra.'

'The princes! Weren't they with the maharaja?' asked Visalakshi.

'No, Your Highness. They had been sent with some troops to assist your father.'

'What happened?' asked Mangalamma.

'They fought a battle at a place called Suramara. They lost.'

Mangalamma started sniffling and Visalakshi put an arm around her to comfort her.

'Have they gone back to Talakkad?'

'That's what the messenger said. They don't have an army worth its name now. The remnants of the army are on their way back. They wouldn't be of any help to us, I'm afraid. The princes, however, were adamant about coming back here and are on their way.'

The queens continued to sniffle and wipe away their tears.

Vedaraya, a confirmed bachelor, stood around uncertain about what to do with two weeping women. He hastily took his leave and returned to his office, leaving behind two very worried queens.

'What do we do, akka?' asked Visalakshi of her elder queen.

'Let us seek the bhikshu's blessings,' said Mangalamma as she got up and made ready to leave.

Devadutta was about to fall asleep when he heard a knock at the door. He waited, hoping that his assistant would handle whoever it was at this time of the night, but then he heard the man walk towards his bedroom door and the soft knocks that followed.

He sighed and got up.

'Yes?' he asked, opening the door.

'They are here to see you,' said the man.

Devadutta nodded and followed the man out to the front of the house. He was surprised. He didn't let on that he was surprised, of course. He wasn't the type of person to do that. But he knew that for them to come here at this time of the night would mean something terribly urgent.

He found them seated on the cushions on the floor. He bowed to them and then took his seat opposite them.

'Something urgent?' he asked one of the men, coming straight to the point.

The man's face split into a smile. 'We won.'

'Where?'

'Manimangala. The prime minister informed the queens earlier in the evening. They came to seek the master's blessings and to know what the future held for them.'

'Aah. And what does the future hold for them?' asked Devadutta, with a wicked smile on his face.

The man shrugged. 'The master gave them the usual sop about it all working out for the best.'

'Any idea when the beaten army is expected back here?' asked Devadatta.

'From what the queens said, it might take another three to four weeks.'

Devadutta was quiet. His fingers tapped a beat on his thigh as he frowned in thought.

'Should we leave now?' asked the other man.

'Not yet,' said Devadutta, coming to a decision. 'We can still be of use to our people. There is still information to be gathered here. You and your master stay there till the army is almost here. I will have a lookout posted on the road and shall send word to you. We can slip out of the gates that same day.'

The two men nodded, rose and left.

Devadutta leaned back against the pillow, a slow smile creasing his face. All the years of living in Vathapi and preparing for just this day were drawing to a close. He would miss the city. After all, it had been home to him for so many years. He looked forward to going back home to Kanchi though.

Commander Prathapa of the Vengi army, and now the master of Parivipura, leaned against the battlements atop the fort walls as he gazed out over the river flowing to the south of the city.

It was midday, but the sun was hidden from view by dark clouds floating in from the south-west. He peered into the distance, perhaps trying to make out the enemy army he was sure was on its way. The messenger had arrived a week or so earlier bearing bad tidings from Manimangala.

The message had been from the king of Vengi, Kubja Vishnuvardhana, asking him to prepare himself for a siege. Kubja mentioned that the Pallava campaign towards Vathapi was a given but that didn't mean that they wouldn't first try to retake Parivipura before veering north-west towards Vathapi.

Prathapa had directed his own scouts to ride out at least sixty miles in the hope that he would get a couple of days' advance notice before the army landed up at his gates. He had already begun preparations for the siege. Ironically, he had had to repair the very walls that the Chalukyas had destroyed in order to get in. He had also sealed off the secret gate at the back through which the Vengi army had surreptitiously entered the fort.

There was, however, something that was nagging him—a nebulous feeling at the back of his mind, a faint whisper of a touch deep within the recesses of his brain, that worried him. He threw his mind back to the happenings over the past few months. He frowned as he recalled the rescue of Commander Dasappa and that other soldier who had proven to be such an obdurate fighter within the palace. It rankled. Having someone go into the dungeon and rescue two of his prisoners reflected poorly on him as the commander. He had thrown the two guards into the dungeon for a couple of months to educate them on the consequences of their actions. After all, didn't the

Bhagavad Gita teach that all men were responsible for their actions and the karma arising out of them?

Prathapa sighed. He went over a mental inventory of the forces at his disposal. There were just about five hundred men under his command. While this was enough to hold the fort when one wasn't expecting to be attacked, it was hardly adequate to withstand a siege by a large army. Not to mention, a large army that had already tasted a resounding victory.

He thought about whether to spare his soldiers the travails of a sure defeat by surrendering the fort, but then pushed that unworthy thought from his mind. His king had ordered him to hold out for as long as he could. And he would do just that.

He turned and went down the stairs. That nagging thought at the back of his mind still worried him. What was he overlooking?

'So, how did you hook up with the captain here?' asked Murugan of young Sadaiyan.

They were lazing around after dinner in a little clearing, a day's march from Parivipura. The Pallava army had started for Parivipura exactly a week after the battle of Manimangala. That one week had been important for many things—for the wounded to heal, for the generals to prepare the army for the battles ahead, and for the army to restock weapons and await a fresh supply of elephants and horses from Kanchipuram.

The soldiers had been grateful for the time. The bandages had slowly come off their upper bodies. Their wounds were still a little raw, but they were healing. They had set a sedate pace in the initial days and then started moving faster as their wounds had healed.

It had taken them two and a half weeks to cover the two hundred and fifty miles to Parivipura. They were only about ten miles away now and had bedded down for the night near a field with a well. The ponds and lakes were all dry at this time of the year and they had to make sure that there was water for the men and animals when they camped for the night.

Sadaiyan had glanced at Muthuvel from the corner of his eyes before responding, 'I met him at Kodimunai.'

'Actually, he saved my life. Broke me out of a Pandya army camp,' said Muthuvel with a grin.

'I see. And from what I hear, you went all the way to Lanka and back with him?' asked Murugan.

'Yes,' replied Sadaiyan.

'So what were you doing before you met the captain?' Murugan persisted.

Sadaiyan looked across at Muthuvel and then decided that there was no point in beating around the bush. He turned towards Murugan and said with a grin, 'I was a thief. I still am, come to think of it.'

'A thief? Interesting,' said the imperturbable Murugan.

'What? A thief? Is this for real?' asked the more excitable Bhatta, looking at Muthuvel.

'Aah yes. I am afraid so. But I am trying to wean him away from that profession. I think he has almost turned the corner now,' he said with an affectionate smile at the young lad.

'Yes. I think I can make more money from going into politics and business than from thieving,' said Sadaiyan as the others guffawed.

'So, what is your plan? Stick around with the captain once the war is over?' asked Bhatta.

'I don't know,' said Sadaiyan. 'Perhaps follow him back to Korkai.'

'Now, why would the captain want to go back to Korkai?' asked Kannan.

Sadaiyan grinned wickedly. 'Why would any man want to go back to any place?'

'You mean …' said Kannan.

'Yes. Anna has someone waiting for him in Korkai,' said Sadaiyan and ducked, laughing as Muthuvel chucked a pebble at him. There was general merriment at this statement.

'Ahha! And you acted the good boy all this while,' said Kannan, slapping Muthuvel on his back. 'So, what's her name?'

'What does she do?'

'Spill the details, will you?

Questions came at Muthuvel from all directions. He held up his hand and said, 'Alright. Alright. ALRIGHT. Her name is Thaamarai.'

'Oooh, Thaamarai,' said Murugan.

'Such a pretty name,' said Bhatta, sighing dramatically.

'And who is she?' asked Kannan.

'A princess!' said Sadaiyan. 'She is the daughter of the king of Korkai.'

'Oh my. Our Muthu is going up in the world. From a mere captain to a potential prince!' said Kannan, laughing.

Chaminda clasped an arm around Muthuvel's shoulder and squeezed it in a friendly manner as his friend blushed and accepted the congratulations of his mates.

Elango smiled. Murugan and Bhatta looked at each other and winked almost simultaneously.

'Well,' started Murugan. 'It isn't as if he is the only captain who has fallen for the wiles of a woman. Am I right, Bhatta?' he asked his friend.

'Oh, absolutely not. It seems to be the season for that. Everywhere you see, there are captains falling in love with damsels. Take our boss here, for example,' said Bhatta.

'What about your boss?' asked Elango, interested now.

'Well, don't you know, the boss has gone and fallen for a girl,' said Murugan, his face serious.

'Yes, and what's more, a girl from the other side,' said Bhatta.

'The other side?' Elango's face showed his confusion.

'A *Ganga* girl! The daughter of the commander of the fort at Asanur. Ex-commander actually,' said Bhatta.

A few of the men whistled. Kannan looked suitably abashed.

'So, are you looking to settle in Ganga lands post this war?' asked Elango.

'Or maybe bring her here,' said Murugan.

'Of course he would bring her here. Who does she have there, now that both her parents are dead?' added Bhatta.

'Will you two be quiet?' asked Kannan. Then he turned to Elango and said, 'I haven't decided yet. Let the war get over …'

'Well, what do you know? The man we thought no woman could pin down has finally succumbed,' said Elango with a smile.

'He isn't the only one who has succumbed to the charms of a woman, is he?' asked General Ilanthiraiyanar, walking into the clearing. The soldiers started to stand up but were stopped by a raised hand from the general.

'Sit down, men.' He took his seat on a little mound next to them.

'So, who else has succumbed to the charms of a woman, General?' asked Murugan.

Ilanthiraiyanar smiled and looked at Elango. Bhatta gave a low whistle. 'Oh boy. This really *is* the season for captains to be falling in love.'

'You know, Bhatta. I have often been very candid in my views about your feeble intellectual capabilities, but I must say that I am amazed at your perspicacity in this matter. You have hit the nail on the head,' said Murugan.

'And I have often thought you a blockhead but thank you for acknowledging my intellectual superiority,' replied Bhatta.

'Look how prettily the three of them are blushing, Bhatta,' said Murugan.

'Yes. They look like shy grooms, don't they?' responded Bhatta.

Everyone laughed and then Kannan asked Elango, 'Well, aren't you going to tell us who she is?'

'She is a spy,' said Elango. 'Works for the general.'

'And her name?'

'Mitra. I mean, Sanghamitra.'

'Oh! Mitra. So much in love that you have a cute little name for her,' said Kannan as the friends laughed.

'Can we have some more wine here to celebrate the impending nuptials of the captains?' asked Murugan as a loud chorus of voices demanded the same from a very hassled cook. Some of the men got up to help him gather the flagons of wine. Cups were passed around the camp as the men drank in joy. General Ilanthiraiyanar looked at his men with a fond smile on his face. *With men like these fighting on our behalf, it makes the jobs of generals like me very easy,* he thought. The revelry went on into the night with the three captains the butt of many scandalous jokes, which they dealt with in good humour.

Ilanthiraiyanar got up and quietly slipped back to the campsite he shared with the other kings and generals. Tomorrow, they would be riding into battle.

32

Harsha's Decision

Vathapi, January 642 CE

The commander in charge of the troops re-read the olai. He had already done it a couple of times, but he read it once again, trying to make sense of it.

He had been sent to the northernmost edge of the Chalukya empire, just south of the Narmada River, by Naganandi, with instructions to ensure that Harsha's army did not cross over to their side of the river. He had reached here along with his army just in time for that.

They had been eyeball-to-eyeball since then, neither side making a move. His army, of course, wouldn't cross the river. He didn't have the authorisation to do that.

And now this olai that had just been delivered to him by the messenger. He looked at the man and noticed that the messenger looked like he hadn't slept in a couple of weeks. The commander motioned to him to have a seat. *Should have told him to do that when he came in,* he admonished himself.

The olai was businesslike, which was very characteristic of the writer. Naganandi didn't have time for pleasantries or frivolity. The message informed him that the Chalukya army had suffered a heavy defeat at Manimangala, near Kanchi, and that they were now retreating towards Vathapi. They were sure that the Pallavas would be mounting a campaign against Vathapi. The commander was requested to rush back home, along with his troops.

'This was it?' he asked the messenger, again. He had already asked this question a couple of times.

'Yes, Sir.'

'Were you at the battle? At Manimangala?'

'Yes, Sir.'

'Was it really bad?'

The man sighed. 'Yes Sir. We were on the ascendancy initially. And then they had some fresh troops come in. I was at the back, behind the reserves. So, I don't know exactly what happened.'

'A lot of casualties?'

'Yes, Sir. Lots.'

'Anyone senior?'

'One of the princes was injured. Probably dead by now.'

The commander mused on this for a few seconds and then said, 'Alright, soldier. Why don't you go and get some rest.' As the man left the tent, the commander called his aide and said, 'Ask the captains to step in here. We need to head back to Vathapi.'

King Harshavardhana was seated along with the King of Ujjain, Raja Rudravarma, in the raja's private chambers. Harsha was contemplating going back to Kannauj. He had had discussions with the Chinese pilgrim Xuan Sang about holding a Buddhist council in his capital city. Harsha was a scholar and the opportunity to gather scholars from across the land, in his city, appealed to him.

A soldier announced a messenger, and the two kings ceased their discussion as the man walked in and bowed to them. He then took out a thin sheaf of a palm-leaf manuscript and handed it over to Raja Rudravarma.

'Who are they from?' asked Harsha.

'The commander of our forces at the Narmada River, Your Majesty,' said the messenger.

Raja Rudravarma opened the stack and started reading. Harsha waited patiently for the king to finish, before asking, 'Well?'

'He says that the Chalukyas have pulled back.'

'Back from the river?'

'No. Back all the way. Apparently, they have packed up and left. It looks like they might be pulling back all the way to Vathapi.'

Harsha gave a low whistle.

'Now, why would they do that?' asked Raja Rudravarma.

Harsha closed his eyes and ran his fingers across his forehead. 'The only reason that I can think of is that their need in Vathapi is greater than their need here.'

'Why might that be?'

'Think,' said Harsha. 'This whole business started because the Pallavas wanted us to keep a part of their army occupied on their northern frontiers. We have done that successfully for a while now.'

'Perhaps they feel confident that we won't cross the river and hence there is no need to tie down a substantial portion of their troops here?' said Rudravarma.

'Perhaps. But I suspect that the Pallavas have been victorious in some battle or the other that we will get to hear about, in due course. And that is the reason that these forces have been called back. Not because they are not needed here. But because their need is greater back home.'

'Do we call our army back, then?' asked Rudravarma.

Harsha took his time responding. Eventually, he said, 'I don't know why we must. In fact, I want you to send your men across the river.'

'But Maharaja! That would mean a renewal of hostilities with Pulikeshi!' gasped Rudravarma.

Harsha smiled. 'Pulikeshi might not have the capacity to renew hostilities with us if what I surmise is correct. We might eventually have to barter for positions with Narasimhavarman. And in order to barter, we need some positions, don't we?'

'So, you are saying …'

'Go grab us some land. Let your army go across, say, halfway to the Tungabhadra River. *Then* we will have something to talk to Narasimhavarman about.'

33
Reconquest

Parivipura, January 642 CE

The Pallava army crossed the bridge west of the city of Parivipura. They could see men atop the fort walls, watching them. They started putting up their tents outside the fort walls, following the usual practice of keeping out of range of arrows. Further back, in the forests, men were cutting down trees to make battering rams as well as ladders to scale the fort walls.

Mamalla stood outside his tent, gazing at the fort. The other members of the inner council of the king stood next to him.

'Doesn't look like much of a fort,' said Mamalla. 'At least, not by Kanchi's standards.'

'Not many forts can match up to Kanchi's standards, Sire,' said Paranjyothi.

'Maybe not, but it still doesn't mean it will be easy to take. Remember that Commander Dasappa and his men held Pulikeshi's forces at bay for over a month …' said General Ilanthiraiyanar.

'… and we don't have that time,' finished Mamalla.

'It's good that we have the other way to take the fort then, isn't it?' asked Mamalla.

The others nodded.

'We ought to give them a chance to surrender though,' said Mamalla. 'Sort of a formal offer.'

'Whom shall we send for that?' asked Paranjyothi.

'Send Mahendra,' said the king, promptly.

'Er, Your Majesty, isn't the prince a little too young for this?' asked the Pallava commander, fully aware that the prince was standing among them. Paranjyothi always spoke his mind—a quality that was much valued by his king.

Mamalla smiled. 'He will learn. There isn't much of a danger here. Besides, didn't Dasappa tell us that it was the young Chalukya prince who made that offer of a truce, when Pulikeshi and his men had attacked the fort?'

'That's right,' said Ilanthiraiyanar.

'Well, then, let's send Mahendra with a flag and see what the current commander of the fort says,' said Mamalla.

Commander Prathapa walked slowly up the stairs leading to the top of the western gate of the fort walls. He had been taking a short nap when a soldier had woken him up with news that the Pallavas had sent a messenger.

He took the stairs slowly, intentionally making the messenger wait. He knew that the Pallavas would be in a hurry. He, on the other hand, had all the time in the world.

He reached the top of the gate and looked down. He saw a young lad seated on a horse, holding the *simha*[17] flag, the

17 Lion

emblem of Narasimhavarman Pallava. He waited for the youth to talk. Presently, the young lad said, 'Are you the commander of the fort?'

Prathapa merely nodded.

'I come with a message from Maharaja Narasimhavarman Pallava.'

Prathapa continued to maintain a studied silence.

'The maharaja would like to take the fort without any bloodshed. He gives his word that should you surrender the fort to us, voluntarily, he will see to it that you and your men are treated well. You will be prisoners, of course, at least for some time, but we will treat you and your men much better than how you treated the former commander of this fort and his men,' said the young lad.

Prathapa smiled.

'And who are you, son?' he asked.

'I am Prince Mahendra, son of the maharaja,' said the prince, with a proud tilt of his head.

'And what happens if I refuse your offer?' asked Prathapa.

'In that case, we will be forced to launch an attack and take the fort.'

'You think that will be easy? I know how difficult it was to take this fort and yes, we have already sealed that secret gate through which we had entered the fort. So yes, knock yourself out trying to take this fort by force,' said Prathapa.

'Is that your final answer?' the prince asked.

'Yes. Go tell your maharaja that the Chalukyas are not cowards and that we will not surrender the fort. If your maharaja wants to take this, he will have to fight for it. He might eventually prevail, but he will lose many good men in doing this.'

Prathapa watched Mahendra hold his gaze. *The young lad has spirit, I will give him that,* he thought. He looked steadily back at the prince, who suddenly turned his horse and rode back towards his camp.

Well, Prathapa, you have landed yourself in a fight now. He walked down the flight of stairs and called his two captains to prepare for battle.

The Pallava archers stood ready. They were just out of range of the archers on top of the fort walls. They knew that they had to get closer to the walls to get their arrows over it, and that in itself presented some danger.

Paranjyothi had spread the archers out instead of bunching them. This had a couple of advantages. The most obvious one was that this would render the volley of arrows from the fort walls slightly more navigable since the arrows would have to target the archers individually. Secondly, by spreading the archers along the length of the fort wall, the attention of the defenders would also be diffused.

Paranjyothi blew a long note from his conch. Immediately, his archers darted forward. Each of them also had a helper who carried with him a large wooden shield as well as several quivers of arrows. The archers dispatched their first arrows into the air, waited a split second to see where they fell, and then ran forward again till they were sure that their arrows would reach the fort walls.

There was an immediate response of arrows from the fort. Most of them fell harmlessly in between the archers. The few that did fall on them were stopped by the raised shields held by the helpers.

Mamalla looked on impassively, his hands clasped behind his back. He saw that Paranjyothi had already moved the men holding the battering rams and the ladders behind the archers, but out of range of the enemy arrows.

'And now we wait,' he murmured to Paranjothi and Ilanthiraiyanar.

'Now we wait,' said Paranjyothi.

Elango was glad that they had brought the torches. The tunnel was dark. It would be, of course. It was dug deep into the ground, under the riverbed. Elango knew where the tunnel ended, but it was Commander Dasappa, the erstwhile Parivipura fort commander, who had shown him where it started. About five hundred of them had cut off from the main column of their army and had lain low, out of sight of the Parivipura fort.

They had waited for the morning and then moved slowly towards the entrance to the tunnel, which was hidden in a little mandapam set amidst a mangrove. The trees shielded them from the prying eyes of the soldiers on the walls of the fort.

Dasappa had asked for torches to be lit and had led the way into the tunnel. The sun had cleared the horizon a while ago. They had delayed going in because they wanted to time their exit from the tunnel such that the Chalukya army would be fully occupied by the Pallava forces.

Thankfully, the tunnel was straight and dry, and they made good time through it. As they neared the end, Dasappa turned around and hushed everyone with a finger to his lips. He went up the long staircase, till he reached the door. He put his ear to the door and stood listening. Elango squeezed next to him and did likewise, then looked at Dasappa and shook his head.

He leaned his mouth towards Dasappa's ear and whispered, 'I don't hear anything.' There was a latch recessed into the door, which had a two-way catch. Elango eased back on the latch. It squeaked and he and Dasappa froze. They put their ears to the door again, making sure that the noise hadn't attracted the attention of anyone on the other side. They stood immobile for a minute or so, before Elango attempted to slide it back once more. The latch squeaked again. It had obviously not been oiled in a long time.

Elango eased it back, bit by bit, his nerves jangling every time the latch squeaked. Eventually the latch was fully withdrawn and the door opened softly. Elango peered through the little gap, but could see only darkness. The door was hidden within a closet in the innermost room of the antahpuram. Given how dark it was, it was obvious that the cupboard was closed. Elango pushed the door open and stepped into the closet.

He hoped that the closet wasn't latched from the outside. He spent a few seconds listening for any sounds outside the closet door. Hearing nothing but silence, he gave the door a nudge. Thankfully, It swung open on its hinges, softly. Elango stepped into the room, sword drawn, and immediately spun around in a full circle. There was no one else in the room. The room itself was in utter disarray. Clothes were strewn all over the place. Tables were overturned. There were shards of broken flagons. Wine stains were all over the floor. It was not how he remembered it from the last time that he had been here.

He motioned to Dasappa, who stepped out next to him. Elango held up five fingers and five soldiers moved silently into the room and took up positions near the entrance. He motioned to the others to stay put.

Elango moved cautiously outside the room, his eyes and ears alert for any hints of enemy soldiers. He walked along the corridor leading to the entrance to the palace. Corridors branched out to the left and right and he motioned to a couple of the other soldiers to go along each corridor to check them for the presence of soldiers. They returned soon and shook their heads at him, indicating that there were no soldiers to be seen. The palace appeared deserted. *Perhaps they have all been called to the fort walls to repel the army attempting to scale it,* thought Elango.

They walked on silent feet up to the entrance to the palace. Elango peeked out and saw a solitary guard at the gates. He whispered something to Dasappa, who sent a couple of soldiers back into the innermost room to guide the other soldiers out of the tunnel and into the palace. Elango meanwhile thrust his sword back into its scabbard and stepped out in a confident manner to the gates.

The attention of the guard at the gate was riveted on the noise emanating from the fort walls. He never heard Elango sneak up behind him and chop down hard on his neck with the side of his hand. The guard collapsed in a heap and a couple of soldiers dragged him into the bushes and trussed his hands and legs with his own veshti.

Elango waved the soldiers over to the gates and then, acknowledging Commander Dasappa's nod, broke into a run towards the western gates about half a mile away. The other soldiers followed him.

Prathapa was on the fort walls directing the defence of the fort and helping his archers pick out targets. He had most of his men lined atop the western and northern walls of the fort. That's where the Pallavas were attacking from, and he didn't think there was any danger of them attacking him from the east. The south was safe since it was ringed by the river.

Suddenly, he heard sounds of a commotion behind him and turned around. What he saw chilled him to the bone. There were scores of soldiers running towards the fort walls. Maybe even hundreds. *Oh Krishna! Where have these soldiers come from?* he thought, starting to panic.

'Captain!' he yelled to one of the men under his command. 'Captain!'

The captain, who was some distance away along the wall, looked in the direction from which the yell had come, spied his commander and waved out to him.

Prathapa pointed down towards the city. The captain looked and Prathapa could almost see the colour drain from his face.

'Gather the men! We have been breached! Get the men off the walls!' said Prathapa, as he unsheathed his sword and ran down the steps, closely followed by his men.

Paranjyothi had watched his archers move forward in an incremental manner, a few feet at a time. While their initial tactic of spreading out the archers had worked, the closer they got to the fort walls, the more accurate had been the shooting from the enemy archers.

His own archers spent more time cowering under their wooden shields than shooting arrows at the fort. Paranjyothi was starting to get a little anxious, as he had not seen any signal from within the fort. *I wonder what it will be*, he thought. *A conch perhaps?*

He looked from his archers to the fort walls, and suddenly noticed two things. First, the hail of arrows from the fort seemed to have come down drastically. Second, the archers and soldiers atop the fort walls seem to have vanished.

That's the signal! he thought.

'Battering rams! Ladders!' he bellowed, and the men handling the ladders and the battering rams ran forward towards the fort walls.

Prathapa realised that they were outnumbered. Sure, they were probably equal in number if you counted all the men he had within the fort, but right here, right now, in this little corner of the fort, they were outnumbered.

He didn't look to see if his men were behind him. He expected his men to follow orders and he had already ordered them to follow him. He ran on ahead, into the narrow lane through which the enemy soldiers were pouring towards them, ducked under an overhanded swing, dropped to his knees, and chopped across the abdomen of his attacker. The man gave a cry and fell to the ground, his internals pouring out of the gaping hole in his belly in a bloody mess.

Prathapa fought on. Doggedly. Ferociously. Cutting. Slicing. Exhorting his men to rally around him.

The ladders went up uncontested. All the Chalukya soldiers on top of the fort walls had rushed down the stairs to counter Elango and his forces within the fort. The first man up was the young archer, Venkata, closely followed by Bhatta and then inevitably, Murugan, Kannan and Muthuvel.

Venkata stood looking down at his city, his arms flashing back and forth between the quiver and the bowstring. His arrows unerringly found their marks on the backs of the Chalukya soldiers. He single-handedly decimated almost an entire platoon. Kannan, Murugan, Muthuvel, Bhatta and some of the other soldiers jumped down and got the massive western gates open, and the rest of the Pallava army streamed in through the gates. It was a short, brutal fight. Not many of the Chalukya soldiers survived.

Control your breath. Focus. Guard up. One at a time. Parry. Parry. Thrust. Duck. Weave. Parry. Swivel. Weave. Lunge. Clean Strike! Breathe. Breathe. Evenly. Not rushing it. Deep breaths. Move to meet the next man.

Prathapa took a quick look around to see where his men were.

Where ARE they? Am I cut off? Have I, in the heat of battle, been cut off from my men? Never mind. Focus. Here they come, again. This one seems a bit heavy. Doesn't move too well. Should be easy. Sword in his right hand. Clumsy movements. Swinging his sword arm all the way back. Heavy muscles. Wants to probably split me in half.

Not so fast, my boy! He weaved his head away as the sword whistled past. *You have overextended, haven't you. Here. Meet my sword. Ugh. Didn't expect that much blood to splash on me. Careful now. Step over him. Here comes another one.*

Slender. Well-muscled, but slender. Light on his feet. Sword held along his thigh. Still. Very still. Balanced. Looks competent. Where have I seen him before? I am sure I have seen him.

Ooh. Watch it! That was close. He nearly got me that time while I was letting my mind wander, trying to remember his face. He is GOOD. Fast hands. Parry. Parry. Parry. *Am being driven back. I hope there are no obstacles behind my legs. Can't afford to fall now.*

Ouch. He nicked me. Got me on my upper arm. Is that my blood? Can't tell. Too much blood all over me. Aargh! He got me again, this time on my other arm. His arms were fatiguing. Weave. Weave. Move. *Watch his feet though. His left foot is extended. Is he waiting to lunge?* His opponent sat down and swept his foot.

Aaargh. That hurt. My back! Didn't see his foot take out my feet. Sword up in the air. Parry. Parry. He tried to calm his breathing. *It is too fast. Too fast. But I can't help it. His blows are coming at a dizzying speed.*

Clang. Clang. Clang. Tschuck! *Aaargh. My right arm feels numb. Where is my sword. Why is the man looming over me. He is raising his sword. Let me deflect it. Can't seem to raise my sword. Where is it? AAAAAAaaaargh. That hurts. My belly hurts. What is that protruding through it? Why is my breath coming so fast now? My eyes are blurring. Deep breaths. Deep breaths.*

I remember him now. That fellow I had thrown in our dungeon along with their commander. What was his name? The commander's? Dasappa. Yes. Looks very much like this other man who has now come into my field of vision. Yes. Same face.

My head hurts. Let me just tilt my head back. What is that? Why does that flag have an unfamiliar shape on it? It doesn't look like our Varaha. What IS that animal? I can't make it out. Why is there a strange emblem on our flag?

I can't see any more. I can't breathe. I feel like I am falling. Stop. Someone. Stop me from falling.

Commander Prathapa breathed his last, never realising that his fort had fallen.

34

Vathapi Prepares

Vathapi, January 642 CE

The corporal at the gate gave a crisp order and the guards opened it with alacrity. The men streaming in through the gates were blank-faced. They shuffled, rather than marched. Only their eyes reflected their misery. Misery at having been beaten, at having to return home defeated. Misery at having to face their fellow citizens, knowing that their enemy was on its way.

There were more wounded than fit men. Their numbers were also vastly diminished. The mood and demeanour of the men was very different from the day a few months ago, when they had set out triumphantly on their campaign. The pomp and pageantry were absent, of course, but more evidently, the soul and the energy they had exhibited that day were missing.

The other noticeable aspect was the utter silence in the ranks. Apart from the creaking of saddles, the clip-clop of the horses' shod feet, the occasional snorts of the horses and the crunching of stones underneath the feet of the marching men, the men themselves did not utter a sound.

They passed through the gates and into the city. Even the onlookers were quiet. News of the defeat had found its way to all the citizens and the mood was sombre. They knew that their city would now come under attack. They had already started preparing for it but watching the defeated army stagger back home gave them a glimpse of what the future might hold for them.

The most disturbing part for the citizens, though, was watching their usually majestic and ebullient king go through the city with his face set and his eyes blank. He, who loved to chat with the citizens, who took every opportunity to connect with them, now couldn't even meet their eyes. His gaze was fixed straight ahead, with unseeing eyes, as his horse plodded its way through the city. A few of the citizens tried to raise a cry, 'Victory to Maharaja Pulikeshi,' but it found few takers, and the cry died down almost as soon as it started. The princes looked equally grim, although they were comforted by the fact that Prince Ranaragha, while still very weak and in need of abundant rest and care, was finally out of danger. The vaidyas had done a remarkable job of not just keeping him alive through the long journey from Manimangala but also ensuring that he was on the road to recovery.

The train meandered through the city. The army men peeled off periodically along the way, and when the king and the princes reached the gates to the inner fort, there were only a few of their men following them. The gates were already open by the time they got there. They dismounted from their horses and walked wearily up the steep stairs to the palaces.

'Who broke the lock to my room?' roared Naganandi. The servants froze where they were. The caretaker hurried over, ashen-faced.

'Sire, the bhikshu …'

'What bhikshu?'

'The bhikshu who was here.'

'A bhikshu was allowed in here?'

'Yes, Sir. The queens allowed it. The bhikshu said that there was something wrong with the room …'

'And you gave him permission to break the lock?' Naganandi hissed.

'Sir, the queens …'

'To hell with the queens!' thundered Naganandi. 'This is my house, and you are the caretaker. Didn't you tell the queens that this room was not to be opened under any circumstances?'

'Yes, Sir, but …'

'And what temerity to actually break the lock!'

'The queens, Sir …'

Naganandi walked back into the room.

'How long was the bhikshu here?'

'An hour.'

'*Hour*?'

'… or so, Sir.'

'Was the bhikshu alone?'

'No, Sir. Two disciples. And then there was another man.'

'Who?'

'I have seen him in the city, Sir. I don't know his name.'

Naganandi looked around the room at the olais and the different maps. It was obvious that they had been touched. Not just touched, but also looked at. He knew how he tied his olais and maps and these had been retied in a hurry.

Naganandi took a deep breath, turned, and with his fury barely controlled, marched out of his house and across the intervening space to the king's palace.

The guard at the palace stepped aside hurriedly as the spy chief stormed in. The palace caretaker rushed out to greet the visitor.

'I need to speak to the queens,' Naganandi snapped.

The caretaker hurried inside. He returned a short while later, saying, 'The maharaja said that he will meet you, Sir.'

'I said that I wanted to talk to the *queens*,' said Naganandi, glaring at the man, who seemed to shrink back under his gaze. Before he could reply, Pulikeshi came down the steps.

'Yes, Naganandi? You wanted to talk?'

'I do want to talk. But with the queens.'

'Why? What's the reason?'

'My room was broken into,' said the spy chief.

'Broken into? By whom?'

'Some bhikshus apparently. And under the supervision of the queens.'

'Is it that room of yours where …'

'Yes,' said Naganandi curtly.

Pulikeshi turned to the caretaker and said, 'Please tell the queens that I request their presence here.'

The room descended into a stormy silence. Naganandi, plainly agitated, stood looking out of one of the windows, playing furiously with the tuft on his head. Pulikeshi had sat down on one of the chairs, his face curious.

Presently, they heard footsteps as the queens came into the room, looking a bit fearful.

Naganandi turned and raked the queens with his eyes. He, however, did not forget to bow to them.

'You called for us, Rajan?' asked Mangalamma.

'Yes, Rani. The spy chief was looking to speak to you about …'

'The room that was broken into, Your Majesty,' said Naganandi, interrupting his king.

'Aah that. Yes, it was under our direction. The bhikshu, a great master, said that there was something wrong with the energy in this place and that it was because of a hidden room somewhere here. When we asked your caretaker, he mentioned the underground room. The bhikshu said that we could get rid of the negativity by carrying out some rituals inside the room. Hence, we asked the caretaker to help break the locks.'

Naganandi's eyes bulged fiercely as he heard this tale.

'I hear there was someone else along with the bhikshu? Do you know who he was?'

'We don't know him, but we heard him being referred to as Devadutta.'

Devadutta? What did that scoundrel want here and how was he even allowed into the palace? thought Naganandi. Aloud, he asked, 'And where is the bhikshu now?'

'Oh. They left about a week ago,' said Mangalamma.

'Left for where?'

'For the caves of course. The master wanted to meditate. They will be in one of the caves on the southern ridge.'

Pulikeshi looked at Naganandi thoughtfully, and then dismissed the queens. Once they had left, he asked, 'Suspicious?'

'Very, Your Majesty. That man Devadutta is a scoundrel. He lives in one of the seediest parts of the town and has dealings with cutthroats and ruffians of all types. I have had to do business with him on the odd occasion. He has proven useful a couple of times but he is not trustworthy at all.'

'And the bhikshu?' asked the king.

'Anyone associated with Devadutta is suspect in my eyes. Also, the olais and maps in the room have been looked at by them, I am certain. We don't know what they have gleaned, but this looks to me like enemy action.'

'Go get them, then,' said Pulikeshi, dismissing Naganandi.

Horses pulled up at the bottom of the steps leading up along the southern ridge. The steps were full of devotees walking up to the various levels to pray to the Gods of their choice, or returning from their prayers. The men ran up the steps, stopping at each of the three levels and looking into the cave dwellings, asking people about a bhikshu and two disciples.

Finally, a priest at the third and the oldest cave told the men that the bhikshus had been living in a cave further up but that he had seen them walking down earlier that morning. The soldiers rushed down upon hearing this and went straight to the man in charge of the hunt.

At the same time, a search party landed up in the lane outside Devadutta's house. The house was quiet and appeared to be deserted. There was a lock hanging on the door and the corporal asked the men to break the lock, which they did, using a crowbar that they had prudently brought along.

The inside of the house gave no sign of a hasty abandonment. As they moved past the outer rooms to the living quarters, they were stunned by the size of the house. It had given the appearance of being a much smaller residence, seen from the outside, but extended a long way to the back. The rooms looked immaculate, as if the inhabitants expected to be back at any time. There were clothes folded neatly inside the cupboards. The inner study was bare. There was nothing at all on the shelves, except a few curios. Nothing to indicate what had existed there in the first place.

The corporal gave it some thought and then, entrusting the search to his second-in-command, rushed out of the house, got on to his horse, and galloped towards the northern gates of the city.

Devadutta and the people with him rode hard. He knew that they would be tiring their horses very fast this way, but they had no choice. The hunt would be on for them, and he wanted to put as much distance as possible between them and the city of Vathapi.

The bhikshu and the disciples had come to him in the morning, even as the army had started to trickle in. Devadutta had been preparing for this day and had already neatly packed the olais that he had wanted to take into a sack. He had burnt the other olais over the last couple of weeks, leaving no incriminating evidence behind.

Of course, the fact that we are on the run is incriminating enough, he thought. He had asked his two bodyguards to find them some horses and they had slowly ridden out of the city from the southern gates.

I am going to miss this city. I have spent nearly half my life here. So many memories. He sighed. *Oh well. I always knew that a day would come when I would have to leave in a hurry.*

Their horses were starting to tire now, and Devadutta slowed his own horse down to a trot and then a walk. The others followed his lead. He asked his bodyguards to find them a way into the woods. Once inside, his men went back out and wiped out the hoofprints of their horses using some leaves that they had broken off from some trees.

'I think we are safe. Even if they follow us down the road, they will have no way of knowing where we got off the main road,' said Devadutta, leading the way into the woods for a mile or so, before turning southeast again, paralleling the road. He was hoping that they would run into the Pallava army soon.

A couple of days after Pulikeshi and his men had returned, there was a fresh arrival from the south. Messengers brought news to the palace that King Srivikrama, Princes Vikrama and Chandra, and the army chief Narasimha had entered Vathapi, with the remnants of his army.

There was a touching reunion between the Ganga king and his daughter, Mangalamma, as well as between the queens and their sons Vikrama and Chandra. Pulikeshi, Srivikrama and Narasimha closeted themselves in a room all day along with Prime Minister Vedaraya and Naganandi, as they discussed their plan of action and preparations for the siege they knew was coming.

That same evening, the forces from the north reached Vathapi. Pulikeshi felt a lot better now about their prospects. They had fresh troops on hand, apart from his own battle-weary troops and those of the Ganga king Srivikrama.

Maybe we can see out this siege after all, he thought.

35

The Pallavas Arrive

Vathapi, February 642 CE

The Pallavas were just a day's march from Vathapi and had camped alongside the road leading to the city.

Paranjyothi, Ilanthiraiyanar, Prince Mahendra, Manavamma, Duraisingham, Elango, Muthuvel, Kannan, Murugan, Bhatta, Thissa and Chaminda were gathered in Mamalla's tent. Ilanthiraiyanar had insisted on the young captains being there. Kannan had, in turn, insisted on the presence of Murugan and Bhatta.

Thissa and his men had joined the Pallava army closer to Vathapi. They had arrived directly from Madurai. Commander Dasappa had stayed back at Parivipura after the battle. The prisoners, the few that remained, would need to be taken care of, and the city put back together.

'So how are we going to do this?' asked Mamalla. 'Pound them with mangonels for a while? Soften them up?'

'That could take a considerable while,' said Manavamma.

'Yes, the fort is quite solid. We could be here a while if we depend on pounding them with mangonels,' said Ilanthiraiyanar.

'Do we have any idea about the fort? Any secret tunnels? Anything at all?' asked Mamalla, looking at Ilanthiraiyanar. 'I thought you had someone on the inside in Vathapi?'

Paranjyothi and Ilanthiraiyanar exchanged glances before Ilanthiraiyanar said, 'Yes, we do have a couple of people on the inside, but we haven't heard from them yet.'

'Is there any way to get at them from behind that hill on top of which the palaces are perched?' asked Elango.

'Not a chance,' said Paranjyothi. 'Our man has thoroughly explored that hill. It is unclimbable, and they have soldiers on the lookout. There is no way to move enough men up that hill.'

'What about out-waiting them?' asked Mamalla.

'They have a freshwater supply inside the fort, and they are sure to have made arrangements for food,' said Ilanthiraiyanar. 'We will have to wait to hear from our folks inside the fort for some information.'

'Do you have a way to get in touch with them?' asked the king.

Ilanthiraiyanar shook his head.

Just then, they heard a commotion outside the tent and a guard came in.

Mamalla looked at him expectantly. The guard bowed low and said, 'There are some people outside, Your Majesty. They want to speak to the general.'

'Who are they?' asked Ilanthiraiyanar.

'They didn't tell me their names, Sir, but there are three bhikshus in the group.'

Ilanthiraiyanar's face broke into a satisfied smile.

'You know them?' asked Mamalla.

'We were just discussing them, Your Majesty. Our folks inside the fort.' Then, turning to the guard, the general said, 'Ask them to come in.'

In walked Devadutta and with him, Sanghamitra, Anjaneya and Jabali.

It took Elango a split second to recognise Sanghamitra with her head shorn of its lovely, thick, lustrous hair.

'Mitra?' he asked, incredulously.

Mitra broke into a wide grin.

'So *this* is Mitra,' muttered Murugan. 'Captain, you didn't tell us that you had fallen in love with a bhikshu?'

'She isn't a real bhikshu, dumbo,' Bhatta admonished his friend. 'She is a spy.' He enunciated his last statement as if speaking to someone with very slow mental equipment.

Mitra laughed that tinkling laugh of hers. Elango's face lit up on hearing that.

'I see now why you fell in love with her, Captain,' said Murugan. 'Pretty laugh to go with everything else.'

Mitra gave him an amused look. 'The captain has been talking about me, has he?' she asked.

'Not really, no,' said Bhatta, taking up the conversational rein from Murugan. 'We had to extract it out of him. The general spilled the beans though.'

'Will someone introduce the visitors to me?' asked Mamalla.

'Sorry, Your Majesty,' said Ilanthiraiyanar. 'This here is Devadutta. He has been our man in Vathapi for the last twenty years or so.'

'And this young lady?'

'She is the spy we had sent with Elango to Ujjain. When she got back from Parivipura, after leading King Krithavarman and his family safely to us, I asked her to proceed to Vathapi. She suggested going there as a bhikshu, with these two young men,' he indicated Jabali and Anjaneya, 'as her disciples.'

The two young men bowed to the king who acknowledged them with a nod of his own.

'So,' said Ilanthiraiyanar, 'you all managed to get out in time, I see.'

'Just in time, Sir,' acknowledged Devadutta. 'Wouldn't have done us any good to have been caught by Naganandi—not after what we did.'

'Oh? What was that?'

Devadutta looked at Mitra and said, 'Why don't you update them about your doings?'

Mitra gave them a quick summary of her activities.

'You were ensconced on top of the fort, near the palace?' asked Kannan, his eyes wide in admiration.

'Not just that. The queens were her devotees,' said Jabali with a grin.

Kannan thumped Elango on the back. 'You, my friend, are a lucky, lucky man.'

Elango appeared embarrassed while Mitra looked at him with a twinkle in her eyes.

'Also, I understand now why you said that it wouldn't have done you any good to be caught by Naganandi,' said Muthuvel. 'He would have been incensed that you all violated his innermost sanctum.'

Devadutta grinned.

'So, anything important that you found in that underground room of Naganandi's?' asked Paranjyothi.

'Yes, Sir. There is a weakness in the fort's structure.'

Devadutta went out and came back with a large sack. He untied the string at the top and put his hand inside, rummaging through the several olais and maps before pulling out a rolled-up silk map. He spread the map on the floor and sat down before it. The king and the generals followed suit while the others huddled around them.

Devadutta pointed to the map and said, 'The northern edge of the fort curves towards the cliffs. That edge of the fort, for about twenty yards, is old and has only a single layer of stones.'

'Aah. We target it with our mangonels then?' asked Muthuvel.

'We can't,' said Devadutta. 'See here? At the very end, the fort curves inwards, trying to mimic the contour of the hill. That is not accessible for mangonels.'

The others looked intently at the map, trying to mentally calculate angles and distances.

'He is right,' said Paranjyothi. 'We can spend the next few months trying to hit that area with our mangonels and we won't make any progress.'

'I had sent out my men to take a look at the wall,' said Devadutta.

'And?' asked Paranjyothi.

'It is flimsy alright. The mortar holding the stones together has fallen off in a lot of places, leaving little holes.'

'What about elephants?' asked Thissa.

'No, for two reasons. One, it is going to be difficult to get the elephants into that little space. And two, it is not likely that the Chalukyas will allow us to bring the elephants right up to the fort walls and not do anything about it.'

'Anybody got any other ideas?' asked Mamalla, looking around. There were many ideas but none that would work.

Paranjyothi looked speculatively at Ilanthiraiyanar and asked, '*Visvaasaghaati*?[18]'

The general raised his eyebrows, 'Now that's a name that I haven't heard in a long time.' He mused for a few seconds before declaring, 'It might work.'

'What is it?' asked Manavamma.

'A kind of fire, Your Majesty,' said Paranjyothi.

'Very hot. Extremely hot,' explained Ilanthiraiyanar.

'How would that help us?' asked Mamalla.

'He,' Ilanthiraiyanar motioned towards Devadutta, 'said that there are cracks in the walls where the mortar has fallen off. If we can get the visvaasaghaati into those cracks and light them up, then …' He shrugged noncommittally.

'Will it bring the wall down?' asked Elango.

'It will loosen the stones at least. We can then batter the walls down with a ram.'

'And how do we get this visghaavaa …'

'Visvaasaghaati,' said Paranjyothi with a smile.

Elango smiled. 'How do we get this visvaasaghaati into those cracks?'

'Someone has to physically go and push it into those cracks,' said Paranjyothi.

'And light it up,' said Ilanthiraiyanar.

'And light it up!' said Paranjyothi.

---

18 Visvaasaghaati was composed of a powder of all the metals as red as fire—or a mixture of the powder of kumbhi, lead and zinc, mixed with the charcoal powder of the flowers of paribhadraka, palasa and hair, to which was added oil wax and turpentine. From the nature of the ingredients of the different compositions, it would appear that they were highly inflammable and could not be easily extinguished. The visvaasaghaati-agni-yoga was virtually a bomb which would scatter fragments of metal in all directions when it exploded.

'How do you make this visvaasaghaati?' asked Mamalla.

'It requires the powders of some metals, the charcoal powders of some flowers as well as turpentine and wax. It is very difficult to prepare, and one needs to take enormous care while making it, else it could actually explode in your hands,' explained Paranjyothi.

'Do we have people who know how to prepare this?'

Paranjyothi looked at his general. 'Well, General?'

'I think I could,' admitted Ilanthiraiyanar, running his fingers through his beard. 'It is finding the materials we need that is going to be a concern.'

'I can help,' said Thissa. 'At least, help gather the materials we need.'

'Alright then. You have one week to find them. It will take us that long to make the mangonels and we can't do much until we have them,' said Paranjyothi.

Night had fallen. Two figures could be seen walking away from the camp. It was pitch dark where they were going, even though the moon was a crescent in the sky. The canopy formed by the trees blotted out any light from up above.

Elango held Sanghamitra's hand as he walked ahead of her, easing his way into the forest, stepping carefully along the path. They eventually came to a little clearing and Elango pulled Mitra to him and crushed his lips on hers with a vehemence that surprised them both. They clung to each other and kissed with a desperation born of a long separation.

Eventually, they both came up for air. Elango had his arms around Mitra while she rested her head on his chest, listening to the thumping of his heart while trying to still the rapidity of her own.

Elango ran his fingers gently over Mitra's bristled head.

'Please don't cut your hair again,' he said.

'Mmm,' said Mitra.

'I mean it. I love your hair. Well, the hair that you had before.'

'That was probably the only way for me to get into the fort,' she said.

Elango tightened his arms around her. 'That *was* something,' he admitted. 'I wonder how those two, Jabali and Anjaneya, didn't give it away.'

'I wasn't too sure of how they would act, but I am very impressed. Jamba will be so proud of them. By the way, where is he?'

Elango stiffened. He had been dreading this moment. Mitra sensed the change in him and raised her head from his chest, drew back and looked up at him. It was too dark to make out the expression on his face.

'Well?'

Elango took one hand from her waist and raised it to her face, caressing it.

'He's gone, Mitra,' Elango whispered softly.

Mitra put her hands on his upper arms, her nails digging into his flesh. 'What?' she asked.

'The battle of Manimangala. He went in along with King Mamalla. He fought bravely. Killed many men. He died a warrior's death.'

Mitra's nails dug deeply into his flesh. Elango didn't flinch but put his arms around her again. Eventually Mitra collapsed against his chest, her body wracked with sobs.

They came to him the next morning. Mitra had obviously told them. Their eyes were red and puffy from crying.

'Do you know where he is buried?' asked Anjaneya.

Elango was startled.

'Buried? We cremated him,' he said.

'But we don't cremate,' wailed Jabali. 'We bury our dead and then plant a seedling over the grave so that it can grow into a massive tree,' he said.

'I am sorry, Jabali. We had no idea. We cremated him with the utmost honour,' said Elango. Then, noticing the tears in the eyes of the two men, he said, 'When this is over, I shall take you to the exact spot where we cremated him, and you can perhaps plant a seed there?'

Jabali nodded, teary-eyed.

The Pallavas trooped in from the south, without much fanfare. They congregated around the western gates of the city, in between the northern and southern gates. They went about their task of pitching tents and getting ready for the siege. This included the building of siege engines and mangonels.

Soldiers ranged out to cut down trees of the adequate height and girth, to be used as the throwing arm. Others roamed around the countryside with carts looking for rocks of suitable weight to be used as missiles to batter the city.

Smithies were set up to work on sharpening the weapons the army already had or to construct more spears, knives and swords. Cooks set up an elaborate kitchen towards the back of the impromptu city of tents. They were one of the first to get set up, since they would need to feed the soldiers, come nightfall.

Men went in search of wells and other sources of water, not just for drinking and cooking but also for bathing and ablutions. A separate space, away from any water bodies, was created for the disposal of bodily wastes.

Mamalla's tent was setup right in front of the encampment. He had insisted upon it. Usually, military practice dictated that the tents of the kings and generals be erected in the middle of the camp to keep them safe from any attempts at assassination by the enemy. Mamalla had made his opinions very clear. He wanted to be out front, where Pulikeshi could see him. Of course, this also meant that now, all the other kings and generals had their tents out in front as well, next to his. It wouldn't do to hide in the centre, leaving the king alone out front.

Ilanthiraiyanar had already sent his men to search the surrounding areas for the materials required for the visvaasaghaati. He and Commander Paranjyothi went around ensuring that work was progressing on the mangonels at an acceptable pace. It would still take them a week to get an adequate number of them built. However, they were seasoned veterans gifted with patience. They could wait.

36
Sneak Attack

Vathapi, February 642 CE

There was a day to go for *amavasya*.[19] The sky, at this time of the year, was clear and the stars glittered in the heavens.

There had been a discussion about when to do this. The mangonels had been ready earlier than expected—five days after they had arrived at Vathapi. They had started pounding the fort the very next day. Huge stones were being hurled into the sky by the machines, their parabolic paths ending on the walls or flying into the city, causing damage, both materially and to the morale of the citizens. The engineers had spent some time trying to work out the angles of the machines correctly. Their initial attempts had seen the stones fall short of the walls. They had slowly brought down the angle until the rocks started landing on the walls or flying over them, depending on the weights of the stones.

19 New moon

The leaders had decided to soften up the Chalukyas for a couple of days near the western and southern gates. Their idea was to concentrate their attack as far away from the northern edge of the fort as possible.

There was further discussion about who would be going along to the northern edge. Kannan, Elango and Muthuvel had volunteered, along with Murugan and Bhatta. Paranjyothi and Ilanthiraiyanar had not been convinced that sending the cream of their leaders on the ground was such a good idea, but the others refused to send their men to carry out such a dangerous task. The generals had finally acquiesced and asked Kannan to lead the group.

Elango had added one more member to their group, the young archer Venkata.

'Just in case the soldiers on top try and take shots at us. I have immense faith in the young man's ability to put a stop to that.'

It was as the men were getting ready that Sadaiyan stole up to them and begged to be allowed to go with them.

'No. Absolutely not. You will stay here,' said Muthuvel emphatically.

'But listen. I have seen those walls. They are tall. I am not sure you big, muscled men can climb up that wall as easily as I can,' pleaded Sadaiyan. Then, looking at Muthuvel, he said, 'Anna, you know I can do this. Let me go with you.'

'We will come too,' said a couple of other voices. Jabali and Anjaneya had followed Mitra when she had come to bid goodbye to Elango.

'We are good at climbing,' said Anjaneya. 'Ask them,' he said, pointing at Elango and Mitra, who nodded their heads.

Kannan looked at them and then said, 'Alright. You three can come with us, but you will follow behind us. You will *only* climb the walls when I tell you to, and you will come back first. Last in, and first out. Understand?'

The three of them nodded.

And now, here they were, lying on the ground, cautiously crawling their way forward. There was no cover for them to hide behind or under, and so they inched forward very slowly, trying to ensure that a chance glance from the top of the fort walls wouldn't lead to their discovery.

They were glad for the darkness of the night. There were torches placed at regular intervals on the fort walls, and, while they threw light in the vicinity of the walls, the torches would also destroy the night vision of the guards. Or so Kannan hoped.

They had chosen to go an hour or so before daylight, the hour when the human body is at its least wakeful. There was another reason they had chosen this window of time. If they did manage to damage the walls, it wouldn't give the Chalukyas enough hours of daylight to repair them before the Pallavas attacked.

Kannan looked back at the other huddled shapes lying on the ground behind him, waiting for him to move so they could follow him. He looked up towards the fort walls, which were a scant thirty yards away, and then to the top of the walls. He noticed a couple of guards desultorily leaning against the wall and having a conversation. *Probably trying to keep each other awake,* he thought. *Well, no point in waiting anymore.*

He looked back again and gave a thumbs up to his comrades, got to his feet, bent low, and started covering the intervening distance to the fort walls. The others mimicked him, and they were soon standing up against the walls, undetected.

They moved quickly around the portion of the fort wall as it curved eastwards to meet the cliff. All except for Venkata. He lay down at a spot where he could get a clear view of the guards, were they to come their way. The guards were at least a hundred yards or so away from this segment of the wall and Kannan had not noticed them patrolling this far.

Kannan knelt as the men gathered around him for instructions.

Kannan, Elango and Muthuvel were the only ones carrying bags. These bags were filled with that inflammable and highly dangerous ingredient, visvaasaghaati. The dense powder had been packed inside cloth bags. A piece of hemp jutted out of each bag, like a wick. The men took these bags out and passed them around. Sadaiyan, Jabali and Anjaneya got the most number of bags since they would be the ones climbing the upper reaches of the walls.

At a nod from Kannan, they got to work. The three young lads climbed up the walls like little monkeys, easily scaling them using the cracks in between the stones and the fissures caused by the eroded mortar. The others started to push the bags into the cracks along the lower part of the wall, and as far as they could reach on tiptoe. It was quick work, and it was quiet work. For the most part. Until Sadaiyan, trying to reach a crevice that was just out of his reach, felt his foot slipping, and gave an involuntary, muffled cry.

The two guards had been chatting with each other, trying desperately hard to keep awake. They both swivelled their heads when they heard Sadaiyan's cry.

'What was that?' asked the first guard.

'You heard it too?' asked the second.

They look towards the northern end of the fort, waiting expectantly for the noise to repeat.

It didn't. The first guard looked at his comrade.

'Should we go check it out?'

'There is no one else around,' said the second man, looking about him. 'Except for those guys near the northern gate. Should we call for some backup?'

'And have them laugh at us if it turns out to be nothing?' asked the first guard.

The second man hesitated momentarily before saying, 'Alright. Let's go and see what caused that noise.'

Sadaiyan, Jabali and Anjaneya clung to the wall, their fingers and toes wedged into the cracks and crevices. Nobody moved. Down on the ground, Venkata had taken his position under a tree with a clear line of sight to the top of the fort. He waited, an arrow notched on his bow. The others had flattened themselves against the fort wall.

Kannan looked at Venkata and noticed the slow motion of his arrow, tracking the guards on top, as the young archer shifted his aim. He looked at the others along the wall and motioned with his hand to stay put.

The arrow kept up its motion in a slow arc. A spool of light appeared on the walls as the torches held by the soldiers illuminated their path. They were holding their torches aloft and peering into the distance. Kannan knew that it was only a matter of time before they started to look closer to the walls. He desperately hoped that Venkata would do the needful, should it come to that. He looked at the young archer and noted that his eyes were fixed along the line of the arrow.

The motion of the arrow slowed further and became almost imperceptible as the guards on the fort walls slowed down. One of the guards came close to the wall and leaned over it, holding his torch above his head and out in front of him. He saw the men clinging to the wall. He saw the men on the ground. He opened his mouth to scream a warning.

Venkata had been waiting for just that moment. He let fly the arrow which had been centred on the guard's chest. The arrow unerringly found its mark and the guard collapsed backwards even as the torch he was holding fell from his lifeless hands on to the ground.

The second guard bent down to check on his colleague, uncomprehending. That movement saved his life for the nonce, as Venkata had shifted his aim and let fly at him. The arrow whipped past his head. The man, understanding that his friend was dead, let out a cry for help, but his cry was cut off by another arrow that buried itself in his throat. He died instantly.

There was an immediate response from the soldiers from the northern gate. Venkata could see men starting to run towards them.

'They are coming,' he said in a loud whisper.

Kannan waited no longer. He picked up the guard's torch that had conveniently fallen near him and passed out a few strips of hemp rope. The others quickly lit the strips from the torch and passed them to Sadaiyan, who had climbed down partway. The young lad took three hemp strips and scrambled up again. He passed two of the lit strips to Jabali and Anjaneya and the trio set about lighting the wicks. The men on the ground were doing the same to the packets which they had placed on the lower reaches of the wall.

'Remember that we have only half a minute before the packets start to burn,' shouted Kannan, ditching all pretence at silence. It was too late for that.

The wicks lit up, sparking as they did so, and then the flames started eating their way up the wicks, fast.

'Down, down! Off the wall, now!' shouted Kannan, and the three young men scrambled down the wall. 'Move, all of you,' he said, waving his hands at the others on the ground. The sounds of the guards running on top of the fort walls came closer. The lights of myriad torches tore through the darkness near them. The men on top started hurling spears down at the Pallava men, missing several of them narrowly.

'Run! Run! Go!' shouted Kannan, trying to get his team safely out of range of the spears. Anjaneya and Jabali jumped the last few feet from the wall and scampered away, leaving only Sadaiyan still on his way down. Halfway down, the young lad noticed that one of the wicks had stopped burning. He started working his way up again to relight it. Kannan, noticing this, ordered him down, 'Sadaiya! Down! Now!'

The young lad relit the wick and then scampered down as fast as he could. A soldier on the top of the wall spotted him. He took almost direct aim at the descending Sadaiyan and prepared to throw his spear down on him when an arrow embedded itself in his chest. The soldier went down, soundlessly. Another soldier appeared in his stead and started to repeat the action with his spear. Kannan had, however, taken up one of the spears that had been thrown at them and landed near his feet. He hurled it at the soldier on top. The spear impaled the man, who toppled backwards.

Sadaiyan jumped down and Murugan, who had refused to leave his captain, took hold of the young thief and started to push him away, towards the others. It was then that the fort wall exploded.

The wicks had burnt down to the powder packed within the packets. The powder had been packed hard. Left in an open area, they might have merely burnt hot. The packed powder, however, was further compressed inside the crevices. As the fire lit the powder, the gases released had nowhere to go. They started accumulating inside and the pressure built up. Eventually, something had to give, and the packets exploded.

The outcome of those multiple explosions was catastrophic. Stones spewed out of the fort wall as if propelled by some hidden hand. The wall itself started to collapse along with the soldiers on top of it. The soldiers yelled as they fell down among the rocks. Many were crushed. The lucky ones fell on top of their comrades and only had fractured body parts to show for it.

The results were calamitous for the Pallavas too. The wall collapsed on Kannan, burying him before he could move away from its vicinity. The others, watching helplessly, heard a lone and despairing cry from him before he was obscured by the tons of stones cascading down upon him.

Murugan, who was a little further away from the wall and who had instinctively shielded Sadaiyan by covering him with his own huge body, was struck by a large stone. The stone hit him flush on the back of his head, crushing it instantly. He fell on the ground, Sadaiyan nestled beneath him, shielding the young lad even in his death.

37
Battle of Vathapi

Vathapi, February 642 CE

A small contingent of Pallava and Lankan soldiers under the command of Generals Ilanthiraiyanar and Thissa had moved under the cover of darkness and stationed themselves opposite the northern edge of the fort walls. As soon as they heard the explosions and saw the fort wall collapsing, Ilanthiraiyanar led the soldiers to the fort at a run. The sight that met his eyes was gut-wrenching.

Young Sadaiyan sat there with Murugan's crushed head on his lap, his body wracked with silent sobs. Others, he noticed, including Elango and Muthuvel, were digging frenziedly towards one end of the collapsed wall, trying to move impossibly large stones out of the way. He realised that they were trying to get to someone.

Bhatta was manic in his activity, hefting stones out of the way as though singlehandedly trying to uncover the buried person. Ilanthiraiyanar threw a quick glance around the men and noticed that Kannan was missing. He motioned to his men to go help with the digging. The addition of another ten men to the group hastened the process of removing the heavy stones until the last stone was removed, revealing Kannan, spread-eagled on the ground.

Bhatta jumped down from the stone that he was standing upon and, sitting by Kannan's side, gently turned him over. He put his head to Kannan's chest and then a finger to his nose. He stood up, slowly, his eyes blinking back tears as he looked towards Elango and Muthuvel and shook his head. Bhatta then looked towards Sadaiyan and the body of his friend and comrade. Bhatta's shoulders bowed as he reached the boy and sat down next to the body of Murugan. He put his arm around Sadaiyan, comforting him even amidst his own overwhelming grief. Ilanthiraiyanar felt profound empathy for the man. He had lost friends in wars as well and the wounds never healed. He motioned to Elango to go towards Bhatta and then gave a crisp command to his men, 'Alright, men. Let Kannan and Murugan's deaths not be in vain. They have opened the fort for us. Let us get the northern gates open.'

'You stay with your men, general. Allow me to do this,' said Thissa.

Saying this, the Lankan general leaped over the stones and scrambled through the opening, followed by his men.

The city had been breached. Ilanthiraiyanar and his men had taken the guards at the gates by surprise and the few men atop the fort walls had been dealt with rather quickly. The Pallava army poured into the city, eager to finish the fight. Mamalla hefted his sword, feeling that familiar weight in his hands.

He knew that it wouldn't be easy. The Chalukyas were a proud people. They wouldn't give up without a fight. The Pallavas would have to fight all the way to the inner fort. He looked back at his army. Many men would die today. Many of them would never see their homes back in Kanchi. Many wouldn't live to see their villages or farms or their loved ones. Wives would be widowed. Mothers would wail for their sons. Young kids would grow up without their fathers. Sisters would only remember the love showered on them by their heroic brothers.

Mamalla sighed. This was a heavy burden. He had always felt it keenly. Kings and kingdoms fought. Ordinary soldiers paid the price for it. Inscriptions would be engraved on walls glorifying their victory. The soldiers might get a few hero stones that their families just might remember for a while. Eventually, even those would be lost in the mists of time.

He felt a hand upon his shoulder. It was Commander Paranjyothi, his eyes full of compassion. He had just brought news of the deaths of Kannan and Murugan. *Such fine, vibrant young men. Gone all too soon. In the prime of their lives. Leaving behind loved ones, perhaps wives or girls whom they were waiting to wed. And all for me. For Kanchi, yes. But ultimately for me. To help me fulfil my promise to my dying father. So in a sense their dying is upon me. All their deaths will be upon me.*

He looked at Paranjyothi and asked, 'Is it worth it, Paran? Is it worth sacrificing the lives of so many young men of our land for my own selfish needs?'

Paran put his arm around his king and friend. He smiled.

'You remind me of another warrior, a long time ago.'

'Who?'

'Arjuna,' said Paranjyothi. 'He was wracked by similar doubts on the battlefield.'

Mamalla scrunched his eyes, sinking into thought.

'You are right. At least I don't have to fight my own family,' said Mamalla with a hint of a smile.

Paranjyothi smiled. 'We all must do our dharma, Narsi. That's about all we can do. The outcome, as you know, is out of our hands.'

'Well, well. A Shiva-bhakta[20] spouting Vaishnavaite philosophy?' teased Mamalla.

'*Hari*[21] and *Hara*[22] are the same, you know. The entirety of creation is one. We all arise and fall within that cosmic reality. Ultimately, even this universe of ours will dissolve into nothingness and then be born again. According to our sages, this has already happened fifty times. We are in the fifty-first such cycle. For the brief period of our existence on this earth, all we can do is our duty to the best of our abilities. What happens happens. There is no surety that even you or I will come out of this alive. But we have a dharma to follow. Yours is the *rajadharma*[23] while mine is that of a soldier.'

'Krishna,' said Mamalla.

'What?' asked Paranjyothi in confusion.

'You likened me to Arjuna. So, I am calling you my Krishna. A friend who guides one during periods of confusion.'

Paranjyothi grinned. 'Well, do you want to go out and talk to your troops before you lead them into battle?'

---

20 Devotee of Shiva

21 Vishnu

22 Shiva

23 King's path

'Maharaja! Maharaja! Sire! Wake up! Wake up!' shouted Queen Mangalamma, trying to wake her husband. Pulikeshi stirred, swatted at her with his hands irritably, and then turned towards the other side. The queen, however, was persistent.

'Rajan! Wake up! The enemy is inside the fort! The prime minister and Naganandi are here, waiting to talk to you.'

Pulikeshi sat up quickly, his eyes heavy with sleep. A look of consternation, born out of understanding, spread across his face. He looked towards the door to his room where his prime minister, Vedaraya, and his spy chief, Naganandi, were standing, with somewhat forlorn expressions on their faces.

'Is it true?' he asked.

The glum nods of the two men gave him the answer that he sought but didn't want to hear.

'How?'

'They breached the fort at the northernmost edge,' said Vedaraya.

Pulikeshi looked sharply at Naganandi. 'The doings of the bhikshus?'

The spy chief nodded.

Pulikeshi stood up to his towering height, his face suffused with anger and grim determination.

'We will make them fight for every inch of their advance,' he thundered.

'Men, this is it. This is the day that we have been preparing for, for over twenty years now.'

A loud cheer filled the air. Mamalla was sitting astride his horse, in full battle gear. The northern gate was already theirs.

Paranjyothi had asked him to speak to the men one final time, before they went in to battle.

'Many of you were young men who fought at Pullalur along with my father and me. I am sure you all remember that day.'

He noted several nodding heads.

'You remember the humiliation then?'

The heads nodded again.

'Good. I want us to remember that feeling. I want us to remember how it felt to lose our friends on the battlefield that day. I want us to remember the sense of hopelessness as we fought valiantly against a force that vastly outnumbered us. I want us to remember that feeling of being defeated as we retreated from Pullalur, back into the fort at Kanchi. I want us to remember how we felt when we couldn't look into the eyes of our loved ones, as we slunk back into the city, vanquished.'

Mamalla paused briefly, to see how his words were being received. The nodding heads had thunderous looks on their faces. *Good,* he thought. *Anger and rage are good weapons to have when one rides into battle.*

'Memories of those tumultuous days continue to haunt us. How many of us have slept well during the last twenty years without having our sleep disturbed by nightmares of that loss? Is there anyone here who has been able to shake off those nightmares?' he asked.

'NO!' rose the scream.

'No, indeed. I know you will not have been able to shake them off because I, too, have never been able to get over them.' Mamalla paused again, and changed tack.

'For all you young men out here, who have grown up hearing about the battle of Pullalur from your fathers and uncles and elders. You must have heard of the promise that I gave my father as he lay dying. Yes?'

'YES!' responded many voices.

'You must have wondered why I hadn't done much about this promise for nearly ten years now. It wasn't because I didn't want to. We had to be careful. Our enemy was strong. We weren't. We were weak. We had to regain our strength. It takes time to regain one's strength. But we never stopped working towards it. Commander Paranjyothi and General Ilanthiraiyanar never stopped working towards it.'

'Nearly a year ago, we set into motion a series of events, the culmination of which is the fight today. We have been preparing for this for a long time. But today—today, we will finish what we started. Today, we will fight to restore Kanchi's honour!'

A loud chant of 'Veera Vel! Vetri Vel!' rang out again and again.

Mamalla waited for the chants to die down and then said, softly, 'Men, war is dirty. War is tough. War is brutal. Men die in war. While I know we will be victorious today, I also know that it is not going to be an easy fight. The Chalukyas are a proud kingdom, and they will fight us with all the tenacity they have. Like we would have done, had an enemy force come inside our beloved Kanchi. There are many who will fall in battle today. I have no right to ask you to sacrifice your lives for me. But I also know that you will not hesitate to sacrifice your lives for me and for Kanchi.'

'Long live King Narasimhavarman Pallava!'

'Long live Mamalla!'

Mamalla looked into the eager eyes of his soldiers and smiled inwardly. He raised his sword high into the air and, turning his horse to face the northern gates, said, 'To victory!'

'Veera Vel! Vetri Vel!' shouted his men as they charged forward.

Progress through the streets was tough, brutal and slow. Mamalla's instructions had been to focus on the Chalukya army and not to trouble the citizens of Vathapi. But that became increasingly difficult as the citizens were in no mood to give up their city. They were helping their army by pouring out into the streets and pelting the Pallava soldiers with stones, rocks, pots, pans, and anything that they could get hold of.

Elango and Muthuvel led the men through narrow streets, their shields held aloft as articles pelted down upon them from the upper storeys of buildings. The Chalukya army hid among the civilians on these upper storeys and flung javelins and shot arrows at their men. There were blind corners around which entire platoons of Chalukya troops hid and jumped out to attack the advancing Pallavas.

The Pallavas had to fight their way through, street by street. They lost many men in these sneak attacks. Several were wounded by arrows. Only the fact that they had formed a canopy of sorts with their shields prevented more damage among them.

Their own archers had trouble losing their arrows at the attackers on the tops of the buildings. Elango, Muthuvel and their men had to clear the roofs of the houses of enemy soldiers, before they could proceed. Many Chalukya men died on those rooftops. Quite a few civilians did as well. It was impossible to differentiate between soldiers and civilians in the heat of battle.

They left behind a trail of death, the wails of the womenfolk following them. For the Pallava soldiers, death was a constant threat. Death could come at them from the rooftops or around a turn in the street—a clean death from a javelin impaling them or a messy one from a sword that could rip their innards out.

Somehow, they found a way to move forward. Inch by inch, foot by foot, into the heart of the city and towards the fort.

They could see the inner fort walls now. The Chalukya soldiers had been pushed back through the streets. The Pallava men controlled all the gates to the city. Paranjyothi had instructed his men to offer and accept the surrender of the Chalukya soldiers, but they hadn't had much success with that. The Chalukya men had fought ferociously and died by the droves instead of surrendering.

They were, after all, fighting for their homes. But they suffered from two serious shortcomings. They were heavily outnumbered by the Pallava troops. And they had also not yet recovered from the hiding at Manimangala, both physically and mentally. To the Pallavas, the battle was a foregone conclusion. It was a question of when, not if. The Chalukyas, however, did not see it that way. They were defending their land and their king. And so, they continued fighting.

The streets were littered with the dead. Street dogs ran among them, sniffing and biting, chased away by the citizens. Vultures soared over a once vibrant city, but one that now was literally a city of the dead.

Elango and Muthuvel had been at the vanguard of the army, and they were the first ones to near the ancient Agastya Lake as they fought their way through. Elango had been shadowed closely by the young archer Venkata. The young man had been outstanding with his marksmanship, enabling Elango and his men to cut through the opposition.

The group had come to the lake from the south. Elango and Muthuvel had split up, with Muthuvel leading his men along the longer route, around the lake. There was a narrow ledge running along the eastern side of the lake that led to the inner fort gates. Elango led his men up this path warily. They could see men at the far end of the lake, guarding the route to the gates.

There was a building along the path and as they came near it, javelins and arrows started raining down upon them.

'Take cover!' yelled Elango, hugging the compound wall of the house. He was bent low, minimising his exposure to the shower from above. Any movement by his men was answered by a shower of arrows or a javelin hurled with incredible power. One of his men scampered forward to grab a javelin and as he turned to throw it back, he was peppered with arrows. The javelin slipped from his grasp and fell to the ground with a thud. The impact of the arrows forced him backwards. He took a step back, then another, and then fell on his back and into the lake with a splash. His body, studded with arrows, floated half submerged, on the surface of the water. The gentle waves in the lake lapped against him, as his unseeing eyes looked upwards at the skies.

Elango yelled at his men to stay in position. He had watched the death of the man with anger. He was angry with himself for being unable to protect him. He looked back and saw the rest of his men hunkered against the wall, their shields held aloft over their heads.

He transferred his gaze towards the north and saw that a detachment of soldiers, who were guarding the fort gates, was starting to come down the path towards them. *We will be ground into dust if we get caught between them and the men on top of this house,* he thought. *I must get up there. There is no other way,* he decided.

He motioned to Venkata, who was right next to him, and to the two men behind him, and quickly whispered some instructions to them. Then, still hugging the wall, he crawled slowly towards the solitary gate that led into the building and waited near it.

He looked back at Venkata and the men and jerked his thumb upwards. Immediately, the three men turned and lay on the ground facing upwards, with Venkata in the middle and the two men lying on either side, holding a shield in each hand. The four shields were enough to protect them from the inevitable rain of arrows that followed.

The two men on Venkata's side had, however, left a small opening, a gap very difficult for an enemy marksman to hit unless his marksmanship was of the Venkata level. The gap, however, was enough for Venkata to take cover and still operate his bow.

The archers on top of the building, who had been shooting down at the Pallava soldiers with impunity, suddenly started sporting arrows on their chests and toppled down off the roof. The others ducked down behind the terrace wall. One intrepid but foolhardy soldier raised his head above the wall with a javelin in one hand only to have an arrow go through his forehead and into his brain.

Elango had been waiting for just this opportunity. He swung open the gate and darted inside the house. He raced on ahead, up the stairs, climbing them two at a time, coming out on top of the roof. The place had an abundant supply of arrows and javelins which explained the incessant barrage that they had been subjected to. He saw men crouching beneath the level of the wall and fell upon them. The men there were mostly all archers and were no match for him. He dispatched them in short order and then stood near the wall and raised his sword up high.

'Alright men, we can move on up …'

Barely were the words out of his mouth when he felt a sudden, sharp pain in his back. He realised that someone had stuck a knife into him. He turned around, the knife still stuck in his back. His sword came up and with one powerful strike, cleaved his attacker's head from its body. The head bounced away to the far corner of the terrace as the man's body collapsed at his feet.

Elango turned again, but felt himself losing his balance. The sword fell from his hands and, as his men watched below, he backed up against the wall and then his momentum carried him over it. He fell on to the ground and the knife in his back went up to its hilt.

Venkata, who had watched this paralysed with horror, raced through the gate and to his captain. Elango lay on the ground, his legs spasming in front of him. Venkata bent down and cradled Elango's head. Elango raised his hand up to Venkata's face and whispered, 'Tell her …'

And then he died.

38

The Lion Falls

Vathapi, February 642 CE

Pulikeshi looked down from the first level of the ramparts of the fort at the battle raging in the city. He had placed himself there with a series of runners in order to manage the battle better. His face had a week's worth of stubble, almost all of it white. His eyes were red with lack of sleep and worry. He seemed to have aged more over the last couple of months than in the previous few years.

The battle wasn't going well for his people. They were being pushed back towards the inner citadel. He had committed both sets of reserves to the battle to stem the tide and it hadn't stopped his enemies. He wondered if he could have done something differently.

He could make out the few cavalry men he had left who were still fighting. He knew his sons were out there making a valiant stand in a lost cause. Once the city walls had been breached, it was only a matter of time before their defences would be overrun by the enemy. *That blasted Mamalla is relentless*, he thought. *Did I underestimate him? Underestimate his resolve? It was only a couple of months ago that I was once again almost at Kanchi's doorstep. How did it all go so wrong?*

He tore his thoughts back to his current predicament. The reserves that he had committed were too inadequate and too late to make much of a difference to the final outcome. He paused and turned slowly to look towards the southern spur that, along with the northern spur on which he now stood, dominated the city of Vathapi. The golden rays of the late afternoon sun shone bright on the city, splitting the dark clouds that hovered over her. He could make out the monks scurrying atop the spur, trying to find a vantage position from which to observe the battle.

They were not scared. They wouldn't be, he knew. It wasn't the way of this land to molest religious people. When two kingdoms fought, the armies fought against each other, and rarely, if ever, did the violence spill over on to the citizenry and almost never to members of religious orders.

And so, the adherents of Vishnu, Shiva, Mahavira and the Buddha watched from atop the southern spur, detached both physically and figuratively from the grim struggle that was taking place on the plains below.

Pulikeshi looked upwards towards the battlements of his inner fort. He could make out his queens and the other members of the royal family as they stood on the upper fort walls, looking down at the battle and periodically glancing in his direction. They, who had prayed for his victory, and who had bid him farewell for the battle at Manimangala with so much hope. They stood almost forlorn now. His queens knew how grim the situation was. He had never been one to sugarcoat things to womenfolk. He didn't believe in doing that. Women, he knew, were incredibly strong. Their ability to bear with difficulty and to remain surprisingly stoic in the presence of calamity was something that he had seen when his own mother had stood with him, all those years ago, as he faced fearsome odds, both internal and external.

In all the years this city had been in existence, there had never been a stage where an external enemy had directly threatened the city. The fact that the enemy was now inside the fort walls and was directly engaged in battle with his army would have left his queens in no doubt about the overall grimness of the situation.

Pulikeshi swung his eyes back down towards the city. He could hear the tumult growing louder and the fighting getting closer to the inner fort walls. He spied the lion battleflag of the Pallavas, held aloft in the hands of a soldier. Next to him, he could make out a man on a horse, showering arrows at his men, as he made his way towards the gateway leading to the inner fort.

Mamalla, he hissed to himself. *The great wrestler.* He smiled grimly as he looked at his rival. They had been on a collision course for a while now. *Not for a while*, he corrected himself. *We have probably been on a collision course since this universe was born out of nothingness. What does the Nasadiya Sukta*[24] *say?*

At first there was only darkness wrapped in darkness.
All this was only unillumined cosmic water.
That One which came to be, enclosed in nothing,
arose at last, born of the power of knowledge.

Perhaps events were set in motion at that point. And this is the culmination of it. Pulikeshi smiled sardonically. He knew emperors had vast egos but this was probably a bit too much even for him. *My mind is wandering. Perhaps trying to postpone the inevitable.*

24 A passage from the Rig Veda

As he once again looked down, his opponent, King Narasimhavarman Pallava, took a break to ease his weary muscles and glanced up in his direction. The two lions stared at each other. The intervening distance seemed to dissolve. Mamalla put down his bow and grasped his sword, raising it up to his face and then in Pulikeshi's direction, a gesture of respect, from one warrior to another

Pulikeshi saw that and inclined his head. They had come across each other at the battle of Manimangala, of course. Then, the tide of that battle had made Pulikeshi turn back. It was different now. Coming to a decision, a set look on his face, he turned and hurried towards the little shrine to Bhagwan Ganapathy, that remover of obstacles. He was wearing footwear and hence did not go into the sanctum of the temple but bowed deeply outside it, his hands folded together, praying to Him to ensure that his sword arm remained strong.

Turning, he rushed down the steps cut across the steep incline, through the gates of the inner citadel, to his enemy.

Mamalla had noticed the nod of recognition that Pulikeshi had given him and watched as he had moved away from the ramparts. *Will he actually come down to confront me?* he thought. *He will*, he answered himself. *The old lion is a fierce warrior, and he won't duck the challenge.*

He took a quick look around. His army had made faster headway than he had anticipated or expected against this enemy. He saw Commander Paranjyothi to his left and General Ilanthiraiyanar to his right. They were on their horses, their sword arms rising and falling rhythmically as they pulverised their way through the mass of Chalukya reserves. Their own reserves had been kept in abeyance until Pulikeshi had committed his forces. Paranjyothi and Ilanthiraiyanar had descended on them from either flank and what was in progress now was a decimation. He also saw his son, Prince Mahendra fighting, behind Ilanthiraiyanar. Mamalla felt parental pride as he saw his son's fighting abilities.

Mamalla watched as the enemy first faltered, and then started to turn back, preparing to retreat, but there was nowhere to go. They were being pushed back to the walls of the inner fort. As they fought on, Paranjyothi paused in his efforts to catch his king's eyes.

'Maharaja!' he yelled. 'Look, Sire!'

Mamalla looked in the direction to which his commander was pointing. He saw that the gates leading into the inner fort were opening. He saw Pulikeshi, armed with a sword and a shield, walk through. Mamalla got down from his horse with only his heavy sword and a round shield for company.

'The emperor is mine and mine alone,' he bellowed. His shout was heard by the soldiers fighting around him. It was also heard by Emperor Pulikeshi as he descended the steps slowly, his eyes fixed on his enemy. Each tread was measured. Men, both his and his enemy's, moved away at his approach, leaving him a clear path to Mamalla.

Mamalla waited at the bottom. He could feel the setting sun beating down on his back. Sweat poured off his face into his beard. His hair was matted and dirty. The tip of his sword was on the ground, and he leaned lightly against it, watching his greatest adversary walk towards him. He didn't register it, but the fighting had intensified as the Chalukya soldiers, bolstered by the sight of their king coming out to fight, made one final push to reverse the tide.

Shouts of *Veera Vel, Vetri Vel* and *Jai Varaha* rent the air anew as the two groups of soldiers clashed with each other. However, just like the eye of the storm registers a calm, missing from its periphery, the noise and hubbub of the fighting moved away from the point where the two kings were coming face to face with each other. Paranjyothi and Ilanthiraiyanar had seen to it that a perimeter was thrown around that spot, leaving it free for the kings to engage in battle.

Mamalla waited, his eyes narrowed, his body relaxed yet wary. He had raised his sword and held it lightly in his right hand, the tip still pointing down. He moved back a few feet as Pulikeshi reached the bottom and took the last step, on to the ground.

The Pallava king looked at his Chalukya counterpart, respect in his eyes. *God, he has such presence*, he thought as his eyes wandered over his opponent, from head to toe. The head, with those long flowing locks, more grey than black now, the face like a rock, the piercing eyes set under bushy eyebrows, the handlebar moustache, those heavy shoulders and chest, the well-muscled arms, still maintaining most of their youthful vigour, and the waist, thickened by the weight of years, supported by two pillar-like thighs. But what brought respect to Mamalla's eyes was something more intangible, an indefinable quality that screamed a message to the world that here was a man. A king. An emperor.

As Pulikeshi started moving in a semi-circle around him, Mamalla mimicked his action. His eyes never left Pulikeshi's for a second.

The battle raged around them, but here, in this little piece of land, all was quiet. Except for the slow movement of the two opponents as they circled each other warily. Eventually, Pulikeshi broke the silence.

'Looks like this,' he indicated with his sword to himself and then to Mamalla, 'ends here.'

Mamalla took his time responding, surprised at the depth of emotion in his voice, as he said, 'You started it, Maharaja. You came to our lands.'

Pulikeshi's face twitched into a wry grin. 'Yes, I did, didn't I? But that's what kings do, don't they?'

'Perhaps … But this was personal.'

'Aah, yes. I heard that your father died bemoaning the defeat he suffered at my hands.'

Mamalla's lips tightened and his eyes flashed. 'Yes. He did. This is payback for him.'

Pulikeshi smiled. 'You think it will be that easy, boy?'

'Look around you, Rajan. We are inside your city. We will win this war. We have already won it,' he said, pointing vaguely around them with his sword.

'I meant us,' said Pulikeshi.

'I don't know. Regardless, you already know that I have won, and that you have lost. Your beloved city is in my control.'

Pulikeshi sighed. He knew that it was a lost cause. It was only kingly pride that kept him going now.

'How goes it with that project of yours at Mahabalipuram?'

Mamalla was taken aback by this sudden change of topic. Pulikeshi noticed his reaction and smiled. 'Yes, I have heard good reports of what you are attempting to do.'

'It is going well. We have some sculptors from your lands, Rajan. Those who have worked previously at Aryapura.'

'I wish that circumstances had been different and that I could have seen those new temples of yours,' Pulikeshi replied, his voice tinged with regret.

Mamalla nodded his head, sorrow and regret creeping into his heart. *He and I aren't that different*, he thought. *We both love the arts. We both love to fight. And we are both ambitious and want to expand our kingdoms. Perhaps, in another life, we might even have been friends. Perhaps.*

Pulikeshi had stopped circling and Mamalla had unconsciously followed suit. There they stood. Two of the three pre-eminent kings of their generation and of this land. Perspiration cascaded down the faces and bodies of the two men. Mamalla rolled his shoulders, working out the kinks. Pulikeshi had started rotating his right wrist slowly, causing the sword in his arm to rotate. The next moment, almost as if propelled by a superior force, they rushed towards each other. A deep *clang* resonated around the area as the two heavy swords clashed.

The first few moments were spent in testing each other out. Each strike by one was met with a counter, using the sword or the shield. The clangs, when the swords struck each other, alternated with the more muted *thud*s as a sword found a shield. Mamalla, the younger man, breathed more easily than the older Pulikeshi as they danced the slow, macabre dance of death.

Mamalla decided that he had tested Pulikeshi's defences enough and rushed towards him, striking vigorously at him. Pulikeshi was hard-pressed, stepping back progressively, countering Mamalla's charge. As Mamalla moved forward, Pulikeshi suddenly stepped in and pushed his opponent using his shield and the full force of those heavy shoulders of his. Mamalla, who had been focused solely on the attack, lost his footing and fell down but instantly rolled over and was up on his feet.

He found Pulikeshi standing in front of him, gasping as he drank huge mouthfuls of air into his starving lungs. Mamalla paused. Pulikeshi had refrained from taking advantage when Mamalla had lost his footing and the younger man reciprocated the gesture by letting his older opponent catch his breath.

The fighting had stopped elsewhere. The Chalukya soldiers were either dead, injured or had surrendered their weapons. Paranjyothi, Ilanthiraiyanar and a few of the soldiers had now formed a ring around the two kings, a sort of impromptu arena encircling the warriors.

Mamalla and Pulikeshi though were locked together in their own world, completely oblivious of what was happening on the outside. Thrust. Counter-thrust. Blocking with their shields. Thrust. Press. Attack. Again and again and again. They were evenly matched. At least at first, as they went back and forth across the ground. Mamalla marvelled at the expertise with which the older man wielded his sword. He looked for some opening, as he started a fresh series of attacks. It came soon enough.

The older man was tiring. His counters were becoming slightly weaker with time. As Mamalla struck his sword and then quickly reversed a strike to the other side, Pulikeshi brought up his shield in response, but the force of the blow loosened his hold on the shield and it was knocked off his hand.

The Pallava king jumped forward, redoubling his attack. As he struck with his sword, Pulikeshi responded by blocking it with his own, leaving his left flank exposed. Mamalla used his shield to hit Pulikeshi's chest from the left, a blow that would have put down a normal man. The Chalukya king was no normal man. He was winded and hurt but he was still standing. Mamalla pressed forward. A couple more blows with the shield followed and this time Pulikeshi went down, his legs slipping from under him as the shield thudded into his chest.

Pulikeshi grunted as he rolled over a couple of times. He took his time getting back on his feet. Mamalla waited. He wouldn't attack a man when he was down on the ground. Pulikeshi stood up slowly, using his sword for support. He looked around and found his shield on the ground and looked at Mamalla, who nodded slightly. Pulikeshi went over, stooped and picked up the shield and then, when he was ready, Mamalla went in, attacking furiously with both sword and shield. Pulikeshi managed to parry a few of the sword thrusts but not all. His arms were tiring, and he was not quick enough to stop the attacks off both flanks now. Cuts appeared on his upper arms and torso, oozing blood. He lunged this way and that, desperately searching to stop this onslaught.

Mamalla knew that the end was near, and it came with an air of inevitability. Yet another series of sword and shield attacks by him led to Pulikeshi exposing his left flank as he bid to stave off the attacks. Mamalla raised his sword for an up-to-down cut but, noticing the weak left flank, reversed his hold on the sword mid-air and thrust down and low. The blade went in smoothly through Pulikeshi's ribs. It made a squelching sound as Mamalla pulled it out again.

The Chalukya king grunted and gritted his teeth, fighting against the pain. He threw down his shield as his left hand involuntarily clasped his side, on top of the gaping wound. Blood poured out of the wound through his fingers, covering his hand in the process and oozing on to his veshti. Pulikeshi went down on one knee as he put the tip of his sword into the ground and used it to bear the weight of his body. He knelt there, gasping for breath, fighting through the waves of pain flooding his body.

Pulikeshi's breathing was ragged. He slowly lifted his head, looked up at the sky and squinted against the rays of the late afternoon sun. He could hear cries of victory as his opponents celebrated but these were drowned out by the whooshing sound of blood in his ears. His eyes seemed to lack focus.

A figure suddenly loomed over him. A tall, muscular figure that blotted out the sun. The figure stooped and knelt in front of him. Pulikeshi recognised him. Mamalla. The great wrestler. His opponent. Pulikeshi looked at him with blurry eyes. He expected to see a grin of triumph.

There was none of that in his eyes. Just understanding. And sadness. Killing a worthy opponent seldom brings with it feelings of satisfaction.

Pulikeshi saw Mamalla reach out and take his right arm, the arm that rested on his sword for support. The sword fell with a clatter as Mamalla supported Pulikeshi and gently lowered him down to the ground, his back against a wall.

Pulikeshi sat there, blood oozing out through his wound and causing a larger and larger stain on his veshti, his legs spread out in front of him. The sun shone down on this great son of the land. As he watched, Mamalla picked up his sword, brought it to him and placed the handle in his right hand. Mamalla clasped his hand around both the sword and Pulikeshi's hand, giving it a squeeze.

Pulikeshi acknowledged the gesture with a nod and then raised his sword slowly to his forehead, in a salute. He had barely got the sword up to his forehead when the last breath left his body. His arm fell to his side, still clutching the sword. His head lolled to one side. Maharaja Immudi Pulikeshi, the great Chalukya king, was no more.

A rousing cheer went up from among the watchers as they saw that their enemy, the man who had caused their old king so much pain and hurt, was no more. Barely had the cheers started when they were cut short by a sharply uttered command.

'No. There will be no cheering here,' said Maharaja Narasimhavarman Pallava.

'There will be no cheering here,' he reiterated, 'not because we haven't achieved what we came here to do. As you know, I made a promise to my father on his deathbed ten years ago, that I would avenge Pullalur, and I have followed through on that promise. But there will be no cheering here because we will demean that act of revenge by cheering the death of a brave man. A great man. A great son of this soil. In another day and age, he and I could have been brothers. We might have fought together. We might have discussed the arts together. It was not to be.

'In another day and age, he might well have defeated me. You forget that I have the advantage of youth on my side in this fight. So no, we will not cheer when such a man passes from this world. The God Yama himself will not stand for that. We are told that we must account for our deeds in front of Dharmaraja when our time is up. I do not want to have to explain to Dharmaraja why I disrespected such a great man at his death.'

Mamalla looked around at the gathering. Paranjyothi's eyes showed compassion, and Ilanthiraiyanar's, understanding. These were seasoned soldiers, and they knew that death in battle could be even more glorious than victory. They knew that valiance must be revered, even if it was that of the opponent.

'I will not have unseemly behaviour from our troops at this moment. A great man has passed away. He died bravely and well. He knew that he was going up against a younger opponent and yet did not hesitate. He fought and died bravely. I just wish, that when my time comes, I will meet death as honourably as the maharaja has done.'

Then, looking at Paranjyothi, he said, 'Commander, please make arrangements for the last rites of the maharaja. Kindly inform his family and ensure that they take part in all the religious rites. There will be no celebrations tonight. We will all pay our collective respects to the maharaja.'

Paranjyothi nodded and gestured to Ilanthiraiyanar to go with him. They left to prepare for the funeral.

The funeral of Immudi Pulikeshi was a solemn affair. Pulikeshi's sons and both his wives were present. Srivikrama was there as well. The inner fort walls had been thrown open to the public. The maharaja's body had been placed on a bier on the first level of the fort. The citizens, weeping openly, came by to pay their respects to their beloved king.

The sun had set long ago, and the place was awash with light from the many torches that had been lit. Mamalla and his generals along with Manavamma and Thissa had placed themselves off to one side, under a small canopy. Pallava and Lankan soldiers lined the walls all along the platform and directed the citizens as they shuffled forward, first touching the feet of their beloved king with reverence, and then moving past the body.

The king's sons stood stoically at the head of the bier while his two wives wailed periodically as they placed their heads against his chest and wept.

The night passed. As the first rays of the sun fell on the bier, the priests motioned to the sons to pick it up and follow them to the top of the fort. A site had been chosen opposite the main palace for submitting the king's body to the fire.

With chanted mantras, the body was placed on the pyre and lit by Pulikeshi's eldest son, Aditya. As the flames licked upwards, the women wailed in despair. Bells sounded and the priests continued chanting their mantras as Bhagwan Agni took his beloved son into His warm embrace.

An hour or two after the body of Pulikeshi had been consigned to the flames, unseasonal showers opened up over the city. The Gods cried for their beloved son.

Epilogue

Vathapi, February 642 CE

General Ilanthiraiyanar stood in front of the huge dome of granite at the bottom of the inner fort. He ran his eyes over it and then decided on a spot roughly at its centre.

'Here,' he said.

A man stepped forward with a hammer and a nail. Ilanthiraiyanar handed his assistant a set of olais.

'Make sure you inscribe these on the wall, starting there,' he said, pointing to a spot about ten feet from the ground.

The inscriber nodded and got to work.

'Carefully! Carefully!' said Commander Paranjyothi. The workmen paused and then, gripping the *murti*,[25] raised it up from its base. It was a black-coloured idol of a standing Ganesha,

25 Icon of a God which has been consecrated in a temple.

the God who removes obstacles. It was shiny and polished with many centuries of worship.

Paranjyothi bowed reverently towards the murti and then, with utmost devotion, took it in his hands. He started walking down the hill towards his tent. He decided that he would carry the murti all the way to his native village of Tiruchenkattankudi, where he would install the Ganesha idol in a temple there.

The murti exists to this day in the temple at Tiruchenkattankudi.

Talakkadi, March 642 CE

She sat on the terrace of her house, watching the road. They had all heard the news, of course. Of Immudi Pulikeshi's death. Of the fall of Vathapi to the Pallava king. She had shed tears for the great emperor. And then she had waited. Waited for that one person to come walking along the road. Hoping for that one person to come walking along the road.

She had watched the road for a few days now. Each dawn had brought hope that the succeeding dusk had crushed. Yet, she hadn't given up hoping and waiting. She saw that the hawkers were coming down the road early in the morning as usual. She wondered if she should go down and buy some vegetables, but she just didn't have the energy to go down today.

She cast her look further down the road. There was someone there, someone she thought she recognised. She squinted her eyes, trying to discern the features of the man. She noticed that he was small and wiry. He walked with a limp. She knew the man! He was never alone, of course. He always had the giant with him and the two of them were always around her man.

But where were the other two? Why was he alone? As he came closer to the house, she looked closely at him. Bhatta saw her and raised his face towards her. His face was filled with pain and misery. It hit her then. Her man was never coming home. Indumathi sat down, her face emotionless. And then a primeval scream came out of her, starting from somewhere deep within her body and exploding out into the universe.

Manimangala, April 642 CE

The three young men walked slowly, led by the youngest of them. Sadaiyan, his face missing its usual exuberance, stopped in the middle of the field at a spot that still showed the remains of a funeral pyre. His companions had told him of the promise that Elango had made them, about taking them to the site of Jamba's cremation. He had promised to show them the place and had asked Muthuvel to go directly to Kanchi, while he had brought the two forest-dwellers here.

'This is it,' he said softly, to Anjaneya and Jabali.

The two young men with him prostrated themselves on the ground, towards the remains of the pyre. They then picked up some of the ash and bound it tightly in a piece of cloth.

'We will take it back to the forest, bury it there and raise a tree over it.'

'It will be a strong tree I am sure,' said Sadaiyan.

'The strongest,' whispered Anjaneya.

Korkai, April 642 CE

She spent every waking hour atop the fort walls looking to the road coming down to her city from the north. Her father had tried to reason with her to stay within the palace, but she wouldn't listen. So he had built a temporary shelter for her where she could at least be safe from the elements. The monsoons had set in, and it rained incessantly. Yet she stayed under that temporary shelter, her eyes peeled to the distance. She would only come down from there to her rooms once it had grown dark.

She took a light repast of fruits and then decided to retire to her bed. This had become her invariable practice over the past couple of months. There was none of the frivolous chatting and laughter with her friends. Her days were regimented. She would get up in the morning, bathe and then go to the temple. She prayed to all the Gods. She prayed for his health. She prayed for his life. She prayed that he would return to her. He had promised to, after all. She would then take up her position on top of the fort walls, come down after sunset, eat alone in her room and then fall into a fitful sleep.

She had just lain down on her bed when she heard someone running.

'Princess!' panted a maid, knocking on the door of her room. 'Princess! They are here. They are here!'

'Where?' she demanded.

'In the king's chambers!'

Thaamarai got up and ran. She ran barefoot down the corridor and then up to her father's chamber. She stopped at the door, out of breath. Tendrils of hair cascaded around her lovely face. She gazed at the backs of the two men talking to her father. Well, one man and a boy.

The man felt, more than heard her presence, and turned around. So did the young lad, a smile splitting his face.

She had eyes only for the man. Muthuvel smiled at her, but she was already on the move. She threw herself at him, her arms going around his neck. Sadaiyan looked away, as did the king, with an uncomfortable cough. Her lips found his.

Kanchi, June 642 CE

The teacher entered the class and there was an immediate hush in the room. Even the noisiest child settled down. She loved them and was kind to them, but she wouldn't stand for indiscipline in her class.

She started teaching them mathematics and then logic. She was patient with their questions but firm. As she taught, the great Shaivite saint Appar walked past the door to the room, with a visitor.

'You have women teachers here?' she heard the visitor ask Appar. The old man laughed that captivating laugh of his and stopped by the door, calling her to him, 'Sanghamitra, child, come and meet my guest. He is a great scholar from Takshashila.'

She bowed to the man and then dismissed her class. She spent the rest of the day with the scholar discussing science, mathematics, logic and medicine. Her hair was shoulder-length now and she knew that she would never cut it again in her life. Elango had loved her long tresses and she recalled his last request to her to not cut it again, ever. She wouldn't.

A tearful Venkata had taken her to the place where Elango had fallen, after the death of Pulikeshi. She had not shed any tears then. Not in front of them. She knew that he wouldn't like that. She had borne herself stoically and had even cremated his body herself. She had gone back to her tent and then, and only then, had she collapsed into tears. Tears that she knew she would be shedding to the end of her days. Till the end of time.

King Vikramaditya, the third son of Immudi Pulikeshi, recaptured Vathapi from the Pallavas in 654 CE.

Acknowledgements

The last book of the trilogy brings with it a sense of closure, tinged with conflicting emotions—happiness and sadness. Happiness at having been able to complete the story, while sadness at having to bid adieu to all the characters that have lived with me for so many years.

As usual, the existence of this book owes a lot to many people, and it would be remiss of me not to acknowledge their contributions.

As always, I want to start by acknowledging my wife and children who have had to put up with my stealing time away from them to write this book. The immediate family bears the brunt of the author's tantrums as he grapples with the stress of everything associated with writing, including writer's block and multiple rounds of editing. I couldn't have done it without them. They are the wind beneath my sails.

My thanks to Appa and Amma for instilling in me a solid work ethic and a love for education and books. A special thanks to Appa, as usual, for being the very first reader of this book. He has always been the first reader for every one of my books. His words of encouragement mean a lot to me.

My deepest appreciation to HarperCollins India for bringing out the trilogy in short order, as promised. Sincere gratitude to Ridhima Kumar for being such a joy to work with and for holding my nose to the grindstone. Thanks to my editor Suzanne Hughe for helping make the book read better through her keen-eyed editing. Thanks to all the other editors who have done an incredible job in ensuring that even the minutest details are not overlooked.

I am indebted to the many established authors—Bibek Debroy, Amish Tripathi, Ashwin Sanghi, Anand Ranganathan, Saiswaroopa Iyer, Abhinav Agarwal, Sunanda Vashisht and Harini Calamur—who have been incredibly kind, yet again, in going through and providing endorsements for the book.

Lastly, and perhaps most importantly, I would like to express my deepest gratitude once again to the numerous readers who have supported me by reading my books. Thank you from the bottom of my heart!

About the Author

Dr Arun Krishnan has studied and lived in different cities across India, USA, Singapore and Japan, before putting down roots in Bangalore. He started off with a degree in engineering and a doctorate, and went on to work in sectors like IT, high-performance computing, bioinformatics, computational biology and HR analytics. He has worked at various corporations, research institutes and also in academia as an assistant professor of computational biology. And then, just to shake things up, Arun went for an MBA and turned entrepreneur. He is a polyglot and is conversant in Tamil, English, Hindi, Bengali, Japanese and Kannada. He loves to sing and plays the guitar, keyboard and percussion instruments. He is also an amateur historian and enjoys visiting historical places. While he has over fifty published articles in journals, conferences and book chapters, The Battle of Vathapy trilogy is his first foray into the world of fiction. You can connect with him on X @ArunKrishnan_ and on Instagram @authorarunkrishnan. More information on all his works can be found at https://authorarunkrishnan.com

HarperCollins *Publishers* India

At HarperCollins India, we believe in telling the best stories and finding the widest readership for our books in every format possible. We started publishing in 1992; a great deal has changed since then, but what has remained constant is the passion with which our authors write their books, the love with which readers receive them, and the sheer joy and excitement that we as publishers feel in being a part of the publishing process.

Over the years, we've had the pleasure of publishing some of the finest writing from the subcontinent and around the world, including several award-winning titles and some of the biggest bestsellers in India's publishing history. But nothing has meant more to us than the fact that millions of people have read the books we published, and that somewhere, a book of ours might have made a difference.

As we look to the future, we go back to that one word—a word which has been a driving force for us all these years.

Read.